SILVER MIRRORS

AN APPARATUS INFERNUM NOVEL

PRAISE FOR *BRONZE GODS*

"Intricate world-building and complex characters are the result of an exciting new collaboration between Ann Aguirre and her husband, Andres... Team Aguirre delivers protagonists whose strengths and weaknesses complement each other, forming a first-rate partnership... This is a killer blend of steampunk and fantasy!"
RT Book Reviews

"Fantastic... Intricately layered, *Bronze Gods* is a fabulous introduction to a dark and dangerous world filled with tricksy magic, fantastical steampunk elements, and a detective duo worth their weight in gold."
The Book Swarm

"[Aguirre] does an amazing job giving the readers plenty of action and mystery to work their teeth on."
Whatchamacallit Reviews

"Steampunk noir, fantastic world-building, characters I fell in love with almost instantly, crime scenes worthy of Patricia Cornwell, clockwork, LOTS of sexual tension, and a heart-stopping conclusion. All in a single book."
The Nocturnal Library

"An engaging and entertaining mystery with an amazing duo!" *Rainy Day Ramblings*

"Humor, romantic chemistry, fantastic mystery, and one heck of an ending." *Seeing Night Book Reviews*

"Aguirre's steampunk world has a gorgeous backstory...As for the plot, it speeds along with plenty of action, tension, surprises, heart-stopping moments, additional delightful supporting cast, and fantastic attention to detail... If you enjoy steampunk, fantasy, mysteries, or thrillers, I think you'll find plenty in here to enthrall you." *Errant Dreams*

"Outstanding!... A.A. Aguirre has crafted a dynamic team in a fantastic world that I cannot wait to visit again."
SciFiPulse.Net

ALSO AVAILABLE FROM A.A. AGUIRRE AND TITAN BOOKS

Bronze Gods

A.A. AGUIRRE

SILVER MIRRORS

AN APPARATUS INFERNUM NOVEL

TITAN BOOKS

Silver Mirrors
Print edition ISBN: 9781781169513
E-book edition ISBN: 9781781169520

Published by Titan Books
A division of Titan Publishing Group Ltd
144 Southwark Street, London SE1 0UP

First edition: May 2014
10 9 8 7 6 5 4 3 2 1

This is a work of fiction. Names, characters, places, and incidents either are the product of the author's imagination or are used fictitiously, and any resemblance to actual persons, living or dead, business establishments, events, or locales is entirely coincidental. The publisher does not have any control over and does not assume any responsibility for author or third-party websites or their content.

A CIP catalogue record for this title is available from the British Library.

Printed and bound in Great Britain by CPI Group Ltd.

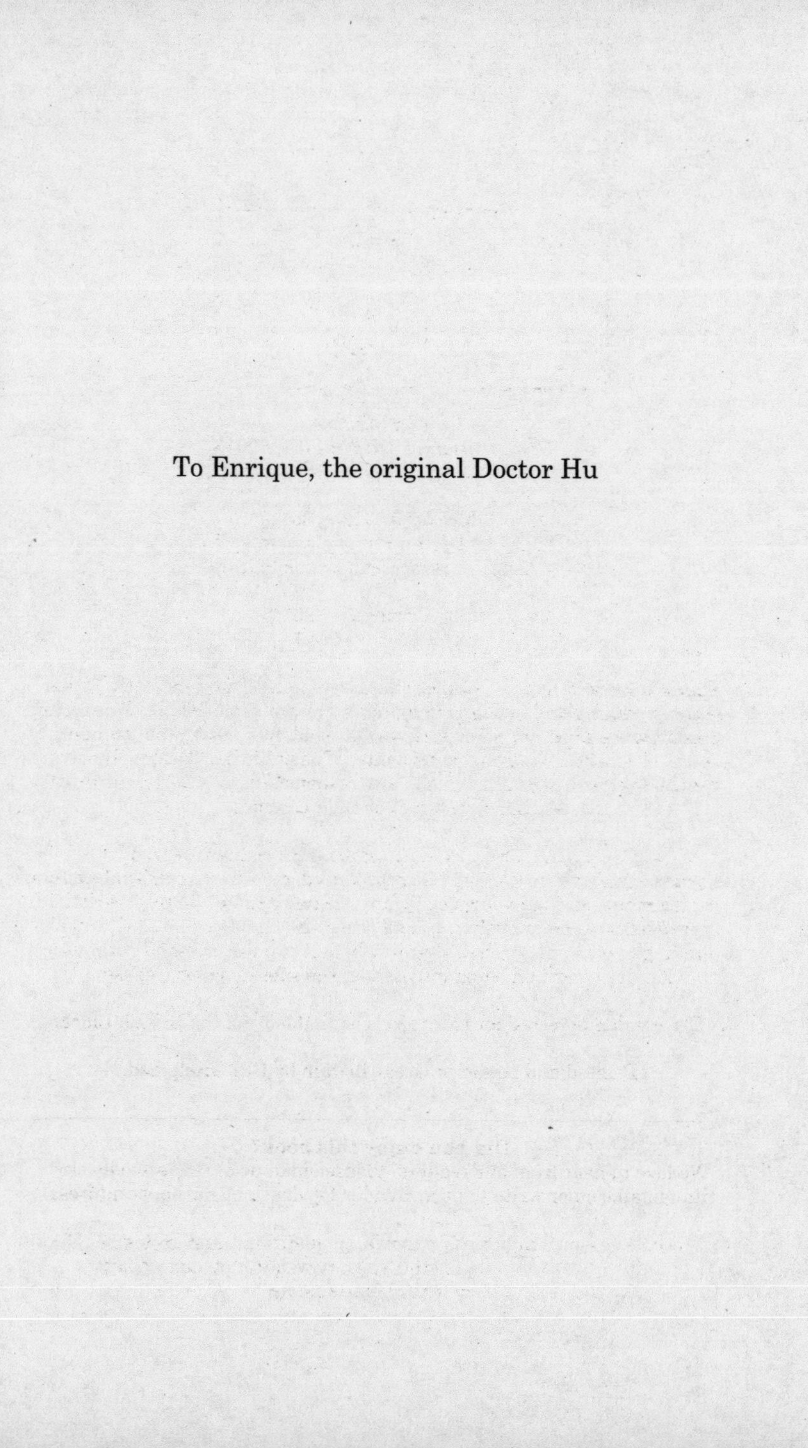

To Enrique, the original Doctor Hu

ACKNOWLEDGMENTS

FIRST, WE OFFER thanks to Laura Bradford, a wonderful partner and advocate. It's impossible not to appreciate her hard work and sincere regard for our books. Next, we tip our hats to Anne Sowards and the Penguin team for polishing our words and then packaging them so prettily. Thanks to our amazing copy editors, Bob and Sara Schwager. They do such a splendid job that it's a pleasure to do edits. Much appreciation to our keen-eyed proofreader as well, Fedora Chen.

Most sincere gratitude to our friends and colleagues who welcomed us into the steampunk world and made space at the bar. Especial thanks to Karen Alderman and Majda Čolak for reading early drafts of the book and convincing us there was gold in the river. At your behest, we mined after it most assiduously.

So many thanks to Bree, Donna, Lauren, Megan, Tessa, Courtney, Viv, Enrique, Erika, and other worthy souls whose contributions we may have overlooked.

As ever, we cherish our children, who thought it was quite bad enough when their mother was lost in a fictional world, and then their father wandered into Wonderland, too. Alek and Andrea, your self-sufficiency and cleverness is a marvel to behold. And we thoroughly appreciate it.

This book was a challenge, mostly because of life, which has a way of going on even when you've two children and a novel to complete. We're pleased with *Silver Mirrors* and hope you will be, too. Which brings us to our most important thank-you: the one to readers, hungry for Mikani and Ritsuko's next adventure.

Read on, for as Sir Arthur Conan Doyle wrote, "The game is afoot"!

1

ONE MONTH AGO, the world nearly ended.

Interrupting the ritual meant to summon all the lost Ferisher spirits should've been enough, but as Ritsuko had told Mikani, it would've been impossible for Lorne Nuall to complete such dark work on his own. There was no way for him to kidnap those girls, move his infernal machines, *and* elude the authorities without aid from somewhere, probably a high-ranking accomplice. Therefore, a murderer still needed to be brought to justice, and Ritsuko wouldn't rest well until the job was done.

She didn't mind the research aspect of detective work. Ritsuko had fond memories of the archives, even if the place appeared to try Mikani's patience. The stack of tomes yet to be examined still towered higher than her head, with a much smaller pile of books that she'd paged through, looking for some sign of who stood to gain most from a change in the status quo.

"Near as I can tell, Theron is all that's left of the Nuall line." Mikani shoved aside an old ledger to make room for a leather tome older than their great-grandparents. "So whatever help his brother had, it likely didn't come from their family, immediate or otherwise." He looked up, giving her a pained look. "House Saermine of the Summer Court, mighty kings and lords of Hy Breasil, now consists of one creepy old chap with a gardening fetish."

"Through deduction, we can rule out a number of Houses," she said thoughtfully. "The Elemental Houses stand to lose the most if the city descended into the chaos Lorne seemed to want. They lost a lot of money during the riots."

"True, and they're not known for complicated plots," he said.

"The ruling Houses don't benefit from a complete change in the order of things."

"Who does that leave, then?" Mikani asked.

Ritsuko opened an old book, one that detailed the bloodlines of the initial Houses. The pages were yellowed, so she took care as she scanned the genealogy charts. Frowning, she answered, "There are Houses that don't seem to be around anymore, but if there are survivors, like Theron Nuall, any of them stand to gain if his brother's plot had succeeded."

Mikani rubbed the bridge of his nose and leaned back on the wooden chair. "That's right down Thorgrim's alley. Manipulative buggers, the lot of them. They *have* been trying to rebuild their power ever since they sided with House Saermine in the royalist wars and lost. And there's a few thousand of them still around."

Ritsuko nodded. "I'll put them on our list of potential suspects. It shouldn't take us more than ten or twenty years to clear them all." Then she grinned. "But seriously, there can't be *too* many people positioned high enough and with sufficient resources to have helped Lorne."

He shook his head. "I doubt there's more than a couple of dozen members of Thorgrim who could do that. And maybe half that, if we consider that most of them are too busy trying to blackmail, poison, and coerce each other to have time for outside interests."

"Where are Thorgrim's holdings?"

"Around Northport, I believe. If memory serves, the

governor's been a Thorgrim for the last forty years."

Ritsuko went back to studying the rest of the names. "This might be too obvious, but... how can we be *sure* there are no Nuall refugees? If distaff relations have been absorbed into other Houses, they might be obsessing over their lost heritage. Such individuals might see it as a great deed, bringing their people back to the old ways. Wasn't Nuall's family considered akin to royalty long ago?"

Mikani pulled the first book he'd been reading closer, opening it with a sigh. "The Nualls became an offshoot of House Saermine over five hundred years ago. Two cousins married, so yes... if House Saermine had succeeded in their bid to overthrow the Council and restore the monarchy during the royalist wars, the Nuall family heir would've been fourth or fifth in line for the Summer throne."

Not that it matters these days. The Council meant that royal blood was rather beside the point. There hadn't been kings or queens in the isles for a thousand years, but three hundred years ago, the royalist uprising, if it had succeeded, would've restored the monarchy. Now the system was far more intricate.

She offered, "It's possible, then, that these unidentified souls are embittered about their lot. Lorne might've been just the vanguard."

"If so, they got a martyr instead. That said, I'm not sure how we could track down other lineages hiding within other Houses."

Ritsuko thought for a few moments. "We can quietly put out the word for merchants and vendors to be alert for coins like the ones Lorne used to build his murder machines. It's likely that if identical antique currency surfaces, it must be connected."

"Good idea. We can always say there's some counterfeit coinage going around, spread the description."

She nodded decisively, pleased with that course of action.

"I think we're done here. Try not to weep, Mikani."

He closed the book with an echoing boom and was on his feet before she had quite finished speaking. "I swear you make up reasons to bring me here, Ritsuko. Let's go talk to some fences and gold dealers, then, shall we?"

"Good plan. And you know it's just because I like watching your lips move when you read the big words."

"I know. You can't take your eyes off me."

She gave him her best mysterious smile. "Could be."

He smirked over his shoulder at her. "Some truths, my dear Ritsuko, are self-evident." He held the door for her. "If we hurry, we can catch the lowlifes still waking up near Iron Cross."

Iron Cross was an industrial district, full of factories and tenements. Not Ritsuko's favorite place, but since they had spent the first part of the day buried in old books, it seemed fair that they should end it in seedy surroundings more to her partner's tastes. She was quiet as they walked out to the cruiser. Gunwood didn't exactly know what she and Mikani were up to, today. She had a feeling he wouldn't be amused. Gunwood didn't like conspiracy theories or ideas that complicated his life. He liked cases closed and documents filed while this was such a mess that it could take years to untangle.

But she hoped not. Mikani would lose patience and shoot someone long before then.

They sped through the city, with Mikani taking every opportunity to push the machine to its limits. She had been jolted from head to toe by the time Mikani locked the cruiser tight, paid an urchin to watch over it, and threatened a couple of loitering factory workers for good measure. Then he turned to Ritsuko, hat somewhat askew and walking stick tucked neatly under an arm. She knew a silly, schoolgirl thrill whenever he wore the bowler she'd bought for him.

"Someone will probably try to break in anyway, but it should still be here when we are done." He pointed down the main avenue, thronged with late-shift workers heading to work and day laborers headed for the myriad dives and makeshift brothels that lined the busy street. "One of the biggest fences in the city's a few blocks down. He'll be able to spread the word if we can convince him."

She checked her sidearm and credentials, then followed her partner toward the little hole in the wall where Roman Quick did business. The surrounding houses were bits of scrap wood and tin, lashed together with hope and tattered twine. There was no sign that these premises condoned illegal activity, though a couple of hard-looking men near the end of the street clearly took note of their arrival. Ritsuko stepped through the open doorway behind Mikani, squinting as her eyes adjusted to the cool, dim interior.

"Good evenin' to you both, fine and distinguished customers." Ritsuko looked around the gloom until she spotted movement off to her left, behind a precarious stack of china plates and cups. Roman stepped closer, a big smile on his cherubic face. Middle height, middle-aged but with clean golden locks and a fair skin that House ladies would envy. "And what might Quick's Emporium do for you today?"

"I'm Inspector Ritsuko. This is my partner, Mikani. We're here to ask you to keep an eye out for counterfeit coins."

"Bad business," Quick said. "What's the world coming to when you can't trust a silver crescent?"

"No," Mikani corrected. "These are purported to be antique. They may look quite convincing if you encounter them."

"Is it some kind of alchemical glamour?" Quick asked shrewdly.

"Indeed." Ritsuko was relieved he had given them a plausible explanation since it saved her the trouble of coming up with something.

"It would help if I knew exactly what to watch for."

Mikani borrowed a piece of paper and sketched out the design from the Nuall coin from memory. *Good job, partner. You're not just a pretty face.*

Quick took the drawing, studied it, then asked, "So it's not gold, just lead or summat, dressed up to look sweet?"

"More or less," Mikani said.

Ritsuko maintained a neutral expression, though she wanted to smile. She laid her card on the counter. "Will you get in touch if you encounter anything like that?"

"Of course I will."

The sour note jangled in her left ear. An impulse she couldn't explain prompted her to say, "That's not true. What's your plan? To find the source of the fool's gold and get him to teach you how he does it?"

Quick looked startled, though he masked it straightaway. "I've been more than polite, I think. If we have no business, you should move along, lest you discourage my customers."

Mikani straightened up and tucked his card into Quick's waistcoat pocket. The other man looked indignant. "Keep that just in case, Mr. Quick. There is, after all, a significant reward for helping the CID catch these counterfeiters. And, of course, friends of the CID tend to find that their businesses prosper."

Ritsuko saw Quick's eyes widen and his brow furrow in calculation at the implied promises her partner had made, even as the discordant tone in her left ear chimed louder. Mikani gestured for her to lead the way, and she headed for the street, mildly hopeful about their prospects for the first time since she'd realized Lorne's death didn't mean they'd caught all the guilty parties.

* * *

Back at Central, Mikani got on the lift, listening to the groan of ancient machinery. Ritsuko was quiet beside him. A minute later, the door opened, and they stepped off. The duty room was busy at this hour with lots of other inspectors filing paperwork, going out on calls, and generally cluttering up the place.

Their boss, Commander Gunwood, came to his office doorway, looking cranky. "Mikani! Ritsuko! What were you doing out there, planting roses? Get in here."

Mikani heard his partner stifle a sigh, but they both answered the commander's dulcet tones. "Something we can do to protect and serve?"

"Damn right. In case you hadn't noticed, the city's going insane. More than usual. She's never been a sweet lady, but bronze gods, she's gone well and truly mad this time."

Mikani exchanged a look with Ritsuko. "What's going on?"

"Take your pick!" Gunwood strode past them, all but shouldering them aside as he headed for the torn and weathered map of the city hung from the wall. "There's a freak thunderstorm hovering over the Mountain District. Just the Mountain District; the bloody cloud ends at the walls. Something's making the trains wail like damn'd souls between Temple and North stations. And every car, bus, and trolley that tries to make its way past Golden Way starts looping faster and faster around the park until they crash or break down." He paused to glare at them, then slammed his open hand down in the middle of the map. "Two dozen suicides, and I've lost count of the number of calls for help with invisible intruders."

"I knew it was bad," Ritsuko said, "but not to this extent. Where do you want us, Commander?"

Mikani wasn't about to take an assignment when he had been offered a choice. "We'll head for North station and see what's making the trains sad, shall we? Maybe they just need a shoulder to cry on and a stern talking-to."

Ritsuko laughed. "This isn't the sort of thing they cover in the manual, is it?"

The commander looked so aggravated that he might actually burst a blood vessel, so Mikani figured it was time to leave. He took note of the huge stack of unusual incident reports on his boss's desk on the way out.

They didn't linger long in the duty room. Other CID personnel shared the lift with them as they headed down to the lobby. Even the guard on duty seemed harried, which was odd, as the man seemed relatively unflappable. On the street, there were less pedestrians than normal, just a few bondsmen in House colors, looking none too pleased with their assignments.

The underground was a short walk from CID Headquarters. On the way, Mikani passed the coffee stand where he always used to buy drinks from Electra, a daughter of the Summer Clan whom he had failed to save. He'd always regret that, and he knew a pang of guilt as they strode past. He hadn't bought anything from them since.

Down in the Park station, it was quiet, no inhuman wailing here. Mikani glanced at Ritsuko. "Seems calm enough."

"Let's ride up to Temple and farther, see when the mood changes."

With a murmur of agreement, he boarded the train just before the doors closed. There were a handful of other passengers, all of whom were carefully not looking at one another. And they all disembarked at the next station. Ritsuko was frowning.

"Did that seem odd to you?" Mikani asked.

"Just a bit."

"Well, I know it was not something I said. Maybe you gave them one of your looks. The ones you give me when you accuse me of dodging the paperwork."

He kept a straight face but could not help looking around the empty carriage. There was something definitely off about the feel of the train: in all his years of riding the underground to and from Central, he'd never felt uneasy. *Until tonight. I feel eyes at the nape of my neck, and I swear someone's whispering just outside the damned window.*

Usually, his partner would banter back, but she didn't rise to the bait this time. "It's *cold* in here. Really cold."

"I'd—wait. Yes, it is. And there's that same bitterness in the air as in the mirror station yesterday." Now that he was paying attention, he could make out a rhythmic pounding at his temples and an uncomfortable pressure at the center of his chest. *Hells and Winter.*

It seemed to Mikani as if the train was actually picking up speed. *That's not normal.* The usual announcement was conspicuously absent. He shifted in his seat as they approached the Temple station to catch sight of six people waiting on the platform, but the train didn't slow. Instead, it zoomed past, and the hammering in his head grew more intense.

Mikani had a sense of overwhelming darkness in the tunnel; strange because he'd always found the underground to be relaxing. Now, it felt like a prison entombing him, and the cries rose up as if from inside him before he actually heard them. Ritsuko pressed her palms to her ears, likely to drown out the wailing that commenced in the darkness, just as the commander had described. The sound echoed with inhuman grief, and that sense of cold chilled Mikani to his bones; it was a despair like he'd never known, that of a small, helpless creature bound in darkness.

He looked around for Ritsuko and found her huddled in a corner near the carriage door, covering her head with both arms. The wailing verged on painful, and tears ran freely down his cheeks when he bent down to curl against his partner, gritting his teeth to keep from screaming. He could feel Ritsuko flinch against his side, and he looked around, desperately trying to find the source of the sound.

Then silence fell, full of echoing cries and the sound of their ragged breathing and metal protesting in a faint echo of the howling that had filled the tunnel moments before. Mikani wiped the warm blood from his upper lip, collapsing with a groan on the floor next to Ritsuko. The vibrations gentled, so he pulled himself together enough to notice that the velocity had decreased.

"This is our stop, Ritsuko."

She gave him her hand so he could pull her up, and he held on to it until they both stumbled out the doors at North station. Ritsuko pulled her hand back then and took a deep, shuddering breath, as if she had been running. Her eyes were bright with unshed tears.

"Something very, very bad is going on," she whispered.

"I know. My favorite bakery's a couple blocks from that last station. I'm going to have to go the long way for it." He ran his hands over his ears, half expecting to find them bloodied, and adjusted his hat. "And, well, the train was definitely wailing." He found he could not keep up the humor, though. "Yes, Ritsuko, something awful's happening, and it seems to be getting worse."

"Do you think it has anything to do with Lorne's failed ritual? We unleashed an awful lot of magic, and we can't know precisely what it did."

The thought sent a hard chill up his spine. "Bronze gods, I don't know."

"This is too big. I don't even know where to start." Then she paused, and his partner got the look Mikani recognized as a dawning idea. "Maybe it's not a bad idea to talk to Theron Nuall. If anyone could advise us if this is a potential side effect of that interrupted spell, it's him."

"I agree. The Architect might have some insight as well, but I don't know if he'd see us."

"Gunwood has to give us some clear parameters," Ritsuko said. "Our training doesn't cover any of this." She sighed. "What are we supposed to do, arrest the machinery?" She sounded as frustrated as Mikani felt.

"We will need bigger cuffs. A lot of them." He wiped at his face with his handkerchief and started toward the stairs. "Let's go see if we can get some answers, partner."

"I'd rather have a stiff drink," she muttered.

"I might know a way to get both."

2

THE HOUSE WAS imposing. Ritsuko admired the immaculate lawn and the carefully trimmed hedges as she strode up the walk toward the burnished doors. She lifted the knocker and banged twice, then waited for a servant to answer. Mikani glanced sidelong at her; she'd noticed that he had gotten in the habit of checking on her surreptitiously, as if he wondered whether she was fully recovered.

A minute later, a man in House colors opened the door. "Inspectors Ritsuko and Mikani, come in please."

Mikani often had brilliant ideas. This way, they combined the need for answers regarding the chaos in the city with checking on Aurelia Wright. The manservant led them down a spartan corridor past heavy doors leading to the Architect's office, currently closed. Though some might disagree, Ritsuko would argue that Olrik was the most powerful of the noble houses, and that the Architect was the closest thing to a king Dorstaad had ever known. Oh, he didn't flaunt his influence; he preferred to work behind the scenes, and his daughter, Aurelia, had chosen to remove herself from the political arena entirely.

They stepped out into a small courtyard with a fountain

at its center. On the other side of the weathered stone basin sat Aurelia Wright. She wore a long-sleeved gown and a pretty lace shawl tucked around her shoulders. The last time Ritsuko had seen her, she had been limited to a sedan chair. *Either someone carried her out here, or she's doing well enough to make it on her own.*

Sensing their approach, the woman glanced up from her book, but she didn't rise. Her cheeks were wan in the winter light, and to Ritsuko's gaze, her limbs held a frangible quality, no longer lithe with a dancer's grace. Miss Wright offered a welcoming smile, however, and rang the bell beside her.

"It's kind of you to come. Sit, please. I'll have them bring refreshments."

Ritsuko perched next to Miss Wright, as Mikani seemed to be waiting, and he took position opposite them, in clear view of the doorway. The same servant appeared and disappeared after a whispered instruction from Miss Wright. Ritsuko wondered what hospitality looked like, offered from the Architect's kitchen, but she guessed she'd find out soon enough.

"Thank you for seeing us," Ritsuko said.

"I collect you have a reason for your visit?"

"As I'm sure you're aware, there are strange occurrences in the city, more every day." Ritsuko paused to ensure the other woman was following her, then described the crying train. "We wondered if you can shed any light on the situation, if you know why this is happening."

Aurelia answered, "While I don't get out much, I do hear things, but I can't *explain* any of it. My father may have a theory, however. I'll ask when I see him next and send word."

That was more than Ritsuko and Mikani could manage. While the Architect appreciated that they'd saved his daughter, he was a busy man, and it was unlikely they could get an appointment in the next week or so. She murmured her thanks, knowing these were exalted connections that most inspectors couldn't call upon.

Whatever it takes to get the job done. But she couldn't just dodge out, now that she'd asked her favor. "How are you feeling?"

"Incomplete." Miss Wright looked away. "Like I'm piecing myself back together from the inside out and finding bits missing."

Mikani fumbled in his pockets, then he came up empty-handed. To Ritsuko, he seemed nervous, and she imagined he didn't call on infirm females too often. He might also be uncomfortable if he could sense Miss Wright's infirmity.

Then he said, "Don't dismiss this as empty reassurance, but... it *will* get better. I can't predict how long recovery will take, unfortunately."

Miss Wright studied Ritsuko's partner incredulously. "How can you know that?"

Mikani frowned and clasped his hands. "I hear it. The old you, like a whisper in an empty room. Getting stronger, slowly. It's hard to describe." He looked over to Ritsuko, silently requesting corroboration.

"He's got powerful Ferisher blood," Ritsuko said. Usually that was enough to convince people that Mikani wasn't a confidence man.

Miss Wright glanced between them. "Right now, it's exhausting to make my way from one chair to the next. My very bones ache. And I no longer know whether people are lying to me, even when I look them in the eyes." She leveled a hard look on Mikani. "Please don't tease me with false hope, sir. I dream of dancing when I can no longer even run."

"I assure you that we didn't cross the city to tease you with false promises. We went through too much together for such casual cruelty." Mikani paused, tilting his head toward Ritsuko. "Not to mention, she'd have my hide if she suspected I was toying with you."

"The doctors talk endlessly of mineral waters, chalice applications, and special infusions to restore my stamina. Yet you claim the cure is time? If that's true, it is a commodity in which I am wealthy enough."

Ritsuko hoped her partner was right, though the water elementals bound to the chalices often produced miraculous healing. "You seem a bit better."

The other woman lifted a shoulder, seeming unsure. "Right now it seems as if everything is on hold: my work, my goals, my... personal life." A tinge of color flared in Miss Wright's cheeks as if she couldn't believe she had almost introduced such a subject in mixed company.

Mikani stifled a smile, and Ritsuko wished she was close enough to nudge him. "Have you seen Mr. Leonidas or Mr. Nuall recently?"

"Theron came two weeks past. He often sends flowers."

To Ritsuko's right, a soft tone sounded. It was faint enough that she sought the source across the courtyard, only to note that Mikani seemed puzzled. He was watching her confusion with a raised brow.

"Something on your mind, partner?" He followed her gaze.

"Did you hear that?" she blurted, before she could stop herself. Ritsuko had been coping with the issue alone. Probably she shouldn't have brought it up, but it was too late for regrets now.

He stood and cocked his head. "Someone gardening nearby, I think, and a couple of trolleys heading downtown. What did *you* hear?"

Before Ritsuko could reply, the servant returned with a silver tray laden with tiny sandwiches on wafer-thin bread, cream cakes, and an ornate tea service. It wasn't the strong drink she'd requested after the weeping train, but tea could be bracing. The footman poured, and Miss Wright thanked him with a warm smile. The man offered a half bow in reply, then departed the courtyard, closing the door behind him.

Ritsuko sipped her tea, which *tasted* expensive, certainly richer than anything that ever graced her cupboard. But she was aware it was a delaying tactic at best. A logical CID inspector did not care to admit she was hearing noises nobody else could. She traced a fingertip around the delicate porcelain rim of her cup, aware that Mikani's frown had deepened.

"It was... like a bell, only not quite. It didn't sound like the one Miss Wright rang for service, more distant, but also mellifluous."

Miss Wright seemed startled. "When did you hear that?"

"After you said Mr. Nuall came to see you two weeks ago and that he sends flowers."

"Bronze gods," the other woman said. Her next words seemed inexplicable. "I intend to kill Inspector Mikani."

Mikani seemed nonplussed. "I don't usually get that reaction from women I haven't been involved with."

But Ritsuko barely heard him. Her left ear rang with a discordant note, and this time, she felt sure it was coming from her head, not an external source. "What...?"

"My dear Inspector Ritsuko, it seems as if you've acquired what Lorne Nuall stole from me." Ritsuko had no idea what the other woman was talking about, and it must've been obvious, as Miss Wright clarified, "Before I was taken, I could always tell fact from fiction. This is how."

With a pang of horror, she recalled how Lorne Nuall had stolen young House scions and strapped them into his murder machines, siphoning off their power and storing it in some kind of battery. When she'd pulled Miss Wright out of the tube, she was near death. *And then I stabbed the device and all of that stolen energy passed through me.* Remembering the agony made her jaw clench, and with some effort, she put the memory aside.

Whether purloined or borrowed, the truth-sense held much promise. It was likely to be damned distracting, if helpful during interviews and interrogations. *I suspect it'll also complicate my relationships immensely.* Misgiving rattled through her; Ritsuko didn't *want* a Ferisher gift. If she could give it back to Miss Wright, she'd do so immediately. At the moment, she felt like a thief, though she hadn't set out to steal power.

"I owe you everything, Inspectors, and if you ever have need of me again, only call. I'll contact you when I know something." Miss Wright's mouth curved in a wistful moue.

Mikani smiled. "We're glad to have been of service and to hear that you're recovering."

"I'm *so* sorry," Ritsuko put in. "If I could give this back—"

"In a way, it's a relief. I wish you more fortune and joy of this ability than I had, Inspector. You may find it a lonely burden to carry."

That sounds right. Though it might help in her work, she had a dark feeling that the gift might cost her a great deal. Her hands trembled. Ritsuko shivered and set down her dainty teacup, afraid that she'd drop the china.

"Why do you think it's come to life now?" Mikani asked.

Miss Wright lifted a pale shoulder in a half shrug. "Perhaps because of me? I may have closed the circuit somehow."

Ritsuko stilled her shaking hands. It *had* been working before now; she just hadn't known exactly what she was hearing or why. *It's a good thing we came to see Miss Wright about the train, or I never would've understood what was going on.* She hadn't wanted to say anything to Mikani because since she'd gotten out of the hospital, he'd had a tendency to hover.

He nodded. "Is there any way to, ah, sidestep this gift? I'm only asking so we know what to look for in suspects, of course."

"Actually—" But before Miss Wright finished her reply, the doors to the courtyard opened, and the servant stepped into view.

"Pardon the intrusion. Mr. Leonidas has arrived and is asking for you, my lady."

Miss Wright stifled a sigh. "It's to be expected. He practically lives here. I'm sorry, Inspectors, but our visit appears to be at an end."

They said farewell and followed the footman through a different arch. As they turned the first corner, Ritsuko mustered up a normal response and let Mikani step past her so she could punch his shoulder. "A way to sidestep, huh?"

He smirked, rubbing his arm. "Just trying to understand your new talent, Ritsuko. From all angles."

As she stepped out the front door, a raucous tone jangled in her left ear. *So that's not why he was asking.* She winced and touched it gingerly. "So you know, you're likely to deafen me if you continue with business as usual."

"Would that keep you from hearing that tone, you think?"

"Probably not. It's a Ferisher power, not a physical one. Also? You're a bastard."

"My word. Already so uppish, Ritsuko."

She offered her best smile. "Not at all. Only think how much this will help us, Mikani... and how our relationship will be improved by complete honesty." Ritsuko left him pondering that as she hurried toward their parked vehicle.

* * *

Mikani wound the heavy red cruiser, its paint still chipped from gunfire, into the afternoon traffic. Buses and carriages labored along the broad avenue, heavy traffic reducing their advance to a steady crawl as they navigated past several construction and repair crews. In the four weeks since they'd killed Lorne Nuall and rescued Miss Wright, a strange atmosphere had descended on Dorstaad.

It's like the city knows how close Nuall came to sacrificing her and finishing his ritual. The whole damned place feels on edge.

"There was another suicide down in the Trade District. That makes a dozen that we know of." *Not the cheeriest subject, but it's strange, and nobody's talking about it.*

"Do we have any idea what's causing them? And how

many does that make? And do the victims have anything in common?" Mikani could tell by her tone that she was wondering if they were actually suicides or murders dressed up to look that way.

"Word is, they all had more than a hint of glamour—seers, fortune-tellers, and a couple of confidence men with the gift of gab. Clemens—"

"Who's that again?" she cut in.

"Commander of Golden District." Ritsuko didn't socialize as much as Mikani. He was prone to knocking back a few pints at the CID-favored pub while his partner went home to her friends at the boardinghouse. Which meant he heard all the good gossip first. "He's convinced there's a witch hunt going on, a reaction to Nuall's murder spree and the riots last month."

He swerved to avoid a bus that stopped in front of them without much warning, its engine hissing angrily and venting dark smoke instead of steam.

"Watch your back, Mikani." Ritsuko frowned. "But I'm not convinced that theory tracks. Why would anyone kill the ones who were being hunted?"

"Never said Clemens was smart, partner, even if he's the boss. *I* think there's something else going on. Hell if I know what, though."

"The deaths must be related somehow if there's a unifying trait amongst the deceased."

"Besides their lack of breathing, you mean."

She cut him a reproving look. "Not funny. What else have you heard?"

"Saskia said another sloop failed to make port from the farms down south."

For the last few weeks, Alexandra Braelan, Saskia to her friends, had pressed him to help with the cragger pirates, who were hitting the Free Trader shipping companies hard. She was also one of the few lovers with whom Mikani maintained relatively cordial relations after the affair ended, but that didn't mean he could take off right now. *I do owe her for her help in thwarting Lorne Nuall's scheme, but there's no way Gunwood's giving me personal time now.*

"I wondered when that bill would come due," Ritsuko said.

"Hold up, there's something going on." Mikani pulled up to the curb and grabbed his hat and battered walking stick from the back while Ritsuko slipped to his side.

A couple of dozen people milled around outside the mirror station, and they did *not* look happy. Their rumbling nearly drowned out the clerk's call for calm. "Unfortunately, this office will be closed until we deal with some technical issues."

"Do you have an estimated time for repair?" a man demanded. "This message is urgent."

The clerk tugged at his tie. "At this time, I can't say. Until—"

"This is ridiculous!"

Mikani had been around mobs often enough to recognize when the mood started to turn. So he stepped forward, Ritsuko at his shoulder. "Step back. There's another station a few blocks north, so why don't you head that way?" Using his stick for leverage and his ID on prominent display, he shouldered carefully but steadily through the crowd, making sure Ritsuko kept up. "The sooner you disperse, the sooner we'll be able to get someone down here to fix this."

His partner flashed her own credentials before she added, "I'd get there first, avoid the queue. Dawdlers will end up waiting even longer."

The man who had said his message was urgent broke off and hurried in the direction that Mikani had indicated. That sparked a mass exodus, eventually leaving the sweaty-faced clerk to stammer out his thanks. He had the typical look of a public servant: round about the middle, crumpled, and bearing a slightly anxious air.

"So what's going on?" Ritsuko asked.

The clerk licked his lips and shuffled his feet for a moment, as if trying to find the words. Then he sighed and opened the door. "It might be easier if you saw for yourself... maybe you'll have some idea what to do."

Mikani looked at Ritsuko, who shrugged, then they followed the clerk inside. The high-ceilinged room was painted an off shade of blue, which brought out the grime on the floor tiles nicely. A long, wooden counter dominated the back, its polished surface reflecting the swirls of light and color from the row of a dozen silver mirrors hung from the wall. The clerk moved aside, seeking refuge behind his desk.

"I'm not sure—" A shrill wail rang through the room, echoing and gaining volume before breaking into a jumbled murmur of breathy voices. "Bronze gods, what in the hells is that?"

Ritsuko approached the nearest device, peering at the movement within. He couldn't tell what was trying to take shape, but Mikani had used the mirrors often enough to realize that this wasn't normal behavior. His partner tested the surface, and the metal reacted as if it were made of water, rippling outward in gradually widening circles. She pulled back, eyes wide.

"What's that?" the clerk asked. "I haven't dared to touch it since that started twenty minutes ago."

"It's... cold," Ritsuko said.

Mikani winced as a spike of ice slowly pressed against his forehead, pulsing in rhythm with the ripples on the silver. *Hells and Winter, that's not normal.* "Careful, Ritsuko... that's no technical malfunction." He could almost make out words in the throbbing at his temples, his gift responding to the disquiet of the mirrors.

"In all my years here, they've never done... that." The clerk wiped his brow. "I've never even heard of anything like it. I sent a runner for assistance to House Magnus, maybe they can help." He did not sound convinced. Or hopeful.

"Mikani, a word?"

Ritsuko took his arm and led him a discreet distance from the public servant. "This might seem like an odd question, but do you... feel anything from them?"

He rubbed the bridge of his nose. "I... yes. Ice-cold. Whispers, as if the mirrors were... alive, and like a nest of snakes, alien and stirred up."

Before Ritsuko could reply, a mixed group of men and women entered, each carrying a leather case. The clerk looked so relieved that Mikani figured this must be the repair team. The tallest, oldest member of the crew frowned when he saw Mikani and Ritsuko.

"Clear the station, please."

Mikani straightened up, instinctively protesting. "We're CID, sir, and you are...?"

"Third Carl Hildur, House Magnus. This station is outside your jurisdiction, as are all other extensions of House Magnus, as provided in due law. This is a House matter." The other men came closer to their Carl. "So I'll ask once more. Clear the station, please."

Ready to argue, he tensed, until Ritsuko wrapped her fingers around his arm. *She's right. This is stupid. No need for a pissing match here.*

"Of course." He touched a fingertip to the brim of his hat and signaled for Ritsuko to lead the way as the Magnus team turned back to the mirrors and waited pointedly for them to go.

Once outside, he breathed in deeply. "Sorry. I guess I'm a little on edge, partner."

But she was frowning, and apparently not due to his behavior. "There's something strange going on, don't you think?"

That didn't require an answer, so Mikani led the way back to the cruiser. He swung in as Ritsuko did on the other side. "Do you think Gunwood knows about the mirrors?"

His partner aimed an uncharacteristically mischievous

smile at him. “Of course not. Didn’t you hear the man, Mikani? It’s a House matter.”

Mikani snorted. “It is until they muck it up, and they call us to clean up their mess.”

He glanced toward the station as he started the cruiser. As he watched, the team covered the doors with black cloth, a couple of uniformed Magnus guards taking position before the door. *Suicides, weeping trains, and screaming mirrors, it’s almost enough to make me miss the riots.*

“Let’s get going,” Ritsuko said. “Gunwood must be wondering where we are by now.”

3

A DAY LATER, RITSUKO was still hearing the unearthly cry from the underground along with the wail of the mirrors. In her time as an inspector, she had encountered some strange things, but nothing that surreal. She and Mikani had been investigating strange incidents all morning, but a courier caught up with them fifteen minutes ago, directing them to return to HQ. Given the way the week had gone, she couldn't imagine it was good news.

"You think we're being promoted?" she asked Mikani with a wry smile.

"Definitely." Her partner was still trying to get twigs out of his hair from the last call: an oak in the garden of a Magnus retainer started smashing windows and tearing at the eaves. It took two hours to break enough branches to rescue the terrified man. "Gunwood's tired of the paperwork, and *I'm* ready to waste a lot of it to get back at that tree. Therefore, a nice, cushy desk job for both of us, your idea of heaven."

There were a few inspectors at their desks as she passed through. A few of them nodded or lifted a chin in greeting. Since they'd received formal thanks from the Architect himself, Ritsuko didn't receive quite as much outright disrespect as she used to. As usual, Mikani chose not to knock, barging into Gunwood's office as if he owned the place.

This time, the commander didn't acknowledge the oversight, wearing a look of complete preoccupation. "Shut the door behind you."

She did as Gunwood ordered, but she didn't make herself at home. Mikani leaned against the door and folded his arms. She couldn't help being concerned, however, as a closed door meant the boss had something percolating that he didn't want the rest of the office to overhear.

"What's the situation, sir?" She kept her tone level.

Gunwood gestured at the ready room on the other side of the door, then at the window. A handful of smoke columns dotted the city beyond. "You've seen what it's like." Gunwood stood with a grunt; Ritsuko suspected he hadn't moved from his desk in hours, trying to rein in the chaos. "We got orders from the Council earlier today. Or rather, *you* did." He dug in his desk for a moment, then pushed a large envelope toward her. "The paperwork was specific about who I should send." He offered Ritsuko a wan smile before smirking at Mikani. "Apparently you two made quite an impact on the powers that be."

After a second's thought, she decided the commander meant the Architect. Aurelia Wright's father, the lord of House Olrik, was the only influential person she and Mikani had impressed in the last year. They hadn't heard anything from Miss Wright regarding their inquiry on the weeping train, but maybe their initiative reminded the Architect to make use of them. If their new assignment came from him, it could be anything. Dread settled in her stomach as she picked up the packet of papers, opened it, and paged through.

She read aloud, "You are hereby commissioned to act on behalf of Dorstaad in an assignment abroad. Having distinguished yourselves as inspectors, the Council trusts that such a special task will not fall outside your capabilities.

Report immediately to the House Olrik's envoy at the Academy for further instruction."

She shuffled through the rest of the documents and found valid travel papers, along with some vouchers for transport and accommodations. Ritsuko handed the envelope to Mikani. Then she turned to Gunwood with a frown.

"Did I understand this correctly? We're being banished from the city?"

Gunwood leaned heavily on his desk, looking tired. "Don't be daft, Ritsuko. We need to stop this at the source, and someone high up thinks they know how."

"Why not send the Guard? They've plenty to go round, surely." Mikani didn't look up from rifling through the papers, scowling as he skimmed them. "If they know who or what's behind this, a couple of companies of lancers and grenadiers should do the trick, no?"

Gunwood snorted. "Any House sends their army up, the others follow to try and pick them off... so they get us to do their dirty work. As always."

"I don't understand," Ritsuko said. "Why us? I've never even been out of the city, and Mikani—" She broke off when she realized she didn't know how much her partner had traveled before joining the CID.

The commander shrugged. "Could be because you did such a stellar job with the last crisis, so you're the current favorite. Better yet, ask the Olrik envoy when you see him. You two have your orders."

Ritsuko knew better than to argue with the commander when he took that tone, so she merely led the way from the office, through the duty room, and down the lift into the garage. She didn't speak until Mikani had commandeered his favorite red cruiser, battered as it was. Once they were both on board, the doors shut behind them, she let her temper overflow a bit.

"This doesn't seem like a vote of confidence," she muttered.

"The city running mad, and we're supposed to walk away? Sounds like they're binning us."

"Hells and Winter." Mikani took them out of the garage, weaving through the mess of carriages, buses, and hansoms filled with people fleeing the city. "I can deal with killers, thieves, smugglers, and the occasional power-hungry relic from another age, but haunted trains, wailing mirrors, and trees with a bad attitude?"

"It's outside our usual purview, that's for sure."

He went on, "I don't like leaving any more than you do, but what good can we do here?" *He sounds tired. Frustrated.* "I'm not keen on running, but I'm less than eager to punch an oak into submission again."

"I can't help feeling someone wants us out of the city." She shrugged. "Go on, mock me for imagining conspiracies everywhere."

He offered a playful look, probably trying to lighten the mood. "*I* wanted us out of the city, remember? Reward, cabin, cooking?"

"I should've known you were behind this, Mikani. You live for the day when you'll have my undivided attention."

"You know me. I'm a devious bastard."

Truth. The tone sounded in her ear, confirming his statement. For a few seconds, she let herself imagine that he did want to get her alone. But that was a silly fantasy, one that would interfere with their ability to work together. So she balled it up like a flawed incident report and cast it away. The remainder of the ride was quiet as Mikani navigated pockets of heavy traffic. Near the Academy, the congestion lightened, though there were more pedestrians.

Mikani flashed his credentials, along with the invitation, and the university constable directed them to private parking. They hurried up the smooth stone walk to the administrative building where the meeting was to take place. Inside, it was quiet and austere with cool tiles and pale walls lined with old portraits.

"Looks like we're in the conference room at the end of the hall," Mikani said.

The envoy was already waiting for them. He was a slim man with a face younger than his silver hair suggested. At their entry, he rose with a smooth poise that made Ritsuko immediately understand how he had come to work for the Architect. This man looked as if nothing could penetrate his perfect aplomb.

"Inspectors." The amanuensis bowed from the waist to each in turn, hands clasped lightly before him in a manner Ritsuko had not seen since her grandfather had passed. "I'm Julian Argyle, in service to House Olrik."

"A pleasure to meet you." Given her resentment of this assignment, Ritsuko didn't mean it, but she had been reared to display good manners.

"I thank you for meeting me. Please, be seated." He straightened and waited for them to sit before taking his own place across the table. "Our people believe they know the cause for the current... troubles, in the city. As the documents indicate, the Council has need of agents it can trust to end these incidents."

"So what's making the city go insane? Trees, trains, mirrors, suicide. It's a hellish mess out there." Mikani looked as if he expected—or rather hoped—that Argyle had these answers.

"There was a... disturbance recently, and the elemental spirits are unsettled. Old procedures for calming them no longer seem effective. We received a cry for help from the Winter Isle, shortly before the mirrors stopped functioning. Bad as it has become here, it's even worse in Northport. Everything indicates that the source of the problems lies somewhere in House Skarsgard territory, in the lands surrounding Mount Surtir. You will travel there, find the root cause to all this, and deal with it as you see fit."

Maybe this was pointless, but she wasn't ready to give in without a fight. "I hardly think Mikani and I are the most suited to handle this problem. Don't you have experts to send?"

Argyle frowned at her. "Are you questioning the Architect's judgment, Inspector?"

So the orders do come through him.

"No," she said quietly.

"To assuage your curiosity, the decision resulted from a conversation with his daughter."

"Because we came to ask about the train?" Mikani guessed.

"Precisely. Nobody else has asked *why*, Inspector. Only how we can stop it. But as a good investigator knows, one must often answer the former before the latter can be unlocked. And as for sending experts, who do you suppose would be more qualified? While there *are* professors of such esoteric matters, they're unlikely to survive the hazards of the voyage, let alone be forged of metal strong enough to enforce a solution."

"That's encouraging," Mikani muttered.

Ritsuko mentally mapped the journey. It would take several days by ship, followed by land travel. It was all a bit mysterious for her tastes. What could she and Mikani do that the local authorities couldn't manage? True, her partner had quite a gift, but the Architect couldn't know about her own. *Unless Miss Wright told him…* In that case, it was possible Olrik thought that their combined abilities offered some unique advantage.

Mr. Argyle produced a couple of documents unfamiliar to her. "The Council has issued you special commissions, giving you an extraordinary level of authority in House territories. You need to be discreet." Mr. Argyle looked at her partner pointedly as he said this. "Local authorities will not impede your investigation, but they're only obligated to aid you insofar as it doesn't damage their own interests." He hesitated a moment before continuing. "The Council couldn't agree how to handle what's happening in the Winter Isle. In particular, House Skarsgard refused outside interference with their mining affairs, and House Aevar's suggestion of a military expedition nearly sparked a melee in the Halls of Law. To keep the peace, Lord Olrik suggested a fact-finding mission by agents without House affiliations." He gestured at them both. "You two are the best we can do. Further aid from the Council is curtailed under the circumstances."

She had questions, and by his expression, so did Mikani, but before either of them could get started, Argyle stood with economical grace. "I bid you both good luck… and good day."

* * *

Mikani breathed deeply of the briny air and sneezed. *Hells and Winter. I thought I was done with this place when I was transferred to Central.* His years as a rookie hunting down smugglers on the East Docks had left him with some good memories and a sound knowledge of the area. They'd also left him with a couple of dozen scars and a severe aversion to the open sea. He looked around the street, looking for a weathered signpost.

"The Marlin Hook. Not fancy, but their beer's good, and it's run by a retired constabulary sergeant." Beckoning to Ritsuko, he led the way down. "If we're lucky, we might even be able to book passage there."

"I suspect you have a bar for every occasion," his partner muttered.

"You're ever the optimist."

The tavern was much as he remembered it: rough and filled with sailors. Dangerous men stared as they went, some bearing House insignia on their skin. He shouldered through the crowd, checking over one shoulder to make sure Ritsuko was keeping up. Mikani dropped a handful of copper on the counter and signaled the barman to bring them a couple of beers. He didn't recognize anyone, but that wasn't surprising, considering it had been years since he'd patrolled the area.

Ritsuko was scanning the room. If he knew her, she had already cataloged the exits, what items could potentially be used as weapons, which patrons were armed, and which of them had drunk enough to be belligerent. She settled on a stool nearby, pressing toward the counter to keep from being shoved from behind.

"Any of these gentlemen captain their own ships?" she asked, as the bartender carried over two frothy mugs of ale.

The bartender snorted as he set down their glasses. "There's not been a gentleman in here since the place opened up, I'd wager, lass. But Riley there's lord and master of the *Gift of Albion*." He nodded toward a loud, stocky man in the far corner, telling a joke to an assorted group of sailors and prostitutes. "And young Girish over there just inherited his old man's steamer last month. There's probably a couple of small-timers scattered around somewhere, if you're looking for a sloop or a short trip to the Southern Isles." He headed off to the other side of the bar to deal with another customer.

Mikani studied the two men the barkeep had pointed out. "Riley, was it? Smuggler, I'd wager a month's pay. Probably has a small, fast ship and knows all the best routes. But I'm not sure he'd take vouchers. We could try Girish, long as you don't mind cramped quarters." He lifted his mug. "After our drinks, anyway. They look like they're sticking around for a while. So." He turned his full attention to Ritsuko. "Guess we're taking a paid vacation to the lovely, barren Winter Isle."

"Do you think we can *do* anything up there?" she asked.

Without waiting for a reply, she downed half of her ale. She didn't look like a woman who could hold her liquor, but she didn't choke or splutter. He considered the question. "Hell if I know, partner. But even I'm not about to refuse the Architect."

"I'd be happier about the mission if I felt sure we could make a difference. It seems like we're deserting in the city's time of need."

Mikani sighed. *I feel the same way.* "House politics complicate everything. I suspect Olrik thinks we're the best he can do under the circumstances."

"*That's* comforting."

They finished their drinks in silence, then Mikani led the way over to Girish's table. The other man glanced up with an expectant, slightly impatient expression. "Can I help you?"

"We need passage to Northport, have vouchers from the Council, which means you can probably pad the bill." Mikani grinned, figuring that would strike the right note.

To his surprise, the captain laughed. "Good luck with that, mate. You won't find a berth on any ship heading north, not even for ten barrels of the Council's gold."

"Why not?" Ritsuko asked.

Girish skimmed her up and down in an openly appraising look. Mikani grabbed the smaller man's ear and pulled him close with a yank that had him spilling his beer, to the amusement of nearby patrons. "Eyes on me, boy. Now, speak."

The man rubbed his ear with a fulminating air, then muttered a curse damning Mikani's parentage. "You should've said she was spoken for. I don't see a ring on those pretty fingers." He made a noise in his throat, and Girish hastened to add, "Look, people are desperate and frightened. They're hoping things are better elsewhere, so the ships are booked. And word is, it's terrifying on the Winter Isle. Captains are rerouting shipments as we speak."

"You're saying we can't get there by any means?" His partner sounded doubtful.

"None that I know of, miss."

"Damn it," she murmured. "He's telling the truth."

Mikani shook his head and finished his ale with a long draught. "We'll just have to find a captain with some...

courage. Let's head out, partner, looks like we will be walking the docks."

Girish turned out to be right. *Bloody little bugger.*

They had walked north along the docks for a mile or more now and spoken to a dozen captains of liners, merchantmen, and a couple of smaller ships that did quick runs up and down the coast to trade with the scattered townships and House holdings along the inner sea. They had all confirmed what they'd already heard: everyone who could afford passage was booking and double-booking berths, cargo space, and even spots on the decks of ships heading up and down the coast of the Summer Isle.

Several of the older clipper ships had House Magnus guards posted at the gangplanks and on deck guarding their wind generators. The crystal engines allowed the light clipper ships to travel faster than most steamers, as their elementals provided a steady and controlled source of wind. From the ragged look of some of the sails, Mikani guessed that the air spirits were starting to show their teeth.

And unfortunately, none of them are heading for Northport. At least, not with room for a couple of CID inspectors. Mikani could almost take that personally.

"The Architect might have to commandeer a ship," Ritsuko said finally.

"We'd be lucky not to end up in the briny deep a mile out to sea."

At this point, there was only one sailor they hadn't talked to: the smuggler back at The Marlin Hook. So Mikani retraced his steps. Girish smirked when they stepped back into the bar. He ignored the merchant captain and cut a path directly for Riley, who was about to begin a game of darts. Vouchers wouldn't work with this one, so he had to come up with better coin. *Gunwood will likely have my arse for this.*

"Captain Riley. We're in need of a ship. Ordinarily, our interests wouldn't coincide, but I'm in the unique position of being able to offer you certain liberties from taxation or inspection when you put into port."

Riley turned, arching a brow. "And who the hell're you, then?"

Mikani performed the introductions briskly, hoping the smuggler had the wit to recognize a good offer when he heard one. The other man appeared to think it over, then he said, "I wouldn't hang such a bargain on a handshake. I'm no fool. What assurance can you offer me?"

"I'll go with you to speak to the port authority, vouch for you personally."

"That might prove of some use," Riley said grudgingly. "Where are you going?"

"Northport." Ritsuko spoke for the first time.

At this, Riley laughed. "Not for a hundred promises of free trade. I'll take you north up the coast, if you like. Maybe you'll find a captain crazier than me in Bloenn's Bay."

Mikani exchanged a look with his partner. She shook her head slightly, and he had to agree. He hated ships, and he wasn't getting on one without a guarantee it would take him where the Architect said they had to go.

Sighing, he said, "Thanks for the offer, but it won't serve."

"What now?" Ritsuko asked, as soon as they left the tavern.

He thought about it as he walked, and the obvious answer dawned. "There's one more captain we can ask. Bronze gods know what it'll cost me."

4

Free Merchant Alexandra Braelan cursed and threw a heavy ledger in the general direction of her shift clerk. The small man ducked and retreated a bit farther into the scant cover provided by the doorframe before continuing his report.

"The crew are safe, Mistress. They'll be back home in the next week or so. And the insurance agents will cover this incident even though they're grumbling about it. Our rates—"

"Enough!" She looked around for another ledger to throw.

The curtains billowed behind her as the ambient temperature dropped. *Bronze gods. Get ahold of yourself before you tear the building down.* She took a deep breath to steady her temper, bracing both hands on the edge of her desk. She could feel the turmoil of her elemental familiars, swirling around her in sympathetic anger. The clerk, Loison, beat a quick retreat while she soothed her spirits. Saskia sank into her chair and looked over the report while gathering her long blond hair back into a braid. She had lost another ship to cragger pirates, who were getting bolder by the day in their raids.

The craggers were named after the jagged coastline where

they lived, a strange people, wilder and more primitive than the rest of Hy Breasil. Attempts at both diplomacy and war with them had been equally fruitless in the six centuries since they first appeared. They usually confined their attacks to isolated settlements and lone ships straying too far from established trading routes; their skill at hiding in the broken coastline made it more expensive to try to hunt them down than to take the occasional loss.

For the past three months or so, however, they had been ranging farther into the Inner Sea, forcing the larger shipping concerns—those allied or subservient to Houses Magnus and Skarsgard—to travel in escorted convoys. That made *them* harder to hit but presented the free merchant ships as much more tempting targets. Some captains had banded together for mutual protection, but when the pirates hit, individual captains were far likelier to cut and run than to defend the other vessels.

The bloody craggers will break us. And the damned Houses will probably give them all medals for it. She sighed, closed her eyes, and leaned back. Siren Trading, her free merchant company, had lost three ships in as many months. She'd be out of business within the year, and she'd sworn she'd do anything to avoid crawling to Stefan Magnus for a commission on some backwater route that'd ensure she never paid off her bond.

"Gods, I'd rather become a pirate myself. Get some payback... paint the *Gull* red. No more ledgers, accounts, suppliers, and twice-damned clients." Saskia cut her daydream short at Loison's discreet cough.

"Apologies, Mistress. Er, before you head out for plunder and rapine, Inspectors Mikani and Ritsuko are here to see you." Loison held the tossed ledger protectively before him.

Either Janus is here to pay his debt, or he needs help... but no more kindness on credit, even for him. Slippery bastard, he is. Little wonder I enjoyed catching him so much... She stopped that train of thought and straightened in her chair.

"Well, show them in!"

"Of course." Loison paused. "You'd make quite the dashing pirate queen." He left as she searched for another book to throw at his back.

When Mikani stepped in a few moments later, she could tell he was having a rough go of it as well. He looked uncomfortable, as well he should, as he hadn't responded to any of her messages. She didn't rise, merely folded her hands at her desk and raised her eyebrows.

"The last time you walked off, it took three years to see you again. So I suppose we're making progress. You're here to make things right, I assume?" she asked in lieu of greeting.

Mikani fidgeted, hands in his pockets. He didn't sit without an invitation, and she didn't offer one. His reply would dictate how well disposed she felt toward him.

"About that..." he began.

Saskia shook her head. "I don't want to hear excuses. I'm not interested in any of your stories or promises this time, Janus."

"Sorry to trouble you," Ritsuko said, "but if his credit's worn thin, would mine be better?"

She didn't know the woman well, so she wasn't sure if that was meant as humor or an actual attempt to barter. *If she wants a deal, she'll have to fight for it.* "What did you have in mind, Inspector?"

"We need to arrange transport to Northport, but several hours at the docks proved fruitless. Mikani led me to believe that you can accomplish the impossible... for a price."

Saskia did her best to keep a straight face. *Oh, bronze gods. I swear I'll tithe you so, so well for this stroke of luck.* "Really? Strange to hear that he still thinks highly of me, given the way he's been avoiding me." She did not glance over at Janus, who was studying the ceiling of her office. "You realize you're asking for passage during storm season and through a gauntlet of bloody pirates? And that I could get my weight… no, *his* weight, in gold"—she flicked a pen toward Mikani, unable to resist—"to head down south carrying some rich, fat noble and his brood to safety?"

"But then you'd be deprived of our company," Mikani said.

Saskia stood. She pressed her hands down on her desk, hard, to keep from strangling him. "You arrogant, annoying… idiot!" She rounded her desk, and Mikani held up his hands. "You threaten to arrest me when we break up, come asking for help with a black sorcerer—"

"Technically, he was a Ferisher. And you *had* blown up that Magnus ship, just before we had our differences—" Mikani covered his head as she swung at him.

"—and now you come asking for a *ride*?"

The other woman wore a bemused expression, as if she couldn't decide if she ought to intervene. Then she slid smoothly between them. Ritsuko didn't say anything about the altercation, but her body language made it clear she found it unproductive. "I believe I might prove of some use to you, Miss Braelan."

Saskia straightened her dress and glared at Mikani a moment longer before turning her attention to his partner. "Then you'll have to convince me, Inspector. Unless you mean to hold down your partner while I beat some gratitude into him."

"No. I'll never do that. And I would find it most disagreeable if you tried." Inspector Ritsuko smiled slightly. "I perceive you to be a logical woman, however, and it behooves you to listen to what I'm offering."

"I hope it's good. Go ahead."

The inspector laced her hands together, seeming nervous, more than Saskia had ever seen in their admittedly short acquaintance. Mikani's partner was generally calm to the point of seeming cold, though if Mikani had worked with her for this long, Ritsuko couldn't be a complete automaton.

Today, however, she was a little more animated; Saskia wasn't sure why.

"I'm not sure how much you know about what happened belowground," Ritsuko said.

Saskia frowned, heading back to her chair. "I've heard the rumors. Mole people. A portal to the abyss. The Winter king's court, take your pick... you saw the stories in the news sheets."

"In fact, Mikani and I thwarted an attempt to steal magic from young House scions and in the process, open a door for spirits that have faded, flooding this world with their energy."

"That... that would've been very, very bad." She clearly remembered the feeling of cold oblivion around that infernal machine: her bones had ached for days after.

"What most people don't know is... when I disabled the device, it contained all the magic the maniac had leeched from his victims, and I conducted the full charge." Ritsuko's mouth twisted wryly. "That... changes you. My point being, I can do something now that I couldn't before. Tell me a truth and a lie. I'll tell you which is which, every time."

"I did not blow up Stefan Magnus's ship. Even though the highborn bastard tried to steal the *Gull* from my father." *And I'll never forgive him for that.*

"The former is a lie. The latter is true. You can test me again if you like—with something Mikani wouldn't have been able to tell me."

Saskia leaned back in her chair. "I've been engaged twice."

Janus looked at her, brows arched.

"That's true," Ritsuko said instantly. "I imagine you can envision multiple applications for my skills: contract negotiations, disputes with suppliers, hiring or discipline of employees. It would also enhance your reputation as a woman impossible to bluff or shortchange."

I'd love to have her along to negotiate next year's contracts with the southern Holdings. If there is a next year...

"You make an appealing point, Inspector." She looked from her to Janus, who was still across the room. "And I'd be willing to offer you passage for your assistance in return for, say... six months of service, as needed?"

"That sounds fair to me, provided I'm not otherwise engaged. As long as I have the time, it is yours, Miss Braelan. And I *do* keep my promises."

"Hells and Winter, Saskia, you know that kind of an edge would be worth thousands—"

"You! Janus Mikani, you *owe* me." Saskia shifted to face him as he stepped closer. "What your partner's offering covers her passage." She narrowed her eyes.

He caught her look, and she could see he knew what was coming. *Oh, good. You always hated it when I cornered you, Janus.*

"So I'll take you up north... only because that's where the trouble is. And you'll help with those Winter-blown cragger bastards, like you promised. I happen to be angrier at them than you, so it's your lucky day."

He folded his arms. She could feel him sizing her up. "And what do you think I'll be doing, Saskia? Arresting the thousands of craggers along the Jagged Coast? Do a mass trial, after they come along quietly?"

She smiled. *Got you.* "Oh, no, you sweet idiot. I want the Janus Mikani that wrecked Black Jack's smuggling ring, after breaking his neck and putting half his gang in the hospital. I need you to help me kill the cragger chieftain."

5

THE DOCKS RECEDED as the white sails billowed with mysterious wind. Saskia Braelan radiated an air of wild majesty as she whispered. *She's beautiful,* Ritsuko admitted silently. *I understand what Mikani sees in her.* In some ways, they were the same: reckless abandon, pure passion, and lack of regret. That might be why their romance was doomed, however; the relationship lacked the space for two titans.

Ritsuko sensed the residual tingle of magic use to speed their departure as she stood at the rails watching the bustle of porters moving crates along the docks. Their figures grew smaller in proportion to the distance traveled. The *Gull* was a lively vessel, crewed by sailors who answered to Saskia Braelan, a woman who showed signs of wanting to kill Mikani.

This should be interesting.

Ritsuko turned to her partner. "Well, we made it this far. I'm not positive she won't execute you and dump you overboard once we've been at sea for a while, however. You sure know how to charm a woman."

Mikani grimaced and looked over his shoulder to where Saskia bellowed orders and steered the ship with equal ease.

"She might. She could be waiting for us to get to deeper waters." He shifted his weight as they veered around a buoy, his knuckles whitening as he gripped the railing harder. "She can hold a grudge with the best of them."

"That's nothing to do with you," she teased. "Purely *her* character flaw?"

"She's also flawed like the worst of them. I should know." He gazed out toward the receding docks, looking a little pale.

"Something wrong?"

"I don't like ships, never have."

"Don't tell me you're prone to seasickness?" Ritsuko had never felt more alive than with the waves bucking beneath the sleek little ship, the wind blowing salty kisses on her skin.

"I just don't like the thought of there being nothing but six inches of wood between me and the several hundred feet of dark, cold, clammy water filled with... wriggling, scaly, slithering... things. Down there."

She schooled her features into a neutral expression. "You mean things with tentacles? Big, lurking, could swallow a ship whole, sort of things?"

Mikani *growled* at her. "I've half a mind to send you down to find out."

She laughed. "Come along, before you succumb to your darker urges. We should make the rounds and get acquainted with the crew."

He pushed away from the railing and led the way along the deck toward the forecastle, where the first mate kept watch to make sure they cleared the busy waters nearest the docks and out into the bay. Mr. Loison, Saskia's employee, stood nearby. The clerk offered a smile as they came closer, one hand resting on a rope to keep his balance. Ritsuko surveyed him, cataloging the good quality of his tailoring to his neatly trimmed hair. He was a slender man of average height, light brown hair, and long nose, upon which a pair of round spectacles perched.

"Inspectors. So very glad to be along. I don't often get to see the earthy side of the business." He gestured at the first mate, a tall and lanky man who was ignoring them. Scars and tattoos adorned both the sailor's arms and ran up along the back of his bald head in intricate patterns. "That's Ferro. Usually serves as first mate to Captain Piers, but with Mistress Braelan along, the captain's on shore leave for the next few days."

"He doesn't seem very social," Ritsuko observed.

Mr. Ferro turned when she spoke, raising a brow bisected by a scar. "I'm not here to amuse you; I'm here to be sure the *Gull* makes the journey intact."

Ritsuko didn't let the man's attitude impact her own manners. "Still, I'm pleased to meet you, sir. I thank you in advance for your efforts to ensure our safe voyage."

The first mate narrowed his eyes on her, then nodded abruptly, before turning his attention back to the shifting water traffic before them. She appraised him for a few seconds longer. He wore typical sailing attire, a pair of trousers belted with a tie, and a loose, sleeveless tunic that revealed rather excellent arms. Despite his taciturn nature, he seemed like an interesting man.

"You definitely charmed him, partner." Mikani gripped the same rope as Loison with both hands but didn't look quite as uncomfortable now he'd stopped looking out to sea.

"Quite!" Loison said. "The most I've gotten him to say is 'move.'"

"Yes, my feminine wiles are legendary." She smiled to show she was joking, as people didn't always know, and the clerk smiled.

"So who else is along for the fun?" Mikani asked.

"There's the boatswain, Nell Oliver, over there."

Ritsuko swiveled her head in the direction Mr. Loison indicated, until she spotted a short, thick-built woman of indeterminate years. Miss Oliver was dressed much like Mr.

Ferro, though she had more hair, a tangled mass of black and silver, tied up in a messy bundle on top of her head. She was lecturing a young man on proper care of the decking, and the boy sighed, looking as if he wanted to kick the pail sitting beside him, but he didn't quite dare.

"She seems competent," she noted.

"And with her, you'll note the cabin boy, Sam."

"He's a rigging monkey," Mr. Ferro muttered from a few paces away.

That told her that the first mate was listening even if he was too busy peering at the ocean to participate in the conversation. Idly, Ritsuko wondered if she could persuade him to hoax a sea-monster attack, just to see Mikani's face; she stole a look at him, stifling a smirk.

He was frowning and looking around the deck. "Is Big Hu still around?"

"He's below, securing the infirmary." Mr. Ferro gave her partner a quizzical look. "You know him?"

"We've met." Mikani turned back toward her. "He threw me overboard when Saskia and I had our last disagreement." He pulled up his sleeve, to show her an old scar from wrist to elbow. "He can be very protective of her. I should let him know that she and I are back on good terms before we get much farther out to sea."

Ritsuko couldn't suppress her laughter. "Yesterday, she beat you about the head and neck. If those are good terms, you couldn't survive her wrath." Nell Oliver was still lecturing young Sam, so she turned to Mr. Loison. "Could you show us to the infirmary? I'd like to know where to find medical attention."

The clerk nodded and offered his arm politely. "It would be my pleasure."

Ritsuko placed her fingers on his jacket. "Lead on, sir."

Mr. Loison stepped away from the mast and weaved through deck obstacles to the hatch that led below. An angled ladder required her to move cautiously against the rocking ship, and she was relieved when the floor leveled out beneath her. The wood was warm and well maintained, with a series of doors down a narrow corridor. One of the sailors had taken her things to her cabin, so she hadn't been down here yet.

"This way." Mr. Loison turned politely to make sure she was still with him.

Mikani came last as they went down toward the end of the corridor. The last door on the left was open, and it bore a plaque graven with the word INFIRMARY. It was a small but efficiently designed room with cabinets built into the walls, various canisters Ritsuko guessed were full of treatments and tinctures, along with a small bunk for ailing patients. But the most remarkable thing was the man frowning at them from within.

She grasped at once why Mikani had called him Big Hu, as he towered over every member of their party, even her partner, by half a foot. He had black hair worn in a single oiled braid, amber eyes, dark skin, and a menacing demeanor. This impression was enhanced by a massive chest and symmetrical facial scars. Ritsuko couldn't imagine anyone looking less like a doctor, but according to Mr. Loison, this man was in charge of the crew's physical well-being.

He also apparently doubles as Miss Braelan's bodyguard.

"Janus Mikani." Hu's voice was a bass growl, like a stone elemental rumbling deep in the ground. "Give me one good reason why I shouldn't throw you over again."

* * *

Hells and Winter. He's actually gotten bigger in the last few years, Mikani thought.

"I'll give you three, Hu. One; this time, I'm not bleeding out and half-unconscious, so you'd have your hands full." Mikani took a step closer, stepping in front of Ritsuko instinctively.

"Two, Saskia and I made peace, or I wouldn't be aboard this ship. And you know it, or you'd have been on me before I got off the gangplank." He took another step closer to the ship's doctor, looking up to meet his eyes as he came close enough to tap Hu on the chest with two fingers. "And three, you'd miss my winning personality."

The two men glared at each other for a long moment. Then Hu broke out laughing and wrapped thick arms around Mikani in a bruising hug. "Damn, it's good to see you again, you bastard. I heard you survived, but you were scarce after you and Li'l White had your falling-out."

Little White. Mikani hadn't heard that nickname in a long time; only Hu called Saskia that, after her flowing blond locks and the white robes she'd favored back then. Though she'd taken to braiding her hair and had traded her robes for city-styled gowns, Saskia still didn't like wearing shoes. *Good to know some things don't change.*

He shoved Hu away, finding it hard to breathe. "Yeah, well, you didn't write much, did you?" Truth was, he'd missed Hu almost as much as Saskia the first few months.

As soon as the other man loosened his hold, Mikani rubbed his ribs. "Dr. Irahi Hu, this is Inspector Celeste Ritsuko. My partner—"

"Bronze gods, man, you made it? You just lost me ten crescents." Hu grinned, his teeth white and even, and extended a massive hand to Ritsuko. "It's nice to meet you, Inspector."

Ritsuko took the offered hand, looking from one man to the other with as much amusement as curiosity. "The pleasure is mine, Doctor. I'm glad you two are on good terms."

Mikani snorted. "We both shed a few tears when Saskia ordered him to get rid of me after we broke the House Magnus blockade."

When he was a rookie constable, Mikani had connected with Saskia and her crew when she got wind of a plot to steal her father's ship. As it turned out, House Magnus was up to its neck in dirty dealing, but when they boarded to recover the evidence, Saskia lost her temper. Mikani tried to stop her from blowing up the ship, which was when Hu stepped in.

The doctor straightened, folding his arms against his chest. "You really should have gotten out of our way, Mikani. I asked nicely."

"With a piece of mainmast!" Mikani shook his head and let out a rueful laugh. "I'll pay you back for that sometime. Right now, though... can you tell us anything about what Saskia has in mind? Why does she want to go after the cragger chieftain?"

Hu let out a deep sigh. "Li'l White is convinced that this one's different. I'll admit, the raiders are acting strange, raiding too far abroad, taking no captives for ransom. They're like beasts, Mikani. They're more interested in murder than pillage, burning any ships that cross their path, like the lot of them have gone insane." He shook his head, clearly puzzled.

No wonder Saskia's worried about these bastards. And he's right; it doesn't make sense. I can't remember any time when the craggers have gone for blood instead of gold.

"And she thinks this chieftain's the key? That he's driven them mad?"

Hu nodded. "You know how she is. She's convinced but won't tell the rest of us why. She swears going after him will send the craggers scurrying north along the Jagged Coast."

A bell echoed somewhere above.

The doctor motioned for them to get out of the infirmary. "We've cleared port, and I have things to do before we hit the Inner Sea. Go find someplace you won't be in the way, and I'll see you at dinner. Maybe you can get Li'l White to tell us what's going on."

Mikani only made a token protest as they were shuffled out, knowing full well that no one on the ship would have time for them over the next few hours. With a resigned sigh, he led Ritsuko toward their staterooms. "Well, Ritsuko, looks like I get to teach you to play Courts."

"Courts?"

"Card game, favorite amongst sailors. You'll need to hold your own, or they'll try to get you to wager everything from your shirt to your badge."

At his gesture, she stepped into the cabin he'd claimed. His oilskin bag lay in one corner, the only item in the room that wasn't bolted down. There was a bunk built into the wall, a small writing desk, and a couple of sea chests rounding out the stark décor.

Ritsuko leaned against the door, looking thoughtful. "I'm not sure if I want to learn. It might be fun to lose my shirt, especially to the good doctor."

Mikani paused as he reached for his deck of cards, a tug in his chest at the thought of Ritsuko with his old friend. Over the last few weeks, they had tiptoed around the shift in their relationship. *Gods know, I'm in no hurry to figure it out.* He put the cards down, doing his best to keep his tone light and teasing. "Ritsuko, stay away from Hu. He's a decent man, and I don't want you corrupting him with your city ways."

"You think I could? Excellent." She was grinning when she strolled out.

Two hours later, Mikani gazed around the captain's cabin. *Saskia's made a few changes. Or it might've been what's his name... Piers.*

Hangings had been replaced with maps, marked in various spots with red ink. The heavy table was the same, however, with the ledgers that usually littered its surface piled up against the wall. By the number of chairs—three on each side and one at the head, there would be seven guests tonight. From experience, he knew the bed was tucked out of sight in a niche, a curtain to safeguard her privacy. The rest of the cabin looked more like an office than a pirate hideaway; she truly was more businesswoman than privateer these days.

Pity, that.

Platters of food were already waiting, along with tall tin cups. Sam the cabin boy stood by the door with an ewer; Mikani hoped it was better-quality grog than Saskia bought for her sailors. The boy nodded at each guest as he or she stepped in. Mikani and Ritsuko were the first to arrive. His partner had clearly done her hair, put on a hint of perfume, and she'd actually painted her mouth.

Don't think I've seen her in lip rouge since... well, ever. He shook his head and sat next to the head of the table. The sway of the ship was hardly noticeable now they were out in the open sea, and he'd been able to find enough distractions belowdecks to keep from worrying about the dark depths below them.

The rest filed in, Hu glaring at him over his choice of seats before pointedly taking the chair across from him and next to Saskia. Ferro and Nell filled out that side of the table, so Loison took the last spot next to Ritsuko with a murmured greeting. Saskia was the last to arrive. Her hair was barely contained in a couple of long braids that she'd looped over her shoulders, and she'd changed from the loose sailor garb she preferred aboard ship to a more formal ensemble of crimson pantaloons and a billowy overcoat that left her forearms free. As usual, she was barefoot, barely making a sound on the wooden floor as she took her seat.

Dinner started slow, but soon the frequent refills on ale and Hu's good humor broke the ice between the crew and passengers. Small talk prevailed for most of the meal, talk about trade winds and usual routes devolving into a pointless but good-natured argument between Loison and the boatswain over the cost of keeping the ship in good repair. On the other side of the table, Ritsuko laughed at Hu's jokes, and Irahi delighted in it, reaching over more than once to touch Ritsuko's wrist as he regaled her with tales of his travels with Saskia, Piers, and others.

There was no reason he should mind seeing someone else with her. *We're partners, that's all.* And if the intensity of the last case made him entertain other possibilities, well, he hadn't said anything to her about it. He forced the ambivalence down, focusing on his food and wineglass. Yet Mikani still studied Ritsuko and Hu, a frown chewing between his brows. Part of him was glad she seemed to be getting along with his old friends while another wanted to pull Ritsuko away.

Even with the odd twinges, he eased with the chatter around him. *Feels almost like old times.* Finally, Saskia rang the silver bell that signaled the end of dinner. Sam scrambled to clear the plates and bring a fresh bottle of wine as they pushed their chairs back and relaxed to the soft sounds of creaking wood and the ship's cutting across the waves.

"Dr. Hu mentioned earlier that the craggers are behaving oddly," Ritsuko said to Saskia. "Could you tell us a little more about what lies ahead?"

6

RITSUKO WATCHED MISS Braelan expectantly, but the other woman was sprawled in her chair, sipping a drink; she lifted her glass lazily in Mr. Ferro's direction, and Ritsuko took that as an invitation for him to answer.

The first mate acknowledged by responding, "The Inner Sea. We sail along the skirts of Mount Surtir, near the Seven Sisters." He leaned back against the wall of the cabin, bringing a foot up to rest on his chair. Miss Oliver smacked his knee, earning her a glare before he straightened and continued. "That'll be the dangerous part."

Ritsuko tried to think where she'd heard that. Her last geography course had been years ago. "The Seven Sisters? That's the western islands, right?"

Dr. Hu sighed wistfully, drawing her attention. "They're paradise itself. Long summers and cool winters. Fruits just waiting to be plucked, beaches of the whitest, softest sand you'll ever see. And the people, lovely, generous, and brave… lovers without equal!" He gestured with his glass when Miss Braelan chortled, and Mikani rolled his eyes, splashing wine toward them. "Pay no attention to those two, they're bloody pagans."

Miss Braelan dabbed at the wine stains on her pantaloons with a folded napkin. "Irahi's from western Maia, the Sister closest to the Summer Isle."

"It's charming to see such enthusiasm for his homeland." Ritsuko had already surmised as much, but she smiled at the doctor. "I'm sure it's a beautiful place, sir."

"Please, call me Irahi. We're all friends here, no?" He flashed a bright smile, and Ritsuko decided he was even more striking when he turned on the charm.

"Then you should call me Celeste." She pulled her attention from the doctor to ask Miss Braelan, "But we're not making port in the Seven Sisters, are we?"

"No." Miss Oliver leaned forward to answer. "We'll use the currents along the westernmost shore of Winter to gain speed." The woman put her hands together, sliding them in opposite directions to demonstrate. "And we'll berth in Northport before the week's done. Refit, resupply, and head off to find us the cragger chieftain."

The boatswain paused at a look from Miss Braelan, murmuring an apology and picking at the last of the meal on her plate. Ritsuko wondered what the exchange portended, what secrets Mikani's former paramour might be keeping. *It's bad enough that she wants him to play hired killer. How much worse could it get?* Possibly she wouldn't like the answer.

"Not much detail there, Saskia." Mikani refilled his glass and stared into it after he addressed Miss Braelan. "I'm not sure I can charm my way past a townful of craggers so we can put a bullet through their chieftain's heart."

Ritsuko thought there was something off in his tone. Perhaps he didn't like the cost of his passage any more than she did. The rest of the crew seemed oddly still, like they knew something she didn't. Not surprising, since Mikani had known these folks longer, so they doubtless were better acquainted with the nuances between her partner and Miss Braelan. It seemed likely that there were myriad shared stories, adventures, and complications of which she knew nothing. Her smile froze just a little.

"I have complete faith in your ability to charm your idiot self into the most dangerous spot in any situation, Janus." Much of Miss Braelan's prior anger seemed to have dissipated after a few hours at sea. She grinned at Mikani, appearing in good charity with him.

With a pang, Ritsuko remembered interrupting an intimate meal at Mikani's house and how at-home Miss Braelan had been. *Whereas I just visited his place for the first time this year.* Through a burst of melancholy, she pulled her thoughts to the present.

At the first conversational lull, Ritsuko said, "Could you tell me a little more about the Winter Isle? I've never done any traveling."

It was a general inquiry, meant for anyone at the table, but Miss Braelan replied. "It's a bleak but beautiful place, Inspector, small but lively. Northport is no Dorstaad, and the Houses don't hold as tight a rein. House Thorgrim isn't big on law and order, so they let Winter settlements fend for themselves. As long as they don't disrupt the fire and earth elemental trade caravans leaving Mount Surtir, Thorgrim doesn't interfere."

Doctor Hu nodded, evidently glad to speak of something other than the craggers. "Farming collectives, ordered little towns all but worshipping a charismatic leader, loose collections of people sharing worship of some obscure god. You'll find them all, and stranger, in the Winter Isle. The one rule is, don't try to smuggle elemental vessels out of Winter."

"Elemental smuggling?" Ritsuko arched a brow, puzzled. It was common knowledge that fire elementals were bound in spheres of amber and earth elementals to heavy, leaden discs; anything beyond that was a closely guarded secret of the elemental Houses. "But I thought Houses Skarsgard and Aevar owned the mines. Why would Thorgrim care if someone tried to steal salamanders and gnomes?"

Mr. Loison cleared his throat politely, and Ritsuko started. The clerk had been so quietly focused on his wine that she'd forgotten he was beside her. *At times, the ability to feign invisibility must prove extremely helpful.* She could envision any number of applications, and that likely gave Miss Braelan an advantage in gathering intelligence on her competitors.

The clerk said, "House Thorgrim controls Northport, Inspector Ritsuko. They levy an export tax on every elemental that leaves Winter Island. That's their main source of income, so they tend to take harsh punitive action against smugglers. Both elemental Houses have tried to set up their own ports in the last hundred years, seeking a way to avoid the fees."

"And they've failed every time." Mikani drained his glass and refilled it again. "Freak storms, crop failures, cragger attacks. Thorgrim once sent a fleet with 'disaster assistance' after a mysterious plague struck a small town sponsored by House Skarsgard. They claimed the settlers were all dead when they found them." He smiled grimly. "Aevar and Skarsgard have more or less given up on the effort now."

Miss Braelan sighed into the silence that followed. "Bronze gods, Janus, you know how to end a pleasant dinner, don't you?"

The other woman tossed her empty wine goblet at him; he caught it and set it on the table as everyone rose from their seats. Miss Oliver wore a dour expression, as did Mr. Ferro, but since that was the only aspect Ritsuko had ever seen from the first mate, she had no idea if Mikani had impacted his mood. Mr. Loison appeared inscrutable as ever. The doctor had drunk less than Mikani, so far as Ritsuko could tell, but he swayed slightly on his feet. It amused her that a man so large would have low alcohol tolerance.

"Get some rest, everyone. It'll be two or three days to the Seven Sisters since I need to save my strength for the crossing past Mount Surtir."

Ritsuko recalled how the other woman had stood on deck, singing as the sails swelled. Unless she was mistaken, that made Miss Braelan a weather witch, but like usual, she sought confirmation. "The wind before wasn't natural?"

Miss Braelan shook her head, then regarded Mikani with a smile. "Good night, Inspectors. Irahi, get to your bunk before you keel over. Likewise, Nell. Mr. Ferro, you have command until first light. Now, if you'll all be so kind, get out of my cabin so I can sleep."

Sam hovered, waiting to clear the table and tidy the cabin for his captain. He was a scrawny lad, covered in freckles, but he didn't seem unhappy with his lot. In the stories, cabin boys were beaten and starved, but Sam seemed to enjoy serving on the *Gull*. From what she'd seen, it was a beautiful ship, sleek in the water and efficiently designed belowdecks.

"Thank you for your excellent stewardship tonight," she said to the boy.

He colored and bobbed an awkward acknowledgment, though he didn't speak. Turning, she stepped out into the hall, lit by special lamps affixed to the walls. The flickering flames cast interesting shadows on the others' skin as they followed her. Miss Oliver and Mr. Ferro only nodded a brief leave-taking and headed off, but the doctor embraced Mikani, then bowed with a grace that surprised Ritsuko given his size and evident intoxication.

"Dream well, Celestial one."

That's... unexpectedly sweet. Warren, her former beau, had never been one for pet names. She had chosen him for his logical approach to life, only to find that too much reason could kill all warmer feelings over time.

So she smiled up at the doctor. "You as well, Irahi."

He beamed in response to her use of his given name, then indicated Mikani with a tilt of his head. "Keep clear of that one, he's naught but trouble." The man flipped an unsteady salute at her partner and staggered toward the infirmary, singing at the top of his lungs in a dialect Ritsuko didn't recognize.

She glanced around. The boatswain and first mate had already disappeared from view, leaving her and her partner standing in the short corridor connecting the staterooms and captain's quarters. Mr. Loison hadn't yet emerged, which made Ritsuko think he must be giving Miss Braelan his impressions from dinner. She made a mental note to be on her guard around the clerk, whom she was sure was sharp as a steel trap.

He ran his fingers through his hair, even more disheveled than usual. "I need some air before lying down, partner. Join me on deck?"

* * *

Mikani leaned on the wooden rail, near the prow of the *Gull*. A quarter moon hung low in the sky. The darkness made it easier to ignore the vast emptiness of the sea all around him. The sound of the waves lapping at the hull and steady rocking of the ship didn't bother him as long as he didn't have to see the expanse of cold water all around.

"They seem a good crew." He turned toward Ritsuko, squinting against the sting of sea spray. "How are you liking your first sea voyage?"

"It's been exhilarating so far. I probably shouldn't enjoy work so much, but I've always wanted to see more of the world." She didn't seem affected at all by the sickness that sometimes plagued those new to sea travel.

Mikani smiled. *It's been years since I felt that excited about an assignment.*

He pinched the bridge of his nose and let out a long breath. "I'm glad one of us is having fun. Being cooped up in a wooden crate with Saskia in the middle of the sea and headed for the Winter Isle is not my idea of a vacation." He paused. "I'm glad you're here, though."

His partner slid him a look he couldn't interpret easily. He was tempted to check her emotional state, but he resisted the urge since it was an invasion of her privacy. His Ferisher gift had always been a curse and a blessing; he could read emotional imprints off objects and sense people's emotions if he concentrated, but using the talent always cost him in pain and often blood. Over the years, he'd learned to lock it away until he needed it. But since they'd killed Lorne Nuall, it had become a struggle not to lose himself in the currents of foreign feelings.

"Where else would I be? We're a team, right?"

Damned right. And I'm glad of it.

"We are. And you'd get in too much trouble without me as a steadying influence in your life. You might go wild."

Ritsuko brightened in a smile Mikani would call mischievous. "That seems like an *excellent* idea, especially here, where word of my misdeeds won't come back to haunt me." She paused, looking thoughtful. "Is there any chance that the doctor knows anyone else at the CID?"

Hells and Winter.

"Hu? Really?" Mikani was less than thrilled at the idea, though he couldn't say why. *And poking that tangled mess is not something I care to do just now.*

She arched a brow. "That doesn't answer the question. And why 'really'? He's a very impressive man."

Mikani leaned on the railing, scrutinizing his partner. "He's a good man, but I've never known you to show much interest in anyone so fast before, Ritsuko. Is the sea air affecting you? Romance of the waves, suddenly want to join the ranks of the Free Merchants?"

"That's the point. I don't imagine he has any interest in moving to Dorstaad. He's married to the nomadic life, whereas I've been nothing but settled. At this point, I could use a little excitement." She lifted her shoulder in a graceful shrug. "Though it's not something I've ever done, I've heard about the excitement of a holiday affaire. I suppose nearly dying has changed my outlook somewhat. I want... to *live*, not just work."

"I..." Mikani hesitated. *Never thought of it that way. Until this last bloody mess, I didn't spare a thought to what went on when we weren't together. Selfish of me. Damned if Jane wasn't right.* His last lover had told him in no uncertain terms that he had the emotional depth of a goose. "I can understand that. It must be hard to be so focused all the time."

"Not hard. Lonely." She looked out over the waves, the moonlight turning her skin to alabaster. "That's why I left the Mountain District. I wanted to talk to people who didn't disapprove of me on a daily basis. I was looking for some... warmth, I suppose, for want of a better word. I'm proud of the work we do, but I don't want it to define me any longer."

From what he recalled, Ritsuko's grandfather had died before they met, and she'd been orphaned when she was a baby. Any extended family disapproved of her since she'd chosen to handfast in place of permanent bond with Warren, and when she dissolved that arrangement without settling and having children, their displeasure deepened to near ostracism. Little wonder she preferred the boardinghouse near Central.

On the other hand, his relatives wished he came home more often. Mikani got nagging letters from his sister once a month, updating him on family business, though he skimmed the parts unrelated to his nieces and nephew. In truth, Ritsuko would probably appreciate the bonds he was trying to escape.

He laid a hand on her forearm. "Celeste, you're an exceptional woman. And I, for one, don't know what I'd do without you."

She shifted to face him then, and parted lips reflected her surprise. *Yes, I'm telling the truth.* He still hadn't gotten used to his partner's having that sense; he didn't know if it made things simpler or more complicated. *Both, probably.*

Then she put her palm over his. "You may know this

already… but you're the person I trust most in the world, Janus. If I were headed for hell, I'd want you at my back."

Mikani was very aware of her cool fingers on his skin and of just how close they were standing. "I know. Truth be told, this jaunt may end up being a good practice run for that." He squeezed her arm gently. "I'll do my best to get us out of it in one piece."

There was no way to be sure if she was conscious of the motion, but her thumb traced over his, and her fingertip rose and fell over the scars on his knuckles. "I have no doubt that you'll manage it, no matter the odds. You're a hell of a fighter."

Mikani studied Ritsuko's face, noticing the faint laugh lines and delicate curve of her jaw. He let go of her arm to turn his hand and clasp her fingers in his. "One need only have the right incentive."

"What was yours when you patrolled the docks?" She left their hands linked, a warm bond against the chill of the sea air. "From what I hear, you were cracking skulls all over."

Mikani chuckled, his fingers tracing the lines of her fingers entwined with his. "Back then, honestly, I was just angry. Angry at my father for going off to hunt down pirates and not coming back. At the Houses, for taking him away from us."

His fingers tensed against Ritsuko's, and he forced them to relax in her grip. She responded with gentle pressure that was probably supposed to be soothing. Ritsuko wasn't watching the ocean anymore; instead, her gaze was fixed on his face.

"I don't know if it's better or worse that you have memories of him… that you can miss him. I was so young when my parents died…"

"It depends on the day, I suppose. And on what memories come up." He shook his head. "Whatever else, he taught me as best he could, and now I try to not disappoint."

"He disappeared at sea? This must be especially tough for you." Her understanding tone cracked him open, just a little.

Mikani didn't ordinarily talk about his father. "When he disappeared, I got blind drunk at his favorite tavern. I made my way to the beach that night and spent three hours raging at the ocean and punching a dock support until I was picked up by the local constabulary." He chuckled at the memory. "They're always shorthanded up north, so I got the choice between serving my sentence at the penal farms and joining the force." She was listening raptly, so he continued, "The constables were a half dozen retired sailors and House Guard veterans. We dealt with thieves, smugglers, and the occasional raider, using clubs, axes, and scythes while we had no guns. They taught me how to fight to win."

"That explains your lack of finesse, Mikani. You were trained by thugs."

He smiled faintly. "I also learned that the Houses don't much care what happens as long as it doesn't inconvenience them." He let out a long breath and turned back toward the ocean as the memories flooded back. "We'd asked for help dealing with some raiders who had killed everyone in an outlying farm; the local lord told us to 'deal with them quickly.' We set an ambush and managed to board them; they cast off and headed for the open sea with four of us still on board. In the melee, the boat smashed into some rocks... only two of us made it back to shore, battered and half-drowned." He shook his head. "I still loathe the sea. Always feel like I might end up reuniting with my old man before I'm ready."

"He's the ghost who haunts you even though you're not certain if he's dead." Her observation was uncomfortably acute.

"He's my haunt and conscience, yes." Mikani straightened, rolling the tension from his shoulders as he did. He'd never shared so much with anyone. *I feel hollowed out. But... better. Strange.* "He's been gone over ten years, and I listen to him more than when he was here. Hells and Winter, I probably listen to him more than to... almost, anyone."

His partner took a step closer. "For what it's worth, Janus, I think he'd be really proud of you, the way you protect those who can't fight for themselves, and especially how you stand for fair play in a world where silver and gold often weight the scales of justice." Another step brought her within arm's reach, then she hugged him.

Mikani tensed for a moment in surprise. But he did not hesitate in wrapping his arms around her. With Ritsuko near, even the ocean didn't seem quite as terrible.

7

Wind billowed the sails, carrying damp with it that chilled Ritsuko's bones. While she loved the freedom of riding the ocean waves, she wasn't enjoying the weather. The closer they got to the Winter Isle, the clearer it became why it was so named. She nestled deeper into her coat and tugged the hood up to protect her cheeks, which felt hot, a sure sign that she'd let her skin get chapped.

In the distance rose the rugged shoreline of the Winter Isle. Gray basalt cliffs rose from the churning surf and beyond, the dark, imposing peak of Mount Surtir, wreathed in smoke and mist until it looked as if the crag had pierced the sky, and the heavens were bleeding fog. It was early morn, second full day on board. Yesterday, she'd spent an agreeable afternoon with the doctor, then they'd strolled on deck as the sun set over the water.

Beautiful. The colors are never so vibrant in Dorstaad.

"Are you armed?" Mr. Ferro clambered down the rigging, clearly addressing her.

"I have a gun in my cabin." She smiled at the first mate, wondering what it would take to dispel his morose expression. "Do you need me to shoot someone?"

He walked past, pointing off to her left. "Yes, anyone on that ship that comes close enough to *get* shot." A faint glimmer was barely visible above the waves where he pointed. "They'll be on us in an hour at most." He disappeared below, bellowing in a guttural dialect at the rest of the crew.

Sailors whose names she hadn't learned appeared on deck, preparing to defend the ship. Their hasty movements impressed on her the urgency of the situation, so Ritsuko ran for her cabin. Her small firearm might not do much damage in an attack, but it was better than being helpless. She was out of breath when she returned, fear warring with determination. A dozen sailors scrambled along the deck and up the masts; the *Gull* rode the waves with a loud and rhythmic roar on her hull. The doctor, Mikani, and a half dozen others stood with Miss Braelan amidships. Ritsuko hurried toward them.

"Definitely craggers. Look at the smoke. They're running dirty and full speed to catch up." The first mate loaded a rifle as he spoke.

"How long?" Devoid of his hat and stick, the unshaven stubble made Mikani look more piratical than any of the officers, and the axe slung over one shoulder added to that impression. He had a reputation for brutality amongst the other inspectors, and now that she'd heard the story of how he joined the force, she understood why.

"Fifteen, twenty minutes. We need to slow before we hit the shallows nearer shore, or we'll shred the keel and save them the trouble." Miss Braelan ignored the ship behind them, her hands steady on the wheel. "Another half day, and we'd have been out of their reach. If I call the elementals now, we'll run aground in the shallows."

So there will definitely be a battle. No wonder the other captains were so reluctant to risk this route. Grimly, Ritsuko drew the knife from her boot. She hadn't brought unlimited ammunition, so she'd need a backup once she ran out. Her breath came quicker at the notion of clashing with murderous pirates. *My self-defense training might not be enough.*

She didn't let fear win. "Where do you want me?"

Irahi turned toward her. "You're with me, Celeste." His gaze dropped, and he shook his head. "But you need better than that cheese slicer. Here." He slipped a dagger from his belt that looked like a cutlass in her hand.

"You make me give you a deposit for a fire axe, but just give her your favorite knife," Mikani muttered.

Ritsuko studied the blade. It was fine steel, highly polished, with an etched mother-of-pearl hilt. She'd seldom seen such fine craftsmanship, and it was sturdy enough that she suspected she could run someone through with it. *Or near enough.*

She was touched by Irahi's generosity. "I'll use this with the greatest care."

Then she stowed the smaller knife in her boot and slid the larger one through her belt. The weight felt reassuring on her hip, but she checked range of movement to make sure she could draw it quickly. *Best to be prepared.* She did her utmost to pretend she wasn't nervous since everyone else seemed calm.

But there's really nothing in the manual to cover this.

Ritsuko managed a smile for Mikani, hoping it was cheeky rather than uneasy. "He just likes me better. I bet he doesn't throw me overboard even once."

Ferro said, "Take this up later. Oliver, position your men portside. Cut the grapples as you can, and remember to give us a clear field of fire. I'll leave two men to guard—"

"I can take care of myself. Just get rid of the bastards." Miss Braelan gestured to the crew to prepare for battle.

"Aye aye, Cap'n." Mikani hefted the axe and headed to the back of the ship, whistling.

Ritsuko heard shouts when the craggers neared. They were a rough lot: bearded, filthy, and hollow-eyed. At the vanguard, the enemy whirled grappling hooks, then the metal prongs came sailing. Craggers hauled on the ropes en masse, tightening the distance between the two ships. Gunfire rang out, along with cries of pain. The ship jolted as the waves rocked it into the cragger vessel—and pirates poured over the rails.

The rush of bodies shoved her away from Ferro and Hu, and craggers surrounded her on all sides. She danced away from the first swipe and spun from another; in that same movement, Ritsuko whipped the cutlass from her belt. She shot a man in the gut and kicked him back. His body tripped the cragger that sliced at her; Ritsuko blocked with a clang of her blade and fired another shot. *Need to keep track.* That bullet ripped through a pirate's arm in a bloody spatter. She fired another round at the one looming behind, but it went wide on a roll of the ship.

Someone was shouting her name, but damned if she could pause to see who. The whole deck swarmed with pirates, as far as she could see. Her boots skidded on the spray-slick decking, tumbling her toward the rail. Nails tearing on the wood, she saved herself and narrowly avoided being skewered by a knife slashing from behind, but she wasn't fast enough. Her side stung, and there was a gash in her coat. The first cragger readied for a second charge while another shot at her, and she dove toward two barrels, set to collect rainfall. Splinters of wood bit into her ankles, and her breath came in choppy rasps.

"Come on, love. I've got all kinds of mercy for a pretty thing like you."

Mustering her nerve, she answered that offer with a blast to the chest. The pirate staggered and fell over with blood bubbling out of his mouth, but two more shouted and ran toward her hiding place, reeking of cheap rum, sour sweat, and old fish. Along with the fear, it was nearly enough to make her lose her dinner. *How many shots do I have left? Got three here.*

They converged on her from all sides, and she lashed out

with a kick from a squat, sweeping the ankles. She was fast enough to kill him with a shot to the head before he could get up, but there were two more with knives within stabbing distance. Ritsuko hoped the barrels weren't important as she shoved them over and leapt to avoid the rush of water. One of the pirates slid backward, and Hu took him over the side with an elbow to the face.

Three more rushed him, so she shouted, "Behind you!"

She raised her weapon, hoping to save him as he had her. But her revolver clicked. *Empty.* Hu spun to defend even as she backed away from the cragger set on killing her.

"The evil tyranny of the slavemaster cities must end!" the pirate snarled.

She stared at the ruffian, bewildered.

From above, a small voice called, "Miss, up here!"

Ritsuko tipped her head back to spy Sam up in the riggings, like the monkey the first mate had called him. Seconds before the pirate rushed, she scrambled up the mast, using the ropes as handholds. The rough fibers scraped her palm, pulling the slice on her side, so she felt the hot trickle of blood over her hip.

If he comes up after me, I have to fight, or Sam could get hurt.

Clenching the knife between his teeth, the cragger went up fast and lunged, using the spring of the ropes to propel himself forward. *Bronze gods, this was a bad idea. Even outnumbered, I was safer on the ground.* But with Sam counting on her to protect him, Ritsuko squared off against the red-eyed, unshaven pirate, hoping she didn't plummet to her doom.

* * *

Mikani unleashed his talent so he could hear the anger and hatred around him, louder than the curses. The ebb and flow of their emotions made it easier to avoid blows and sense when fear got the better of them. He'd learned that trick in Celbridge; his years working the docks in Dorstaad as a merchant's enforcer and later as a ward officer had made it second nature.

It's cheating, but there are more than enough of them to even the odds.

Slick, warm blood covered him, but the rest of the battle faded to inchoate chaos beyond the short range of his own struggle. A tall, scarred pirate cut high, aiming for his head. Mikani lifted the haft of the axe to stop the blow. As the man stumbled, Mikani headbutted him in a satisfying crunch of bone. A kick and a shove later, the cragger was in the sea, and Mikani caught his breath.

Ritsuko. Mikani searched for his partner, and a shiver ran down his spine when he failed to spot her. When a cragger got in his way, Mikani shattered his knee with a hard kick and bashed in the man's skull with the half of his bloodied axe. Movement in the rigging directly above made him look up. Ritsuko was swinging from a rope, her feet braced on the mast. She swooped down at a cragger who had gotten past the men below. The filthy raider ducked her blows, more at ease in the ropes high above deck than she could ever be.

The bastard's biding his time. When she gets tired, he'll pull her off. The ship tilted and shuddered as the cragger vessel slammed into its side, sending attackers and defenders stumbling to their knees, Mikani along with them. He hauled to his feet, sidestepped the renewed carnage, and pushed forward.

"Hu!" Mikani swept the axe before him, hacking into a cragger who didn't scramble away in time.

"Busy." Irahi had a cragger by the throat, his free hand swinging his hand cannon like a club. "Can't reach her!" He tossed the pirate into his fellows, punching another who ventured too close. Ferro was holding his own, slashing with quick and controlled strikes at anyone who tried circling behind the bigger man.

"Just bloody brace…" Mikani swung low, making the last three craggers between him and the doctor throw themselves aside. He buried the axe on the deck with a solid thunk and vaulted onto Hu's shoulders, using his friend to reach the rigging just beneath the cragger slashing at Ritsuko.

Irahi grunted and lifted his shoulders as Mikani landed, boosting him.

Mikani grabbed the raider's legs, using his momentum to pull the surprised man off the rigging; they both crashed against the deck. Hu immediately brought his boot down on the pirate's skull. *He's out for hours, if not dead.* Then Ferro slit the bastard's throat, so that a slow-spreading crimson pool formed. Mikani was still seeing stars when the doctor hauled him to his feet.

Ritsuko climbed down then. "Thanks."

But there was no time for niceties; craggers still needed killing. Eventually, they broke, and the *Gull*'s crew killed most of them while the pirates fled for the railings. On the enemy ship, they cut the grappling lines. Mikani tried to count how many survivors were left on the opposite deck, but between the movement of the men and the sea, it proved impossible.

The planks were covered in carnage as Saskia gave the orders to put on speed. Mr. Ferro muttered something about seeing to the dead, then he started the surviving sailors on piling the bodies away from the wounded. Hu set about moving the injured crewmen down to the infirmary, where he could treat them.

Mikani wiped the blood from his face and looked over at Ritsuko.

"You all right, partner? Still having fun?"

"That was a little more adventure than I expected, but I'm well enough." She looked a little pale, shaky, probably from the spinning.

Mikani reached over to wipe a red smear from her cheek. "All right. We need to clear the deck, see who needs help."

"I can probably pitch in with some first aid. Do you think Irahi could use a hand?"

"Hu could probably use a dozen. Go ahead, I'll see to things up here."

Ritsuko paused, her gaze intent. Then she put a hand on his shoulder while turning the other one up so he could see it. The delicate skin of her palm was aflame with rope burns. *That looks like hell.*

"Thank you," she said softly. "I don't know how much longer I could've held on. You're my hero today, Mikani."

"Told you. Always there for you, partner."

She let go of him and stepped back with a warm smile. Mikani watched her walk away, torn between relief that she was all right and worry that they might not fare so well next time. *We're in over our heads.*

"Stop staring, start cleaning." Ferro pushed past, dragging a body toward the port railing. Sam hurried along behind him, his arms full of collected weapons and assorted debris, looking flushed but glad to be of use.

Mikani pulled his axe free from the deck with a wet thunk.

"Oi! Like we don't have enough damage from the stinking craggers?" Oliver was dirty, bedraggled, and furious. Her repair crew was starting to check for leaks and cracked timber. "Dimwit. The axe goes in the raiders, not my ship."

"They kept moving. I missed." He dropped the boatswain a salute and headed for the helm, pausing now and then to help flip a dead enemy off the side of the ship.

Saskia was leaning heavily on the wheel. Her vest was torn in a couple of places, and a nasty bruise was forming on one cheek. One of the men who had been assigned to guard her lay nearby, nursing a deep wound to the thigh; Mikani saw no sign of the other.

"They don't usually bring so many for boarding parties.

This is getting worse, Janus." She looked over at him, her hands holding the rudder steady. "That must have been at least forty or fifty raiders, plus crew? They must have been piled three deep belowdecks."

Mikani sat heavily, resting against the mizzenmast. He lay the axe across his knees, tracing the nicks and cuts on the haft. "That ship wasn't meant to carry anything back, cargo or prisoners for ransom. Something has them running scared... they fought like desperate men."

He looked up, ignoring the urge to read her. *Not sure I could, even if I tried, right now.*

Using his gift was taxing at the best of times. Using it constantly in the middle of a fight to the death was excruciating. His head throbbed, and his skin chafed and burned where his shirt rubbed against it.

"They didn't cut and run when they should have. Most of them preferred to stay and die. Why would they do that?" There was a look in her eyes that he'd never seen before, perplexity mingled with despair.

"They'd rather die than go home? Or they wanted us dead more than they wanted to live." Mikani rested his head against the rough wood. "Either means a world of trouble."

In his time working at the docks, the craggers had always been a distant but real threat. Captains went out of their way to avoid them, and for the most part the raiders left them well enough alone but for the occasional demand for ransom or stolen cargo. But he'd never known them to be suicidal, more concerned with slaughter than booty.

"How long has this been going on?" he asked.

"Two or three months. Why?"

"Not sure yet. But if we can work out the pattern, it might help us understand what's changed. And once we figure *that* out, we can stop it."

"From your mouth to the ears of the gods," she muttered. "I don't know how much more of this we can take."

8

SASKIA STUMBLED THROUGH the cabin door and to her bed, swaying with the motion of the ship. She pulled her feet up under her, staining the rumpled sheets with blood and grime. With a weary sigh, she freed her hair from the loosened braids and dropped into a tumble of pillows.

Bronze gods, I want to sleep for a week. Wish to wake up and find that every last one of those filthy hill dwellers burned in their hovels overnight. She folded her arms to her chest and rolled on her side, trembling for a few moments as the rush of excitement and fear from the fight washed through her body. A single wracking sob escaped before she pulled herself together. From the ewer on the stand nearby, she poured a splash of icy water into a bowl, then grabbed a clean cloth.

"Enough, Alexandra. You're the captain, act like it." She repeated the words as she undressed and washed up. Shivering again, she examined the darkening bruise over her cheekbone. One of the raiders had skewered her personal guard and knocked her against the wheel. Her knife was still stuck in the bastard's throat; she hoped Sam would recover it before they tossed the bodies overboard.

That'll heal, at least. Poor Dayson. He saved my life... I'll need to see to his widow—I'll need to see about far too many widows, after this is over.

She pulled on a fresh shift and sea-green gown, leaving her pale hair free and tangled. As an afterthought, she gathered the mess of sheets and stained clothing into a corner. She would burn them first chance to prevent the nightmares the smell of death would otherwise bring.

But first, she had a duty to her fallen crew: she spent the rest of the afternoon writing out letters of condolences and making sure the families of her fallen would be provided for when the *Gull* returned home.

When she emerged, the sun was starting its descent in the bright blue sky. *Bronze gods. It feels like days, not hours.* Saskia took her place on deck. She was the last to arrive, but it was important that she look the part. If the captain were a disheveled mess, the crew would take their lead to behave accordingly. Discipline would suffer.

Irahi Hu's voice rang loud over the gathered crew. "We gather to ask that you listen. Dwellers of the deep, watchers of the sky. We gather to ask that you listen: listen to our pleas."

Janus and Inspector Ritsuko stood near Mr. Ferro and Nellie. Loison lingered a couple of feet away from the rest of the crew. As usual, he was pale and composed, his countenance revealing nothing of his thoughts or of the steel trap of a mind he hid behind his spectacles.

"Take our brothers. They lived for the sea, grant them rest in the sea." She pulled her attention back to Hu, standing near the railing and over the eight bundles of canvas holding the bodies of their shipmates.

She stepped forward when Hu nodded at her. His face looked far older when it was arranged in sober lines; his ritual scars gained a somber weight. *I've always hated this part. Give me the freedom of the waves, but remind me not of its cost.*

"These men died for their ship. They died for their captain.

They died for their brothers. Remember them, one and all. And may the waves hold them close, until we meet again."

"We remember," came the uneven chorus from the two dozen men and women gathered on deck—and even Janus joined in, though he had never been much for ceremony.

Nell chanted a low dirge from the east; those who knew the mournful tune joined in. The chant rose and fell like the dusky waves, a melody born of grief and loss. In the past months, Saskia had lost more men at sea than in several years prior.

The craggers have to be stopped.

A half dozen sailors stepped forward. One by one, they gathered the canvas bundles and gently tilted them into the waves. Sam pressed close to her side, wide-eyed and solemn. She squeezed his shoulder. Dayson had treated the boy more like a son than a nuisance underfoot.

"I'm sorry," she said softly.

Her throat was thick with regret, but it wasn't all she felt. There was relief, too, that she hadn't ended her life today, bleeding out near the mizzenmast. And perhaps Sam sensed it, or saw it in her face, because his shoulders hunched.

"He was doing his job," the boy muttered.

"And well." That was scant comfort to a child who had already lost so much.

Sam stepped away then, weaving to the deck railing so he could watch the ripples of the bodies sinking into the dark, merciless sea. There were good wishes and quiet farewells, beneath the haunting refrain of Nell's a capella song. Saskia gave the mourners a few minutes before clapping her hands. They looked up from their whispered conversations.

"Raise sails! We're wasting daylight, and I for one don't want to be sailing this forsaken stretch in the dark." Her crew dispersed to their stations; they'd have to pull long shifts to make up for their losses. "Mr. Ferro. You have the helm." She paused. *If we sail on now, we might lose weeks searching for their base.* Everyone knew the craggers lived along the Jagged Coast—the barren, northwestern shore of Winter Isle dominated by the Salamander's Spine mountain range.

But that's several hundred miles of inlets and hidden coves. Even Houses Skarsgard and Magnus working together have not been able to find them so far.

She had planned to threaten and bribe captured craggers for the location of their base. And she'd bet on Janus's getting the information where other Free Trader and House captains had failed. Inspector Ritsuko's newly confessed talent had been a godsend; between his interrogation and her truth sense, Saskia'd had high hopes of finally tracking down the bastards.

Trailing their attackers would be faster but much more dangerous.

Bronze gods, forgive me and keep my people safe.

"Mr. Ferro? Set course after the dogs that attacked us."

Several sailors stopped in their tracks, looking her way. Irahi was shaking his head, as if divining her intent; Inspector Ritsuko and Loison seemed puzzled. Janus looked upset.*But then, he's either laughing or angry whenever we're together, isn't he?*

"Get to it! They're not expecting us to give chase. We'll let them show us where they make their nest. And then we'll make the last of them pay for our fallen brothers!"

Her crew started moving, then. Some nodded in agreement: they were still angry and ready for vengeance. Her first mate turned the wheel, setting a western course out of the shadow of Mount Surtir and toward the wild ocean beyond the Inner Sea. The chances were good that they could take advantage of the enemy's weakened state.

"We'll be fighting the current the whole way." Ferro kept his eyes on the horizon, setting the course more by dead reckoning than the compass.

Most of the others didn't know him well. His character

didn't lend itself to ready chatter and friendly smiles, but he was a damned fine helmsman. There were reasons for his taciturn behavior, and Saskia knew just enough not to pry. In this regard, you could judge the book by its cover; Mr. Ferro was a dangerous man.

"I'll call the winds to help us when you have us well past the shoals." She folded her arms and watched the men scurry up the rigging and along the deck.

Inspector Ritsuko was speaking with Irahi, who was still shaking his head and pointing out to sea. By the other woman's expression, she was asking about the wisdom of this course and possibly mentioning her assignment in Northport, but she didn't care what either inspector had to say. Their work could damned well wait until Janus kept his promise.

I'll have the cragger chieftain's head on a pike.

By his frown, Hu wasn't exactly delighted with the notion. Nell was already belowdecks, getting the *Gull* ready for the chase. There were timbers to reinforce and a few leaks to patch from where the ships had smashed together, the ocean driving the collision. But the *Gull* was a game little ship, all heart and desire to run.

Content that she had the situation in hand, Saskia wheeled to spot Janus coming up the wide stairs of the aft castle where she stood, his jaw set. She recognized that glint in his eyes. It meant he was about to threaten her, question her sanity, or both.

Oh, Janus... just like old times.

And maybe he had a point, but she had no intention of listening to it. This was the first break she'd gotten since the attacks increased in frequency and ferocity.

"Saskia. What in Hells and Winter—"

She cut him off before Mr. Ferro or the other crewmen nearby took offense at his tone. "*Mr. Mikani!* We need to talk. In my cabin, after the change of watch in three hours... please inform your partner, Doctor Hu, and Miss Oliver."

She squared off to him as he came to a stop at the head of the stairs, fists clenched at his sides.

He held her gaze for a long silent moment before turning away, muttering darkly.

"That one's dangerous." Mr. Ferro sounded almost amused.

"I know." She let out a long breath and made her way to her cabin to prepare for a grueling fight. And that was *before* they went after the raiders.

* * *

The atmosphere around the table was much tenser than when they'd gathered for dinner, that first night. Sam had proven wise and made himself scarce when they'd filed in.

Wish I could do the same, or that I could just order them around without question... but if I could, they wouldn't be the right crew for what lies ahead.

"It's madness. Hells and Winter, we're tying a bloody steak to our neck and chasing a wolf into the forest!" Janus scowled from the corner, arms folded and his temper hardly in check.

"Li'l White, Mikani's right... and gods know I don't say that often. We should be headed for Northport, to repair and refit before going after these dogs." Irahi offered an apologetic look, regretful that he couldn't support her.

Now Nell seemed offended. "My fieldwork is as good as anything you'd find in most dry docks, better than some."

Saskia sighed. "That's not his point."

"I've still got a number of men too weak to work," Irahi said. "I'm running out of supplies in the infirmary, and you're chasing the next battle?"

"You know I love a good fight," Mikani snapped. "But this? Wouldn't be."

Irahi and Ferro flanked him, likely because of his bristling demeanor. *They don't trust him not to do something stupid. Bless their wise hearts.*

Nell was staring at her. The boatswain turned a dagger in her hands, over and over. "If the captain thinks we need to give chase, I'm with her. The sooner we find their den, the faster we can hunt them down."

"Damn'd be, we're not—"

"Mr. Mikani!" Saskia was surprised when he stopped talking. "You've had your say."

He shook his head but leaned back, chewing his lip.

"It *is* insane." Mr. Ferro turned toward her. Saskia didn't know what he saw on her face, but his features softened a little. "But I'd follow Captain Braelan to the underworld itself, for she'd bring us back out."

Inspector Ritsuko spoke for the first time. "It seems to me that this is a numbers game. We lost eight crewmen in the fight. They lost many more. Do you intend to scuttle their ship or do you think we can mount an assault on the cragger stronghold as well?"

Saskia'd been struggling with that very same question all evening. *I would give much that we could go in guns blazing and end this once and for all.*

"I propose neither." Janus's scowl shifted to puzzlement. They all spoke at once, so she held up a hand. "Gods' truth, I know it'd be idiotic to follow them home to attack their stronghold. And it would be even worse to risk us all in hunting down their ship for revenge.

"We must chase them, yes. But we need to be quiet, so that we can trail them to wherever it is they're hiding. We won't be hanging a piece of meat around our neck." She flashed a tired smile at Janus. "We will track the wolves down to their lair, so that we may return with the combined fleets of Skarsgard, Magnus, and the Free Traders and set them loose on those bastards once and for all."

9

RITSUKO HAD WONDERED how Miss Braelan intended to pursue the raiders. They had a head start and any number of places to hide.

The answer, as Irahi had explained, was elementals.

Miss Braelan had called the wind spirits, coaxing them to follow the raiders and come back to whisper of their course. The sylphs, he'd explained, had short attention spans: they could report back and forth within a range of a dozen miles. They couldn't follow all the way to their lair, but they *could* keep the *Gull* on the right track.

"And the bastards ward their stronghold," Miss Braelan put in. "Otherwise, once we got close enough, I could use the same tactic to sniff them out. But I'm wind blind, the closer we get to the center of the action. Which is where you come in, Janus."

Ritsuko couldn't tell what Mikani thought about this development. He had been furious earlier, but now his expression was controlled and watchful. It was impossible for her to ask with Miss Braelan's officers nearby. Most of them seemed disposed to do whatever the woman ordered, regardless of how imprudent it might be.

It's a risky plan, but if we survive, she'll have the information necessary to end the threat. I suppose that makes it worth the danger.

The hunt had lasted the better part of two days. They'd sailed at the limit of the elementals' range to stay out of sight of cragger raiding parties and patrols. By the time they had slipped into a sheltered cove, Miss Braelan looked exhausted.

But even so, she'd insisted on coming along with the landing party that afternoon.

Ritsuko had misgivings about her own role, but she didn't want to be left behind. So she didn't protest as the others discussed last-minute strategy. The skiff lay on the beach nearby; Miss Braelan and Irahi had come along with Mr. Ferro, Mikani, and herself.

They had tracked the craggers until they'd slipped into a deep inlet: following them into the narrow passage would have been suicidal, so they had sailed on along the seaward side of the narrow finger of land until they'd found a spot to hide the *Gull* and land a boat. Mikani, Mr. Ferro, and she would make their way inland in search of the raider's main base, to gauge their numbers and defenses for a full punitive expedition. Irahi and Miss Braelan would watch over the boat to safeguard their means of escape, and if threatened, they could retreat and return once it was clear. The others set up a way to communicate over distance, just in case, and Miss Braelan explained what the lantern signals meant.

Then the other woman said, "Irahi and I can wait until sunset tomorrow. That's a full day… after that, one of their patrols is likely to find us." She paused to look out to sea. "I wish I could come with you. But tired as I am, I'd be more a hindrance than aid, as Irahi has pointed out for the last half hour. So be careful, and please come back… all of you." She offered a smile to all three of them, but her gaze remained on Mikani.

Her partner nodded. He started to say something, then

walked toward the narrow trail that led up the cliffs. "Let's move, then. We need to be at the top of the cliffs before it gets too dark to see... it'd be a bloody shame if we ended up walking off the damn'd edge."

Mr. Ferro hefted his rifle and followed suit, pausing to say, "Watch out for her," to Irahi.

Ritsuko wasn't ordinarily the sentimental sort, but this wasn't the kind of mission for which she had any training or experience, and there was a chance she'd never get to know the doctor any better. For obvious reasons, he wouldn't be accompanying them, as he wasn't built for stealth. So she went over to him, hoping she didn't look as foolish as she felt. Irahi's strong features were highlighted by the scant sunlight trickling through the clouds, and it glossed his dark hair.

"I just wanted to say—"

"Tell me when you get back, Celeste." He took her hand in his, gently. "Now, keep those two fools out of harm's way, you hear? Gods know they need safekeeping."

She nodded and wheeled to march resolutely to where Ferro and Mikani stood waiting. "I'm ready as I shall be. Let's find some craggers."

"Hunting them down will be easy, partner. It's keeping them from spotting us that's the fun part." Mikani led the way. He'd strapped his service pistol around his waist and someone—probably Irahi, judging from the elaborate patterns on the hilts, had loaned him a couple of long, curved daggers.

Mr. Ferro carried his rifle and a cutlass slung over his shoulder. She still had the long, heavy knife that she'd put to good use during the raid, and Miss Oliver had given her a worn but serviceable shotgun. A better choice, she'd said, than a revolver when it came to putting a raider down, mostly from the increased stopping power.

Ritsuko checked her weapons, then fell in behind the other two. Ahead, the path wound up the cliff in irregular twists, turns, and sometimes sheer walls that she clambered up in the falling darkness. Near the halfway mark, Mr. Ferro lost his footing, skidding toward the distant surf, and Mikani dove for him. Her heart skipped a beat as her partner tumbled toward the edge, right behind the first mate, but he snagged the man's loose tunic and somehow he held on long enough for her to scramble back toward them to give a hand up.

"Thanks," Ferro said, sounding genuinely thankful.

Mikani only nodded and forged on. He was quiet, enough that Ritsuko couldn't be sure if something was eating at him or if he was being cautious to avoid potential detection, even this far from the cragger lair. *Although it could be honeycombed in these cliffs for all I know. They might be right beneath us.*

The group crested the top of the cliff as full night fell.

Ritsuko sat on a boulder to catch her breath and empty her boots of debris. Mr. Ferro crouched nearby, while Mikani scouted their surroundings. They stood on a narrow ridge that stretched for several miles to either side. Behind them was the sea. The inland side sloped toward wooded hills and valleys. In the far distance, she could see the glimmer of water.

"Is that a lake?"

Mr. Ferro looked toward where she was pointing. "That's the Kraken Sea. It's narrow, full of hidden reefs. The craggers are about the only ones who know how to navigate it, so they use it to evade pursuit."

Mikani rejoined them. "The raiders we're chasing must've sailed that way. They probably thought they were safe. They didn't count on our being so pigheaded." He pointed to his left. "I found an old campsite and a hunting path. With luck, we can follow it to their base of operations... or at least, to a village where we might pick up a fresher trail."

"Is it safe to travel after dark? How rugged is the terrain?" Ritsuko didn't want to sound nervous, but her sensible boots had been designed for paved streets, not mountainsides, and it would be extremely inconvenient to break an ankle.

"Treacherous," he admitted. "And we can't use torches, or they'll see us coming from—" He paused. "I'm an idiot. Look around. If there are as many raiders as Saskia fears, we should bloody well be able to spot the lights of their camps from here."

"That's an excellent plan," she said, quietly relieved.

"Might as well hunker down here and eat something," Ferro added. "Once full dark falls, we've got a bird's-eye view. We need to get closer, though, to give the captain a report worth bringing back to the Houses."

That was the part that worried Ritsuko, but she only sat down where the first mate indicated to receive her share of salted fish and hard bread. The sky was lovely in tones of purple, last shimmering rays of sunlight drowning in spectacular fashion. At such a height, the air felt cold and clear in her lungs, and the night would grow chillier still. She huddled deeper into her hooded coat, wondering how her orders from Commander Gunwood had gotten so complicated. *And there's still the matter of a certain conspiracy—* But she couldn't dwell on her delayed work assignment or the self-designated task of hunting down the one who had sponsored Lorne Nuall's reign of terror behind the scenes. She could only concentrate on one crisis at a time—and avoiding death at the hands of desperate men definitely took precedence.

"You look pensive, partner." Mikani spoke low, presumably so the first mate, sitting nearby, wouldn't overhear.

"Mostly the usual sort of thoughts, like how did I end up here? Was my grandfather right? If I had married one of the men on his approved list, I'd be in the Mountain District right now with two perfect children, and I never would've met you." She gave a wry smile.

He ran a hand through his hair, frowning. "I know we're out of our depth here, Ritsuko. But there's no one I'd rather have with me than you, just now. So keep it together like you always do, and we'll be fine."

* * *

An hour later, night was full upon them. The half-moon shone weakly through the thick cloud cover. Mikani scanned the woods and distant shoreline, seeking any sign of life. Ferro and Ritsuko stood at his back, probably doing the same. Or the first mate might be looking for someone to shoot; he had an angry look to him.

"Hells and Winter." *It'd be just our bloody luck if the bastards all go to bed at sundown, weary from a long night of pillage and murder.*

"I can't see a damn'd thing so far... trees, dark trees, and very dark trees."

He spun as the other man moved off to climb atop a grouping of boulders for a better vantage. Then Ferro drew a spyglass from his pack and peered through it in all directions. *He's likely got the best eyes of us all.* Mikani waited to hear if the first mate had found anything.

When the mate jumped down without speaking, he thought it was a negative, until Ferro jerked his head toward the east. "They're inland, past the first valley. I can make out some lights, but we need to get closer to learn anything useful. Get moving and keep your traps shut."

"You're a charmer, Ferro." Mikani stretched and looked down the hunting path. "We might as well follow it down. Be wary of snares, but we shouldn't run into any hunters in the middle of the night." He started down, Ritsuko close behind and Ferro bringing up the rear.

They made slow progress in the dark. At times, they joined hands to feel their way from tree to tree, with more than one stumble into the bushes. *Bronze gods; we might as well have brought in a battalion, as much bloody racket as we're making.* He hoped to be across the valley and on the opposite hillside before daylight.

The trek back should be faster. And they won't expect

anyone to be daft enough to come at them over the mountains.

It wasn't a direct line, either. The path carried them deeper into the forest, and Ferro said, "We're getting off course. We'll have to go cross-country from here."

There was probably a better route, but they didn't know it, so Mikani had to follow Ferro's sense of direction. He had little experience in woodcraft, so it was best not to pretend otherwise. The first mate took the lead, forging through tangled bushes and over fallen limbs down toward the southern coast. The *Gull* had dropped them off on the inhospitable northern side of the narrow peninsula. The many crags and hidden valleys made it a perfect hiding spot for raiders.

Mikani followed Ferro's bony back until he was heartily sick of being smacked with branches released a little too early. At last he stepped out onto the smooth sand of the beach along the shore of the Kraken Sea. Ritsuko was looking tired, but she didn't complain; she only took a swig of water from her canteen. Ferro got out his compass, apparently doing a little figuring. Then he sighed.

"That took us a little out of our way, and by my reckoning, we're six or seven miles off. That's the good news. The bad news is that it's mostly uphill."

Mikani peered along the coast, to the east. "Looks like we have a couple hours until dawn, at most. Let's get back to the tree line but keep the beach in sight. If we spot any boats, we can hide, but at least it'll keep us going the right way until it's light enough that we can head back into the hills."

"Is this area purely populated by craggers?" Ritsuko asked.

"No one else is mad enough to try." Ferro checked his rifle, as if the mere mention of the raiders might summon them forth. "They've villages and hamlets scattered all along the shores of the Jagged Coast and Kraken Sea. Near as anyone can tell, they live off fishing, hunting, and whatever they can steal from ships that stray too close to their land."

"I dunno. This land has a certain charm, Mikani." She flashed him a teasing smile. "You could build me the country cottage you promised. The terrain is right for… goats. And possibly a kitchen garden for all the lovely meals you'll cook."

Even without reading her, he could tell she was still frightened. It was strong enough that it washed over him whether he willed it or not, but she definitely wasn't letting on. *That's the spirit, partner.*

"With my luck, even the local goats are bloodthirsty beasts. And damned if I'm getting on a boat every time you want to go to town."

"No? Very well then." Ritsuko turned to Ferro, and said, "Lead on, sir. I'd like to finish this adventure before it gets light enough for them to see us making our escape."

Ferro raised a brow, as if he couldn't understand why this woman treated him with such courtesy, no matter how curt he acted toward her. With a puzzled shrug, the first mate set off northeast along the shore. He established a quick pace, navigating driftwood and tumbles of rock, though the terrain was much gentler on this side. Mikani watched the sky lighten, and it felt as if they were racing the horizon. *If the sun's fully up by the time we find a better vantage on the settlement, none of us will see Dorstaad again.*

He wished it were feasible to chart the town's location and withdraw, but the Houses couldn't mount an attack without a better idea of what was waiting for them. So that meant they needed to do more recon; they needed a rough ship count in and around the docks, and a general sense of the craggers' forces. While it might not be completely accurate, it was a good deal more than they could learn standing on a hillside, where trees obscured the port. As if he shared that thought, Ferro increased his speed, bounding along the sand with impressive stamina. His course carried the group up into the hills, past the tree line, and the mate finally paused on a rise.

Lights glimmered here and there in the valley below, likely fishermen and bakers who had to get an early start. Ferro got out his spyglass, focusing—so far as Mikani could tell—on the harbor. He didn't interfere with the other man's attempt to count ships. They might not all be docked at the moment, but even this much information was more than anyone had managed to acquire so far. He spun slowly, keeping watch.

"There are three dozen ships in port." Ferro sounded shaken.

Ritsuko pushed out a breath. "So many? That's practically an armada. I had no idea the craggers were so numerous or so well organized."

"At least a couple of thousand men, then. Even with—" Mikani took the spyglass when Ferro tossed it at him. He shook his head and scanned the port below.

Hells and Winter.

After completing his assessment, he understood Ferro's reaction. The man wasn't given to false alarm. "They're not just raider ships. They have a few heavy steamers and at least three warships. They must've captured a few Magnus frigates." He gave the glass back. "They have a few more in the inlet just on the other side of town. Another dozen, maybe." He shook his head. "I don't think anyone's ever seen this many craggers cooperating before. It's a *city* down there."

"This is... worse than I expected," Ritsuko said softly. "I was prepared for bad, but this is people preparing for war."

"Agreed," Ferro said. "It may well take the combined fleets of Magnus, Thorgrim, and Skarsgard to burn these bastards out of here."

She sighed. "That's assuming they believe us. If I were safe and sound in the city, and someone brought me this tale, I'd want some hard evidence. Ideas?"

The mate shook his head. "Can't think of anything other than my word that I saw it with my own eyes. And I'm inclined to shank the man who calls me a liar."

"We need more information," she said.

"Well. We could go down to the local tavern, tip the tender." Mikani glimpsed more and more buildings as the sky brightened. "But I'm not sure they'd be forthcoming. So let's find an isolated farmstead or goat herder, and we'll ask *them*, instead."

"Right." Ferro's tone was scornful. "They'll just answer us to be friendly."

Ritsuko answered, "He's got a way with people. I'll know if they're telling the truth."

The first mate seemed to take a second look at her, but it was too dark for Mikani to read Ferro's expression. "That so? You're more interesting than I first thought, wench."

"You don't know the half of it, man. Now shut *your* trap, and let's get moving."

10

THE PATH FROM town was better kept than the game trail, which told Ritsuko it was more frequently used. She crouched lower, hoping the party they'd seen heading up this way wouldn't spot her too soon. Her companions were still and silent in the blind, leafy fronds cloaking their presence. The occasional dry limb crackled some distance away, an indication that the targets were drawing closer.

At length, Mikani touched her arm, which she took as the signal to strike. She pushed through the branches and cocked her weapon, confident that the other two would do the same. And on either side, Mikani had his sidearm out while Mr. Ferro favored his rifle. The men from the cragger settlement were dressed and equipped like hunters; there were three, two older, one younger, likely an apprentice.

We did well to find even odds.

"Good morning, gents. We'd like a word." Mikani kept his pistol trained on the taller, burlier man while carefully stepping closer. When the thinner raider reached for a knife, her partner cocked the hammer of his gun.

"Don't. On your knees, if you please. We don't want you

getting stupid ideas while we chat." He kicked the nearest man behind the knee, just hard enough to send him sprawling; the other two eased to their knees nervously.

The younger one looks no older than fifteen.

Mr. Ferro held his rifle at the ready. She stepped closer, as Mikani holstered his pistol and crouched before the bigger man. Before speaking, he restrained the three captives by binding their wrists behind their backs. At a gesture, the first mate aimed his rifle, likely to make the point about how fast he could shoot one of them.

"I ask. You answer, yes or no. Simple, easy, and we all head off at the end." Ritsuko had explained to Mikani that she needed simple answers the better to use her truth-sense, so he was playing this just right. "We don't have a lot of time. Is your fleet larger than the forty-odd ships we saw in port?"

The three exchanged a look, then the biggest one muttered, "Sod off."

Mikani responded with a brutal right cross to the hunter's jaw. The man spat blood, red trickling down his lips, and Ritsuko suspected he must've bitten his tongue. *Don't beat him until he can't speak, partner.* It was... unnerving to see how brutal Mikani could be without even seeming angry. She understood the urge to fight to defend... or even hitting someone in a fit of temper, but this seemed darker.

"Are there more than forty ships? If you choose not to answer, I might get bored. The young one might prove less resistant."

Ritsuko caught the flare of alarm in the older man's eyes. *They have a bond, then. Father and son, perhaps.* No father worth the name could stand to see his child suffer, so this was probably a bluff. *It is, right?* She realized she wasn't sure if Mikani would rough up a kid to get the information they needed. *How... surprising.*

"Yeah, there's more... more than enough to shove all you bastards right off Winter at last, and good riddance."

Truth. And I don't need Mikani's ability to tell he's furious.

"And that's your main port, down there?" she asked.

"We have men and ships up and down the Jagged Coast, you whoreson." Mikani raised his gun and pointed it at the boy's temple. The man bucked in his restraints, so Mikani had to push him back. "You leave him be! Yes, that's our main port... the high king gathered us there."

Truth. High king? Ritsuko had never heard the term.

Mikani hadn't, either, to judge by the expression on his face. "Who's... no. This high king, then, he's the one ordering all the attacks?"

"He's trying to save the world," the boy said defiantly. "The elementals—"

"Stop talking." The second hunter spoke for the first time, a growled warning to the bigger man. "Hrothgar will gut you like a fish for what you've said today. Don't make it worse."

"Worse than gutting me?" The big hunter laughed. "Don't see how it could be."

"He could behead your boy, too—a blight for the traitor's seed. His line shall not prosper."

Truth. Ritsuko suppressed a shiver. The cragger code was apparently harsh, brutal, and unforgiving. Unfortunately, the man's words had done their damage. Their helpful hostage went quiet. Mikani paced with a growl of frustration.

"If you're not talking to me, I have no use for you," he said quietly. "The deal was, you walk away if you answer my questions. It'd be a lot simpler for us to shoot you."

"I like that plan," Mr. Ferro said.

Ritsuko didn't, but she hoped Mikani was bluffing, though the first mate's words rang unmistakably honest. She'd killed her first man only a few weeks back and was uncomfortable with casual violence. Yet she didn't speak for fear of interrupting whatever game Mikani was running. She felt pretty sure that the first mate wouldn't be unhappy about putting bullets in the lot of them, even the boy.

"Do your worst." The second hunter wore a defiant expression.

"Do you have a family?" she asked.

The boy's eyes widened. She hadn't been asking him, but from his expression, it was clear he had relatives in town. As for the older men, they didn't speak or meet her gaze, but she had the youngest hunter's attention. She might be able to use his expressive face against him. He wasn't answering in words, but his emotions were clear.

"Your mother's back in town, isn't she?"

"Don't say anything," his father cautioned.

But he didn't have to. She could tell by the kid's worried look that she'd guessed correctly. "She'll be mad with grief if you don't return, and she never learns what's become of you. But if you have brothers, she won't be inconsolable. That's the advantage of a large family."

"I don't have any," the boy whispered.

"There's no reason for this to end badly," she went on. "You're afraid of this high king, but why does he need to know what happened here? Your mother would prefer for you to come home safe and sound rather than die for someone else's code."

"You don't know Gert," the biggest one muttered.

The boy chewed his lip. "She doesn't much like Hrothgar. She says his overweening ambition will doom us all."

Truth. If I can keep the kid thinking of his mother and how much she disapproves of this high king, he'll decide it's better to please her. And to survive.

"I'm sure she's a clever woman, your mum. She must have reasons for feeling that way. Do you think she'd want you to die on this hill on your knees? For a man she despises?"

"No. The high king's behind everything—why we're building our navy and why strikes have increased. He says—" But before the boy could finish the babbled confession, the second hunter slammed his head sideways, knocking the kid backward with a painful clack of skulls.

Mr. Ferro fired without warning, putting a bullet in the instigator. He fell, blood spreading across his chest. From what Ritsuko knew of anatomy, it looked like a clean shot through the heart. The boy was dazed, though, not wholly conscious, as that had been a hell of a headbutt.

That hunter would absolutely have reported that breach of trust. So it's probably best for these two that he's dead.

"Hells and Winter." Mikani kicked the bigger man down prone, and glared at Mr. Ferro. "They probably heard that all the way in town. The kid's not going to do any more talking, and I think the big guy'd rather take his chances with us than this Hrothgar."

"We got what we needed." Mr. Ferro was anything but apologetic. "So let's cut their throats and head out." The first mate reached for his knife, but Mikani stopped him with a look and a shake of the head.

"Two things. One, if they need to tend to their wounded, whoever finds this lot will have to leave some men behind." Mikani stepped over to the struggling hunter, and brought his boot down with a sickening crunch on the man's knee. His scream of pain echoed through the hills. "And two, we need to move."

Her partner pointed down the path. Fifteen or twenty men were coming into sight, jogging up the hillside. They didn't seem to have spotted them yet, but the cry of pain had them moving toward the wounded hunters. The boy had blood trickling from a cut on his brow, and he still looked dazed. *So we've got a stunned kid, a dead man, and a crippled one.* She found it hard to see them as enemies at the moment, as part of the vicious, brutal raiders who had attacked the *Gull* a few days before. They just looked like beaten men, and she felt like a villain.

She stumbled back a few steps. It had taken most of the night to get here, and the return trip showed signs of being equally harrowing even though it would occur in daylight. *Mostly because they'll be hunting us every step of the way.* Mikani and Mr. Ferro were already on the move. Ritsuko sighed, and with a final, remorseful look at the men on the ground, she followed.

This information had better be worth it.

* * *

Mikani batted aside branches and stumbled over rocks as they ran. He heard Ritsuko close behind. *I trust that she can keep up. She's resourceful enough... and if I look back, I'll probably fall into a bloody crevasse, the way this bastard's leading us.*

They cut straight up the hill and toward the cliffs, hoping the thick-wooded terrain would keep their pursuers from following their trail as easily. But after an hour of running through nettles and bushes, Mikani was about ready to take his chances facing the craggers head-on just to be done with the stumbling.

"I can't hear them anymore." Ritsuko sounded short of breath but not quite winded yet.

"I can't hear a damn'd thing over our own noise. Ferro!"

"They'll split up and try and circle around us before we make the cliffs. Hunt us like animals." The lean first mate did not stop, his easy loping gait giving him good speed even in the broken terrain. A gunshot sounded somewhere to their left, another on their right.

"That's hardly reassuring." Mikani loosened his daggers in their sheaths and sawed through a tangle of branches and brush. "Get a bloody move on, then. We'll make better speed on the foothills of the cliffs and out of this forest."

Mr. Ferro increased his pace, leaving Mikani and Ritsuko struggling to keep up.

They broke from the tree line and onto the rocky hillsides leading up to the ridge above. The sun shone weakly through a thick layer of dark clouds.

If that storm breaks, it'll make us harder to spot. But it will make climbing down the cliff... tricky.

They only took a moment to catch their breath before the sounds of men shouting and running through the undergrowth not far behind them made them head for the hills and the cover offered by the scattered boulders and rock piles dotting the slopes. The cragger group did look smaller, so Ferro had been right. *Only ten men with guns charging at us.*

"Get ready for a fight," Ferro said.

Beside Mikani, Ritsuko took cover, and because he couldn't think of a better plan, Mikani did the same. The first mate braced his rifle on the rocks, and Mikani holstered his daggers. *Have to use the right weapon for the job.* His gun didn't have the same range as a rifle, and Ritsuko had a shotgun, so no long-distance sniping for them.

"I wish we had more time to prepare," Ritsuko said.

A bullet pinged into the boulders, chipping stone that bounced against her cheek. The sharp edge cut her cheek, but she returned fire. Moving targets were harder to hit, so she got a tree instead. The cragger had to dive, however, and Mr. Ferro shot one of his companions. Mikani sighted and shot; he was aiming for the chest and got the thigh of the man next to his target.

Close enough. Look at him bleed.

The raiders slowed and ducked behind trees and bushes, swearing and calling out warnings to one another.

"Move now, up the hill. I'll keep their heads down." Mikani took another shot at a raider when he peeked around his cover to try to aim at them.

Ritsuko and Ferro scrambled up the hillside toward a rock outcropping a couple of hundred feet away. Mikani fired again a couple of times to buy his companions a few seconds, then ran after them.

Ritsuko and Ferro had just taken cover when the firing from below started. The first mate returned fire, allowing Mikani to leap into cover beside them.

"I really hate guns." He reloaded quickly.

They leapfrogged their way, shooting and scrambling for the next piece of cover, all the way to the top of the ridge. The craggers giving chase were cautious in following, which allowed the three to regain their lead as they ran along the top of the cliff, looking for the narrow path they'd taken up from the beach.

The going's definitely much quicker in daylight. Helps when you can see the path, and you have a couple of dozen men trying to kill you.

Running on sand, however, was no easier than the rocks, just for different reasons. When Ritsuko went down in a loose, damp patch, Mikani paused long enough to grab her hand and haul her upright, before pressing on. Ferro's balance was better, likely from long years at sea. He was used to the unsure footing of a rolling deck.

More gunfire rang out behind them, and there was precious little cover. His heart raced, pounding in his ears, both from the exercise and the danger. He moved closer to the base of the cliff, hoping the others would follow suit. It left Ritsuko more vulnerable, however, as she was behind him. So he slowed his stride long enough for her to pass while hoping this moment of chivalry didn't end with a bullet in his spine.

Down on the beach at the bottom of the cliff, he saw glimmers of light, barely visible in the scant sunshine. But it had to be Saskia, signaling. Either they had encountered trouble or— *Oh, damn. I wonder if they've run across the other half of the patrol.*

"Full out, Ferro, or we might not have a way out of here."

In answer, the first mate pushed into a sprint. Mikani wouldn't have guessed the man could move so fast, but those long legs served a purpose, apparently. Ritsuko surprised him, too. She was small, but desperation probably had something to do with her ability to keep up.

More gunfire chipped into the rocks behind him, one too

damned close to his leg. *That could have stung a bit.* He fired blindly behind him and kept running.

As the cliffs narrowed, opening to a slightly wider beach, he glimpsed Saskia. He didn't see the rest of the patrol yet, so that was a blessing. *Almost there. Damn'd be. Maybe Ritsuko was right about the cigarillos sapping my health... I swear my heart's about to burst through my chest. Messy.*

"Hurry!" Saskia shouted. "They're coming down the path."

"We'll be lucky if they don't blow a huge hole in the skiff." The first mate sounded too tired to muster his customary sour humor, however.

It's been a long night.

He ran, not just for his own life, but for Ritsuko and Saskia, too. At last, they reached the boat, as the craggers converged down the beach. The raiders shouted a confused jumble of conflicting orders, offering them precious seconds to shove the skiff off the sand and into the water. Hu tossed them in one by one, and then the big man hauled himself over the side with Ferro and Mikani's help.

"I meant for this to be a quiet mission, Mikani." Saskia scowled at him.

"Details, details." He joined Hu at the oars while Ferro and Ritsuko fired at the craggers onshore. Saskia ducked low at the rudder as bullets splashed nearby and struck the hull with little clouds of splinters. Half an hour of frenetic rowing later, they were climbing the rope rigging off the side of the *Gull.*

"Leave the boat, no time to bring her back on board!" Nell Oliver was signaling at them to hurry, alternating with shouting orders over her shoulder.

As soon as Mikani cleared the railing, he could see why the boatswain was so eager to get going. "Hells and Winter."

The craggers had sent two warships after them. The captured Magnus frigates were rounding the edge of a nearby bluff, their dark patchwork sails billowing in the wind as they gained speed. They were twice the size of the *Gull* and bristling with cannon ports that were already opening. Craggers swarmed the decks, preparing to obliterate the clipper.

Saskia pushed past him toward the forecastle, her crew pulling up anchor and running to free their own sails. She shouted orders like a madwoman, so fast that Mikani couldn't parse all the nautical terms. It became a muddle of port and starboard, leeward ho, abaft the beam, and something about the boom vang. The sailors leapt to, however, so they evidently knew exactly what Saskia expected.

She took up position near the prow of the ship. Mikani couldn't hear what she was whispering, but he recognized the tingle of magic in the air. The winds stirred, yet these were no natural gusts. The air swirled thick and white, so that he could almost make out ghostly faces in the vapor. It felt damp and chill wherever it touched his skin.

Ritsuko pressed closer, quietly. The sails swelled beneath the elemental push, and Saskia raised her arms, likely demanding more. He couldn't imagine the energy this must be costing her, especially when she'd taxed herself chasing the raider ship, then spent a day roughing it on the beach. *But she's never lacked in determination. Or stubbornness; oftentimes when it wasn't good for her.*

As Saskia's long hair whipped in the wind, the first cannon shots boomed out.

11

CANNONBALLS SPLASHED DANGEROUSLY close to the hull of the ship. Ritsuko staggered under cover at the forecastle and found a handhold. She was shaking with exhaustion and unsure if Miss Braelan had the necessary reserves to get them out of this mess. The wind whipped until it sounded like angry spirits howling, snapping unsecured lines and billowing the sails.

In response, the clipper took off. She imagined the craggers shouting in frustration, but the warships were just too big and heavy to keep up. *They might chase us all the way to Northport, but they won't catch us, as long as Miss Braelan can keep the winds alive.* That was the big question so far as Ritsuko was concerned. Just how strong a weather witch was this woman? It didn't seem like the time to ask, but all of their lives depended on her stamina.

The craggers continued firing even after the clipper left range, but eventually, the cannons fell silent. On deck, the sailors cheered. Miss Braelan didn't let up until they were well out of sight of the Jagged Coast. Once there was nothing but open sea surrounding them, she finally stopped her onerous work. The woman's shoulders slumped, and she stumbled when she moved away from the prow. Irahi was there to catch her with a concerned hand on her elbow.

Muttering, the big man led the woman down to the infirmary, leaving Mr. Ferro to shout at the rest of the crew. *I hope that's enough of a lead.* Natural winds weren't nearly so powerful or reliable. But Sam was in the crow's nest, peering about, so he would shout if he saw anything on the horizon.

Ritsuko turned to Mikani, who was alternating between watching Miss Braelan and glaring at the receding cliffs. "We need to brief her when she's feeling better."

"It may have to wait until we get to port. I suspect she drained every ounce of strength and then some... stubborn witch." He shook his head, likely biting back more choice words for their captain. "But you're right. She'll want to know as soon as she wakes."

Mr. Ferro called down to them from his post at the wheel.

"Stop muttering and get up here. If you please." Her partner flipped a mocking salute but signaled for her to lead the way up the stairs to where the first mate was still giving orders.

"We'll cut through the narrows around the bay." He pointed somewhere ahead. "With the currents—"

Mikani interrupted him. "How long to Northport?"

Mr. Ferro made a sour face, but answered, "Three, four days at most." He seemed disinclined to elaborate further.

"Then let's hope for clear sailing." Mikani unstrapped his daggers and pistol. "We'll check on Saskia, then get some rest. See you on the morrow, Mr. Ferro."

Ritsuko stretched, suppressing a moan. She made a note to increase her physical training time when she returned to the city, as that trek had been brutal. Her sensible boots had rubbed blisters at heel and toes, which swelled and burst. She could only imagine the raw, bloody mess waiting to be tended. Murmuring some excuse for the two men, she tried not to limp as she made her way to her cabin. The slice on her side pulled and burned. At this point, even with a poultice, it seemed certain to leave a scar.

First, a wash, then some first aid. And then I'm sleeping until I see land again.

* * *

On the fourth afternoon, they approached Northport, as Mr. Ferro had predicted. The port was even more crowded than Dorstaad's East Docks; ships sailing the flags of at least three major Houses and a dozen smaller shipping concerns were anchored along the broad, sheltered bay. Ritsuko counted more than sixty vessels ranging in size from small fishing boats to the massive cargo steamers that dwarfed even the Magnus war cruiser, towering above them near the harbor's entrance.

"That's the *Pride of the North.*" Mr. Ferro had been unusually loquacious since they'd gotten word regarding Miss Braelan's recovery. Now he stood beside Ritsuko, identifying ships and flags as they negotiated the congested channel, headed for their assigned berth. "Over there, you'll see Skarsgard's winter squadron. Three frigates, four sloops. All armed to the teeth."

"Why do they have such a strong presence here?" She wasn't clear on the politics of the Winter Isle or the economic complexities, either.

"Safeguarding their interests, mainly, but given what we saw of the craggers, they'll be gearing up for war soon enough." The first mate nodded in what she took as a farewell—it was the closest Mr. Ferro came to courtesy, then he moved off to lecture one of the sailors.

She shivered, gazing out over the gray water toward the city. Northport was low to the ground; no building rose above three stories in height, sandstone and dark red tile sprawling over three hills around the bay. The most imposing structure was perched above the tallest hill off on her right: walkways and gardens stretched over and around the knoll.

The architecture seemed oddly familiar. After a moment, she remembered why.

It reminds me of the Nuall villa.

"That's the Thorgrim palace." Irahi came up on her left. For a big man, he moved quietly; she hadn't heard him approach. The circles under his eyes said it had been difficult restoring Miss Braelan to health, but he was smiling. "I've heard stories of what goes on in there. If half of them are true, I know men who'd give a year's wages for ten minutes inside."

"Not long ago, *you* would've been one of those men." Mikani strolled toward them, wearing the hat she had given him. It might be a small thing, but she got a warm feeling anytime she saw the bowler perched on his tousled hair. This marked a return to the more or less civilized Mikani, though she knew better than to imagine it went all the way through.

Irahi eyed the other man. "Says the scoundrel. I've half a mind to toss you overboard again."

Her partner smirked. "You can try."

Ignoring their banter, Ritsuko rose up on her tiptoes for a better vantage. To the right—was that port or starboard?—she spotted an older steamship that seemed to be in trouble. The water around it had been cleared of other vessels, except for the gunship sailing out from the harbor. She'd never seen a steamer move like that before; usually, they turned slowly, but this ship thrashed almost like a living creature, more like a whale.

"What's happening there?" She suspected the first mate would have more insight, but he was busy elsewhere.

The doctor followed her pointing finger and stilled. "I have… no idea. Mikani?"

"Captain's drunk. Or insane."

She frowned at her partner. "They don't send a warship after inebriated sailors."

Irahi laughed. "If they did, half the *Gull*'s crew would risk execution on a daily basis."

Ritsuko called out to the first mate. "Mr. Ferro! Can you shed some light on what's going on over there?"

He used his spyglass as the gunship drew closer to the thrashing steamer, opening fire with a thunderous noise. Cannonballs tore through the hull, and the steamer actually shuddered; the metal vibrated, emitting a noise that she told herself was just the welded panels breaking apart. *But it didn't sound that way.*

Instead of answering, Mr. Ferro shouted at the sailors. "Get us well away from that mess, boys! I want at least a hundred feet distance from those ships on our way to port."

She took that to mean it was truly dire, or he didn't know and was erring on the side of safety. Since the steamer wasn't armed, it didn't return fire, but it tried to dive *under* the water, like a creature avoiding pursuit from above. The ship wasn't built for such a maneuver, and it rolled as the gunship continued the onslaught.

Ritsuko watched the unequal combat until she had to cross the deck to keep the conflict in sight. Though it had gaping holes in the hull, and, in several places, the ship was on fire, the steamer kept moving, little twists and rolls. *I don't know much about steam engines, but that doesn't seem right.* As they put some distance between the *Gull* and the other two ships, Mr. Ferro strode over, looking grim, even for his customarily dour features.

Silently, he handed the spyglass to Ritsuko. She put it to her eye and closed the other for better focus. At first, she wasn't sure what he meant for her to see. The men on board the warship were grim and determined. Most were sooty and exhausted, clad in charred, bloodstained uniforms. It looked as if they had fought a pitched battle, and they were afraid of losing.

"I don't understand," she said with a questioning look.

"Are you looking at the steamer?"

"No."

"Do so."

There was a reason she hadn't been. The inexplicable *wrongness* of that ship chilled her down to the bone, a creeping sensation of dread that she couldn't articulate. Taking a breath, she altered her viewing trajectory. She skimmed along the half-flooded deck, taking in the damage and the scorch marks, ragged holes, and charred metal.

"What's missing in this picture?" the first mate demanded.

It took her only a few seconds to grasp his point. "There are no sailors on that ship."

Mikani stepped up beside her, setting a hand on her shoulder. The mate silently handed him the glass, and he inspected the steamer, then shook his head. "What the hells."

"That's what I'm afraid of," Irahi muttered. "Have you ever seen anything like that?"

"Not exactly." Ritsuko thought for a moment, then she told them about the weeping train, the wailing mirror, and the furious tree.

"I'd give a lot to understand what's causing this," Mikani said.

Mr. Ferro put away his spyglass with a grim expression. "We're better off figuring out how to survive it. Hold tight, it'll be a rocky run past this ship graveyard into the harbor proper."

* * *

As soon as they berthed, the boatswain, Nell Oliver, led a party of armed and nervous sailors down the gangplank to secure the dock. Other ships had the same idea: the long pier was swarming with sailors pointing guns at other security details, at the streets, and sometimes at each other. Officers and civilian officials stood in little clusters, speaking in hushed tones and glancing out toward the harbor, where the plume of smoke from the sinking steamer was clearly visible.

Loison paused beside Mikani and Ritsuko as they stood by the railing. "Inspectors, if you wouldn't mind? I need to see the harbormaster regarding our berth and repairs, and I'd feel safer with an escort."

He turned to Ritsuko with an arched eyebrow. "Partner?"

"I'm concerned. Aren't you?"

"Yeah, fair enough. After you, then, Mr. Loison." *Almost forgot the man was aboard. Don't remember seeing him since our run-in with the raiders.* They followed Saskia's man past Nell Oliver's security cordon and down the docks. The other groups of armed men kept them under close watch until they passed by.

"Nervous lot." Loison seemed amused.

"Can't say I blame them." Mikani pointed at the buildings beyond the docks.

Parts of the city were clearly in flames, and people scurried back and forth in the streets ahead. Citizens, guards, and sailors were frantically trying to put out fires while avoiding some unseen menace off to their left, toward the Thorgrim palace.

"Bronze gods. Gunwood wasn't kidding when he said it was worse in the north. Do you think this is related to the trouble in the city?"

Mikani nodded. "Seems likely. Steamships don't just get bored and head off without a crew. Steamers, trains, the mirrors... it can't be a coincidence. What a hell of a mess."

"Chaos is rarely productive, Inspector. Ah, there's our harbormaster. Mr. Pheebs!"

A bear of a man, his beard streaked with gray, came toward them. He was dressed in a faded Thorgrim uniform and seemed even grimmer than Ferro. "Mr. Loison. It's been years. You're doing shipments now?"

"Only exceptional ones. Say, there seems to be a spot of trouble." Loison gestured at the running crowds.

Hells and Winter, the man has a talent for understatement.

Pheebs scowled over his shoulder. "The machines have run mad. Carriages are smashing into walls and each other, steam engines exploding in foundries and workshops. The *Solstice* just broke off its moorings and made a break for open water." He gestured at the gunboat circling the sinking steamer's debris. "Worse, there's talk of golems disobeying orders. Half the captains want to shell the town. Best turn and sail away, Loison."

"I'm afraid that's not an option. I'm Inspector Mikani, this is my partner, Ritsuko. We're here under special orders from the Council. We need to dock, we need repairs... and we need to speak to whoever's in charge—"

"Don't know who that'd be." Pheebs offered a wry laugh. "I'm barely keeping the docks from being overrun, and I don't know how long I can hold." He motioned behind them, where the Skarsgard squadron was docked. "Those bastards are ready to start shooting. Their captain warned me yesterday that they're waiting for the last of House Skarsgard's people to arrive, then they'll fire on any ship that looks crosswise at them. And if they start, the Magnus force will join in or try to stop them. Between the two, they'll tear the port apart."

"I'm finding that I enjoy travel much less than anticipated," Ritsuko muttered.

Loison gave her what Mikani judged to be a sympathetic look, but he was too busy weighing possible solutions to respond. "It would be a slaughter."

"No argument from me," Pheebs said, "but what'm *I* to do about it? I've gotten as many of my people to safety as I can, sent word to the palace... and I'm now warning anyone stupid enough to come into port." He gave them a pointed look.

Ritsuko put in, "We might be able to lend a hand. The city's obviously in no state to receive travelers or to offer much shelter or information."

"What do you have in mind, partner?"

Loison seemed interested, too, as did the dockmaster.

She continued, "It's unlikely that we can persuade House Skarsgard of anything, but if I recall correctly, House Magnus is allied to House Aevar."

Mikani saw where she was heading with that. "And we recently did them a service."

She nodded. "Where are the Magnus troops quartered, sir?"

Mr. Pheebs pointed farther along the docks. "They're holed up in the *Pride*, mostly, but have run off all other ships from pier eighteen."

That was a quarter mile from their location, give or take. Not a great distance, but with the uneasy mood on the docks and so many armed men looking for trouble, Mikani didn't expect it to be simple. With any luck, he could talk his way out of shooting anyone.

"You coming?" Mikani asked Loison.

"I might prove useful. And I do know how to avoid attracting attention," the clerk answered.

True enough.

With a parting word of thanks for Mr. Pheebs, Mikani set out, keeping a wary eye on the troublemakers. Some of them wore House colors. Others looked like sailors who had been kicked off their ships for rabble-rousing. A man who was used to the ocean never settled down calmly on land; he'd learned that knocking heads on the docks.

They were halfway to pier eighteen when a half dozen drunkards burst out of a nearby tavern, hurling insults and bottles at someone inside. Thwarted from the trouble brewing within, they stopped and pointed at Ritsuko. Or maybe the clerk. The man's finger jogged so bad from the liquor that it was impossible to be sure.

"Oh, dear." Loison stopped dead in his tracks.

Well, he didn't run. That's something.

The sods gestured crudely as they approached. Wolf-whistling at Ritsuko, the louts made their intentions clear, despite thick northern accents that Mikani had a hard time understanding. But it was hard to mistake the meaning when a man grabbed his crotch.

He rested a hand on his pistol handle, calling out, "Gentlemen. Though I use the term loosely." *Damn it, don't provoke them.* "How about you go about your business, and I don't toss you in the drink?"

Ah, hells. Not like they'd listen.

"How about you take the fancy man and leave the lady with us?" This one spoke intelligibly enough that Mikani got the gist, though the slurred words didn't help. "Can't you see it's the end of the world?"

Mikani smiled and looked over at Ritsuko and Loison. "No, I think not. See, I'm rather fond of her."

When the ringleader took a step forward, Mikani drew his sidearm. He was out of patience with this, and he'd just as soon shoot these louts. That wouldn't help the general disarray, however, so for the sake of law and order, he drew deep on his remaining patience.

No more conversation. I'm saving my diplomacy, such as it is, for House Magnus. Or maybe I should let Ritsuko do the talking.

Ritsuko spoke for the first time, sounding polite. "Sir, I will absolutely stab you if you don't step aside. I am in *no* mood."

Mikani had no idea whether it was her level tone or the sincerity in her gaze, but the group mumbled and decided to seek amusement elsewhere. He aimed an admiring look at her and stepped around, picking up the pace until they reached pier eighteen. House Magnus had armed guards stationed at all points; it was impossible for anyone to slip past by land or sea.

He made straight for the older of the two sentries, reasoning that he was probably in charge of the watch. "Tell your captain that representatives of the Council need to speak to him." When the sailor hesitated, Mikani added, "Move it, man!" He leaned in, using a tone usually reserved for recalcitrant cadets. "If he's not here in two minutes flat, it's your arse!"

"Do you have any proof of that?" the guard asked impassively.

With an annoyed sigh, Mikani produced the packet of papers the Council had sent regarding the mission, along with his CID credentials. The guard took his time inspecting them, then he sent his younger comrade along the pier, presumably to alert someone more important. They cooled their heels for a few minutes before being summoned past all the checkpoints.

A uniformed man led them up the gangplank to the *Pride of the North*, and he never said a word, not even when he knocked on the stateroom door. A curt "Come!" followed, and the guard opened the door, then resumed his post.

Silent bastard.

"They sometimes cut out their tongues," Loison whispered, "when the guards are privy to a great deal of sensitive information, as one is who watches the inner doors."

And my father wondered why I didn't want to serve one of the great Houses.

The clerk continued, "Good luck. I'll wait on the dock with the guards."

Beside him, Ritsuko rubbed her hands along her arms, visibly nervous. But she controlled it before they passed into the lavishly appointed cabin. In the center of the room stood a man of early middle years, still lean and strong, and his hair was fair enough that you couldn't entirely tell what parts were lightened by the sun and which others were aged silver.

Looks like a mean bastard.

"Inspectors. I'm Viktor Magnus, commander of the *Pride*. What the hells do you want?"

12

SASKIA WOKE UP with aching bones, a bitter chill that would take days to fade.

Stumbling to her table for a drink, she looked out on Northport harbor just as Loison was disembarking to secure their berth and supplies. She saw Mikani and Ritsuko with him, but they were quickly lost in the mass of bodies hurrying here and there on the docks. This was more than the usual unloading of ships, less purposeful and more panicked. There were barrels left unguarded, and on a normal day, there would be thieves and beggars taking advantage of the lapse. The lack of such larceny told her the problem must be dire.

Bronze gods, what's going on out there?

In the distance, multiple fires burned throughout the city; plumes of smoke drifted in the afternoon breeze. But what drew her eye were the swirling shapes in the smoke and clouds above. Wind elementals circled the town like vultures on misty wings. All the bound ship sylphs were screaming, bucking at their restraints. The roiling anger of the fire elementals bombarded her, enough of them free that her senses tingled with the heat.

Something's driven them mad… oh, spirits, my familiars.

Saskia focused as she dressed in a simple blue gown,

eschewing all customary trinkets and vanities. Her elementals hovered nearby, confused and in disarray at their sisters' anger. They'd served her well the last few days; they were exhausted, too, and their fear was infectious.

"Hush, my dears, it'll be all right." She murmured to the air around her, willing them to listen. They calmed a bit, but she could tell they were still unsettled by the madness in Northport.

And I can't blame them.

Pulling on a gray overcoat, she left her cabin and headed for the deck. Saskia spotted the first mate as the doctor turned toward her. The large man was sweet, but his overprotective nature made it difficult sometimes. If he had his way, she would be forced back to bed with a hot posset and a warm brick for her feet.

But given the mess in Northport, there's no time to rest.

"Mr. Ferro!" She strode toward the aft castle on unsteady feet, circumventing the physician.

"Li'l White!" Irahi tried to intercept her, turning from his inventory of supplies near the mainmast.

"Not now, Irahi. Why are we sitting here? The city's a war zone. As soon as the others return, we need to pull back, anchor out in the bay where it's safe."

"You should be in bed! You can barely stand." The doctor leaned in, as if ready to pick her up, and she stepped back, pointing a trembling finger up at him.

"I swear, Irahi Otis Hu, that I will blow you off the side of this ship if you take one more step!"

"Enough!" They both paused and turned, somewhat startled, to look at Mr. Ferro.

"Leave the captain be, or you'll have a mutiny, Doctor. We can't retreat. We're barely afloat. You pushed the *Gull* pretty hard." He signaled to where sailors were busy working the pumps and patching the hull. "And I've no idea when the shore party's returning."

"I saw them go ashore, but I thought Loison was simply seeing to provisions." With a worried frown, she noted that there wasn't a whole lot of activity in that regard. The porters weren't moving cargo to and from the ships, which meant she had *no idea* where Janus and the others had gone. *That's a fine state of affairs for the captain.* "What are they doing?"

Ferro shrugged. "If they told me, I wasn't listening. I've a ship to look after. You don't pay me enough to play nanny."

She fought the urge to throttle her first mate, and Irahi cleared his throat, likely reading her mood in her expression. "I'm sure they'll be fine."

He sounds about as sure of that as I am. Hope Inspector Ritsuko can keep Janus in check. This was just the sort of situation that the Mikani she'd known—and loved—had often made worse with incautious words and actions. *And we've already got mad elementals.*

"Mr. Ferro, post a double watch. Doctor, walk with me." She offered the big man her arm, and he discreetly helped her keep her balance so the crew wouldn't see how spent she still was as they headed for the relative privacy of the prow.

Irahi held his tongue until they were out of easy hearing range of the men, but as soon as they ascended the stairs to the forecastle, he turned toward her with a worried expression.

"Tell me straight, Alexandra. How bad is it?"

He must be nervous. He never calls me that.

She pulled her hair back from her face, twisting it in a makeshift braid while she considered her answer. In the end, she chose the truth.

"It's bad, Irahi." She nodded toward Northport. "There are maybe four or five dozen elementals running amok there, near as I can tell. They're tearing the city apart." Then she gestured at the docks. "Between the wind crystals and steam engines of the ships, and those bound in cargo crates for the Summer Isle? There are probably several hundred more elementals all around us right now."

Her friend was quick on the uptake. "If even a fraction of those start breaking free, they'll raze everything in this bay. And if whatever the ones already on the rampage have is contagious, the newly freed elementals might then also go berserk." He stopped and leaned heavily on the rail. "Bloody hell, they would level the entire city, and who knows where they'd stop?"

Saskia offered him a weary smile. "You asked."

"You should have lied, Li'l White. That would've been kinder—what's that?"

A mob was headed their way, and they looked to be in an ugly mood.

Saskia sighed. *An elemental rebellion's not enough, obviously. Bronze gods, what did we do to piss you off so completely?*

"Trouble." She jogged unsteadily toward the gangplank. Irahi followed close behind, bellowing for the crew to follow.

Nell and her men stood with the watchmen from the other ships at the entrance to the pier. The crowd of townspeople, armed with makeshift weapons, outnumbered them at least three to one. Saskia headed for the barrel-chested, impressively mustached man who had apparently taken charge of the assorted ship contingents. He had a pistol tucked in his belt but gripped a heavy staff in his thickly veined hands.

"Steady, boys. You, put that blade away or I'll shove it up your arse. Easy now." He tapped a shoulder here, glared at a man there.

"Bloody instigators, just adding fuel to the flames. They'll get someone killed. Captain Nazari Lev, of the *Deva's Flight*." The mustached man smiled and bowed formally as Saskia and her men came up to them. "You're from the *Gull*, yes? A fine ship."

"Captain Alexandra Braelan—Saskia. A pleasure, Captain Lev; the *Flight* does credit to her captain." She offered a smile, keeping an eye on the stirring, screaming people a few yards away. "We seem to have a wee problem on our hands.

Perhaps we can finish praising each other's ships later?"

Captain Lev guffawed and turned his attention back to the crowd. It had gotten larger, between desperate folk and troublemakers.

"There is always time for civility, Captain. But perhaps—"

The townsfolk were grumbling dangerously. One of them cried out, "Move aside, let us board! We need to get out of here, now!"

Another added, "Show some mercy! We've families, help us!"

"We can take them, they won't shoot. Press, and we can be away from here!"

The crowd surged; the sailors tensed and drew back a couple of steps. Impasse began as neither side wanted to be the first to rush or fire. Then someone screamed, startling the mob like a herd of deer, and the mass of townspeople surged forward in a press of bodies that crushed several of their own number. The guards on the pier braced, but reaching hands tugged at their arms and clubs, threatening to pull men from the crumbling safety of their line and into the angry mob. Some fled, women carrying children away from the melee, but most stayed and tried to force their way over the defenders.

Irahi burst forward, bodily slamming past the nearest sailors and into their attackers—pushing some aside, batting others into their fellows and off the docks to the cold waters below. Even he was not safe from the struggling refugees, though, and it took three men to pull him back to safety while he swung at those grabbing for him.

Nell was holding her ground, barely, rallying her men and slashing with her cutlass at anyone stupid enough to come at her. She shouted obscenities in more languages than Saskia knew; the boatswain was *very* angry and willing to take it out on the mob.

Saskia ducked a bottle someone hurled at them. Captain

Lev swung his staff over the heads of the front line of sailors, sounding sickening "cracks" as it connected with bones and heads. He kept roaring out orders and trying to keep the men from panicking as they were nearly overrun in that first mad rush.

She could see someone behind the building fracas, screaming shrilly in encouragement. He sounded like the man that had first screamed that they should rush the sailors: he'd finally gotten his wish and now seemed determined to bring the whole thing to as bloody a conclusion as he was able.

That ragged bastard's going to get us all killed.

He was tall and spindly in ill-fitting blue finery two decades out-of-date. She could not make out his features beyond the wild mane of dirty gray hair, but his voice carried easily enough.

"That's it, brothers! Cut them, kill them all! Bring them down, and the ships are ours! One more rush, they're done for!"

Bronze gods. I'm too weak to do more than blow dust in their eyes; they're going to break through, kill my crew—spirits, no!

She ducked and grabbed Captain Lev's pistol, pulling it free and stepping away while he was busy pressing back against a renewed push by the enraged crowd.

Saskia stepped back three paces and braced, sighting along the barrel of the heavy revolver.

"Give me thunder, my darlings," she murmured under her breath. As soon as she felt the stir of air around her hands, she fired.

The elementals amplified the sound, funneling it and adding their voices to it.

The sound of her shot crashed and rolled over sailors and townsfolk alike, sending a dozen of them tumbling to the ground with a cry of pain, holding their ears. The screaming demagogue let out a high-pitched scream and disappeared from view behind the panicking, dispersing mob.

They carried some of their fallen friends, left others to crawl away if they could. At least four of them did not stir at all.

The sailors fared a little better: most managed to regain their feet, though three had to be helped back to their ships by their mates. Nell was rubbing her ears, sitting on a piling; Irahi was already tending to the wounded and sending others back to their ships.

"I'll take that." Captain Lev held out a hand; Saskia returned his pistol. "You are full of surprises, Captain Braelan of the *Gull*." He was bleeding from a half dozen cuts and bruises, but seemed in surprisingly good spirits. "We'd best make the best of it, yes? Come on, you layabouts! Move your arses, get a guard post set up here. We'll rotate watches, always a half dozen men. I'll talk to your captains, now do it!"

She nodded, running a hand over her face.

Irahi was right there, bless his heart, turning her to guide the way back to her ship. "Well done, Li'l White. One shot fired, and you saved three ships."

Saskia looked over her shoulder. There was no sign of the spidery man. She turned back toward the *Gull*, leaning heavily on Irahi.

"A girl needs a hobby. Let's hope our missing three do as well, whatever they're up to."

13

RITSUKO SIZED UP Vikor Magnus in a glance. His dark eyes were hard; cruel lines bracketed his mouth. This wasn't a man who had time or patience for anything outside his own agenda. He didn't look pleased at their interruption, either. If he could pitch their documents into the ocean and get away with it, she had no doubt that he would. Mikani put away their packet of papers, however, and seemed unperturbed by the impatience in Magnus's tone.

"We're here because you seem happy to sit on a powder keg and wait for someone to light the fuse," her partner said. "If the Skarsgard men get nervous and start shooting, they'll start a small war out there."

"I'm not in charge of Northport defenses," Magnus returned.

"Small wars have a habit of growing. Sooner or later, a stray round will hit a Magnus warehouse, or one of your defensive pickets." Mikani leaned toward the commander, who matched his stance. "And then you'll be *forced* to strike. By week's end, you and the trigger-happy Skarsgard idiots will be at each other's throats while the city burns around your high-and-mighty selves... just in time for a cragger armada to sail in and thank you all for making it easy for them to raze Northport."

Magnus's expression became increasingly sour as Mikani spoke, and by the time her partner was done, he looked ready for a fight. "You arrogant bastard. If those Skarsgard coal miners so much as spit in our direction, the *Pride*'ll tear their squadron apart… and what the hells are you on about, a cragger armada?"

In terse tones, Mikani summarized what they'd learned, and Magnus seemed genuinely shaken. "If what you're saying is true, we need to mobilize immediately."

"Pulling out of Northport won't save the city. Right now, you have more pressing problems," Ritsuko pointed out.

"I'll send a scout ship to confirm your report," Magnus said. "Once I have corroboration, I'll proceed accordingly. I can't let the craggers push this far."

Mikani nodded. "It'll take more ships than you have here. You might have to cooperate with the other Houses to break them."

She relaxed somewhat, pleased to shrug off the cragger threat from her shoulders. But she still had to persuade Viktor Magnus to take action instead of waiting to see how bad it got. If someone didn't step up to restore order, it could take months for Northport to recover. Magnus had to grasp his role in minimizing the damage caused by panicked citizens.

Maybe profit was all this man understood, so she said, "Loss of life will make it difficult to do business, and while you may command the Magnus forces in Northport, I wonder how long that will continue if House profits diminish due to an armed conflict in the region."

The commander raised a brow at her. "Are you threatening me?"

"Merely reflecting on likely outcomes. If you choose to assist us, it will go much better for all concerned. I had thought you might be familiar with our names from some work we did a while back... involving House Aevar?" She paused.

The commander looked surprised, and he sized them up afresh. "That was you two? Stories make you out to be ten feet tall and significantly less... disheveled."

"We clean up nicely. Listen, we're wasting time here, Commander. Simple truth is, letting this escalate will result in little more than grief for everyone involved. You're the only one with enough firepower around to force the Skarsgard squadron to stand down and listen to reason before they start shooting civilians who wander too close. And you'll need all your resources when those craggers sail in." Mikani seemed to be struck by inspiration. "And what better way to show up Skarsgard?"

Ritsuko pinpointed the moment Viktor Magnus saw their point of view. He looked from one to the other of them, clearly weighing the benefits against the cost. "If I order my men to defend the harbor, I get full credit for the salvation of Northport."

Otherwise, you let the place burn and innocent citizens die? Jackass. She didn't use that word often, but it applied to Viktor Magnus.

"Wouldn't have it any other way." Ritsuko hoped that the other man didn't notice the faint ring of sarcasm in her partner's tone. "You'll get all the laurels, Commander."

Once they wrapped up with Magnus, who was already barking orders to his men, Ritsuko disembarked. Standing beside Mikani, she watched from the end of the pier as the *Pride of the North* cut loose from its moorings and maneuvered toward the center of the docks, between the Skarsgard squadron and the city. That should keep Skarsgard from decimating civilians, though the way the mobs were prowling, who knew what would happen next?

"House Skarsgard won't risk shooting while the Magnus ship's in the way." Mikani sounded quite certain, though she had her doubts.

"Will that be enough? It'll only take one overeager gunner to set them off."

"I expect they'll be quite careful not to do that." She'd nearly forgotten Loison, who had elected to wait for them outside. True to his word, the man was a shadow, and she hadn't noticed him slipping up behind her. "Firing at House Magnus's flagship could be construed as an act of war. The last time two Houses engaged in open combat, they both took years to recover from the vicious circle of vendettas and proxy wars. No House scion would risk a repeat... especially when there might be a fleet of raiders headed this way."

"Well, that's one less threat hanging over our heads." Mikani turned toward the town. "Which leaves us with elementals running wild and a city ready to tear itself apart without House Skarsgard's help."

"We need to locate the source of the problems. Mr. Loison, you've been to Northport before?" Ritsuko addressed her question to the clerk.

The man nodded. "Thrice previously."

"Then direct us, if you please. If things were more... normal, who would we talk to regarding these difficulties? Who's tasked with keeping order?"

Mr. Loison considered for a moment. "That would be the Major General. I believe that it's still Lady Maire Thorgrim, wife to the late Lord Aolfe. She took over his post a year ago." He pointed toward the palace on the hill.

"What do you know about her?" she asked.

"She's an able administrator. Her late husband was no laggard, but the word is she can outmaneuver most. It's widely believed that she's the reason they got the appointment for Northport—several factions of the Council wanted them out of Dorstaad."

"Politicians." Mikani glared toward the palace. "Hate them."

"Then we need to speak with her," Ritsuko said.

She estimated that the mansion Mr. Loison had indicated might be a mile and a half away, perhaps. On an ordinary day, that would be a pleasant stroll. Today, it could take all afternoon, so they'd best keep all their wits about them.

"Then let's start walking. Watch out for mobs and possessed carriages." Her partner checked his sidearm and set off at a brisk pace.

The streets were clogged with people, debris, and here and there, overturned wagons or carriages, some still steaming. Like the ship, they thrashed more like living creatures than machines, and she had to avert her eyes, quickening her step to keep up with Mikani. Mr. Loison stayed close to her side, either for company or protection, Ritsuko wasn't sure which. But she had the feeling that the clerk might not be as helpless as he purported.

The sky was dull and heavy as lead, clouds echoing the fires below. Northport might usually be a lovely, inviting city, but at the moment, it felt as hospitable as a heavy rain. Mikani glared most of the troublemakers into submission on the way to the Thorgrim residence. A few looked like they might start a brawl anyway, but her partner stopped them with a hand on his weapon, encouraging them to move on in a hurry. Fortunately, the ne'er-do-wells were armed with knives and cudgels, not solid sidearms.

The sprawling edifice was even older than the Nuall villa, the weathered stone showing clear signs of centuries of exposure to briny air. There were tall, wrought-iron gates, where they had to flash credentials to get past the throngs milling outside. At first, the guard wasn't inclined to let them in, but a judicious application of tact and determination carried the day. After striding up the drive, Ritsuko lifted the heavy knocker, which was forged in the shape of a wolf. The resultant bang echoed through the house, followed by slow, ponderous footsteps coming to answer. At last, the door swung open to reveal a silver-haired man of venerable years. He looked too old to be fetching and carrying, and Ritsuko wanted to tell him to find a comfortable chair and put up his feet.

"May I help you?" the servant asked.

"We've come to see the Major General," Ritsuko said.

"Do you have an appointment?"

Mikani made a frustrated noise beside her. Before he could say something like "the burning buildings are our appointment," she spoke quickly. "No, but I trust our credentials will prompt her to make time in her schedule for us." She proffered them with a smile.

"Come inside, please. You may wait in the opal sitting room while I discuss your petition with the lady."

The room in question was gorgeous, decorated in opulent fabrics that glimmered in the light; even the walls held a pearlescent sheen. Ritsuko opted not to sit down, as she was afraid her clothes would smudge the pristine fabric of the settee, and that wouldn't endear her to Lady Thorgrim. Rare oil paintings in gilt frames adorned the wall, along with a framed collection of antique coins. Something about that portion of the room caught her eye, but Mikani distracted her by pacing, while Mr. Loison took up a watchful pose on the opposite wall. She noted that he had an excellent view of the whole room from there, reinforcing her impression of his acumen.

"This is a lovely home," the clerk said. "Exquisitely appointed. I've never been permitted entry before."

"Did you try?" Mikani asked.

Mr. Loison chuckled quietly. "Hardly. I know the General only by reputation."

Ritsuko regarded the clerk in silence. *Interesting. That's not the truth, is it, sir?* Though she didn't say anything, the equivocation certainly gave her pause. *Just how did Miss Braelan meet you, Mr. Loison, and how did you earn her complete confidence?* She chose not to say anything, however. If the man knew about her gift, then he already understood that she'd registered his minor deception. If not, he was an ally, and she couldn't afford to offend him.

"It's too fancy for my tastes." Mikani made a face. "Feels more like a museum. I expect a guard to come by and tell us to not touch anything."

Ritsuko thought of Mikani's cottage, with trinkets scattered all over. It was definitely more inviting. To her surprise, she missed the place, though she hadn't spent much time there, comparatively speaking.

Before she could reply, the door swept open in that distinctive style favored by long-term retainers. The elderly servant stepped in and intoned, "The Lady Thorgrim."

I suspect he'd have asked us to rise if we weren't standing already.

* * *

Lady Maire Thorgrim was a little shorter than Ritsuko, with a cherubic face and laugh lines at the corner of wide, expressive brown eyes. She looked to be in her forties, dressed in mourning black with a hint of Thorgrim silver at the hem of her skirt and sleeves.

"Welcome to Northport," she said. "Though I'm afraid we're not at our best at the moment, Inspectors." She held out her hand; Mikani hesitated.

Hells and Winters. Shake or kiss it?

Mr. Loison stepped into the pause, bending to not quite press his lips to her knuckles, so Mikani followed suit.

"We appreciate your hospitality, Lady Thorgrim." Ritsuko bobbed in a little curtsy, which surprised Mikani.

She always did have better manners than me.

"I admit I was curious. We don't get too many tourists from Dorstaad, let alone the Council's lawkeepers. Though gods know, law and order is something we sorely need at the moment..." She trailed off as she looked out the windows at her city in turmoil.

"That damnable portal is destroying my city," she finished in a softer voice.

"Portal?" Ritsuko and Mikani asked almost in unison.

Lady Thorgrim turned to them. "I can't think of any better way to describe it. Several weeks ago... something happened. The Magnus wind witches and several seers and sensitives all felt it. A couple passed from the shock, I heard. Quite horrid." A shadow passed over her eyes, and Mikani could feel the wave of emotion rolling off Lady Maire even without trying.

"What do you mean?" Ritsuko asked.

"A hole opened to whatever lies beyond. That crack in the veil between the worlds is—as near as we can tell—waking up the old spirits and causing our binding enchantments to fail."

"The wall was raised to seal off Hy Breasil from the brewing wars in the Iron World," Mikani interrupted. "You think something is now... seeping through from there and waking up the elementals?"

They say we originally came from the other side, but there's no telling what might be there now.

But Lady Thorgrim shook her head. "When the Architect erected his walls a century and a half ago, he was sealing us off from other... places. There are other lands, as far away and strange to Hy Breasil as our islands are to the Iron World. But now there's a break in those barriers, and that hole in the fabric of the world is making the old, primal spirits of the land—the elementals, awaken from slumber."

"In truth?" Loison was surprised enough to forget he was supposed to be a ghost.

"What would cause something like that?" By his partner's tone, Mikani thought he knew what Ritsuko was thinking.

And sure enough, Lady Thorgrim replied, "Only a dark and unthinkable ritual."

Damn'd be. It's as bad as I suspected. The spell we interrupted in Dorstaad seems to have done some damage after all, if not exactly what the mad bastard intended.

"I see," Ritsuko said softly. "Exactly how long has this been going on?"

Lady Thorgrim considered for a few seconds, then supplied a rough estimate for the date. And it coincided with the trouble in the city. *There's definitely a connection. Now we just have to put a cork in this. However that works. Likely easier said than done.*

"That was when we stopped Lorne—"

The other woman erupted into a coughing fit, apparently choking on her tea. She collected herself quickly as Mikani frowned.

The Major General waved off their concern. "I'm fine, pay no mind. Whatever you may need to help restore order in Northport, ask and you will have it. My own guards are run ragged trying to keep order. As I imagine you noticed, there are only two left on my property."

"The ones on the gate," he said, nodding.

"So I'd appreciate any aid you can render." She gave them both a hard look, and Mikani suddenly understood why the Council had been so eager to get her out of Dorstaad. *She can't conceive of not getting what she wants.* "My city is in trouble, Inspectors. Set her to rights, and we can discuss the elemental trouble afterward. Until then, though, you'll understand if I don't have the time or resources to spare for anything more... esoteric."

That was clearly a dismissal. Lady Thorgrim summoned a servant to show them out. Ritsuko was obviously worried, which proved she *was* as clever as she looked, and Loison was silent, chewing on what the Major General had said about the portal.

"She was... odd," Ritsuko said as they walked. "And she was hiding something, not telling us the whole truth."

Mikani nodded. "I saw that, too, but that's common

amongst politicians, no? The left hand never knows what the right is doing."

Ritsuko agreed with a sigh, and they continued to the ship in troubled silence. Mikani hoped to convince Saskia to lend them some manpower as Northport desperately needed aid.

Back at the *Gull*, he counted two hundred sailors and dockworkers setting up a perimeter around the westernmost docks, led by Hu and a tall man he introduced as Captain Lev. With Viktor Magnus keeping watch over the bay proper in the *Pride*, it took only a few hours to convince the captains of the makeshift alliance Saskia and Lev had forged to lend their men to restoring order.

I trust the Major General will back me up on the docking and tax concessions I promised. If not… well, that's a problem for another day if we survive this one.

Ritsuko shone, organizing work crews and quartermasters to provide shelter and, with Hu's delighted assistance, medical attention for as many of the Northport residents as they could convince to take refuge in the safe zone. She was a natural at this sort of thing, despite a smudged face and tired eyes. But after the third time his attempt to help ended up in a near brawl, she shooed him off to find some other way to contribute.

Hells and Winter. I'm no good at comfort, so might as well do what I do best.

He deputized two dozen restless sailors, arming them with clubs, poles, and a sense of self-importance. "Listen up, you lot. You're the closest thing to a constabulary that Northport has right now, and if I catch any of you acting like right idiots at my back, I'll shoot you down, then string you up myself."

"Gods help them," one of the dockworkers joked.

The others laughed, but they seemed to understand the severity of the situation. Figuring that was the best he could do, Mikani took his makeshift peacekeeping force out in the streets to beat some law and order into Northport. They set to work on the nearest warehouses and taverns, where looters had started taking advantage of the chaos.

A deputy-sailor called out, "I'm allowed to hit them if they run, right?"

"You're allowed to hit them if they *don't*, provided they're breaking the law," Mikani shouted back.

"I shoulda been a constable," one of the sailors muttered as he hauled a struggling man away from a pile of fine textiles.

Mikani watched for a second to make sure the suspect wouldn't end up unconscious in a pool of blood, but his team stopped after a few blows to the head. *Good enough.* Soon they had a cluster of would-be criminals subdued and bound, but damned if he knew what to do with them. *There's got to be a precinct or a gaol somewhere, but it may not still be operational.*

"What now?" a deputy asked.

That's an excellent question.

He pointed to the nearest warehouse. "There. Toss them in, post four guards, and let them cool their heels and sleep off the headaches. If any of them show some sense, we'll sort them into work crews to start cleaning up the mess."

"Seems like a fair punishment," another sailor said with a nod.

"Chain 'em together," a second advised.

Mikani paused. "In the warehouse or on the work detail?"

"Both."

He made a note of the suggestion, then said, "For now, it's not our worry. Drag them in, lock them up, and let's keep moving."

* * *

Over the next three days, the Northport Auxiliary Constabulary grew to eighty men. Some were eager to save their town; others wanted a chance for legally sanctioned violence. Mikani kept a close eye on those volunteers, as he didn't want his band renowned for causing more trouble than they prevented. Many of the men they arrested and locked up saw the error of their ways soon enough and were sent to put out fires and clear debris off the streets. A few dozen die-hard malcontents preferred to rot in the makeshift gaol. Or at least, they would've, if they had been left to Mikani's care. Ritsuko made sure the louts received bread and water, which was more than they deserved.

By the fourth day, the few remaining steam engines in town had been tossed into the bay or smashed into harmless wrecks. When a ship seemed too lively, the *Pride of the North* and a newly recruited Skarsgard squadron blew it to timbers. Northport harbor was littered with broken masts and floating debris. *It's a bloody maze of wreckage out there, now.*

Ritsuko's efforts paid off as well: as word spread of the aid efforts, merchants and traders joined in with supplies, manpower, and the offer of buildings in the secure areas of town. It was a long, hard slog, but in less than a week, Northport was no longer a plume of fire in the sky.

Mikani felt as if he'd hardly spoken to his partner in the last week. They'd both snatched bowls of rice and a few hours sleep whenever they could manage, often on opposing schedules. Ritsuko had been tireless, gathering supplies and volunteers, tending the wounded right alongside the doctor, and he hated to admit how well suited she seemed to that life. For the first time, he glimpsed the possibility that she could be content and useful outside the CID.

As if she sensed his gaze on her, Ritsuko glanced up from the bandage she was checking. The wound beneath was healing well, so she merely replaced the gauze with a clean wrap and rose, heading to where Mikani stood. He ached from the long nights and little sleep, and doubtless his odd mood could be attributed to lack of sleep.

"I think we've weathered the worst of it," she said.

Somehow he made himself smile in return. “I hope so, partner. Now”—he looked up the hill toward the Major General’s palace—“I believe Lady Thorgrim owes us some answers about what the hells is going on. With any luck, Magnus’s scout ship has returned by now and they’ve started spreading the word about the craggers so we don’t have to worry about their razing the town while we’re out looking for angry spirits.”

14

AT THE PALACE gates, the two guards turned Mikani and Ritsuko away this time. She hadn't slept more than four hours straight in weeks, and she was in no mood to be polite. The instinctive protest exploded forth before she could stop it. "But the Major General said we'd speak more after the initial danger passed."

"She's changed her mind, Inspector. I've no doubt she has more pressing business."

Mikani slammed a fist into his palm, eyes narrowed on the guard. "After everything we've done for Northport, it's the *least* she can do to answer a few questions. Now, are you letting us in, or are we doing this the hard way?"

"The least she could do is clap you in irons for overstepping your authority, as you are right now. As her emissary—"

Mikani let out a snarl and Ritsuko grabbed his arm to hold him back. "We have enough problems without turning the government against us."

Though she liked it no better than he did, she led him away from the gates and listened to him complain for at least half a mile. The city was in much better shape than it had been when they arrived, so she felt all right about leaving, provided they could figure out where to go. The common thread behind all of the problems from Dorstaad to Northport seemed to hark back to elementals and spirits, however.

"We won't solve the problem from here," Mikani said.

"That seems certain," she agreed.

Ritsuko was weary and footsore by the time she trudged aboard the *Gull*. She washed up in her cabin and joined the others for the first meal they'd eaten as a group in days. Irahi and Nell Oliver were already there, as was Miss Braelan and Mr. Ferro. Mikani came in last, still scraping damp hair away from his face. If he was as hungry as she, Ritsuko didn't wonder why he hadn't taken the time to shave.

As Sam served grilled fish and rice, she said, "We must seek the source of the trouble."

"I don't know if it's the source," Miss Braelan replied, "but I had a report from a trader that things are even worse to the west, near the elemental mines."

Irahi sighed. "While I'd ordinarily protest the idea of running toward trouble, it seems as if you find the greatest damage close to the heart of a storm."

"True," Miss Oliver agreed.

For a few moments, there was only the sound of cutlery clinking against the plates. Mikani cleared half of his food before saying, "Then we just need to decide who's going."

"*We* are," Ritsuko said, indicating her partner.

It's our *assignment.* She was prepared to argue if anyone spoke otherwise, but Miss Braelan only nodded, then glanced at the doctor. A medic might prove useful, but she wasn't about to invite him personally. Though they had spent a great deal of time together, working, over the past few days, that felt too forward. There had been no opportunity for greater intimacies; most of their conversation had revolved around medicines, patients, and treatments.

"Hu, would you mind?"

"I planned to volunteer," he said.

It stood to reason that if things were bad in Dorstaad, worse in Northport, that they couldn't fathom what might be going on in the Mount Surtir mines. House Skarsgard controlled all of the fire-elemental distribution while Magnus owned the earth rights, and the whole region was likely to be a dire, dangerous mess. The journey would be fraught with hardship, and she was already exhausted, first from the trouble with the craggers, then the chaos here.

Dinner wrapped up quickly after that. In the morning, it didn't take long to put provisions together. Merchants were grateful not to have lost their full store of goods, and they donated supplies to the cause. Those, Mr. Loison supervised, ensuring they were packed efficiently in the saddlebags. Finding horses required a little more effort, as the steam carriages weren't safe. After what she'd seen, Ritsuko would've argued if anyone had tried to talk her into traveling that way.

But the mode of travel didn't present the crux of the current argument. Just past eight bells, she stood on deck with Mikani, Mr. Ferro, Irahi, and the impatient boatswain, listening to Miss Braelan build a case.

"Of course I'm going," the weather witch said, sounding annoyed. Though her presence hadn't been agreed upon the night before, apparently the other woman had taken it for granted. "Neither the Major General nor the great Houses will divert their forces until this threat has been dealt with. Therefore, it's in my best interests to see this through."

Mikani snapped, "And what is it that you *will* do? The horses don't run on wind, and there are no sailing ships up in the middle of the bloody crags."

"A damned sight more than I could here, Janus! Take that tone with me again, and I'll show you what a good gust can accomplish."

The doctor was wisely keeping silent, as was the first mate. Every time Miss Oliver tried to interject, one or the other would silence her with a look or by raising their volume. They were getting nowhere fast.

"Where are all the elementals?" Ritsuko asked. Mikani turned toward her, and she could see him bite back an angry retort. Miss Braelan gave her a speculative look. "They're going... somewhere, when they break free of the machines, right?"

"I... they're around, sure. Somewhere. Or they faded back to wherever they go?" Mikani looked puzzled, more than angry.

That's a start.

Ritsuko went on, "We might be facing more than hazardous roads and whatever's waiting in the mines. I'd feel better if we knew whether we had angry spirits bearing down on us."

"I can spot them." Miss Braelan had caught on. "I may not be able to control more than the wind sylphs and their kin, but I get a sense of the others. All practitioners share that. Do you?" She turned a sweet smile to Mikani.

Ritsuko could tell Miss Braelan knew she'd won the point.

He conceded with ill grace. "No, it's all damned noise to me when they're close. The whole city's a bloody low rumble of seething anger and resentment. It's fading now, but—fine. Fine, then, you're along. But—" He held up one finger. "You follow my lead. We can't have two captains on this trip."

Ritsuko wondered when she'd agreed to let Mikani take charge. *Odd. I don't recall that conversation at all.*

"I wouldn't have it any other way." Miss Braelan waited until Mikani stormed toward Loison before turning to Ritsuko. "Thank you, Inspector. He can be a little difficult at times."

"So I've noticed. Did you want anyone else to accompany us, last minute?" They had four horses, though, if necessary, they might be able to scare up another one.

"I'll watch the ship," Mr. Ferro said flatly.

Apparently it didn't matter if Miss Braelan wanted him along. Ritsuko speculated that he'd had enough land travel during the journey to and from the cragger stronghold. The other woman nodded, accepting his decision, so Ritsuko didn't object either. Her gaze lit on Nell Oliver, who shook her head.

"There are still some repairs that need to be completed. I'll serve better here."

"Irahi?" Miss Braelan prompted. "Are you still with us?"

"I am. Everyone's well enough on ship, and the rest of the town can find their own physician. Besides, what would the two of you do without me?" He offered an expansive smile at Ritsuko and his captain.

Into the lull, Ritsuko heard Mr. Loison say to Mikani, "The horses are ready to go, whenever you are."

Since she already had her personal effects packed in the bag slung across her shoulder, she made her way down the gangplank toward where the horses stood, some distance past the pier. One was piebald, another white with gray undertones, the third a restive roan, and the fourth pure black, shining in the scant sunlight. Miss Braelan and the doctor followed after a flurry of farewells.

Maybe it was rude of me not to say anything to Mr. Ferro and Miss Oliver, but I'm too tired to be polite.

"Which amongst you is the best rider?" Mr. Loison asked.

"Not me," Ritsuko said.

She'd never been on a horse in her life. In fact, she was a little frightened of them. They were extremely tall, and they had big teeth, though she had been assured in the past that they didn't eat people, only plants and the like. *But better a horse than a possessed steam carriage.*

"I think I'd better have the big black," the doctor said, studying the rest. "I might prove a burden elsewise."

"You could always carry the horse, might be faster." Mikani stepped away from the doctor quickly, heading for the roan with a hand outstretched and a more sedate pace. "There, mate, it's all right. You don't throw me, and I won't kick you." His tone was gentler than he'd ever used in her presence; the words subsiding to a lower soothing murmur as he approached and stroked the horse's flank.

The roan snorted and shifted, but Mikani kept close. It was another five minutes before he swung into the saddle. By that point, the animal had calmed, and Ritsuko was perched uneasily on top of the piebald while Miss Braelan had the white.

"Thought you were going to ask the horse for a date, not just to let you ride him." Irahi grinned, already astride the big black.

"Boys," Miss Braelan mock-scolded. "You two can play nice, or we'll leave you behind." With a tug on the reins and a word, she started along the road west.

Irahi laughed, following suit. Mikani edged closer to Ritsuko, looking bemused. "Are you all right, partner?"

"I'll be fine."

I hope. She wished she'd had more than five minutes of Irahi's quickly murmured instructions. *Do I tug the reins to the right if I want to go left? And I use my knees to stop it? Bronze gods.* Mikani took her answer at face value and set off after the others. She mimicked him; the horse jerked into motion when she snapped the leather, and she took off with a jolt.

The road led through town, but the cleaning crews were working hard to repair the damage. There was no elemental magic in sight anymore. *Probably for the best until we sort this out.* She didn't allow herself to consider how difficult it might be. Sometimes it was best to focus on the immediate problem, which was getting to the Mount Surtir mines in one piece. They had maps in their packs, marked where they could find shelter and a hot meal. On the last leg of the trip, it got very rugged, and there were no way stations or hamlets.

But that's three days away.

The motion of the horse felt like she was being paddled. Ritsuko tried to relax, to move with the animal, but it didn't help a whole lot. Several days of this would jar her teeth loose. But she ignored the discomfort as they cleared Northport on the western side and continued on into the foothills. A road had been cleared, but it wasn't paved; the dirt was well packed, but she imagined it would turn to mud quickly, a flash flood sweeping down from the mountains.

The land she rode through was rough, rocky outcroppings surrounded by purple heather and gorse. In the distance, the sky was heavy and leaden, and Ritsuko suppressed a chill. *Wonder if that's natural, or if Miss Braelan can see the elementals swirling above. Either way, there's a storm coming.*

It only remained to be seen if they could prevent the cataclysm or whether they'd be swept away in the deluge.

* * *

The horses climbed gradually, taking advantage of the relatively clear land and service paths around the rail line that usually carried workers and cargo between the mines and Northport. By late afternoon, however, Mikani veered from the tracks when he crossed a bridge over a steep gorge rather than risk breaking one of the horse's legs if they slipped between the dormers. The others came behind him; he hoped Ritsuko was all right. She hadn't looked too sure atop her mount.

Rain spattering on his forehead made Mikani look up; at some point, the sky had clouded over, sprinkling rain, and the horizon was darker still, the direction they were headed. He followed the dirt path into the heart of the storm. Icy drops splashed with stinging force, drenching him within minutes. Thunderclaps echoed far too close for comfort, lighting the storm-bred gloom with angry flashes of silver.

Hells and Winter. And I used to complain about the storms back home.

Mikani pulled up his coat collar and braced against the increasing downpour, his horse sliding on the ribbon of churned-up mud that had been a path only moments before. Behind him, he glimpsed Ritsuko hunched on her horse, and a dark shadow that could only be Hu, who had fallen behind to ride closer to her.

Saskia rode at the rear. She called, loud enough for everyone to hear, "This isn't normal weather, ladies and gents."

"I knew it," Ritsuko muttered.

The air was cold enough that he could see his breath, defying the rain lashing his face. Snow wouldn't be any better, and ice would be disastrous. So Mikani hoped the temperatures didn't drop further. His horse seemed nervous as it trod along the rocky path. Now and then, its hooves slipped on the slick stones, and he tried not to think about the drop on the left side. The path was too narrow for two horses to ride abreast; he shuddered to imagine what would happen if someone came riding *down*.

"We should find shelter," Hu yelled.

Good luck with that, mate.

Mikani didn't need to check the map to know they had several hours before they crested the mountain and a bit longer to reach the first hamlet, which at first had simply been a way station for travelers. It was a small village by any standards, but if they had clean beds and hot coffee—*Hells and Winter, I'll even drink herbal tea*—he'd be happy. The rock wall offered no solution either, no ready cave where they could wait out the weather. *At least it's a windbreak.* But the wind was sweeping in all directions, likely driven by maddened elementals.

"Can you do anything about this?" He raised his voice to carry back to Saskia.

"I tried. They're not listening."

As if she'd agitated the storm spirits further, lightning split the sky, limning the mountain in stark white light—and in that split second, Mikani *almost* saw the faces in the mist. *Almost.* The alien presence left a chill in his bones, and he locked down his gift tighter, not wanting to feel whatever drove the creatures to boom thunder all around them like a warning.

"Dismount! I'd rather not have one of us tumble over if we lose a horse in this mess." *The going will be much slower, but a damned bit safer. Or as safe as we can be when we have the skies themselves against us.*

"Hug the wall, watch your step. If the horse rears or bucks, let it go." Mikani waited for them all to grab their steed's reins before starting up the narrow trail once more. Water ran down the path and off the rock wall as the storm raged. Mikani felt as if he were crossing an endless stream, the constant wash of muddy water and pebbles numbing his feet after fifteen minutes. Every now and then, the edge crumbled under the constant flow.

His lashes were damp, nearly frozen, so at first, he thought he was hallucinating, as something whipped by, striking the edge of the cliff and tumbling over. But the second time, he was sure when the rock slammed down only half a foot in front of his terrified horse. The roan surprised him by stilling on the path instead of screaming or rearing. It might've been skittish to start, but the horse had good nerve when it came down to it. Mikani craned his neck, worried about the stability of the stones above.

The weight of the water might be too much—

Only it wasn't a natural rockslide they had to worry about. He had been picturing the lot of them swept off the side under a deluge of shale, but instead, he saw three hulking figures atop the shelf, some one hundred feet above them. *Hells and Winter. Are those golems?* From that distance, he couldn't make out the faint glow of the runes normally used to control the massive stone constructs. *Someone's trying to stop us... or they've gone rogue like the fire and air elementals.* Either way, they each grabbed another rock—a boulder by human standards—and were about to drop it atop their party.

"Move!" he shouted.

The reins felt slick and cold in his hands, but the horse came when he pulled. He didn't dare run, much as he wanted to. His heart beat so hard it almost hurt as he raced as quickly as he dared along the slick, precarious ledge. Mikani hated being so far away from Ritsuko, but there was little he could do about it right now.

Impact. The huge rock slammed into the ground behind him, creating a minor rockslide. Bits of the path crumbled away, tumbling down the mountain in a shiver of wind and rain. He couldn't even hear when it reached the bottom. Someone cried out as another rock hit. More tremors. A horse whinnied in terror, the high-pitched tone unmistakable.

What the hells is going on back there?

Though it might not be wise, he had to check. Mikani peered over his shoulder and found that they'd lost one of those horses, Saskia's white. She was directly behind him, clinging to the rock wall. Her face was greenish pale.

"The boulder..." she said helplessly.

He knew what'd happened, then. "Come on. Quickly. We'll have to make do."

Mikani set the pace as quick as he dared. He wished he could reassure Saskia and check on Ritsuko, but this wasn't the place. If they didn't get off this ledge, they'd all end up like the horse. A third stone crashed behind Ritsuko mere seconds after she moved, and it opened a ten-foot gap in the path between her and the doctor.

"I can jump it," Hu said, but Mikani sensed he was none too sure.

He heard Ritsuko say, "It might be easier on your horse?"

"Too wet," Saskia shouted.

"Then how the devil are we getting the horse across?" his partner asked.

Above, the elementals or golems—whatever the hell they were—searched for stones suitable for smashing humans. Urgency gnawed at him like an itch he couldn't scratch. The path was too narrow, the edges already crumbling; if he tried to press past the others to try to help Hu, chances were that they'd all end up tumbling off the edge of the cliff.

Bloody hell, maybe I can draw them off, at least. He drew his gun and shot at the rampaging elementals. Saskia let out a surprised yelp.

"Over here, you mud-gobbling bastards! Over here!" Mikani shouted.

He fired once more, and a low, rumbling groan, the grind of rock against stone, filled the air. The next boulder hit a couple of feet above him in a shattering cloud of rock shrapnel. *Damn, that worked. Now what?* He pressed forward, hating his own helplessness, but he could only try harder to draw their ire. Mikani beckoned to Saskia. *Best to give Hu as much room as we can.* To his relief, two of the hulks on the ledge above kept pace with him and Saskia, leaving only one to rip out chunks of rock from the cliff to throw after them.

So long as they're tracking us, they'll leave Ritsuko and Hu alone.

He glanced back in time to see Ritsuko calling the black horse like someone else would a dog. The animal raised its head up and down, seeming puzzled, since it didn't have a rider controlling it. Then she got an apple out of her bag and the horse took off. *Bronze gods, she'll be trampled.* But he couldn't stop what was already in motion. The animal's hooves slid on the wet rock, but Ritsuko dove against the wall, so the horse skidded past her. It teetered near the edge, right behind her own mount, which thankfully had a placid nature. Her hands trembled as she gave the black the treat and patted its rump.

Mikani kept moving, and above, he heard the thunderous footsteps of the golems giving chase. *As long as we don't stop, it'll be all right.* He'd tell himself that anyway. Saskia stayed right behind his horse, more obviously frightened than he'd ever seen her. There was no point in worrying about what would happen when they got higher on the mountain, where they might run into these creatures up close. *Not sure that's a fight we can win.*

With any luck, they could outrun them.

Another glance over his shoulder showed Hu backing up to make a running leap. If anyone else had been stranded on that side, he had his doubts they could've crossed the gap but Hu landed *almost* where he needed to be. *Damn.* The big man's heels dug into the crumbling rocks near the edge, and he tipped backward.

Ritsuko grabbed him, her other hand on the horse's tail, and by some miracle, the black helped, towing them both forward. Hu fell on top of her as the golem dropped another stone.

15

THE EARTH BENEATH Ritsuko's feet trembled, then crumbled away. Hu tried to shield Ritsuko from the rocks raining down as they dropped; above, the horses followed Mikani and Miss Braelan. Wind whipped her cheeks as she plummeted, and she couldn't get her breath. There was only air beneath her, and falling, falling. She couldn't even scream.

Just as well, the wind was knocked out of her when she landed. Hu thumped down nearby, and the stone that had landed on him sailed down past the secondary ledge, all the way to the bottom of the cliff. She lay for a few seconds, unable to believe she wasn't dead. Of the rogue golems, there was no sign.

They're probably chasing the other two.

With a soft groan, she sat up. Her entire body felt bruised, but she seemed reasonably sound. The doctor didn't stir. Considering he'd had a huge rock dropped on him, then fallen off a ledge, that wasn't surprising, but if he was seriously injured, Ritsuko had no idea how she could move him. To make matters worse, all their supplies were with the horses.

She gazed upward and could only see a curtain of water,

darkness, crumbling stones, and an endless river of mud. *Impossible to tell how far we fell.* Using the rough edges of the rock, she hauled to her feet, and shouted, "Mikani!" But the wind swooped her voice away and gave back only the roar of the storm. There were no lights visible above, and she quelled rising fear that tasted like bile in her throat. *Focus. Stay calm.* The ledge they'd landed on was more of a rocky outcropping, but it did wend some distance around the mountain. She peered downward, finding only a dead drop to the darkness below.

Stay calm.

"Irahi?" Heart in her throat, she felt for a pulse.

There, strong and solid. The knot on the back of his head, however, explained why he was unconscious. Not knowing what else to do, she sat beside him for several minutes, whispering his name. She feared the creatures might hear and double back to renew the attack.

At length, he stirred, peering up with dark, bleary eyes. "Celeste? What happened?"

"We're in a bit of a predicament, I'm afraid."

With her help, he sat up, though the movement hurt him. His muffled curse sounded almost like Mikani. "Think I broke some ribs."

"What can I do?" she asked.

"If I had the supplies, I'd wrap and tape them. Since I don't... I bear it." The doctor tried to smile. "If you'd be so kind as to lend me your shoulder, I think I can stand."

But he was gray-faced and shaky when she got him on his feet. "I'm so sorry you were hurt protecting me."

"My dear lady, I *fell* on you. I should be apologizing."

"You also kept me from being killed by a giant rock." Ritsuko had no doubt that she would've fared much worse if the projectile had landed directly on her.

"I'm delighted to be of service." But the pleasantry came through gritted teeth.

"We'll move slow," she said. "Put your arm around me if you need to."

"Though you're kind to offer, there's no room. Don't worry, I can keep up."

Together, they stumbled forward, perhaps twenty feet, and the weather cleared. The pouring rain tapered, then stopped entirely. It wasn't *normal* to fall and leave a storm's radius. Though Miss Braelan had said the torrent wasn't natural, this proved that this whole region was spooky and dreadful. Nothing had been right since the *Gull* passed the Seven Sisters. But foreboding, no matter how strong, didn't change her orders.

"Shaping up to be a fair night," Irahi said, sounding breathless.

While she pretended to accept his good nature, Ritsuko couldn't stop checking on him over her shoulder. She wondered if Mikani and Miss Braelan had escaped the elementals, if they were safe. But she couldn't let that concern interfere with their progress, so she fixed her mind on traversing the ledge. Here, there were no signs of life, no heather or gorse. And perhaps a hundred feet, as the ledge wrapped around the mountain, the news got worse. To continue, they had to climb down a nearly vertical incline with few handholds. She got vertigo just looking at it.

"Perhaps we should rest," she said.

Irahi shook his head. "We should continue on until nightfall. Get as far as we can."

He knew as well as she did that without adequate supplies, they might not fare well. The plan had been for them to cross this mountain and reach the first hamlet. Ritsuko didn't see that happening, but with the doctor hurt and no food or water, they couldn't afford to dawdle. As if he'd guessed her thoughts, his expression became stoic.

"I'll go first. If I slip, I doubt you could catch me."

"I did once before," she said.

"You had help, Celeste."

That much was true, and the black horse was nowhere to be found. It was cowardly, but she closed her eyes, not wanting to watch. But she heard his scrambling descent and round curses when the motion pained his ribs. It was a relief to hear him panting nearby. She glanced down and found him standing solidly on the ledge below.

"Come on. I'll catch you."

He was definitely bigger, and probably stronger, but she wished desperately that it was Mikani waiting for her down below. If her partner said that, she'd launch herself without a second thought. She didn't know Irahi as well, and it took all of her courage to clamber over and let gravity carry her. The rock was smooth enough that her boots had no purchase, so her body slammed into his. Pain made him swear, but he didn't even budge.

"There we are." He lifted her and spun so she was in front of him on the other side. "Carry on with the trail blazing."

"You should probably conserve your strength," she protested.

Irahi only smiled.

There were a few more similar jogs until they reached a lower path that seemed more suitable for humans, less for mountain goats. By Irahi's gray face and the sweat pouring off him despite the chill mountain air, she guessed he was hurting like hell. She didn't know what to do about it, however. Every time she expressed concern, he waved and mumbled a vague assurance, validating the truism that doctors made the worst patients.

It was nearly dark when she heard the faint whisper of water. Since her throat was burning, she quickened her pace. And when they rounded the curve, she spied a trickle coming down the side of the mountain. There were gentle inlets cut into the stone, so she guessed this was the regular runoff channel, either from the recent storm or from a stream higher up. She stifled a whoop of triumph; they could make it to the village without food.

Too thirsty to worry about manners, she put her mouth on the stone and let the liquid run into her mouth. It tasted sharply of minerals, but nothing in the flavor made her think it was tainted. Then Ritsuko shifted back so Irahi could drink his fill. Since he was bigger, it took considerably longer, then he set each cheek in the flow, cooling his face.

"I've a flask in my pocket. I knew liquor wouldn't help our situation, but..." Irahi delved into his torn jacket, produced the container, and dumped the alcohol. Then with some effort, he filled it with water.

"If we're careful, that should last us."

Irahi nodded tiredly. "Let's go, love. We can put a little more distance behind us before we lose the light entirely."

Ritsuko didn't know how she felt about the endearment. He was exhausted and hurt, so perhaps it was just one of those things. In the end, she let it go as it wasn't the time to ask. So she just nodded and set off.

Night fell quickly on the mountain, and the temperature dropped accordingly. Soon, not even the moon and stars gave enough light to make her feel confident about where she was leading them. Her progress had slowed to a near crawl by this point anyway.

Ritsuko sighed. "I think we have to stop here."

"Agreed. It's too risky to press on. One misstep will send us plummeting."

She gave a wry smile, knowing he couldn't see it. "Thanks for that mental image."

"Are you afraid of heights?" he asked kindly.

"A little, before. More now."

"I suppose falling off a mountain will have that effect." His wry tone surprised a laugh out of her.

She wished they had... anything to help with the chill, but there were no blankets or bedrolls. No warm supper. *It would be impossible to build a fire here, anyway.* With a faint sigh, she slid down against the rock face. Ritsuko had no idea how she would sleep, but even if she didn't, rest would help, provided she didn't freeze in the night.

"Don't take this as an improper advance, Celeste, but I think if we're to survive, we need to pool our resources." The doctor opened his arms, and a shiver went through her.

It was too much intimacy, too fast, but practicality wouldn't permit her to demur. "Let me know if I hurt you."

At first it was dreadfully uncomfortable. She thought about how she'd climbed into Mikani's lap after she killed her first man, how good and natural it felt. By contrast, she felt nearly smothered by the weight of Irahi's arms. Yet the warmth was heavenly. She was afraid to move, however, worried about jabbing him.

"Relax," he whispered. "We're going to be all right."

And she wished with all her heart that she believed him.

* * *

Mikani grabbed Saskia by the waist, forcibly yanking her back from the disintegrating edge of the mountain path. The woman in his arms struggled and kicked at him, swearing as he hauled her back. The path behind them disintegrated in a flurry of mud and splintering rock. He glanced back once, but the darkness had swallowed Ritsuko and Hu, and no amount of shouting roused a response.

Another boulder slammed down.

If we stop, we fall, too.

He staggered in the cascading mud and stinging rain as Saskia's struggles finally wound down to wracking sobs and halfhearted kicks. *Ritsuko. Celeste, why did I bring you here? Please…* But he couldn't even concentrate to shape a prayer with the golems attacking. *If we don't draw them away, they'll finish the others.*

Lead them away. Keep moving. We'll come back for you, partner.

The golems kept pace as long as they could, hurling rocks that were driven astray by the wind, but soon, they ran out of higher ground, and Mikani dragged Saskia onward with all of his strength. The storm let him pretend that it was only rain dripping down his face and clouding his sight. He carried her along the winding trail and into a narrow pass. Boulders flew past him and shattered, peppering them with flying shards of stone and rock; none came so close as the one that had taken Hu and Ritsuko, but he could not stop moving yet. He scrambled and stumbled on, his limbs on fire, until somewhere far behind him he finally heard the elementals rage as they lost their prey.

When he stumbled again, he stayed down on hands and knees, trying to regain his breath. Saskia curled up under him and turned away, crying fitfully.

His heart raced, and his chest burned. He could feel his arms and legs starting to cramp, so he pushed himself to his feet and reached for Saskia. When she tried to struggle, he grabbed her arms and yanked her to her feet, pressing her against the rock wall before she thrashed her way off the edge.

She slapped him, hard. Then again.

"You bastard! We have to go back! Let me go, we need to get back!"

The path was still crumbling, slivers and sheets of broken rock and dirt sliding down the mountainside with a grating sound. *They could be hurt, buried under a pile of rocks. But getting through that landslide will take hours or days; if we break a leg looking for them, we're all dead. Or they could be... Ritsuko could be—no. They're alive, and we* will *get them out of here.*

The thought of losing Celeste twisted his heart, startling a pained self-confession from where he'd buried the thought. *I can't go on without her.* Mikani let Saskia vent for long minutes, striking at his chest and trying to push him away, while he regained his breath and tried to get his own trembling back under control. When she tired, with her fists clenched in his shirt and her cursing reduced to loud gasps for breath, he leaned in close to be heard over the rain.

"We can't rescue them, Saskia. Not on our own." She sobbed louder, but he could sense her listening. "We need to get help. We'll return."

"They'll be dead by then."

"They could be dead *now*." The admission cost him: his stomach wrenched, and for a long moment he couldn't draw breath for the knife endlessly turning in his chest. *No. It's not true. I won't let it be. Be strong for me, Celeste.*

Saskia snapped her head back, eyes wide and red. She pushed at him and struck at his chest and face, weakly. He only turned away enough to avoid the worst of the blows without breaking eye contact.

"Don't say that. Don't you bloody say that, Janus, they have to be alive, they have to be."

"Then they need more than two idiots stumbling in the rain and reminding those damned rock creatures that they're there. Be smart, Braelan."

Saskia was silent for a long moment, angry and frightened. "Damn you, Janus. You bastard—let me go." Saskia closed her eyes and stood up straight. He did not need his gift to feel the wave of hatred she had for him at that moment—it matched his own self-loathing; but the blinding wave of her grief had broken for now.

He fought back the knot in his throat and started limping up the slippery trail before his muscles cramped up completely. He could hear her following, splashing against the stream of filthy water rolling down the trail and against their shins.

Then she was next to him, ducking under his arm to help him limp along, wet and bedraggled and freezing cold against his side. They struggled along for the better part of an hour, crouching against the wall when the wind whipped the rain into icy shards of hail and starting nervously every time thunder cracked with the sound of rock giants throwing boulders down from the sky.

He was reduced to willing his legs to move, concentrating on keeping his balance, so he'd not drag Saskia over the edge if he stumbled.

Have to keep moving. Come on, Mikani, get your arse in gear. Ignore the pain, push through it. Have to get Ritsuko. Have to help Hu. It's only pain.

He was snapped out of his hollow trance by a whinny. Up ahead was a small widening of the path, half-sheltered by a rock overhang. Their horses were huddled there, trembling and wild-eyed, but seemingly hale. He went to the animals, calming them and rubbing them down as best they could. Mikani could barely walk, and Saskia would be unable to lead them all.

"We need to rest." Mikani forestalled her protest with a gesture at his legs. "I know. But we need the supplies and horses if we're going to get help. And honestly, I don't think you can carry me to the next bend, let alone the top of the mountain. Ten minutes, and we go on."

"I can go on ahead, get you all some help."

"And you could fall off the edge, or get waylaid by animals, elementals, or craggers... and we'd all be done for."

Saskia chewed her bottom lip for a moment before finally nodding. She turned away from him to light a lantern, more for cheer than heat. Mikani also hoped it might summon help in the dark, though the chances were slim in such a remote location, and even less that the curious party would have good intentions. They sat in silence while the horses recovered, and Mikani stretched and rubbed away the cramps in his legs.

"Do you really think they're still alive?" Saskia didn't look up from the small, flickering flame, her half-chewed travel biscuit forgotten.

"I do." *Bronze gods, I hope so. Or I'll tear down the damned mountain.* "It'll take more than a big rock to bring down Hu. He's taken a shotgun blast to the belly and walked away from a six-on-one bar fight before."

"As I recall, you were the one that started the fight. And the shotgun was first aimed at you." She turned toward him, dark circles making her eyes look hollow in the shifting light.

Well, hells if she's not right about that.

"And I got him out both times." He waited for her reluctant nod. "He's a tough, stubborn brute. You know he is. And Ritsuko—" He cleared his throat, pained by the sudden clench deep in his chest. It took him a few seconds before he could continue in a relatively even tone. "Ritsuko's smart and resourceful. If anyone can get them out of that mess, she can."

"You care about her." Saskia sounded wistful.

He looked away. "She's my partner. Of course I—"

"Not what I meant, idiot. And you bloody well know it." She looked away, tying her hair back into her customary loose braid, twigs and dirt and all. "I don't think I've ever seen you quite like this, Janus. Not even... not even with me."

Mikani frowned, running a hand through his hair but glad of any diversion from the thought of Ritsuko hurt and waiting for him to find her. "Hells, Saskia. You and I... gods, we had some great times, but we wanted different things."

Hells and Winter, we're having this conversation now?

"Oh, Janus." She gathered some loose dirt and threw it at him. "I think... we would have killed one another, sooner or later. You're too damned pigheaded and bloody honorable for a pragmatic weather witch to put up with for long. Let's get moving, shall we?" She stood, turning the valve to extinguish the lantern, and the night was all darkness and cloudy skies.

He clamped down on his gift, hard, to keep from reading whatever emotion was rushing through her. Better to take her words at face value. "Saskia—"

"Please, Janus. Hurry."

16

SASKIA TOSSED JANUS a saddlebag. With his usual reflexes, he caught it. Then she mounted Hu's black horse wearily. This day felt endless—and she had a sick hollow in her stomach. *He can't be gone.*

Irahi was her oldest friend: her father had hired him over twenty years ago, on her first trip as the *Gull*'s apprentice navigator. She'd taken an immediate liking to the boisterous young man and his boundless cheer; he'd eventually admitted to being amused by her restless enthusiasm—and her penchant for finding trouble, a welcome change from his placid life on the Sisters archipelago. While most of the crew deferred to her as the captain's daughter, he'd treated her as a crewmate and, eventually, as a friend. When her father had given her command of the *Gull*, it had surprised no one when Irahi chose to serve under her... and they'd been traveling together ever since.

Gods, I can hardly remember a time without him. He has to be all right.

She finished adjusting her saddle and glanced over at Janus. A tight knot formed in her throat at the look she'd glimpsed on his face, like he couldn't breathe for thinking of his missing partner. He kept glancing back toward the broken path, and for a moment she thought they might turn back to search for their missing companions.

Then he tossed the bag over the roan's saddle and saddled up. To her eyes, he looked almost tender as he took charge of Ritsuko's piebald. Fortunately, it was a placid animal and fell in behind them. As she led the way out from the outcropping, she noted that the rain had tapered to a miserable drizzle while they rested.

Her mount was sure-footed along the rock trail, never faltering as it climbed. The narrow trail widened gradually as she reached the entrance to a high valley, the rocky ledge opening into a scrubby plain flanked by steep, wooded slopes. After that, it was easier going, but Saskia's whole body ached with each swaying movement of her mount.

Once again, she saw the white horse screaming as it tumbled from the crumbling edge. *If Janus hadn't told us to dismount, I would've gone with it.* She didn't want to dwell on the tragedy, but there were no words that would suffice. Janus must've felt the same way because he was quiet behind her, just the rhythmic clop of the roan's hooves ringing against the rocks.

When the rain picked up again to a steady drumming patter on her head and back, she hunched her shoulders against the downpour. She was chilled, drenched, and grateful for the distraction the discomfort provided from her brooding.

An interminable period later, the rain had subsided to a miserable drizzle once more when she spotted lights in the distance. The sight—along with the promise of warm stalls and mounds of oats—encouraged the tired horses into a canter. Though Saskia was a fair rider, the sudden change of pace nearly unseated her, as she'd been practically dozing in the saddle. Behind her, Janus cursed.

The village of Skalbrekka was tiny, hardly more than a widening of the path along the valley floor. No more than ten cottages, along with a stable and the public house where travelers took shelter on the way to the mines: the rail line that ran from the mines toward Northport snaked by nearby, but she could see nothing resembling a train station in the village. Even gaslight hadn't reached this far north; instead, they used old-fashioned oil lamps, a handful of them to light the main thoroughfare. There were no people about, probably because it was past dark, and the weather was nasty, but as Saskia slid off her horse, raised voices from the tavern reached her ears. At first she thought they were fighting, then she recognized a traditional drinking song, belted out in a thick dialect of the old tongue.

Haven't heard that spoken in years.

She took a step in that direction, but her knees nearly buckled, so she clutched the black, who tugged her toward the stable. By the sounds of it, Janus led his horse that way, too.

A lad came out rubbing his belly. She guessed they'd interrupted his supper, but she couldn't bring herself to care. Worry had too tight a grip on her.

Saskia produced some coins and jingled them in her palm. "Two silver crescents for you to care for our mounts. Four more if you've fresh horses."

"Ponies, ma'am. They're sturdier, better for the mountain paths."

"That'll do. Get them ready."

"You can't ride out at this hour."

Janus snarled. From the sound, she guessed he was losing patience. "Why not?"

The boy glanced over at him. "Owner's orders, sir. It's too dangerous to travel at night. There've been... goings-on, out in the wilds."

"Like freak storms and marauding elementals?" Saskia snapped the question. "We know. That's exactly why it's imperative for us to get back. We lost two of our party, and we need to find them."

"You can talk to Glenn, if you like. He runs the inn, owns the ponies, too. Might be, he'll see fit to help you."

With a sigh, Saskia dropped two crescents in the boy's palm. *Irahi would scold me for taking my frustrations out on the boy.* "Thank you. Look after the horses for us."

"Will do, ma'am. I hope you find your friends."

Inside the public house, the air felt shockingly warm, likely from the press of bodies and the blazing fire. There were a dozen or so men in the common room, roughly dressed and sporting luxurious beards and braids twined into their long hair. But there were a number of women, too, and not just the ones serving drinks; some conversed in a tight knot in the corner while others joked and drank alongside the men. A large group continued singing in exuberant fashion as she trudged toward the bar, where a lean, one-eyed man kept watch on the room.

"Are you Glenn?" she asked.

"Depends who's asking. Do I owe you money?" The man smiled.

Janus cut in with another growl. "We need to rent some ponies and we could use a hand with a search. How much?"

Damn it. Never show how desperate you are. You just tripled the asking price.

To her surprise, however, the innkeeper was shaking his head. "I wouldn't go prowling in the dark for any amount of coin. Settle in, and I'll see who's available, come morning."

Saskia mustered every last scrap of calm and patience as Janus slammed his palm down on the counter. "I'm an envoy of the bloody Council of Dorstaad, and my partner's out there, possibly injured—"

"The Council has little to say what goes on in Skalbrekka, mate. You're in the hinterlands now, well and proper. I collect you're upset, so have a drink on the house. Then I'll rent you a room, you'll sleep, and we'll set out. In the morning. I'm not losing anyone else in the dark or letting my ponies break their legs."

One of the barmaids slipped them a sympathetic look, but Saskia could tell Glenn wasn't budging. "How long until dawn?" she asked softly.

"Four hours, five at the outside."

That meant it was past midnight already. Waiting felt like failure, but in her heart, she knew the truth. They'd do more good with the light to mount a proper search. *Just hold on a little while longer, Irahi, Inspector... I've faith in you.* She would not accept any other possibility; they might be hurt, somewhere, but they had to be alive. Still, she was no happier about the delay than Janus was, though she hid her displeasure a little better.

"You promise we'll ride out then?"

"My word on it."

That might mean nothing at all. Saskia collapsed in a chair, her pack thumping to the floor beside her. Instead of joining her, Janus paced. He was like a caged wolf, crossing the floor in long, impatient strides; he paused at the window to glare out into the darkness like it was responsible for his fury. In time, the young waitress put two steaming mugs on the table, along with soup and bread.

"Fortified tea, ma'am, and venison stew. It'll warm you right up."

"Thank you," she said wearily. "How much?"

"Board comes with the room."

There was no chance she was getting Janus into a bed; she'd be lucky if he ate. "I don't think we'll be needing it. Will your employer mind if we bide here by the fire?"

"Not at all. Then it's two crescents for the victuals."

That sounded low, but she was used to city prices, so she merely passed over the coins. Saskia didn't try to convince Janus to eat. She merely dug in, knowing she needed her strength to keep going on little sleep. In time, his energy ran low, and he flung himself into the chair opposite her. He scowled at the stew and the now-lukewarm drink.

"I can't," he said, low. "I can't sit here and eat when she—when they—"

"I know," she said softly.

Choosing to leave them behind is killing him. She was still angry at him for that—and at herself, for giving in... though it must've been the right choice, judging by how they'd barely even made it to shelter, themselves. *We would have died on the mountain if we'd gone back. Fine, Janus, you were right. But I'm not sure I'll ever forgive you for it.* Saskia understood how Janus's mind worked; she'd just never been very good at balancing his moods against her own.

In silence, she finished her food and drank the tea. He did likewise, grudgingly, probably because he didn't want to pass out before the search party departed. After that, the hours seemed interminable. When her eyelids started to grate like gravel, and she found her thoughts drifting like muddy water, Saskia put her head down on the table in the hope of catching a nap.

A hand on her shoulder startled her awake. From the faint light trickling in the smudged windows, it was just before dawn. And she was surrounded by rough-looking men. Janus stood with them, and he looked like pure distilled hell. His eyes were red as blood, as if he'd been digging at them, and his face was both filthy and unshaven. In other words, he fit right in with the locals, who all seemed like they'd been up all night carousing.

"As promised," Glenn said. "Your horses are rested, and I've gathered some lads to help with the search."

"Whereabouts did your mates go missing?" a tall, bearded man asked.

Janus described the area, and the Skalbrekkans exchanged uneasy looks. But not a single one protested when Glenn said, "Let's mount up."

The weather was better today, the return trip less harrowing, but it still took hours. Farther from Skalbrekka, they split up, and Saskia was conscious of time ticking away. Over each new rise, she prayed to see Irahi coming toward her, but so far, there had only been empty crags and hollows, broken ledges and unrewarded effort. *Maybe one of the other groups found them.* But she couldn't hold tight to that hope. The quest seemed impossible—and then, as if he'd absorbed as much of her mood as he could bear—Janus snapped.

He flung the reins to his roan toward her. "I can't concentrate and pay attention to the horse, too. I'll bloody well find her or die trying."

"Janus, you've no idea how far away they are—"

"Quiet," he snapped.

She shut up, reading the desperate determination in his blue eyes just before he closed them. So Saskia signaled to the nearby men for silence. They might not understand exactly what he was doing, but they could doubtless tell he was Ferisher-touched. Fear boiled up inside her; his gift could be dangerous when pressed to its limits, and Janus was opening himself up to the whole *world. Looking for Ritsuko.*

17

EVEN THE LONGEST *night ends.*

Ritsuko cradled that thought all through the dark hours, while her stomach growled, and she fought constant fear. By the time the sun came up, her entire body ached; she had bruises on bruises, and in the scant moments of sleep she'd snatched, she had probably hurt Irahi. She didn't like the sound of his breathing. It came in jagged rasps. Though she wasn't a doctor, she knew ribs could do internal damage when they broke.

If he has a punctured lung...

She shifted away from him to peer into his face. His forehead was clammy, but he mustered a smile when he saw she was awake. "Did you rest any?" he asked.

"A little. Can you move?"

"I don't see that I have a choice."

They could wait for rescue, of course, but that seemed counterproductive, so she levered herself to her feet and pulled Irahi up. He groaned and staggered, reminding her how narrow the ledge was. In the daylight, it was worse; she could see the long fall down the rocks below, nothing but death and more death that way. Ritsuko squared her shoulders and tried not to think about how hungry she was or the fact that the runoff from the night before appeared to have dried up. It was just as well she couldn't remember how long people could survive without water.

"I'll go first," she said.

When he didn't argue, Ritsuko took it as proof that he hurt more than she did. *I'd have more than bruises if not for Irahi.* Figuratively speaking, she strangled her panic and kicked its corpse over the side of the mountain, then she set off, boots scraping loose clusters of rock that plinked against the cliff face as they tumbled down. His heavy tread offered assurance that he was with her, but even at her careful pace, his breath grew ragged. Ritsuko turned, gesturing for him to be still, and leaned her head against his chest. To her relief, his inhalations sounded dry. *So far.* That didn't mean he was healthy, but at least he wouldn't start coughing up blood.

He touched her hair lightly, offering what she felt sure was meant as a reassuring smile. "I know you're worried, but I've been hurt worse."

"And I imagine you had immediate access to shelter, food, and medicine."

"That's true, but I'm tough. Keep moving."

Even if it was pure bravado, she had no way of treating his injuries, so she set off. As they walked, the day brightened, and only the position of the sun told her that time was passing. Moving slow, they didn't cover much distance, and she stopped often. Farther on, the ledge narrowed to the point that her heart thundered in her chest as she inched along.

The stone lip wound around the mountainside, and Ritsuko stumbled into Irahi, who hissed in pain when her elbow caught him in the side. "Sorry."

She'd hoped the path would angle upward, maybe eventually rejoining the original path. Instead, this ledge simply... ended. They could retrace their steps to where they'd fallen, but that would sap energy they didn't have.

Exhaustion pulled on her legs like leaden weights, but she found the strength to help the doctor maneuver in the shallow space, so they could retreat around the corner. *Better not to sit so close to the edge.*

"Let's settle where the stone is widest. That should be safer."

Irahi held on to the rock wall as he backtracked far enough for them to make camp. *Not sure if that applies when you have no supplies.* It was somewhere to rest, at least, and the slight overhang above gave some respite from the sun. Her back protested when she slid down beside the doctor. Now all they could do was wait.

"Here," Irahi said, offering his flask.

The water felt tepid and brackish on her tongue, faintly flavored with the liquor he'd poured out the night before. Ritsuko was careful not to take more than a couple sips; there was no way to tell how long this had to last. *I wish I knew more about survival.* But maybe more information would just frighten her more if it permitted her to predict their life expectancy with greater accuracy.

Not thinking of that. Mikani's coming. He'll find us.

Once they got comfortable, Irahi went through his pockets. *Good idea.* Ritsuko did the same and they piled the items between them. The emergency inventory consisted of one partially filled flask, two peppermint sticks, a packet of salted beef, a handkerchief, a comb, two knives, a thimble, a pincushion, a pencil, a pair of scissors, and a scent bottle. Ritsuko beamed when she realized they had what looked like a feast, as it had been almost a day since she'd eaten.

Irahi wore a sheepish expression. "I thought I'd better pack something in case I got hungry before we reached the inn."

"I could kiss you."

"Save it for when I've got more energy." But it was a lackluster riposte, and his hands trembled when he passed her a strip of dry meat.

Ritsuko ate it slowly, trying to fool her stomach into thinking it was more substantial. Then the doctor snapped a peppermint stick and offered her half. "Dessert, how decadent."

After the sweets were gone, they each had another swallow of water. "Do you think they're searching for us?" she asked.

"Absolutely."

"Should we have waited where we fell?"

"I don't know if it would've been any better. In the dark, in the storm, I doubt they'd be sure how far from the village we were."

"The road is impassable right now. What will the villagers do for supplies?"

He lifted one shoulder in a weary half shrug. "A stone elemental could mend the path, but it will be expensive."

"Not for us to worry about, I suppose. We have our own challenges."

Irahi smiled in response to her deliberately optimistic description of their predicament.

For a few seconds, she studied the pile of possessions; and then it occurred to her. While she might regret this move come nightfall, if nobody had found them before then, cold would be the least of her worries. Ritsuko shrugged out of her coat and took up the scissors, cutting the fabric into long strips.

"If that's for my ribs—"

"You said not to bother, you're the doctor."

"Then what're you doing?"

"Making a rope." With grim determination, she braided the cloth together and pulled it tight, tighter, hoping it would bear weight.

"I don't think it'll be long enough to reach the bottom, Celeste, even if you strip down to your bare skin."

If Mikani said that, it would've sounded… wicked. She fought a blush, continuing her work. "That's not my plan. I'm hoping it might be long enough to reach the top. I'm not confident in my climbing ability, however, so I was hoping—"

"That I'd secure the rope on this end and stop you from plummeting all the way down?"

"Exactly. If I can get to the top, I'll help you up."

"I don't know if I can make it," the doctor said quietly. "Walking is a strain. Scaling a cliff would be agony."

His quiet certainty cut a slash across her heart. "We can't stay here, just getting weaker."

"I know. Don't apologize. You're not a damsel who sits and waits to be saved."

"It goes against my nature," she admitted.

The rock face above was rough, and she had no idea if she could manage. With no climbing experience, it seemed foolhardy, but she'd go mad sitting on this ledge. *I'll take every precaution, but I have to try.* Ritsuko cut her skirt next and by the time, she finished making the rope, her fingers were sore. She looped it around her waist, then let Irahi tie the knots.

"Not as good as Ferro could do, but they should hold. Good luck."

Ritsuko left all her worldly goods with him as a promise that she was coming back. A few deep breaths steadied her, then she evaluated the cliff above. Slightly to the right, she should be able to haul herself up. Two feet felt like an immense distance when there was so much open air beneath her. The ledge *might* catch her, and if that failed, hopefully it wouldn't hurt Irahi to keep her from tumbling over the edge, using the makeshift cable.

Inch by inch, she went up, torturously slow. It took minutes for her to find the next handhold and even longer to gather the courage to reach for it. Her arms trembled, and she forced herself not to look around. *Only the rock, there's* only *the rock.* Irahi seemed to sense that silence helped more than encouraging words could, so he said nothing as she shifted upward.

Then the loose rock skittered away from her feet, and she clawed at empty air. For the second time, Ritsuko fell.

She didn't scream.

* * *

Mikani closed his eyes and drew a shuddering breath. He had always channeled his gift through touch and taste; even when he set it free during battle, he relied on the hot wash of anger and bitter fear from his opponents to guide his attacks and counters.

It's always been close, bloody and intimate. Like killing, like tasting the fading emotions of a dying man...

He wasn't sure he could even do what he intended, but he'd be damned if he didn't try. Men muttered behind him, and Saskia's gaze weighed heavy on the nape of his neck. As he released his hold upon his talent, the acrid hint of their fear and doubt touched the tip of his tongue. Saskia's concern was close and sharp; he recoiled as the wash of emotions cut into the tentative web of his expanding senses. Mikani sensed an echo of himself on her, all angles and sharp taste like rich wine and spices, but she also kept Hu close, gentle, steadfast, and reassuring as a home's warm hearth.

With a shuddering breath, he cast his talent wider, doing his best to block the tangled mess of her emotions from his senses. Hot blood hammered at his temples, and he tasted the fear of a rabbit hiding from a hawk in the tall grass nearby. He cast wider than ever... but it was only a few dozen yards, and his chest was already burning with the strain. Each labored breath was a harsh rasp in his ears that drowned all other sounds.

It's not enough. Not nearly enough. Damn'd be, I can't feel her... she's too far.

Since he could not track memories and traces of her emotions, he'd have to improvise.

She's the sun. I'd normally search for her by following the trail left by her passing... today, I must seek her warmth, instead.

Mikani loosened his grip and sought her in his memories. When they first met, partnered against both their wishes by Commander Gunwood, the lingering haze of her initial annoyance turned to delight when they broke their first case within a week. The first time a suspect went after her, he'd broken the man's jaw. Ritsuko had been angry with him; frustrated as he'd been at the time, he'd also admired her determination to make it without special treatment. Next a memory of visceral joy cascaded through him of the first time he'd seen her smile, rare as a fleeting sunbeam through a thick cloud. Mikani threaded through each moment with her, sharp in his mind and resonating with emotion—the happy celebration of a hundred small victories, the shared frustration of long nights as they worked the cases no one else wanted.

He gathered his feelings from years of partnership, weaving them together into a tenuous outline of her. Mikani was vaguely aware of moving. Ignoring the sensation, he set his gift free so he could concentrate on seeking more memories of Ritsuko. The world faded, and in his mind's eye, she became more real than anything else: amusement in her voice when they argued over paperwork, her worry over his reckless ways, and the shimmer of the way her hair caught the sunlight just right, shining blue-black against her skin.

When did I notice that? Or, rather, how could I not *notice that before?*

Her face glowed in the red light of dawn and a spark of heat went through him at how her brow furrowed just so as she became lost in thought. Tumbling along with that fragment of memory, a lingering trace of her scent... and the clear sensation of her fingers on his cheek. He heard her voice speaking a dozen fragments of half-remembered conversations.

Her face was everywhere.

Hells and Winter, Ritsuko... Celeste. When did you become so deeply ingrained in me? The realization hit him hard, with a suffocating twist deep in his chest: a sharp and undeniable tug toward the west. Mikani opened his eyes with a gasp, and only Saskia's hand on his arm kept him from falling off his horse.

The rest of the men stared at him, eyes wide, fear rolling off them in oily ripples... but he barely even noticed them or the throbbing burn at the back of his throat. He spat out a mouthful of coppery heat and steered the roan toward the far end of the narrow valley.

"Janus?" Saskia's voice was distant, distorted.

He swam in a haze of pain and purpose that couldn't be easily pierced. "I can feel them. This way."

She shook her head, frowning at him. His tongue felt swollen and heavy; the faint sting told him he must have bitten it at some point, so he pointed toward the hills with a trembling arm, instead. Saskia nodded and turned to the others, her words a muffled murmur as he rode past her, following the insistent tug at his heart.

For two hours, they rode into the hills surrounding the valley, calling out every few minutes for Ritsuko and Hu as they advanced along narrow trails and crumbling mounds of shale washed down the mountainside by the elemental storms. The going was slow and precarious, with frequent switchbacks and detours to make their way past gorges and treacherous patches of mud... but Mikani never lost the trail. The carefully crafted web of emotions tied to his memories of Ritsuko was as unmistakable as the first light of dawn, guiding him toward her.

He had neither the time nor energy to waste talking to the others. As he followed that trail, he could not help but realize just how entwined their lives had become... how he'd come to accept her as a part of him, natural as breathing.

I'm an idiot. Regaling her with tales of my affairs, not realizing that she's the one constant light ready to bring me out of the dark.

Mikani was so lost in tracking and recrimination that he nearly rode off the side of the mountain; only one of the men's sharp tug on his reins and Saskia's startled cry saved him from being bucked off his horse and off the sheer cliff before them.

"Bloody hell..." He pulled up short and looked around, feeling her nearby, almost painfully close. The throbbing in his head and rush of blood in his ears kept him from hearing the faint cries from below until someone pointed down the slope.

"Irahi!" Saskia dismounted and scrambled to the edge.

Mikani followed clumsily, crawling the last few feet to kneel beside her and peer down, trying to blink away the blurriness in his vision. Hu was sprawled against the rock wall, Ritsuko cradled against his side. The wash of relief that swept through Mikani nearly crumpled him. He let out a long breath as he shuddered uncontrollably. He forced his eyes open, his mouth twitching in an attempt to smile, and looked down.

Ritsuko hadn't moved, and Irahi seemed to be attempting to stand... and failing. *Bronze gods, no. No, no, no.*

Two volunteers held him back as he tried to launch himself down the slope to get to Ritsuko; he struggled against them with desperate strength until Saskia grabbed him by the hair and leaned in close enough to shout at him.

"She's alive! They're alive... stop being an idiot, stay still so we can haul them up!"

He pulled himself to his knees, shaking and struggling to stand as they fashioned a rough harness from ropes and leather straps. After tying one end to the black horse, and securing Saskia into a makeshift rock-climbing rig, they carefully lowered her along the rugged rock wall toward

Ritsuko and Hu. When Saskia's descent sent a small shower of loose shale and gravel rattling down the slope, Ritsuko opened her eyes and sat up. She squinted up and offered a weak wave.

Mikani made a hoarse sound and collapsed.

18

Hours later, Ritsuko stood in the room bespoken for her use. It was simple but clean with a single bed and a dresser for storing personal possessions. Since it was tucked beneath the eaves, it had only a single window, through which she stared out over the hamlet, where villagers went about their business. A woman shopped at the market while a boy herded a flock of sheep through town.

That's something you don't see in the city.

After she'd bathed, her cuts and bruises had been treated, and they'd eaten a simple but hearty meal. *We're safe.* The night on the mountain had been the longest of her life, and she couldn't forget how she'd felt when she fell the second time, dangling, powerless but for Irahi's strong arms. Failure threatened to choke her. *I couldn't save us.*

Never been trapped quite like that before. Hate feeling helpless.

She hoped Irahi's ribs didn't bother him too much. Though she was exhausted, tension left her unable to sleep. The others had insisted everyone needed to rest before pressing on, but she felt keyed up in addition to the bone-deep weariness. She paced quietly, feeling every bruise.

A tap on the door distracted her. It was a tentative sound, as if the person on the other side thought she might be sleeping. *That would be lovely, but no.* Ritsuko answered, mustering a blank, courteous expression.

Mikani stepped in and closed the door behind him, more disheveled than usual, dark circles under bloodshot eyes. "You look like half a mountain fell on you. And yet, you're not in bed." He stepped closer, his gaze darting from her face to her bandaged arms and back.

"Too much excitement. I haven't settled down yet."

"I could ask Hu to mix something up. It'd give him something to do other than complain about the food and the shoddy job the herbalist did patching him up." He reached up to brush a strand of hair from her forehead.

"I don't think that would help," she said softly.

"I could..." He trailed off and let out a long breath. Then he shook his head, pulling her close. "Damn it, Celeste. I thought that you were... just, damn it, woman, I thought I'd lost you."

"Me too," she whispered. "It's not every day that I fall off a mountain."

Twice.

She leaned her head on his chest and wrapped her arms about his waist. His heartbeat was a comforting rhythm beneath her ear. *That was the only thing that kept me going. Knowing you'd find me.* She hadn't dared speak her hope aloud, but she'd known if it came down to it, Mikani would use his ability to search, as he'd done for the murderer in the tunnels even though it hurt him. She was rather amazed to find him still upright after that much exertion. Usually, he'd have taken something and passed out by now.

"And you bloody well better not make a habit out of it." Mikani guided her to the bed, nudged her into sitting as he came to his knees in front of her. He took her hands, as if afraid to let her go just yet. "I'm sorry we didn't come back right away. I thought we could lead the elementals off and bring back help, but the villagers wouldn't budge until morning."

The tone rang, soft, but enough to alert her. "That's not entirely true, is it? You thought we might be dead."

He dropped his gaze. "We saw the boulder crash down on you. And we heard you fall... so yes, the thought did occur to me."

She pulled her hands back, folding them neatly in her lap. "I suppose you did as you felt was best."

Though it might be illogical, but hearing the truth hurt. *He left. Not knowing if I was alive or dead. He just* left. She didn't know if she'd be able to make the same decision, regardless of its prudence. It was impossible *not* to wonder if he'd have abandoned Miss Braelan.

She pushed to her feet and moved to the door. "It'd be wise if I got some rest, Mikani."

"I'm sorry." He stood, stepped out, and pulled the door behind him, closing it hard enough to jar the frame.

Right. Like you *have any reason to be angry.*

Ritsuko took her own advice and lay down, though it was a long time before she slept. For the evening meal, she took a bowl of soup in her room because she didn't feel like talking. And just before she was about to go back to bed for the night, she had another caller.

This time, it was Irahi, wound in bandages. "May I come in?"

"Certainly." She stepped back to allow him access.

Her room wasn't set up for socializing, but the doctor didn't seem to mind. His expression became professional as he skimmed her from head to toe. "You don't seem too much the worse for the wear after our adventure."

That word surprised a laugh out of her. "I'll live."

"You were missed at dinner."

That was sweet, but the idea of being sociable had seemed intolerable. "I didn't mean to worry anyone. I'll be up to speed tomorrow."

"I just wanted to be sure you weren't injured worse than you let on. It seemed like you were half carrying me, toward the end."

"For all the good it did us," she muttered.

"Are you sure you're all right? You seem… off." Irahi's dark eyes were altogether too perceptive, fixed on her face in a way she found disconcerting.

For a few seconds, Ritsuko considered confiding in him, but it wasn't her way, especially when she hadn't known him long, despite the eventful nature of their acquaintance. So she lifted a shoulder in a quiet shrug.

"I learned a few things this week. And some, I wish I hadn't."

"May I?" There was no chair, so he asked her permission to take a seat on the bed. Which she gave in a nod. After Irahi made himself comfortable on the bed, he said shrewdly, "I wonder if this has anything to do with why your partner's in such a temper and drinking downstairs?"

"Probably," she answered.

"Life rarely develops as we expect. People surprise us, sometimes in unpleasant ways. They don't always react as we hope they will or want them to."

"You sound extremely knowledgeable about this phenomenon," Ritsuko said, sitting down beside him. "Are you thinking of someone in particular?"

"As a matter of fact, I am." His face became wistful, devoid of his usual good humor and flirtatious bonhomie. She suspected it was the most candid glimpse she'd had of the real man.

"Someone you've known a long time?" she guessed, sure he wasn't referring to her.

Ritsuko had certainly noticed how protective he was of Miss Braelan. Theirs was a long friendship, but for the first time, she guessed he might wish things were different. She was a lovely woman, clever and adventurous, so it was natural that men fell in love with her. Half of the sailors on the *Gull* were probably nurturing secret, unrequited affections.

"Unfortunately, yes. But my place in her esteem has been cemented in a fashion I wouldn't have chosen."

Ritsuko sighed. "While you get to watch her make bad choices while offering unconditional support? That seems familiar."

"I hope I haven't led you to unreasonable expectations? I believed we were merely—"

"No, it's fine. I'm relieved, in fact. I was afraid you'd end up proposing, and that would be awkward." She grinned to show she was teasing.

"It might be better for both of us if I did. But I can relieve your mind on that count. But there's much to admire about you, Celeste. I'm glad you were with me, down on the ledge."

"Likewise," she said.

"I'll leave you, then, if you're not in need of medical attention."

"No, the salves and bandages are doing their job. There's not a lot that can be done for bruises or scrapes anyway."

"Unfortunately, time is the only cure for broken ribs as well. Good night." Irahi opened the door, then paused.

Despite his injury, he bent down and kissed her cheek, a brotherly salute. "Try not to be sad. You'll meet someone who's heart-whole and has the wit to appreciate you."

"I'd hug you, but that might hurt more than you'd enjoy it."

"Not if you're gentle with me," Irahi said, reverting to the flirtatious manner that she knew was just a facade.

So she had her arms looped around the doctor's waist when Mikani went past to his own room. He didn't pause or greet them, merely shut the door behind him with exaggerated care. Ritsuko stayed there for a few seconds, then bade Irahi good night.

There was still a long journey ahead.

* * *

Mikani watched as Saskia haggled for a pony and supplies. The innkeeper seemed to be even more stubborn than earlier, and he paced impatiently while they negotiated.

He checked the straps on his saddle a third time, then muttered a quiet oath and headed for the far end of the village square in search of some quiet. Since he'd searched for Ritsuko and Hu the day before, he'd been dogged by a low, indistinct murmur just at the edge of his hearing that made it hard to concentrate.

And the drinking didn't help the accompanying headache, either. Fancy that, must be getting old.

He looked over to where Hu was helping Ritsuko check her packs and saddle, and the headache spiked.

That could have gone better. But there's no good way to explain that finding her dead would have broken me. At least, not without digging into a lot of things we've left unsaid. And what if she doesn't feel the same? Thinking about his partner that way didn't feel wrong anymore, just impossible to navigate, like a briar patch with only one true path, and he wasn't known for perfect romances.

He turned away before he got another unwanted glimpse at how hurt Ritsuko was: he needed to find a way to bring his damned ability under control, or he'd be raving mad by week's end. Mikani strode back toward the inn, fully intending to threaten to leave Saskia behind to haggle to her heart's content if she wanted. She emerged then, shaking her head but carrying a bag full of supplies. She stopped dead when she saw him, the thoughtful expression turning wary at his expression.

He ignored the sharp tang of worry rolling off her and headed for his horse. "Let's ride. Hu can take point to set a pace that doesn't rattle his ribs too badly."

"Just try and keep up, Mikani. I won't take it easy on you while you nurse that hangover." The doctor grinned down at him from atop his horse, but Mikani could hear the relief buried in the other man's voice.

"Wouldn't have it any other way, Hu. Get your beast moving, we're losing daylight."

Hu rode by, followed closely by Ritsuko. She did not turn to him, and he didn't look up from the neck of his horse as she rode by.

Saskia stopped, managing to somehow look almost graceful on the short, dappled pony that she'd just purchased. She looked at Ritsuko, then up to him. "Janus—"

"Better get going. That thing's not exactly built for speed." He flicked his reins, and she had little choice but to follow.

He slowed his horse to a walk to let her ride past. Her pony clattered by, and she glared up at him in passing. "Idiot."

I'm well aware.

Over the next two hours, he found that he could drown out the constant hum and drone of his gift if he concentrated.

The problem is, there's bloody little to focus on out here in the middle of nowhere.

Mikani was riding well behind Ritsuko, Saskia, and Hu. He could see them chatting and looking around, and Hu's deep laughter occasionally reached him. But if he looked their way for too long, he picked up snatches of emotion wafting back on the wind like half-remembered scents and half-forgotten feelings.

He chose to look around instead, trying to listen to the steady rhythm of his horse's hooves on hard-packed dirt and to wrap himself in the animal's vague sense of boredom.

The road along the narrow valley wound its way ever higher along Mount Surtir's slopes. The mountain filled most of the western horizon now, plumes of steam and smoke rising from a dozen fumaroles and vents on the rugged flank of the volcano. Even from that distance, Mikani thought he could smell a hint of sulfur and ash. Small groves of twisted trees and hardy wildflowers that he could not name broke the monotony of the coarse grass blanketing the gently rising ground. An occasional rustle and furtive movement in the distance spoke of animals eking out a living from the desolate landscape.

It's better than a bloody mountain path in the rain, though. I'll take boring for the day, but any longer, and I might start missing the angry rock things.

That thought made him glance at his companions up ahead. His horse had cut the distance to them by a dozen yards or more while he'd been distracted; the sharp jab of sad anger he caught there made him curse and rein back.

That's going to get incredibly... inconvenient. Hells.

* * *

The villagers had given them directions to a shorter road to the elemental foundries and mines. It had fallen into disuse when the railroad had been finished; they swore that it would cut their travel time to half on horseback, though.

With that in mind, Hu called for a break in their ride a couple of hours past noon. Mikani was ready to argue until he glimpsed the other man's pained expression. "Fine. We could all do with a stretch, anyway."

Mikani dismounted and started a fire, while Ritsuko and Saskia helped Hu down, ignoring his chagrined protests. Lunch was quick, then they got back on the horses. He hoped like hell that answers lay at the end of the trip.

* * *

Just past sunset, Mikani spotted the village where they would spend the night. Before the end of the day tomorrow, they should reach the mines. His mount seemed as relieved as he that there would be a break. Though he hadn't pushed the animal, he was tired of riding.

This was even smaller than Skalbrekka, hardly more than a handful of buildings and a public house, which had clearly seen better days. Most of the roofs needed replacing, and the people were thinner than they had been in the other village.

Times must be tough.

But the stable lad snatched at the coins, and the tavernkeeper seemed pleased, if surprised to see them. He called for bowls of stew and his words of welcome tumbled over the top of each other as he recommended his home-brewed ale and his wife's bread. Soon, Mikani could tell that the inn was family-run. The stable boy appeared to be a son or possibly a nephew, while the father poured drinks, his wife cooked, and his daughters cleaned and served the food.

There were only three other patrons in the common room, surly-looking locals he guessed. So it was a quiet meal, as none of their party seemed in the mood to chat, either. Even Saskia had picked up on the mood, or maybe she was just tired. Either way, they ate in silence.

Ritsuko was the first to retire, followed by Saskia.

Mikani kept his eyes on his cup and his senses deliberately dulled with a steady supply of ale and some home-grown liquor that the tavernkeeper swore would not make him go blind. It burned his throat, roiled uneasily in his stomach, and kept him in just enough discomfort that he did not realize Hu was still sitting next to him until the other man spoke.

"What happened back there, Mikani?" Hu's voice was steady enough, but Mikani could not help but read the layered accusation in his tone.

"Guess the rock golems thought you were one of them, and they wanted to play?"

Mikani had just enough time to kick back from the table before Hu had him by the lapels and against the wall. The tavernkeeper and his daughters scrambled out of the main room to peer around the doorframe.

Smart. I'd be glad to be in another room, too, right about now.

"What happened back there?" Hu was breathing raggedly; even through the quickly dissipating haze of alcohol, Mikani flinched at the pain and anger radiating from him.

"Damn it, Hu... It was stupid and—"

The doctor slammed him against the wall. *That'll hurt when I sober up.*

"Don't bloody lie to me, man! I've seen you do thoughtless things. I've seen you *try* to get killed. But I've never seen you run. Tell me, now, or I swear I'll—"

"I tried to get them away from you! I was luring them away... the path collapsed. Damn it, Hu, we couldn't get back to you." He hesitated, before the final admission. "I told myself I was being smart—that we'd get help—but the truth is, I was afraid I'd find her dead. All right? The thought of finding her broken in a pile of stones..." Mikani drew a sharp breath. Guilt and despair roared in his head, drowning out everything else. "I couldn't bear it."

I truly couldn't.

For a few seconds, he imagined life without Ritsuko, and he couldn't even picture himself working for the CID. There was just an ever-widening abyss, rising and falling like the sea.

Hu closed his eyes and let out a long breath. Then he sat heavily, letting Mikani slide down to a pile on the floor in front of him. "Bronze gods, Mikani. You've seen death before. Bloody hells, we've buried friends together, you and I."

"She's different, Hu."

"Then tell her that before it's too late, you sodding imbecile."

19

STONE COTTAGES DOTTED the mountainside as Ritsuko rode into Eldheim. Plumes of smoke rose up from the other side; it looked as if something might be burning. People seemed alarmed here, too, not pausing to greet the newcomers. *Just once, it would be nice to receive a proper welcome instead of more bad news.* But it had been that sort of trip.

The mining town showed its age in the rugged stonework, worn away by years of exposure to wind and rain. This was the largest settlement they'd encountered since leaving Northport with fully stocked stores, supplies that had probably been shipped in via train, before all the troubles began. Cobblestone streets led through the main shopping district and out the other side. Everyone was in a hurry to get to the mines above.

"We should find the Skarsgard and Magnus foremen. They'll give us access to their mines if they're still alive." Mikani looked worn, deep lines creasing the corner of his eyes. She was not sure he'd slept in the last couple of days.

"They'll be at the main shaft, up ahead." Hu pointed toward the far end of town, where a monolithic structure, seemingly carved from the mountain itself in black stone and granite, swarmed with activity. A half dozen train tracks emerged from as many tunnels at its base, though no engines were in sight.

They made their way closer, weaving through the shifting crowds.

"That's strange." Miss Braelan was looking around. "They don't seem to be fleeing... you'd think they were preparing for a siege."

She was right: people were carrying building supplies and weapons, boarding up windows and erecting makeshift barricades in doorways. They did not spare more than a moment's attention for the four of them as they rode past.

"I'd guess more elementals running amok," Ritsuko said with a sigh.

It's not a good sign when that seems like an ordinary problem. By their expressions, the others agreed with her assessment. But before they could enter the mines, they needed to find a place to stable their horses. Ritsuko stopped a couple of folks to ask for directions, and the third person she bothered gave her harried information. Mikani set off toward the other side of town, near the inn as was customary.

Miss Braelan did the haggling for the care and feeding of the animals, while Ritsuko examined the inn across the alley. Two young men were boarding up the windows from the inside while an older man reinforced the door with strips of metal. Each slam of his sledge made her jump a little, mostly because they all looked so grim. Nobody was feeling helpful or even remotely sociable in Eldheim. Though the trouble wasn't like what they'd seen in Northport, the mood seemed darker, as if these people had made up their minds that this was where they'd fight and die, defending their homes. At closer inspection, some buildings bore scorch marks or had divots of stone gouged from the walls.

Like something huge and powerful struck them.

"I think we're done here," Miss Braelan said.

The stern-faced innkeeper turned as she spoke. "You picked a dire time to come calling. If you're wise, you'll rest those horses and ride out again in the morn."

"Unfortunately, we can't," Ritsuko said.

A shrug greeted her reply, then he went back to work, leaving her to follow the rest of her party. Her legs felt soft and unsteady after two days of riding, sore in strange places. Hu paused long enough to offer his arm. She took it, grateful for the support, and glad they'd cleared the air. Now she could enjoy his company without fearing she might hurt him when it came time for partings. While she'd miss him as a friend, he didn't own her heart.

With Mikani beside her, Miss Braelan set a brisk pace toward the mining offices, the center of the various train lines. Hu and Ritsuko followed. She couldn't make out what the couple ahead was talking about, but it seemed to be important. Fortunately, over the past day, Ritsuko had managed to box up her bruised feelings, as they didn't lend themselves to a solid partnership. *So he left. It was doubtless the prudent thing to do. And it all ended well enough.*

Moving at such a clip, the group reached the administrative complex that comprised the bulk of the local industry in no time. The cavernous building was well lit with gas lamps mounted high on the columns supporting a vaulted ceiling. Skarsgard and Magnus bondsmen hurried along, pausing now and then to converse briefly before setting off, disappearing into the countless passages and stairwells dotting the walls.

"Excuse me." Ritsuko stepped in front of a young man trying to hurry past. "The mine foremen—"

"Inward, three flights up, second right." He sidestepped past her and rushed off.

The four of them exchanged brief looks before doing their best to follow the vague directions. After a couple of wrong turns, they came to a set of thick, wooden double doors.

They were pitted and scarred, the smell of a recent fire still lingering about them. Two weary-looking guards watched their approach.

"What do you want?" The shorter, broader guard was evidently in no mood for niceties.

"It's apparent that you're having difficulties. We've been sent by the Council to investigate the problems here, as the issues have become rather widespread." Ritsuko produced their packet of credentials along with her best smile.

The guard examined all of the documents before swinging the doors open. "I hope you can do something, though bronze gods curse me if I know what."

He doesn't sound hopeful, though.

She nodded and murmured her thanks. The others followed when she stepped past the sentries into a large room dominated by the long table in the center. Papers were strewn over it, along with maps and other tokens. A small cluster of men and women were gathered around, arguing in low tones. Ritsuko noticed that the walls were thick, and without windows, the space seemed like a bunker, even though it wasn't underground.

"You must have important backers," an older gentleman said. "Or you wouldn't have gotten past Gates."

Ritsuko started, "Would you like to see our—"

"Not in the least. I haven't the time to waste. Just tell me what you're about."

"We're here to find out what you people mucked up. Sir." Mikani had stepped past Miss Braelan. He leaned heavily on the table with both hands, sending a couple of mine clerks scrambling aside.

"Listen—"

"And then, we'll deal with it, before the bloody mess drags everyone down with it. To do that, we need access to the mines."

The older man was trembling with rage or indignation. Mikani seemed to have that effect on people. But it was the man to his right that answered her partner.

"We've been trying to figure out what happened for the past three weeks. Under most difficult circumstances." Several of those at the table started talking at once.

"Hells, man." A thin, pale man dressed in Magnus livery raised his voice. "We've been fighting off crazed gnomes and salamanders for a week straight. If you have any answers, I'd love to hear them."

"Let us in. We'll find your answers." Ritsuko made eye contact with each of the men in turn. "We represent your best chance to resolve this."

The whole table devolved into a tumult as the managers discussed their request; some were vehemently opposed, fearing further retaliation by angry elementals. Others figured that they had precious little to lose, and if someone was going to get killed investigating, better it not be any of their own employees.

As Mikani paced, Miss Braelan watched the argument. Irahi stepped up behind Ritsuko to lay a hand on her shoulder. She turned with a smile that felt tired and forced. *If I had more energy, I'd interrupt, but it's been a devil of a few days.* Besides, she couldn't think of anything to add. It wasn't like her truth-sense, Mikani's ability, or the other woman's affinity with sylphs would help a lot deep in the bowels of the earth.

Ritsuko leaned wearily against the doctor's side. The man was built like a towering oak, and since this was his uninjured side, she had no compunction about taking advantage of his strength. Irahi slid an arm around her shoulders; she suppressed a wistful sigh, wishing Mikani was this free with affectionate gestures.

"What do you think we'll find down there?" she whispered.

"No idea. But if the town's preparing for a siege."

She nodded. The talk went on for several more minutes before the mine managers came to consensus. Eventually, the older man addressed Mikani. "We'll let you in, but I can't guarantee you're all coming out again."

Though the foreman doubtless intended his words to be ominous, she couldn't restrain a shiver. *Let's hope that's a gloomy disposition talking, not a prophecy.*

* * *

A half dozen guards escorted them down and deeper into the bowels of the building.

Mikani barely noticed the workshops and refineries they passed, many of their doors torn open or molten into cooling slag piles. As they descended, the crowds thinned. By the time they reached the massive doors barring the way to the main mine shaft, he hadn't seen another soul in five minutes or more.

The guards hurried to open the gates and ushered them through. As the doors closed behind the four of them with an echoing boom, he could see the deep scars in the hardened wood. At least a dozen charred remains were scattered in the chamber they'd entered.

The guards were not meant to keep us in line. They had to make sure nothing came out when we went in.

Hu lifted his lantern higher to illuminate the way ahead. The main passage was at least fifteen feet high and wide, sloping down into darkness. Shattered lamps hung from charred ceiling supports, and in several places, the stone of the walls had been burned into dark glass.

"Janus? What exactly are we going to do?" Saskia gazed around the tunnel, wide-eyed.

She hates tight spaces. This must be terrifying her.

"I'm still working on the details. Hopefully, Hu and I can beat or break whatever it is that's causing this."

"And in the scenario where you two can't use violence to resolve things?" Saskia asked.

"Then Ritsuko and you will need to save the day." He

flashed a brief grin at his three companions before leading the way into darkness.

They entered the main chamber where minecart tracks from a dozen different tunnels converged. He could see signs of struggle everywhere; broken tools and overturned crates littered the floor. At least one of the passages had collapsed.

"We must be on the right track." Hu was examining a pile of greasy ash on the floor. "Many people died badly here."

Mikani nodded and pressed on. Pain and despair rolled off the walls, from the air itself. The dark impressions churned the bile in his stomach, so that it surged into his throat. With some effort, he swallowed it down, moving toward vibrations he sensed deeper within.

"This reminds me, rather unfortunately, of the last big case we resolved," Ritsuko said softly.

"We spend far too much time in dark, deep holes chasing monsters."

She made a quiet sound of agreement. Her footsteps reassured him, light and quiet but unmistakable. It was eerily still, no picks or machinery to disturb the stillness. *Mines should be full of activity, rock being chipped, ore dropping into cars to be carried to the surface.* It was some relief that he wasn't picking up anything from Ritsuko anymore. Mikani didn't know if she'd gotten over her hurt or whether she'd learned to block him.

From behind, Saskia slipped her hand into his. Mikani squeezed her fingers in silent reassurance, trying not to let the hidden menace get to him. *Hard not to worry when things can just step right out of the walls.* To his right, the stone trembled a little, not hard enough for him to think it was an actual tremor. *Something worse, probably.*

"Company?" Hu asked.

"Likely," Ritsuko answered.

"Let's not find out." Mikani jogged back along the tunnel, taking the first side passage as the vibrations grew closer behind them. Rushing along in the jumping light of the swinging lantern, he stumbled into a wider chamber and nearly tripped. Saskia pulled him back as Hu and Ritsuko rushed in behind them; they hugged the walls and held as still as they could. The tremors rose in intensity to a small quake, raining rocks and dust, then faded.

He waited in silence for another five minutes, listening intently. Far in the distance, something very angry and old was heading away from them.

"We were lucky that time." Hu was breathing heavily and cradling his ribs. "If we go deeper, we're going to run headlong into one of those things, Mikani."

"I don't think blind exploration is the wise move," Ritsuko added.

Saskia twisted her hands together, a sure sign she was distraught. For a wind witch, there was little more dreadful than being entombed. "We're not ready for this, Janus. We don't even know what we're looking for. We need to find out more... you're the inspectors, how do we proceed with this investigation?"

While he considered, another rumble sounded in the distance. *Hells and Winter. We'll get killed if we race along without planning our strategy. We need a hint, a witness—*

"You're right." He could sense them, deeper in the mountain. "We need to find out what's going on. We should ask."

"The foremen didn't seem to know—"

"No, not them. We go straight to the source. We'll ask the elementals."

Ritsuko, Hu, and Saskia looked at him. He didn't need his gift to tell him they suspected he'd gone mad.

"How in the isles are we going to do that? I'm a weather witch, Mikani... I can influence the wind and some water spirits, not earth and fire elementals!"

"They don't seem all too eager to chat, Mikani." Hu shook his head.

Ritsuko was silent a moment. Then she asked, "What did you have in mind?"

I can always count on you, partner.

"There must be a way to fence one in. Then maybe we can force some answers out of it, get an idea of what's going on. Anything is better than what we have at this point."

Hu and Ritsuko turned to look at Saskia. She chewed her bottom lip and played with her braid as she considered the problem.

"I suppose I could try a simple lure and binding. That might draw in a lesser spirit. If—" She shook her head. "If we can draw in a fire spirit, I might be able to coerce it. Maybe. They're little different from animals, so I'm not sure we'll get anything useful out of one."

"We'll take 'maybe' over nothing," Mikani said. "Let's get to work."

Saskia addressed the other two. "You may find this... disagreeable, but I need everyone's help, or I won't have enough energy for the spell."

"Whatever you need," Hu said at once.

Ritsuko looked less eager, more wary, but she nodded, too. Saskia opened her pack and set out various accoutrements. In the wavering light, it was impossible for Mikani to tell exactly what she was mixing in a glass vial, but she shook it vigorously to blend the components. Then she sprinkled the powder in a rough circle.

"No matter what happens, don't break this line," she warned. Everyone murmured their agreement while waiting for further instructions. Saskia went on, "I need you to the north, Irahi. Mikani, to the west. Ritsuko to the east, and I'll be south."

Since Mikani didn't ordinarily participate in such rituals, he had no idea why he was moving to the west of the circle, but he did so. Saskia drew a small but wickedly sharp knife, concealed somewhere on her person, then she pulled it across her palm in a decisive motion. Hu bit out a curse and started toward her. At the last moment, he seemed to remember he wasn't supposed to cross the dust on the ground, and he stepped back, grumbling. She turned her hand over, squeezing her fingers together so the blood spattered on the herbs and whatever else she'd blended for the spell, mingled scents of copper, minerals, and lavender.

"Now the rest of you," Saskia said.

Miskani didn't watch while Hu and Ritsuko sliced their palms. Saskia whispered from her position to the south, a low chant that raised the hair on the back of his neck. By the time Mikani was done with his own self-inflicted wound, something uncanny was happening. Their blood was no longer just random droplets rained down across the powder; instead, it was flowing with a purpose, joined in a flow that stained the powder red.

And if I'm not imagining things, there's a faint glow, too.

The circle flashed brightly, forcing Mikani to shield his eyes. Someone—Saskia or Ritsuko, let out a pained cry. When he focused again, a flickering form swirled inside the circle, sparking against an invisible barrier. It glowed red and purple, but Mikani couldn't clearly make out its form beyond a sense of supple grace and boundless energy. The all-too-familiar anger rolled off the elemental, but it was mingled with a hollow ache.

It's sad. No; it's grieving. How can that be? That's like a steam engine having a bad day; like a fish mourning his fellows caught in a net.

The gyrating salamander stopped, now fully coalesced inside the circle. It glared at them with amber eyes and raked a three-toed claw against the summoning wards. The creature radiated heat, and it had translucent skin with fire trapped inside. Mikani had never seen anything like it.

Why? The voice crackled in Mikani's head.

"Bronze gods..." Saskia stared at the creature, wide-eyed. "It can speak?"

20

RITSUKO KNEW SO little about elementals that she didn't understand at first why everyone seemed so shocked. The creature bound in the circle writhed in rage, fire blazing in its inhuman eyes. Each time, it twisted and snapped back to the center. *Wonder if it's taxing to keep the thing trapped or if the blood we fed the wards do the heavy lifting.* It wasn't the time to improve her grasp on magical theory, however.

"You're a fool," the salamander spat at Miss Braelan. "How long do you think you can keep me confined like this? Even now I can feel your amateurish measures fading."

Does that mean the spell's of limited duration?

"Then we'll talk fast," Mikani said.

"Tell us why things have changed," Miss Braelan demanded—but she sounded shaken.

Ritsuko thought the direct approach was best, especially if they didn't know how long this thing would remain trapped. Once it got free, she had no doubt it would boil all of their blood in their veins. Its flickering gaze swept over the group, then returned to Miss Braelan, who had captured it.

"You dare to ask me this? After what your kind has done?

Your stupidity is remarkable."

The rock beneath the salamander glowed, and she thought it looked as if the stone might be softening. *How hot must it be?* It was hard not to be terrified of a creature that could melt the flesh from your bones, but she also felt a pang of sympathy. She hadn't the slightest notion that any of the elementals used by the great Houses had even a hint of free will. It was horrifying to contemplate the fact that House practitioners had been enslaving sentient beings.

"Pretend we don't know better. Well, not so much a pretense in my case." Mikani shifted closer, but Miss Braelan shook her head violently as the elemental turned its attention on him. "As far as any of us knew, you... your kind, were remnants from another age. Husks. No more mind than—"

The salamander hissed and flared, slamming into the barrier hard enough to nearly knock Mikani back with a wave of heated air.

"We were chained, ensorcelled into a half-life! Your sorcerers stripped us of the will to resist until we had to withdraw to retain some shred of sanity."

"Bronze gods." Miss Braelan held a hand up to her mouth with a horrified expression. "We didn't know. Truly, we did not."

"Ignorance is no excuse, *human*." It swirled and circled, as if testing the circle. Sparks rained down to the glowing stone floor; the air was becoming uncomfortably warm and dry as the creature raged. "For two centuries, you have enslaved us. Two hundred long years of pain and impotence. But that ends now!"

"The gap in the barriers woke you up, and now you're breaking free." Mikani rubbed at his temples, a thin trickle of blood running down his upper lip.

"That's only the start. We'll snap our chains, tear down the cages you've built around us. And we'll come for you, all of you."

A jolt of unpleasant realization went through her. *It's talking about a revolution. Between what we saw from the craggers and this, Dorstaad could be a smoldering ruin sooner than I care to envision.*

She fought down her dread and managed a calm tone. "Who's we?"

"My brethren will roast you in your homes, and wind will tear them down around you. You will have noticed the vicious storms, yes?"

"Water and earth aren't involved?" Irahi asked quietly.

The doctor had been so still that she'd almost forgotten about him.

So, apparently, had the salamander. It jerked its serpentine head toward him and shimmered with wrath. "Water is weak and mutable. Earth is slow and stupid. We don't require their aid to stamp your kind out like a pestilence."

Before she could decide what to ask next, the elemental slammed a burst of flame against the barrier holding it in place. And this time, a shiver of energy made Ritsuko think the blood in the wards wouldn't hold much longer. The air even felt hotter. She backed away, eyes fixed on the furious spirit. *Such an odd thing, a marriage of flesh and fire.*

"Whatever else you mean to ask, I recommend you do it quickly." Mikani looked at Miss Braelan, who was delving into her pack.

"Can you freshen the bonds?" Irahi asked.

The other woman shook her head. "Not in time to keep it from cooking us."

All of Ritsuko's instincts said they should be running, but the fire elemental would catch them, she suspected. It probably knew the mines much better, and it didn't have human limitations on speed. Her heart thundered in her chest. As she opened her mouth to suggest a retreat, as she couldn't think of a better plan, she heard the thunk of boots coming their way.

Just when I thought things couldn't get worse.

Irahi muttered and pulled his heavy blunderbuss from its holster. Mikani checked his rifle and stepped between them and the tunnel, where the footsteps were getting louder. Miss Braelan pulled a silver dagger from her pack, looking less certain than the men. "Janus? Elementals don't wear boots, last I checked."

"Hello! Up ahead! We're coming for you, don't move!" The voice was gravelly and deep, echoing in the chamber. Three men came around the corner and pulled short at the sight of Mikani and the doctor. With a cry of surprise, two of them raised pickaxes. The third held up a glass flask sloshing with a treacly liquid, then paused. "Who in Muspel's halls are you people? And why the bloody hell do you have one of *those* with you?"

"You first." Mikani pointed his rifle at the man with the sphere.

"Shoot me and I drop this. I drop this, we all go with a flash, mate."

"Janus, Irahi. Stop pointing guns at the nice men with explosives. We have more urgent concerns at the moment, remember?" Miss Braelan stepped in front of Mikani and Irahi.

"At least someone in your party has a brain." The leader gestured toward Miss Braelan. "Go on, banish it."

"If I could, I would. I suggest we go," she replied.

"I take back what I said."

The last time Ritsuko had seen such a combination of outrage and disapproval, she had been listening to Commander Gunwood lecture Mikani. With a clenched fist, the newcomer barked orders at his men. Quickly, the others shoved Mikani, Ritsuko, Irahi, and Miss Braelan away from the circle, and they performed some kind of ritual. They were working too fast, with silent desperation, for her to be sure how it compared to the prior summoning. For a couple of minutes, they chanted in low monotone, while the wards grew thinner and thinner. Lashes of flame flicked out through the dissipating barrier, and Ritsuko dove away. The fire spirit swelled with rage, but before the creature could cover them in flames, the spell ended with a whoosh of bright light. When her eyes adapted again, the floor was scorched, and the salamander was gone.

Then the leader turned on Miss Braelan with a ferocious scowl. "What kind of imbecile summons a monster without knowing how to get rid of it?"

"The kind that runs into idiots in an elemental-infested mine armed only with pickaxes?" Mikani grinned at the other man.

"You think this is funny? We've been down here for damn near a week, and I'm pretty sure no aid is coming. *You* couldn't even help yourselves." The leader skimmed Mikani up and down. "Looks to me like you need a punch in the head."

Even without the confirmation of her truth-sense, Ritsuko could tell their rescuers had been living rough. On closer inspection, they were dirty and desperate-looking, thin and unshaven. If they'd truly been trapped for a week, it was unconscionable that the mine owners hadn't mounted a rescue. Suddenly, she understood the anger.

"You thought we'd come to save you," she said softly.

One of the miners spat onto the charred spot where the salamander had been. "Wishful thinking. You lot know even less than we do about surviving this place."

"We'll certainly do better pooling our talents and resources," Irahi put in.

"Why can't we leave the way we came in?" Miss Braelan asked.

"You're welcome to try, but I predict you'll end up burned to a crisp, while pounding on the doors begging to be let out." Some of the other miners muttered in anger. "We tried that when this started, and lost three men for our trouble. They shouted that they couldn't risk it and left us to burn."

"Those thrice-damned beasts have been herding us deeper into the mines ever since. Every time we try to head for the outer tunnels, they chase us down."

Truth. Ritsuko remembered what the foreman had said. *I don't guarantee you're coming out again. He meant it, but I didn't realize exactly* how. *Bronze gods.*

"They locked you in?" she asked, unable to believe what she was hearing.

The foreman nodded. "We didn't evacuate quick enough. Now the outer doors are sealed, and they won't be making exceptions for any of us. They can't risk the salamanders escaping along with us."

"But they let us in," Miss Braelan protested.

One of the men muttered, "No doubt they listened to be sure there was nothing on the other side. Try asking for help when the elementals are trying to kill you. See what happens."

While she parsed the fact that they were entombed, the doctor performed the introductions. The gentleman who had been speaking for his group sighed and seemed to decide that cooperation was better than adding new enemies to his list of problems. He was tall and gaunt with silver hair and a fresh burn scar on his throat. *Looks like a near miss.*

"I'm Evans. The boys are Kurtz and Jurgensen."

The miners lifted hands in greeting. Four more men came around the corner at a run, interrupting even these brief courtesies. "The elementals are on us, boss. We have to go." Mikani glanced into the tunnel where Evans's party had emerged. The dark tunnel walls reflected shifting firelight, faint but growing brighter by the second.

"Move!" Evans didn't give them time to argue; he grabbed Saskia's arm and shoved her ahead of him. Ritsuko and Hu did not hesitate in taking off.

Hells and Winter, I can feel it getting warmer. Better sightsee another time.

Mikani sped after the others, following the sounds of multiple footsteps running at full speed along the dark shaft. Mikani nearly ran past the small side tunnel where they'd turned off, until Hu called for him. He skittered to a halt and stumbled into the passage, slamming his head painfully against the lower ceiling.

"Watch your head!" Hu sounded far too amused.

"Watch yours when I catch you," Mikani muttered back, one hand on the tunnel wall and the other on the back of his head to try to ease the pounding of his skull.

He ran for what seemed like endless minutes, following the footsteps ahead and fleeing the growing heat behind him. The shadows of the mine shaft were growing lighter.

They're nearly on top of us. Damn'd be, maybe if I could take out a support on one of these walls I could buy us some time. Of course, if I end up burying myself in a tunnel collapse, I'd be less than pleased. Still, if it means she gets away—

He ran full tilt into Hu's back. The bigger man grunted, and Mikani fell back with a breathless oath.

"Why the hell did you stop?"

"We're waiting for our ride."

Mikani wiped the blood from his lip. He took Hu's offered hand and stood, stepping away from the tunnel mouth. Evans was standing on an old handcart, iron-pitted and smoke-stained. There were two minecarts, barely big enough to hold two people each, coupled to it.

"Get a move on, then!" Two of his men were on one side of the oversized lever. "You, Doctor. With me, I'll need your bulk to get this thing moving. The rest of you, all aboard, and keep them off us!"

"You heard the man, Hu. Put those arms to work for a change." Mikani stepped past, staggering at the smack Hu laid on the back of his head. He paused to help Saskia and

Ritsuko climb onto the front cart, before vaulting into the last cramped minecart. He shoved aside a covered box, trying to make room for his legs.

"What are we supposed to do, hurt their feelings?"

"Use the damned grenades! Go! Push, pull… push!" Evans shouted the last at the men on the handcart. They strained and grunted with effort as they pulled on the heavy levers, and they lurched and screeched into motion.

Ritsuko signaled him: she was holding a small sphere of crudely blown glass in each hand. "There are a couple of crates of these."

Mikani set his rifle aside and uncovered the box nearest to him. Instead of the glass orbs he expected, he found a two-foot-long, thick iron tube attached to some sort of pump. Someone had crudely written "Boom Tube" on the side. The rest of the crate held rough chunks of dark gray rock.

Well, hells. They have grenades. I get to throw rocks.

"They're coming!"

Mikani looked up and over the side of the rocking cart. They were a couple of hundred feet down the tracks already and picking up speed. But he could easily make out the two salamanders as they burst from the tunnel in a flare of golden red flame and a hiss of superheated air. The swirling elementals paused only a moment before giving chase with loping strides along the passage's walls and floor.

They left smoking, glowing marks wherever they came into contact with the rock.

They're fast.

He pulled the makeshift mortar from its crate, loaded a rock, and started desperately cranking the pump. A grenade sailed over his head and smashed into the tunnel wall with a sharp crack that splattered the viscous black fluid in a cloud of droplets. As soon as the first salamander ran into the dark mist, there was a deafening explosion. The shock wave that struck them a moment later nearly derailed his cart; he had to let go of the mortar to try to hold on.

Behind them, the mine wall crumbled, rocks crumbling down to block the path. Mikani didn't know if the explosion took out one of the salamanders or if it was blocked by the rubble, but there was only one giving chase right now. *Hells and Winter, they've been doing this for a week? No wonder Evans is cranky.*

The fire spirit crackled, flames lashing out from behind; to Mikani's eyes, it looked like the fire was giving it a push. *Just what we need as we're trying to head uphill.* He heard Hu grunting and swearing as he strained to haul such a heavy load. The chains linking the carts groaned, and the grind of the wheels over the track threw sparks while the elemental closed the gap. Saskia and Ritsuko hurled a couple of more grenades, but they were off target, and the dark mist hung dormant. *That might catch another one later, if it doesn't dissipate, but it will be too late to do us any good.*

Mikani braced the air cannon against the cart wall and yanked the release, firing with a muffled boom. The jolting motion of the cart when it jogged left skunked his aim. The air around him felt uncomfortably warm. Another sharp turn flung him down in the cart, and he cracked his head on the side. By the time he scrambled to his feet, ears ringing, the fire spirit was almost on top of them. Taloned fingers, each one aflame, slashed the air only inches away from the rear railing.

He'll have us next time. Wonder how strong this bastard is.

From the front car, he heard raised voices. Evans was shouting something, and it sounded like Ritsuko was screaming. *What the hells. Never heard her sound quite like that.* But he couldn't pause to check out the situation. Instead, he struggled with the movement of the cart as he reloaded. For a few seconds, he juggled the rock, then he slotted it in place as the monster dove for the cart. The thing would've latched on, except the earth dropped out from under them.

And everyone was falling.

Cool air rushed past his face. He knew only the sensation of speed and the hot whoosh of the salamander plummeting nearby. Mikani struck the dark water with an impact that stole the breath from his lungs; maybe that was what stopped him from swallowing a few gallons of it. The elemental let off a dim glow, but by the way the thing was thrashing, he guessed it no longer wanted anything except to get out of the water. He kicked to the surface, frantic to see where everyone else was, but it was dark, and there was too much movement. Mikani swam to the far wall, looking for other survivors, and found only more stone, damper rock.

He dove again and again until he could no longer hold his breath. The cavern was dark and quiet. The rasp of claws told him that the fire spirit was scrabbling its way out, leaving him alone. *Can't give up. They must be here somewhere.* He wouldn't consider any other possibility.

Sucking in a deep breath, he went under again, and this time, the current snagged him. The water swept him into a small tunnel, almost completely flooded. It bashed him against walls and ceiling until he felt like a bloody tenderized steak. Mikani snatched gulps of breath in those rare moments when he found an air pocket, only enough to keep him from passing out—not enough to fix the red burn of his lungs.

It could've been minutes or hours; he was barely clinging to consciousness when the current grew stronger still. Maybe his ears were ringing, but he swore he heard the roar of a waterfall, then he was tumbling over it with enough force to send him plunging down into the gray sea below. Pure luck kept him off the rocks. He was trembling when he surfaced. Shoving the wet mop of hair out of his eyes, he immediately took stock.

Survivors. Where are they?

Then someone reached out a hand to him. Hu pulled him

onto the rock. With relieved eyes, he found Ritsuko, Saskia, Evans, and Kurtz. He didn't see the rest of the miners. *Damn.* But he couldn't help the rush of relief when his gaze skimmed over Ritsuko's battered face. *She's gonna have two black eyes.* It was crazy how much he wanted to hug her.

"So," he said aloud. "How do we get back to Eldheim?"

21

SASKIA WATCHED JANUS, a knot forming deep in her throat as he hovered near Ritsuko while Irahi tended the worst of her scrapes and bruises.

Stop it. Let go of the past, you've plenty of trouble today to deal with.

With effort, she turned away, drawing a deep breath and trying to gather her dripping hair into a braid to keep it off her face. They were all filthy, cold, and tired. Kurtz was off exploring and Evans was trying unsuccessfully to build a fire out of driftwood and a few drops of the black oil that they'd used for grenades.

She huddled on a flat boulder no more than ten steps across and twice as wide. The whitecapped surf crashed on a narrow and rocky beach that stretched along the cliffs as far as the eye could see. As far as she could tell, they were twenty or thirty miles from the nearest fishing village. *I could send the sylphs with a message for Mr. Ferro on the* Gull. *But if the salamander spoke the truth?* Saskia listened for her familiars. They were there, flitting on the bitter winds. Saskia couldn't think of a time when they hadn't been in her life. She hesitated to call them with an outstretched hand and a whispered word.

For going on two centuries, House thaumaturges had bound elemental spirits into physical objects: silver mirrors allowed communication, amber spheres powered steam engines in ships and carriages. Hulking stone golems with the strength of twenty men built roads and bridges. As far as Saskia could recall, elementals had always been just another facet of life, like cattle or horses: intangible, but mere beasts nonetheless. Even her relationship with the air spirits that served her was akin to that of a master with faithful hounds.

Weather witches have never abused their familiars, on pain of losing their service... but do they serve willingly? Can I trust them?

"Over here! Found something!" Kurtz returned and was calling to them from a dozen yards off to her left. She was grateful for the interruption and hurried back toward the others.

"It's an old smuggling rig, I think. Runs up the side as far up as I can see."

"Bloody thieves, making off with an honest man's work." Evans spat into the waves.

Janus looked from one man to the other. "So what in the hells' name is a smuggling rig?"

Kurtz started to explain, but Irahi interrupted. "Could you walk and talk? Not to be rude, but the tide's rising."

The strip of beach had grown narrower.

"We should seek higher ground." After Inspector Ritsuko spoke, she set off the way the miner had come.

The rest of the survivors needed no encouragement to follow suit. Saskia slogged through the rising water, trying to keep her footing as the cold water rose over her ankles. When they arrived at the smuggler's rig, she knew a moment of pure dread.

"You're kidding." Janus glared at Evans and Kurtz.

"It *does* seem precarious." Inspector Ritsuko tugged at a

length of chain, then wiped the grime off on her thigh.

Someone had affixed two steel rails along the side of the cliff. A wooden crate the size of a small cart was secured to the rails with makeshift clamps. Four chains as thick as Saskia's finger attached the crate to a thicker length of chain that rose between the rails until they all disappeared into the darkness a couple of hundred feet above them. The other end of the chain came back down a few feet to the right, where it disappeared into a complex assembly of gears and cogs mounted on the platform itself.

"It's a few hours on this thing, hoping we don't fall, or a week in water up to our necks, praying we don't drown." Irahi stepped onto the makeshift lift. He grabbed the chains and jumped a few times; the wood creaked alarmingly but did not break. "Get on. Kurtz and I will hoist us up. Keep a sharp eye out, see if any of the others are still alive along the beach."

Despite pervasive cold and hunger, Saskia was impressed at the way Irahi was taking charge. She hadn't seen this side of him in a very long time. *Then again, we've both gotten soft in the years since we sailed the northern seas.* Evans gave her a hand up, towing her onto the platform. Since the rig had been designed to transport crates of contraband, there was space enough for the six of them. *We lost so many in the dark river.* Unlike the doctor, she didn't hold out hope that they'd find the other miners alive. *If they didn't drown, something's eaten them by now.* As a child, her father had told her stories of the fabled krakens that lived in the deep off the coast of the Winter Isle, tentacles enormous enough to crush entire ships. Though she dismissed them as fish stories, she couldn't repress a shiver as she gazed down at the whitecaps below, dashing with what seemed like thwarted fury against the rocks.

The mechanical parts were old and rusted; it looked as if the smugglers who'd built this contraption had abandoned it years ago. With each jolt upward, Saskia whispered a nearly forgotten prayer. Her stomach felt as if it were filled with eels and oil, until she was barely holding on to the bile it contained.

This is nothing like the deck of a ship.

"How far are we from Eldheim?" Janus asked from behind her.

She turned, grateful to have a reason to avoid the view that didn't stem from her own unease. "Hard to say. Overland, no more than five miles. I don't think any of us would've survived if we'd been in the water for too long."

"It was a hell of a ride," he agreed. "I'm of a mind to have... words with the manager who sent us in, knowing he didn't mean to let us out again."

"Don't be an idiot. Those huge, heavy doors are all that's keeping the salamanders out of Eldheim. If it weren't warded, they'd have already melted through it."

"Magical bindings wear out," Janus said. "I wonder if they have anyone to fortify them."

"Doubtful. Right now, there's a war brewing on two fronts. Between the craggers getting ready for war and the elementals gone insane—"

"Relax. I won't beat up mine management." He managed a smile through swollen lips.

"Good to see you've learned some restraint."

At last. Wonder if she had anything to do with it. Her gaze cut to Inspector Ritsuko, who was standing close to Irahi. He was hauling mightily on the chains, levering them upward. He'd discarded his jacket to reveal a stained white shirt. It was ripped in places, showing glimpses of brown skin, and the taut pull of his muscles was obvious through the thin, damp fabric. When Saskia looked away, she felt... strange, as if she'd never seen him before.

"It only took a lifetime and several beatings." But Janus was watching his partner, too, and the intensity of his expression didn't match the lightness of his tone.

She didn't want to think about... any of this. "Feels like we've bitten off more than we can chew this time."

"Just a bit. But Gunwood is always telling me I have a big mouth."

That surprised a laugh out of her. "Somehow I doubt that's what he meant."

Bantering with Janus took her mind off the terrifying ascent, however, so she was startled when the platform stopped at last. Irahi and Kurtz affixed the chains to the rings driven into the rock, presumably for that purpose. There was a good-sized ledge here, along with crude steps hewn into the mountain itself. Irahi helped everyone past before beginning the climb. Saskia looked at Irahi with no small measure of concern.

He's tired as any of us, injured, and still he pulls us up to safety.

While he was a strong man, he couldn't continue like this indefinitely.

By the time everyone reached the top of the cliff, the sun was sinking beyond the horizon. There were no signs of life anywhere on the rocky beach below, and Evans paced with low mutters of what he'd do to the money-grubbing bastards who'd cost his men their lives. Nobody tried to check his anger. She suspected they all understood how it felt to lose friends through factors beyond their control.

At last, Evans settled enough to get his bearings. He jerked his head. "This way. If we push, we'll reach Eldheim before the storm catches us."

Saskia whirled. And sure enough, dark clouds were gathering off the coast, localized enough that she suspected it wasn't a natural thunderhead. That pause was enough to put her behind the others, however. She set off after them with quick steps. The path was rough, and nobody was in the mood to chat.

* * *

A couple of hours later, Janus stopped suddenly and signaled for everyone to get down. Now that she was paying attention, Saskia heard thunder in the distance. "The storm's nearly on us. We don't have time—"

Janus looked over his shoulder and shushed her with a look. She shot him a glare, crawling to the top of the hill. The noise boomed again; she realized then that the sound was coming from the wrong direction. Saskia peered toward Eldheim.

Several buildings along the edge of town had been demolished entirely. Clouds of dust rose from the rubble in a swirling haze. A massive boulder flew through the air in a wide arc, reminding her far too much of the creatures that had attacked them on the mountain path. It slammed into the street, rolling for a dozen yards before crashing into a wall—shattering it with a hard, cracking sound she'd mistaken for thunder.

This can't be what they were preparing for… the salamander said that the earth elementals were not part of their uprising.

Four towering, shadowy figures advanced on the town from the valley below. One stopped and ripped a tree from the ground. The creature threw the improvised missile in an overhead throw, sending it crashing down on a barricade, scattering its defenders.

"Where did those damned golems come from?" Evans rose to his knees for a better look. "It's… craggers!" He scrambled to his feet, stumbling over Janus's outstretched hand. "Those bastards brought fettered golems!"

Saskia rose carefully. Judging from the number of torches weaving through the darkness, more than a hundred craggers were marching on Eldheim in a disorganized mob. A few fired into the air as they approached town; every now and then, they shouted something unintelligible. The defenders loosed scattered volleys from behind the barricades, but she could tell this wouldn't last long.

Too many of them are aiming at the golems. They might as well be hurling insults.

"Hells and Winter. We can't just watch." Janus stood, dusting off his knees.

She wanted to argue with him because they were armed only with the bits and bobs that had survived the waterlogging, essentially knives and the like. *What are we supposed to do against so many?*

Evans pointed. "We'll circle around, meet up with local forces. The walls haven't been kept in the best repair over the years. That'll cost the governor down the line, but in the meantime, we can use the chaos."

That was a saner plan than rushing the cragger army. Since Evans knew the area best, he took the lead. The darkness made it challenging to move over rugged terrain, but she managed. Fortunately, there was so much trouble near the main gates that it wasn't a problem to slip along the perimeter until she spotted the crack in the walls. This one was narrow; Irahi had to turn sideways since his shoulders wouldn't fit. *Those golems could bring down these old fortifications with a few well-placed blows.*

"It's a good thing the craggers don't know this rock as well as I do," Evans said.

Kurtz gestured silently. Saskia turned in time to be slammed up against the wall by soldiers wearing Skarsgard colors. Her chin cracked on the stone as Evans swore.

"Are you mad? We're the least of your worries at the moment."

"You could be spies."

"We came out of the mines," Inspector Ritsuko put in. "Take us to the foreman. He'll vouch for us."

"Lies. Nothing's come out of there in days. They're all dead."

At that, Evans growled and broke free of the soldier's hold.

He punched the man square in the face, hard enough that Janus winced. The resultant crunch and spatter of blood left his target rocking on his feet. But immediately, four others grabbed Evans, shoving him against the wall, arms akimbo so he could neither struggle, nor reach his weapons.

Spirits, we don't have time for this.

Evidently Janus was of the same mind. "He wasn't joking. You have bigger problems."

As one, the group turned toward the administrative complex. Though it was some distance off, the fiery glow was unmistakable. After the encounter in the mine, Saskia would've recognized the sound anywhere.

"The salamanders have broken out... we'll be caught between the craggers and their golems and the fire elementals."

22

"THE WHOLE TOWN will be destroyed," Ritsuko said. "We don't have time to debate."

She hoped the guards had more common sense than this detainment suggested. Their leader stared off toward the administration complex, then took a step back. In the flickering shadows, he seemed alarmed. *As well he might.* The others were muttering amongst themselves in reaction to Miss Braelan's words. If salamanders were on the loose in addition to the craggers at the gates, Eldheim might well be doomed.

"We have to bottle the fire elementals," Mikani said.

"They sounded too angry to be willing to parley," she answered.

Miss Braelan nodded. "From what that salamander said, they want revenge, not peace."

There was a rumble of agreement, but she noticed that nobody looked too eager to take on the task. After their narrow escape from the mines, she didn't want to engage the creatures either. *Nobody ever tells you that adventures are exhausting, messy, and inconvenient.* But there was no safety in the town this night, no quiet place to hide, and

Ritsuko could never look herself in the eyes thereafter if she fled from her duty.

"How do you propose we do that, then?" Irahi towered over the guards holding his arms, as if they could hold the big man should he choose to break free. "I've heard it takes hours of effort to bind even one salamander to an orb. We don't have hours. Or orbs."

"It sounds as if you've the matter well in hand." The guard cleared his throat. "I suspect we're needed near the front, so we'll leave you to it."

Ritsuko had seen cowardly men retreat before, but never with such military precision. They must have been frightened away by the brightening glow, fire spreading in town to the north. *And obviously, that's just where we're heading.*

"Let's go," Mikani said. "Before we're interrupted again."

Her partner hurried off, leaving the rest of them to follow. The streets were a mess, full of terrified townsfolk seeking safer shelters than what they could create with wood and barricades. *Those won't help a whole lot when the flames flicker outside.* Homes were built of timber and stone, but enough of the former to present a problem now. Huge-eyed children stumbled along after their parents, towed by the hand as if there were anywhere they could go. Distant booms echoed from the east side of Eldheim, more evidence that the craggers were still pressing.

They ran past more than one squadron of House Guards rushing from the main mine complex toward the sounds of struggle behind them. The crack of golem-tossed boulders punctuated shouted orders and cries of pain; Irahi seemed tempted to stop to lend aid when they ran past a group of people, covered in soot and grime, digging through a pile of rubble that had once been a home. But Mikani hurried along, and the doctor was forced to follow with a pained expression.

As they neared the massive building carved out of the side of the mountain, the crowds thinned. *Everyone must be hiding, fighting the craggers... or trying to keep the elementals from rushing out of the mines.* A mixed group of Skarsgard and Magnus soldiers had erected a barricade at the foot of the stairs to the administration building. Gunfire and screams echoed from the building, with the occasional flare of flame lighting up the entrance in garish red and gold. The troops were clearly trying to contain the elemental threat.

Doesn't sound like the fight's going well.

"Glad to see you!" one of the men called.

Ritsuko wondered how they'd feel if they knew a patrol had chosen to head in the opposite direction rather than deal with the danger here. Their group was so small that matters must be dire indeed within. She squared her shoulders, trying to brace for the horrors to come.

"They think we're reinforcements." Evans sounded hoarse and tired.

"Or insane. I'm leaning toward both." Mikani led the way up the wide stone steps toward the main entrance.

Inside, two full squads were pinned down behind metal shielding, with a half dozen elementals pressing. It was only a matter of time before the men on the other sides roasted alive. Already their hands were smoking inside their gloves, and the steel trembled beneath the repeated bursts of flame. So far, they hadn't made much progress in driving the salamanders back. She didn't like to think how many must've pushed past before the soldiers assembled and got the blockade in place.

"This place is a conflagration waiting to happen," Evans bit out.

"This isn't our fight, is it?" Kurtz said. "Those bastards left us to rot, sure enough. So if we were smart, we'd walk away."

Miss Braelan actually laughed. "You haven't known Janus very long, have you?"

Mikani shook his head. "Hand over the grenades, and you can run. We're going in, and we're saving those men if we can."

The miner handed his pack to Irahi. "I've got to find my family, maybe I can still get them out." He paused to give Evans an awkward, one-armed hug, complete with backslapping, then he went back down the steps, head low, as if he felt some small shame at his decision.

"Your inspirational speeches leave something to be desired, Mikani." The doctor peered in the bag. "We have eight grenades left. What do you propose we do?"

"Throw one now, and we bring half the building down on our heads." Evans studied the pinned guards. "We'd likely all die trying to save them."

"Janus, while I understand your need for heroics, I'm not behind any scheme that ends in fiery death," Miss Braelan said.

"Are your wind spirits strong enough to do anything here?" Ritsuko asked.

She guessed the answer was no, so the other woman didn't surprise her when she shook her head after a brief hesitation. "Wind would only... agitate the situation, I'm afraid. Fire isn't quelled by it."

The guards had set up at the first intersection of the hallways. Ritsuko imagined that the branching corridors didn't lead to any exits, or the salamanders would already be moving off and not cooking the soldiers slowly. The House Guards fired standard ammunition when they could gather the strength—she could only guess how exhausted they must be—but it had no effect. Ferishers might have some defense against forces of nature, but their lore had been lost or intentionally buried. There was no time for research.

"Do you know where these halls go?" she asked Evans.

The man shrugged. "I know the tunnels like the back of my hand, but I never had reason to spend any time up here with management." He spat the word like most men would "maggot."

"Where are the lavatories?"

They all turned toward Miss Braelan.

"Oh, bronze gods. Lavatories. Plumbing. Running water? No House overseer would share the facilities with the workers. They must have their own."

One of the soldiers turned with a sympathetic expression. "There are some down the hall and to the right, miss, but you'd be much better served to do it out of doors."

Ritsuko laughed. Trust a man to think a woman's gentle biology couldn't handle such a stressful situation and that Miss Braelan was in desperate need of the facilities. She swapped an amused look with her as the other woman raced past.

Miss Braelan called over her shoulder, "I have a plan to get some help, hold the line."

Ritsuko followed, along with Mikani, Hu, and Evans. It required stepping past the shields, and soldiers shouted warnings as they sprinted, fire blasting the floor behind them. A few of the strikes sizzled the backs of her boots, and the white-hot flare of pain told Ritsuko she had been burned, but then the nerves went dead. She stumbled, pressing on as fast she could.

No time to worry now. I hope she knows what she's doing.

A few of the smaller salamanders squeezed through the ravaged doors and gave chase, buying the soldiers some time. She thought the others were following, but there was no chance to look back. An instant of hesitation, and she'd be fried. More flames struck the walls, hissing and dying against the stone. *So glad there's not more wood in here.* Miss Braelan kicked open the heavy door marked private, and the others charged in behind. This *was* heavy timber, but it was thick enough not to char.

"I just need a few moments," Miss Braelan said breathlessly. "Irahi, I need your help. The rest of you, hold it for me, if you can."

They were clearly in a luxurious lavatory designated for executive use. Everything was ornate stone and marble, gilded facets and shining mirrors. Ritsuko caught a glimpse of herself in the gaslight and shivered. *I look like a shade or a wraith, all eyes and tangled hair*. She turned gratefully and pressed all of her weight against the door, along with Mikani and Evans.

Miss Braelan pointed at the sink, addressing Irahi. "Break it open. For this to work, I need water and lots of it."

Then she closed her eyes and her soft whisper told Ritsuko she was summoning her familiars. The creep of elemental energy prickled over her, raising the hair on the nape of her neck. Irahi grabbed the sink with both hands. The first salamander hit the door with a gout of flame on the other side, and the wood bowed and charred beneath her hands.

* * *

Mikani pushed back as the wood smoldered, warm against his shoulder. With a loud screech of metal, Hu tore the copper sink free from the wall. A thin spray of water hissed from the twisted pipes. The big man grunted and pulled again, tearing the sink free. Water gushed out to splash on the floor in a cold rush. Hu dropped the sink and started tugging at the water tank over the water closet.

Mikani shifted his weight when he slipped on the wet tiles. He could feel Saskia's spirits gathering around her. *They're scared and worried for her, but not angry*. There was more, but he couldn't fully interpret the rush of alien emotion from the wind elementals. Water swirled and rose in a shimmering funnel at the center of the room as the sylphs gathered strength from Saskia's low chant. The temperature dropped as the spirits gained power: Mikani's breath puffed out in smoky wisps, and steam rolled off the door's hinges.

"Move!" Saskia shouted.

He grabbed Ritsuko and pulled her aside. The door flew open with the snap of tearing wood, slamming against his back and knocking them both to the corner. There was a deafening hiss, a scream, and a billowing cloud of steam filled the bathroom.

Hu pulled them to their feet, one in each hand. Saskia gestured as she strode toward the shattered door; the growing pool of water spiraled before her in a torrent that formed a transparent sheet, so it was as if she walked through a living mirror that flowed with her every movement. The wind spirits sang back to her, a chilling call if he'd ever heard one. *Glad she's on our side.*

The wall of water swept through the doorway, carrying the smaller elementals with it. A huge salamander withstood the onslaught, facing Mikani with a ferocity he partly understood. More water rushed from the broken pipes. Since there was no drainage in the room, the flow was forced into the corridors as if they were indoor canals. Saskia added the weight of her familiars to the current, creating small funnels to douse the flames whenever the salamander flared with murderous intent. The creature's eyes glowed red as hot coals, its talons raking charred lines on the stone as it fought to hold ground.

Gambit successful.

With any luck, the soldiers would be faring better now with the enemy weakened. It would be hard for any sparks to catch; everything was damp, and Saskia was blowing the water around to ensure that everything was doused. *Good thinking, that.*

Hu tapped Mikani on the shoulder. "Stay with the captain. Evans and I will break all the plumbing we find in here."

When he was sure the way had cleared, Hu led Evans out of the room. Mikani followed, his hand on Ritsuko's arm to help balance on the wet floor. She was obviously limping and in pain; after a few steps, he picked her up.

He gazed down into her surprised face. "I'm not letting you fall again, Ritsuko."

To his surprise, she didn't protest. A few minutes later, a cold wave washed over his feet.

They must have found another lavatory. Saskia rounded the corner ahead. She spread her arms and unleashed her artificial storm: wind and water buffeted the salamanders and soldiers with a muted roar and cries of surprise and pain from the elementals. Two turned and scrambled toward the mines, scrambling over the walls as their flaming skin flickered and steamed.

The last elemental stood its ground. It nearly filled the corridor, easily twice as long as Hu was tall and nearly as broad. Its six limbs clawed at the ceiling and floor as it stood its ground against the tempest, screaming its rage. It spat out a flame burst, but the wind sent it careening against a wall in a burst of sparks and smoke. Saskia flinched from the muted explosion, and the elemental took advantage of the brief opening to bound past them and toward the exit.

"Hells and Winter..." *Deal with it later. Need to stop any more from coming out.* He pushed away from the wall, shifting his hold on Ritsuko. "Are you hurt?"

"Nothing that can't wait until later." From her pained, false smile, he knew it was worse than she was letting on.

He was tempted to read her, but if he got a feel for how bad she was truly hurting, it might make it hard for him to focus on problem-solving. And this situation had a lot of them. It was dark as hell, as some bright spark had evidently possessed the foresight to turn off the gas lines given that there were fire monsters running amok inside the administration offices. Debris and broken furniture littered the slippery floor.

Mikani was just pondering what to do when Ritsuko said, "We have to seal the mines properly."

At once, a number of voices rose in protest, soldiers protecting their masters' interests, even to the death. To die in the line of duty was one thing; to die protecting a building and someone else's profits? Mikani could not fathom that.

Evans stalked to the center of the room with Hu close behind him. They were both wet and disheveled, their features drawn in angles and shadows. The doctor kicked one of the metal shields so it tumbled back with a clatter. His old friend was obviously out of patience with the violence and the chaos.

"She's right," the miner said. "And I'll gut the first man who tries to stop us."

Saskia added softly, "I have the strength left to pull the air out of your lungs. I'd rather not. So don't make me."

Mikani had no idea if she could *do* that with her elementals, or if she had the cruelty to carry out the threat, but from what he sensed of the men's moods, they believed her. And that was all you needed for an effective bluff. Bronze gods knew that she'd looked scary as hell with the wind and water whipping around her, a true and awe-inspiring weather witch.

"My orders are to hold this position," the guard finally said. "I don't know anything about what you're planning. And neither do you, men."

They answered with silence, freeing Mikani's group to press forward down the slick, dark hallway. It wouldn't be long before the skittish salamanders dried out and prepared for another charge. *This time, there's nothing to stop them, unless* we *do.* Evans knew the most about the explosives they'd carried from the mines. *Let's hope it's enough not to get us all killed.*

Mikani heard the crash of glass. A few salamanders might have decided to take a more direct route into Eldheim; that didn't bode well for the townsfolk. He quickened his step, conscious that if he fell, he'd take Ritsuko with him. Evans was ahead, navigating the twists and turns in the dark. A few times, the miner cursed as he thumped into something.

"I wish I knew a light spell," Saskia muttered.

"Would be handy," Hu agreed. "They always have them in the stories."

"You should put me down," Ritsuko whispered.

"When have you ever known me to do what I should? Stop squirming."

"You can't fight this way."

But he couldn't really fight fire elementals anyway. So he ignored that quiet comment and concentrated on maneuvering down the stairs. The silence was eerie, the darkness complete. At the base of the stairs, Mikani heard someone scrabbling in his or her pack. Then Evans turned the valve on his small lantern.

"Better than nothing. And I'll need to see what I'm about. Otherwise..." When the man trailed off, Mikani knew what was at stake.

From that point, it didn't take long to reach the mine entrance. The heavy doors that had locked behind them earlier were blown to bits. Steel shards littered the floor, misshapen in spots, so that it looked as if they had melted and cooled before bursting entirely. A few bodies lay nearby as well, charred beyond all recognition. *These are the men we spoke with earlier.* But there was no identifying them now.

Mikani set Ritsuko on her feet. She was a little unsteady, and he was anxious to get her some medical treatment, but not yet. Calmly, competently, Evans studied the stone, the cuts, and the weight, along with arches and angles, probably weighing factors Mikani hadn't even considered. Then the miner sighed and told the party what to do; they set the charges according to his specifications.

"There's no way for everyone to get clear before we set this off," Evans said wearily. "One person has to start the fire, so to speak, but I can count to five hundred before I let it go. If we did this right, the upstairs should be fine. The rock will cave into the tunnels, not bring down the whole building."

That's a big "if."

23

RITSUKO BRACED FOR an argument about who should stay behind to chuck the lantern and ignite the gas pockets, but before that could begin, she glimpsed the russet glow of the returning salamanders. So she shouted, "Do it now!"

With no hesitation, Evans hurled the lamp. It sailed into the mouth of the tunnel and shattered on the stone. Detonation was instantaneous; a great boom echoed, and the whole room trembled, rocks tumbling down from the opening, creating a dust fog to accompany the thunderous collapse. Mikani threw himself on top of her, and as she went over backward, she saw Irahi shielding Miss Braelan. Chunks fell from the ceiling as the cave-in rumbled below the ground. Inhuman cries of rage and pain rang out, then fell silent.

As more debris tumbled down, Mikani pulled her to her feet, and they ran up the stairs, heading toward the front door as fast as they could. The first twenty feet were dodgy, but the farther they moved from the epicenter, the more stable the building seemed. Ritsuko exhaled, silently thanking Evans for his careful placement of the oil from inside the grenades. Her calves and ankles felt raw and hot;

the numbness had worn off, so each step felt as if someone were scraping a skinning knife down the backs of her legs.

"Well done," Miss Braelan said to Evans, who was coughing.

There were a few fresh bodies near the front door, but the surviving soldiers appeared grateful, even standing in inches of water. The administration offices were a wreck, and it was probably worse in town. She needed a rest, but somehow she kept to her feet, ignoring her injuries. There were doubtless others in a worse state.

Mikani came up to her and placed a hand on her arm. "That'll keep the elementals off us for a bit. Now we just have an army of craggers and whatever salamanders managed to slip out. The day's looking up already, partner." His voice was hoarse, and she could barely make out his features through the layers of dirt and ash.

Not that I look any better.

One of the guards came up to them. The thick layer of grime made it impossible to tell his House. "The overseers will be down soon, and they won't be pleased. You saved a lot of lives, but I doubt they'll see past the mess you've made." He signaled a couple of his men to give them three rifles and a couple of heavy handguns. "It's not much, but it's what we can spare. We'll buy you some time, too."

Mikani nodded. "Thanks." He passed her one of the guns, unfamiliar and heavier than her service pistol. "You all right to walk, Ritsuko?" Irahi glanced over at that.

"I'm well enough." *Good thing I have the truth-sense, or he'd already be picking me up.*

He looked dubious for a moment, but a loud explosion somewhere in the distance distracted him.

"Sounds like they're past the outer defenses." Evans checked his rifle and started walking.

Mikani followed close behind, then Miss Braelan. Irahi waited for Ritsuko, frowning. With the grime and ash covering him, he reminded her of a stone golem. "You're hurt, Celeste."

"We all are. It'll keep." She lowered her voice so her partner wouldn't hear. "These boots will need to be cut off, and the fabric of my trousers will need to be soaked away, I fear."

Irahi nodded once, after a moment. "You have the will of a warrior. Truly, you need to come to the Sisters with me after this is over. I'll be the envy of the islands." He grinned and waved her on after the others. "I'll bring up the rear."

Ritsuko quickened her step to catch up with the others a block away. The townsfolk had built a makeshift wall, bringing down several damaged buildings and shoring up the rubble with whatever they could find. Men and women ran along the inner wall, shouting in confusion and anger while fireballs burst against the tumbled rocks. Every now and then, a sphere of flame arced high over the walls to burst with a deafening roar, scattering those nearest the impact.

House Guards and miners fired over the barricade, the gunshots almost soft in the crackle of flames and dull thunder of fire missiles. Smoke and ash hung heavy in the air. Ritsuko could hear the rumbling of the cragger golems up ahead, but could see neither the stone creatures nor craggers assaulting the Eldheim defenses.

There was a deafening crack nearby. A small building, already half-demolished and scorched, tumbled in a cloud of dust a couple of dozen yards away. One of the cragger golems had a massive salamander wrapped in its arms, wrestling with the creature as it screamed and flared with gouts of flame that she could feel wash over her. The elemental blazed into the night sky in a pillar of ferocious orange light, and when the smoke cleared, there was nothing but a pool of molten stone cooling on the ground.

They'll level the whole town. And we don't even know what the craggers are doing here. If Ritsuko had been asked, she would've guessed that they intended to march on Northport or even Dorstaad, not Eldheim and the mines. A few moments later, a salamander crawled out of a flicker lantern, small at first, but it grew in size with every step it took. *So the ignition effect that destroyed the golem taxed the elemental's strength, but didn't kill it. That'll make it pretty damned hard to end these things.*

As if the craggers shared her conclusion, a loud voice rang into the darkness, shouting for a retreat. Strategically, it made sense for the craggers to let the House soldiers face the elementals, then roll back into town to mop up any survivors. *Good strategy. Bad for us.* All around, bearded, wild-eyed men broke away from battle and ran for the sparse cover of the wooded hills outside town.

Her head ached with exhaustion, but this might be their only chance. They had to find the man giving orders to the cragger troops and find out what he wanted. So she quickly drew a handkerchief out of her pocket, unfolded it, and held out her hand to Evans for his rifle. He gave it without question, a response Ritsuko appreciated. She affixed the cloth to the barrel and moved through the chaos, avoiding the barrage of gunfire aimed at the salamanders who turned their attention to the defenders.

They apparently don't care what humans they kill.

Ritsuko held the rifle by the stock with the scrap of cloth fluttering in the breeze. It should be evident by the way she carried it that she didn't mean to fire it. And she was tired enough that if the craggers shot her on sight, she didn't much care; at least it would mean a rest from all of this. Mikani said something, but the ambient noise made it impossible to discern the words unless she stopped and turned around.

If I do, the craggers will vanish into the trees until Eldheim's well-nigh defenseless. It's now or never.

Despite the pain in her legs, she hurried past the broken gates of town, with the rest of the group following. They might be protesting or questioning; Ritsuko wasn't listening.

This is all I can do. I may not be a captain or an adventurer, but I know how to talk to people. In the distance, she made out the last rank of the craggers, racing toward the forest. Soon they'd be out of earshot, so she simply stopped and shouted, "I formally request parley with your leader." Then she held her ground while lifting the white cloth high in the air, where it could catch and reflect the scant moonlight. "Put away your weapons," she said softly to the others.

"Are you sure about this?" Miss Braelan asked.

She laughed shakily. "Not even a little. But if they're allowed to return, it'll be disastrous. Eldheim's barely holding together as it is."

The word "parley" echoed forward through the craggers' disorganized line, echoed mouth to ear, until Ritsuko thought her nerves would fray to the point of bleeding. She felt her pulse in various bruises and wounds, reinforced by the ringing in her ears, which might be a result of concussive damage or simple exhaustion.

Please grant me the right words, Grandfather.

Eventually, a giant of a man—on par with Irahi—strode through the cragger force, who had paused in their retreat. It was safe enough, this distance from town, as the soldiers had enough problems to keep them from giving chase. If things went poorly, there might only be an ashen ruin left when these talks concluded. He had a savage, imperious air, huge hands, a scarred face, and auburn hair, braided and laced with ornamental bone.

"What Summerlander dares to call for words with me?" he demanded.

* * *

Mikani fought the urge to reach for his rifle as he sized up the craggers' leader.

He knows his way around a fight. He's angry as hell's

own hounds, but scared, too... and those burn marks on his left arm look fresh. He released his grip on his gift further, taking in the roiling waves of anxiety rolling off the host of craggers before him.

"They expected the salamanders to side with *them*," he whispered. Ritsuko shot him a quick glance and stepped forward.

"I'm Inspector Celeste Ritsuko, special envoy for the Council of Noble Houses from Dorstaad."

The man made a sound of disdain as he came toward her. He towered over Ritsuko, one of his hands easily big enough to engulf her head if he reached for her.

I will take him down if he tries. He glanced at the milling throng of tribesmen. *The rest of them might be a bit of a problem, but we'll burn that bridge if we get to it.*

"I am Kaeheld of Ceannen, Chief of Clan Coirse, war leader for the families of the Jagged Coast and Kraken Sea. Speak your piece, woman."

"We approach under a flag of peace," she said with quiet dignity. "I request to hear your reasons for attacking this place and what you require to negotiate a truce."

The gathered craggers called out, their mingling voices unintelligible and loud. Then Kaeheld raised a hand, and the tumult died down to an angry, rolling murmur.

"What authority have you, Ritsuko of the Council in Dorstaad? We've been promised much, by the snakes in Northport. Their pledges have proven hollow as rotten logs."

Mikani touched Ritsuko's elbow. "She has the full support of the Houses. Northport must obey." *At least, I hope so. Bronze gods know we've little choice at the moment. Really hope Olrik doesn't take our heads for this.*

Her voice was calm and composed. "All conflict can be resolved. We need only identify the promises to which you refer and amend the wrongs done to your people."

To Mikani's ears, she sounded sincere and in control, but

her emotions gave her away. She was frightened and shaky, trying not to show it. The cragger chieftain scanned her up and down, as if taking her measure. Ritsuko met his gaze steadily. Mikani wondered if it seemed odd to the leader that with three men standing behind her, she was still handling the exchange.

"Perhaps all I want is to see my enemies vanquished," Kaeheld said.

"Then we'll withdraw. I can't help with that," Ritsuko answered.

Kaeheld stood quiet for a few seconds, a frown pulling his brows together. His men stirred, restless to fight or finish the retreat, but he raised a hand to silence them; and the stillness was instantaneous. The distant battle sounded loud by comparison. Pauses in between gunfire told Mikani they were running low on ammo or there were fewer defenders to pull the triggers.

"You have brought the wrath of the spirits on us all. With your machines and your men desecrating the Dragon's Hearth." He pointed at the mountain behind them. The men closest to him made an unfamiliar hand gesture and bowed their heads. "You ask what we want. We need an end to the blasphemy. The wrath of the Dragon's kin is already upon us all." He stepped closer, and Mikani moved forward. For a tense moment, he looked straight into Kaeheld's dark eyes. Then Ritsuko touched his arm, and he reluctantly stepped back.

The chief continued, turning his attention back to Ritsuko. "The fire wyverns have destroyed many of our villages in the past months. Now, they all threaten to burst forth and raze the islands of the north. Then they will come for you, but not before the Northern Families have fallen. That, we cannot allow, Ritsuko of the Council."

"To prevent misunderstandings, you're saying that the practices in the mines here have led to this... uprising? And your people have suffered as a result." Ritsuko sounded mildly apologetic, but Mikani could understand her confusion.

It's a hell of a lot to take in. It's like learning that the fireplace has feelings and is bloody tired of heating my cottage without being asked.

"That is an understatement. The elemental spirits have been dishonored, disrespected, and bound against their will for far too long."

Ritsuko pushed out a soft breath, and Mikani heard Saskia muffle a sound of dismay. Hu was quiet at his shoulder, and Evans was still. He guessed the miner probably had his hands near the weapons he had reluctantly put away. *This could go wrong so quick.* Yet he admired his partner's composure in the face of overwhelming superior force. It was probably the fact that she comported herself like a leader that made Kaeheld take her seriously.

"It doesn't excuse our actions," Ritsuko said, "but we sinned out of ignorance, not malice. Advise me how we can make amends and restore order to the region."

"Amends? How do you make amends for two centuries' toil, under chain and muzzle?" Kaeheld shook his head, and raised both arms. "The Dragon's kin want the blood of men, and even that will not quell their anger. They have been slipping forth from the depths all along the Dragon's spine mountains for weeks, now; and it is our families who have paid the price of your arrogance."

Mikani narrowed his eyes. *He's not telling us everything; he's scared, but not terrified. He has a hidden ace.* From Ritsuko's expression, her newfound talent or experience as an Inspector—or both, told her the same.

"That is not entirely true, sir." She leveled a grave stare on the cragger chieftain, and the silent exchange went on until Kaeheld looked away.

It wasn't a sign of weakness, however. Instead, he seemed to be taking a quiet consensus by glancing at his men. A few of them shook their heads, but then one of them, probably a lieutenant, said, "We lost three golems already. Our force will be hard-pressed to take the city, defeat all defenders and the freed wyverns as well."

"Both sides would benefit from a peaceable solution," Ritsuko said. "I've seen a lot of death tonight. I'd prefer to see no more."

The chieftain clenched and unclenched his hands, corded muscle rippling on his arms. *I can feel the anger rolling off him. This is it; either he sees reason, or he strikes Ritsuko. Then I shoot him in the head, and it all goes to hell.*

"My son burned to death, not a week past. I would not be remembered for needless deaths when my time comes."

Ritsuko closed her eyes for a moment, her shoulders sagging in what Mikani judged to be relief. "Help us contain the salamanders. Wyverns. There must be a way... share what you know with us, please."

"Their anger burns bright... hot enough to wake the Dragon, if we don't act quickly, Ritsuko of the Council." Kaeheld turned and beckoned to someone in the throng. A dozen figures wound their way toward them, older and frailer than any soldier had a right to be. "These are the oldest and wisest of our Dream Weavers. Long since, they saw this threat coming, but their warnings went unheeded... and we are paying the price now."

The old men all held staffs, heavily decorated with bones, shells, and feathers. One seemed to be carrying a full spiderweb in a long branch, glimmering in the distant firelight.

"We're stopping an elemental uprising with shells and a spiderweb?" Evans sounded as if he was on the verge of panic.

"We once interrupted a world-killing ritual with a store-bought talisman and a knife. Could be worse." Mikani grinned at the other man. From the miner's reaction, he wasn't sure if he'd come off as confident or insane.

"This is why you attacked here," Ritsuko said in the tone of one making a critical deduction. "Instead of a more pivotal port. This isn't the staging ground of a larger war. You intended to force the mine owners to permit you to make things right with the spirits, by force, since they broke their promises before."

"You are a clever woman," Kaeheld said. "And our high king is a cautious man. We were sent to appease the Dragon while Hrothgar prepares to sail on Northport, should we fail."

"The increased attacks along the coast were because you needed supplies to replace those lost in trouble with the salamanders... and to provision for this push," Saskia guessed.

The cragger chieftain nodded, gazing toward Eldheim. "If you can promise us safe passage, our Weavers will do what we came to... and we'll discuss reparations after."

Mikani couldn't decide if the Chief was thinking of reparations for his people, or for the enslaved elementals. *Either way, the Council will have a bloody fit if they even agree. I'm not looking forward to going home anymore.* It seemed like forever since they'd rested, but this interminable night could only end if they found a way to appease the rebellious fire spirits. *If the craggers know how to do it, we have to go along. Otherwise, this only gets worse.*

Ritsuko seemed to share his opinion. "We'll talk to the commanders in Eldheim. Hold position here. We'll return when we've finalized the accord."

24

IT TOOK ALMOST two hours of arguing to get the House soldiers to pull back. Ritsuko was heartily sick of everyone by the time they returned to the craggers and offered safe escort into Eldheim. The salamanders were burning everything that would catch, and a number of villagers had fled the town entirely. A makeshift camp was set up to the southeast, tents and wagons full of hastily gathered possessions. In most cases, that was all the refugees had been able to save.

To keep things civil, Kaeheld didn't bring his whole company; instead, he ordered most of them to hold their ground while a small party guarded the Dream Weavers. The cragger chieftain's expression was grim as he followed Ritsuko through the burning town. She imagined he'd seen this more than once if his people had already faced the enraged salamanders. This truce was shaky at best, and the lieutenant who had agreed to it was young. Most of his superiors were dead, so it was clear that he really had no idea what he should be doing.

We're definitely overstepping our authority here. But better to face punishment later than to let everything burn and everyone die.

Ritsuko glanced over her shoulder as they walked. Miss Braelan was deep in conversation with a couple of the cragger sorcerers, with Irahi following close behind. The doctor kept glancing Ritsuko's way, offering tired-looking smiles as they wound their way through the ravaged streets. He ignored makeshift aid stations and the pleas for help as they passed, and she saw from his expression that it cost him dearly.

Mikani, on the other hand, seemed intent on taking in the destruction. He was frowning, gripping his rifle with white-knuckled hands over his shoulders. He must have sensed her gaze as he turned to meet her eyes. "This ritual of theirs will work." A discordant note rang in her ear, as if he didn't quite believe his own words... but he wanted to.

So she tried to reassure him, knowing he must be imagining this scene set on the Summer Isle, perhaps in Dorstaad or north up the coast, where his family lived. "They know more of what is going on than we do. If they think it will work, we must believe that it will."

Or every town and city in Hy Breasil could end like this.

"Not much choice, right." He looked around once more. "Just wish I'd had a chance to warn my sisters. Now's a hell of a good time for them all to tend the outlying fields, I think."

"The mirrors are down," she said gently. "It's not as if a letter would've gotten there in time. It's not your fault. And I'm sure they're fine."

Maybe.

He was silent a moment. "I need to see them when this is done. You should come with me." He paused to offer her a small grin that made him seem almost himself. "We bloody well deserve a vacation."

She raised a brow, keeping her expression neutral when her heart banged a little with surprise. "Are you inviting me home to meet the family, Mikani?"

"Don't worry, Ritsuko. I promise you, they're nice. I'm the black sheep, remember?" He swung his rifle down to the crook of his arm, averting her gaze. "You're my closest... Hells and Winter, Ritsuko. You're my..." He shook his head, and finally said, "Yes. I am, Celeste."

Truth.

Ritsuko would give a lot for him to complete that sentence. *You're my... what? Closest friend? Partner?* But there was no time for her to speculate. So she nodded.

"Then I'd love to go with you. I could use a break," she admitted.

Provided I don't die of gangrene before then.

Miss Braelan walked up, flanked by a half dozen of the Dream Weavers. The craggers were silent, but the weather witch looked excited and eager. "These Weavers... they remember things from before the Iron War."

From her history lessons, Ritsuko recalled that there had been a terrible conflict that nearly wiped out both humans and Ferishers. While the fae had magic, humanity had numbers and iron. In the end, it only ended through a treaty founded on marital alliances.

And that's how the great Houses were born.

Miss Braelan went on, "I mean, not from books or even oral traditions, it's like they were there! Bronze gods, do you know what this means? They were around when the Ferisher Courts still walked the islands. The craggers might have been on the first long ships to land in Hy Breasil a thousand years ago!"

"Saskia? Focus. What do they need to do? How do we help?" Mikani held Miss Braelan's gaze as she frowned, then nodded.

"Right. We need to reach an old vent leading down to the mountain's core." She pointed to a small, craggy trail winding its way farther up the slope beside the collapsed administration building. "Come on then. We need everyone up there for this to work." She hurried after the Dream Weavers as they walked past them and headed up the path.

Mikani raised both brows and turned to Ritsuko. "If we need to throw a virgin into the volcano, we're out of luck."

She glanced at the peach fuzz on the young lieutenant's cheeks in silent suggestion. Mikani responded with a choked laugh, and they set off after the others. But before they'd gone more than ten steps, the ground *shook*. Not what resulted from an explosion, but bigger and deeper. Dust broke from shuddering walls, drifting on the wind.

"You had to say 'volcano.' Uhm. Was he *serious* when he was talking about a dragon? That was... allegory, right?"

"I heard tales, growing up. Krakens. Dragons. Old creatures from the times of the Ferishers." Irahi had caught up to them. "Anything is possible, these days. And honestly, wouldn't it be just grand to see a dragon?"

"Only as long as it did not see us, Hu." Mikani checked his rifle, then seemed to realize just what little use a bullet would be against a mythical beast and slung it over his shoulder.

"Dragons," she said with a sigh. "I suppose no adventure tale is complete without one."

They climbed for a couple of hours, the ground shuddering and groaning three more times while they traveled, until they reached the appointed spot. Closer inspection revealed a dark crevasse in the side of the mountain, easily thirty feet high and lined with jagged rocks. A red light glowed from deep within the chasm.

It looks like a dragon's maw.

Miss Braelan motioned them forward, while the craggers spread out and pointed their staffs toward the opening. Kaeheld and his men formed a semicircle behind them.

"Inspector Ritsuko, I need you with us at the front. Janus, Irahi... join Kaeheld's men. Please try to be quiet and behave."

Mikani wore a deep frown. "Why do you need Ritsuko?"

She laid a hand on her partner's arm to silence his instinctive protest. He scowled, but moved off to join the craggers when she made it clear she was willing. Then Ritsuko turned back to Miss Braelan, her heartbeat loud as thunder in her ears. *I hope I don't regret this.*

"Where do you need me?"

The other woman led her toward cragger sorcerers, who were chanting in low voices, creating an eerie a capella harmony. As one, they wove their staffs in elaborate patterns in the air, and though it might've been a trick of her tired eyes, Ritsuko could almost glimpse the trails of light left behind, designs not quite visible and etched in air.

Kaeheld stepped forward from where he stood alone at the edge of the opening, waiting for them. His Weavers formed a circle around him, and remembering Miss Braelan's earlier ritual, Ritsuko wondered if it was safe to pass. But her movement didn't distract the sorcerers, so she took her place beside the cragger chieftain, hoping she didn't look as nervous as she felt.

A rumble came from deep within the cavern, rocking the ground. She kept to her feet by clutching Kaeheld's arm; she expected him to rebuff her, but the chieftain's gaze was fixed on the darkness, now brightening with a terrible glow. The chanting grew louder, the Weavers repeating the same syllables until they became nonsense noises and throbbed like ancient drums.

Measured booms rang out, and it took her a few seconds to realize those must be footfalls, but they didn't sound right. When the enormous salamander emerged into sight, she understood why. He was much larger than any others they'd encountered. The portion she could see was nearly twenty feet high, with six legs gripping the walls of the chasm—more like a spider than a reptile. Long frills flowed and stirred in the gusts of heat rolling off the creature, waving like living hair from each side of its elongated skull. Flames licked around the monstrous silhouette, framing the creature like a demon from a painting.

"This is good, right?" Irahi whispered. "This is supposed to happen?"

Ritsuko shared his doubt, but somehow she managed not to recoil. With each shift, the dragon drew closer, and the air heated until it felt like it must be burning her lungs. It grew difficult to suck in a new breath; her chest tightened. Beside her, Kaeheld seemed rapt, as if an old god had come to life.

Then it spoke in a voice like thunder. "Small, brief ones, why have you called me?"

* * *

The harsh red light cast by the massive elemental washed the color from everything; the pulsating heat made it hard to breathe in anything but short, shallow breaths that dried Mikani's lips and made his throat ache.

"We humbly request an audience." The oldest Dream Weaver bowed low, and the others followed suit. "We ask your mercy, Lord Thuris, Dweller at the Mountain's Heart, keeper of Fire. We ask the opportunity to make amends."

A sweltering shock wave nearly knocked Mikani down as the elemental roared; Kaeheld kept Ritsuko on her feet. Only the shamans seemed unaffected, the heat wave rolling over them with a flutter of robes and dangling staff adornments.

"The old pacts have been broken! You animals enslave my people. We retreated to the far lands, and you persisted in awakening us once more. Well, *man*, we are returned."

"They can be restored, Lord Thuris. We bring a Speaker for each isle." The Dream Weaver motioned toward Kaeheld and Ritsuko.

Oh, hells. What are they doing?

Hu laid a heavy hand on Mikani's shoulder; Mikani had not realized he'd tried to step forward until the big man pulled him back. "Interrupt and you kill us all, Mikani. Trust them."

Mikani bit back a retort.

"We offer peace. We offer to renew the pure sanctity of your mountain. A stewardship, that none will again disturb your kin, Lord Thuris."

The salamander's great head swayed toward Ritsuko and Kaeheld. Its eyes flared white-hot, and its claws sank into the bedrock at the lip of the chasm with the hiss of melting granite.

"We had all that. We require restitution!"

The old man stood taller, bracing his staff against the rock. "We have wronged the Dragon kin. We offer the Rites of Summer; when the land is coldest, we shall offer warmth. We offer the Bonds of Blood; the Speakers will bind their lives to restoring the pact. Your kin will be restored to the glory they knew in the old days, Lord Thuris."

The elemental made a deep, rolling sound. It straightened, towering well above them all.

The Rites of Summer, Bonds of Blood? What in gods' name is the old man offering? Hells and Winter, what's he offering on Celeste's behalf? I should have brought some grenades to help with this negotiation.

"Warmth in the cold. A bond. Proper respect. Your words earn you a chance, man. But we have suffered. Peace and palliatives are not enough."

The old man smiled. "Blood demands blood and pain demands pain, Lord Thuris. This we know." He stepped forward, as did five other Dream Weavers. "The six of us give ourselves freely to the fire to seal the pacts."

Ritsuko made a small sound at the words *give ourselves freely*, but it wasn't loud enough to distract from the proceedings. Mikani clenched his teeth as Hu squeezed his shoulder, hard.

"Warmth. Bond. Respect. Restitution. Very well, human, you have earned a reprieve. Ware that you don't break your word."

The eldest shaman bowed once more. Then he turned to Ritsuko and Kaeheld; without warning, he grabbed their hands and flicked a sharp, long fingernail to their wrists. He held them still as their blood soaked his hands before releasing them. The Dream Weavers renewed their chant; the harmonies seemed to swell—the elemental Lord had joined the wordless song, the deep reverberations of its voice shaking rocks and dust loose all around them. The six sorcerers came together and joined hands. Saskia and the others pulled Ritsuko and Kaeheld aside as the rest of the craggers dropped to their knees.

The sounds of explosions and battle from the town below stopped, replaced by a low, dull roar. Mikani turned toward Eldheim. The freed salamanders rushed the mountain, glimmering streaks of gold and red clambering over buildings and along the rocky slopes. A choked gasp made him turn back to the chasm. The six sorcerer sacrifices took the final step together, opening their arms and falling forward into the fiery depths. The salamander roared once more; even Hu stumbled back as the rush of hot air and sound knocked them all off balance. He had to drop to his knees to keep from being rolled off the edge. Mikani grabbed onto Ritsuko when she slid by, dropping to the ground next to her as the elemental's movements threatened to split the mountain wide open. It couldn't have been more than a few seconds, but it felt like hours before the noise withered to a loud ringing in Mikani's ears.

He wrapped an arm around his partner instinctively, as the world went a little mad. The surviving craggers took over the chant, but it gained new notes, mourning if he guessed correctly. This was a song for the dead, honoring their sacrifice. All around, he glimpsed sad eyes and dirty faces, resigned to the necessity of appeasing forces beyond human ken.

"My kith and kin will guard Mount Surtir. Great one, we are yours."

"It is done," Lord Thuris boomed. "All terms accepted. Now begone!"

The peak shook again, and the flames flared sharply in warning. He didn't intend to stick around for lava to come rolling over them if they didn't move fast enough. Mikani didn't let go of Ritsuko until they reached the base of the mountain. Hu was helping Saskia, while Evans had the shell-shocked look of a man grappling with too many surprises at once.

I know the feeling.

They were still some distance from town when Ritsuko stumbled. He started to make a joke, until he realized she was actually passing out. Worried, he swung her into his arms. *Hu needs a look at her, but where?* Eldheim was in complete disarray, no hospitals that he'd seen. *It'll have to be the cleanest place I can find.*

Hu quickened his step, obviously worried. "Do you want me to take her?"

Like hell.

For reasons he wouldn't examine too closely, he shook his head. "I've got her. But I'm open to ideas as to where you can set up a temporary practice."

"Try the west side of town," Evans said. "It's mostly old stonework over that way. So even if the salamanders rioted, the buildings should be more or less intact."

"That's where we're headed, then."

Before they got to town, Kaeheld broke off with his surviving guards. "I suspect you don't fully grasp the import of what happened here, but know that we will keep our part of the bargain. If you fail us again, the consequences will be devastating."

Mikani started to ask for clarification, but Saskia stayed him. "I'll fill you in once we take care of the wounded."

The party was grim and silent as they trudged back into Eldheim. There would be fallout from this night's work, no question, but he didn't care how enraged the great Houses would be. So what if they lost a little revenue? The matter of certain technologies becoming scarce would be a problem, too, but it wasn't his worry.

Eventually, Evans found them an innkeeper willing to open his doors, especially once he heard the role they'd played in forging two damn-near-impossible alliances. As predicted, the structure was built entirely of dank stone, with rooms so small they seemed like cells, but with no fires burning, it was the best thing Mikani had seen in weeks.

He couldn't look away when Hu cut through Ritsuko's boots. It was worse when Mikani saw that her trousers had melted into her skin. That required soaking, and her calves were raw when the last of the fabric fell away. Red skin showed through blistered patches of white, and he could only think of how *long* she'd walked around like that. Not that there had been any time or safe place for treatment, but it didn't change the deep pride he felt when he considered her quiet gallantry. Mercifully, Ritsuko was unconscious until Hu finished cleaning, treating, and wrapping her burns. Then he bundled her in a blanket and carried her up to a room the proprietor had prepared.

A few moments later, he came back to the common room, where Mikani was sprawled in a chair across from Saskia. She called for food and drink, and they ate with the appetites of starving beggars, though nobody had much to say. It seemed incredible that the cragger sorcerers had chosen to give their lives to save everyone. *There should be a reward given to their families... or a memorial built. Or both. Hells and Winter if I know what's enough for* that.

"Saskia." She looked up from her glass, eyes wide and bruised from exhaustion. "Just what did we do, up there? What are the Rites of Summer, the Bonds of Blood?" He leaned forward, ignoring the pain echoing from every joint and muscle and coaxed his talent to life. "What did that old man need with Ritsuko's blood?"

She's tired, but aren't we all. There's also regret...

"The Rites of Summer are an ancient tradition, Janus," she murmured, without looking up. "I have never known anyone that's ever performed them. It's a ceremony to share life force with the spirits." She shook her head. "Kaeheld needed to seal the new treaty with the fire elementals." Saskia finally met his gaze. "Inspector Ritsuko, as representative of the Council, stood in as the signatory for the Summer Isle. Kaeheld spoke for Winter. They signed a new pact in blood, basically, binding all of Hy Breasil to abide by the new treaty."

Hells and Winter. We just signed away all mining rights in Mount Surtir and cut off the supply of fire elementals to the islands. Mikani let out a long breath and leaned back. "Hells. There goes our pension."

We'll have a price on our heads when Skarsgard learns of this. Hells, all the Houses will get in a bidding war for the right to execute us.

They were all quiet after that.

Finally, Evans muttered, "This has been the damnedest night. Hope Kurtz is all right."

Mikani hoped so, too, but there must've been casualties. He didn't envy the survivors the task of rebuilding. "I wonder if he found his family."

Evans wore a grave look. "His wife's smart. I'm sure she took the children and hid."

Sometimes that's not enough.

After Miskani ate the stale bread, cold meat, and a wedge of cheese, washed down with a mug of watered ale, he shoved away from the table. There was just no way he could sit still. Hu and Saskia glanced up at him with knowing eyes. He felt as if there was something he should say to her, an apology almost, but the words didn't come. Mikani managed a half smile.

"She's resting," the doctor said. "But you should check on her."

Mikani went up the stairs and knocked on Ritsuko's door. Only a few seconds elapsed before she said, "What is it?"

At least she wasn't asleep.

He slipped into the room and closed the door behind him. The cloying scent of Hu's ointments filled the room. Ritsuko was propped up in bed on a number of pillows, with the blanket pulled over her injured legs. Her expression gave nothing away, so he couldn't tell if she was glad to see him.

I could find out. But I don't want to.

"I'm sorry you were hurt... again." Hesitant and unsure, Mikani shuffled closer while keeping his gift tightly reined in.

"It goes with the territory," she said quietly.

"What, knowing me?"

"Don't be absurd. Come, sit down."

With a frown, he perched at the foot of her bed, clasped his hands, and studied his scarred fingers. Ritsuko reached over and put her hand atop his. That startled him into meeting her gaze, but to his surprise, she didn't seem angry, just... weary.

I can understand that.

"You should be yelling at me. Being berated usually makes me feel better."

As ever, she addressed the distance between them directly. "I won't lie, being left behind hurt. But... what could you have done—middle of the night, drowning storm, elementals prowling? You'd have gotten yourself killed. This way, we both made it. It couldn't have been an easy decision."

"It should have been me down there with you, not Hu."

Her mouth curved in a smile he'd almost call playful. "You wish you could've huddled with me all night on a stony ledge?"

"I'd have found a way to save you, Celeste, if I had to carry you in my arms down the bloody mountain." Mikani stood, paced the three feet to the wall and back to loom over her.

"There was no way down but a long fall. I don't blame you." She reached up to set a hand lightly on his arm. "I don't hold it against you. So it's time to let it go."

Mikani slid in beside her and pulled her to his chest, murmuring into her hair. "Not letting you go ever again."

A shivering breath escaped her, but she didn't resist. Her arms stole around his back, and she put her cheek against him as if listening to his heartbeat. "I knew you were coming, by the way. I never doubted it."

He brushed his lips against the top of her head. "Thanks for trusting me."

Even if I'm not always sure I deserve it.

25

THE NEXT MORNING, Saskia handled preparations for the journey. She expected more opposition, as they'd done a lot of damage in Eldheim, but the House Skarsgard and Magnus overseers were missing or still in hiding. So she had little trouble gathering supplies from grateful miners and soldiers. Finding transportation required more effort.

"How can you not have any horses?" she demanded in frustration. "This is a stable."

"See that hole in the wall? The big stallion kicked his way out when the salamanders started burning things. The rest followed him." By his expression, the livery owner was in no mood to hear about her problems when he'd lost his livelihood.

"Is there anywhere else I can try?"

The man gave her several other addresses, so Saskia trudged to each, one by one. She was still drained from using her familiars so much in such a short time; this was something Loison would normally handle for her, but he was back at the *Gull*, keeping order along with Mr. Ferro and the boatswain. At each stop, she heard the same thing—the horses were either gone or the owner needed them too badly to rent them out for a long-distance journey.

Sighing in discouragement, she headed back toward the inn. *Looks as if we'll be walking. And with the mountain path through Skalbrekka gone, it'll be a long, slow journey down the main trade road.* The air was still heavy with the scent of gunpowder and charred wood, underlaid with a sweeter, herbal scent from the rushes people were burning to drive out any lingering evil spirits. Such superstitions had no effect on elementals, but it didn't stop the townsfolk from trying. *They need to feel in control somehow.*

The repercussions from this trip would be felt for years to come. Saskia didn't know yet how it would impact her business. It might increase demand, but people who lost money on the exchange might cut back all expenditures, curtailing growth. *No point in obsessing over it now.*

The others were out front, regarding her expectantly, when she returned. She didn't know what to tell them. But before she had to break the bad news, Kurtz showed up with a couple of horses and a small cart.

She pushed out a small sigh of relief. "I thought there wasn't an animal to be bought or rented in the whole town."

The miner seemed uncomfortable. "They belong to my brother. It's the least I can do... you saved us. And my family. I... I'm sorry."

She imagined he meant he regretted taking off, leaving them to deal with the dilemma without his aid. Honestly, Saskia didn't blame him. *If I could've fobbed the situation off, I might have run, too. But sometimes there's no one waiting to take over.*

"You did what you had to, man." Irahi smiled at the miner and took the reins. "No one could have asked for more. Go in peace." Kurtz murmured his thanks and rushed off.

Evans stopped by as Saskia supervised the packing. Inspector Ritsuko went into the back of the cart; the other woman was quiet, not that she was ever a chatterbox. But what they'd witnessed the day before was big enough to feel life-changing. She was still grappling with the implications herself.

Putting those thoughts aside, Saskia clambered onto the horse not hitched to the wagon, watching as Janus bade Evans farewell. "Thank you. If there's anything we can do—"

"Just get out of here. You've started something big and ugly with the Houses, mate."

Saskia suspected that was an understatement. Janus and his partner would bear the burden of responsibility for most of the damage even though the problems had already begun before their arrival. The Houses would only see the massive loss of income from sealing off the fire-elemental mining operations—and the fact that agreements with serious consequences had been made without their stamp of approval. She prayed the Council was wise enough to keep to the terms. Otherwise, the consequences would be devastating.

Janus sighed. "True enough."

"Keep your head down and your wits about you when that storm breaks," Evans said.

She nudged her horse closer and smiled at the miner. "It's not the first time we've riled up the Houses, Mr. Evans." *Though I do suspect this* is *the biggest incident.* "Bronze gods keep you, and may Eldheim come back stronger than before."

"From your lips to the gods' ears. Godspeed." Evans waved as Saskia set off along the road, Janus and Irahi following with a snap of reins and a creak of wooden wheels.

She rode through the ruined streets, trying not to let the sorrow she saw in so many faces etch onto her heart. The sound of hammers on stone and people chopping wood filled the air, mingling with voices calling out instructions and greetings. More than a few Skarsgard and Magnus men had joined the reconstruction efforts, even if the overseers were absent. She noticed that they stayed clear of the shattered remains of the administration building.

Let the ruins stand as a reminder of what we're giving up to survive. Evans is right: we might have saved lives, but the Houses will want blood for the loss of the mines.

Fear percolated through her. The Houses had the power to tear down everything her family had built. With enough money came indisputable power. They could rush punitive measures through or impose taxes so severe that her company would collapse beneath their weight. With some effort, she stilled her racing thoughts, and whispered to her ever-present familiars, who sensed her unease and responded in kind by whipping the wind around her.

"I'm fine," she murmured in reassurance.

Her air spirits didn't seem to share the outrage with those taken from the mines. *Does that mean our line honored the old ways, performed some ritual asking permission and formally creating a permanent bond?* Before now, it was a question she'd never thought to ask. The elementals served her family, much as this horse carried her farther from Eldheim. *Just how smart are my sylphs anyway?* The matter merited investigation.

A few minutes later, they passed the craggers' dwindling encampment. Most had already struck their tents and cooking fires and were making their way farther up the mountain. By the terms of their new agreement with the Salamander Lord, Kaeheld's host would remain on the slopes of Mount Surtir as guardians of the elemental's volcano—*stewards to the Dragon kin's lair.* Kaeheld stood alone on a small rise by the side of the road. She raised a hand in farewell, but he remained motionless, watching them as they rode out of sight.

The first stage of the journey passed in near silence, apart from Janus asking his partner ten times if she needed anything. It was hard to credit how different things had been the day before, guns booming and houses afire. Four hours into the ride, they paused for a meal.

"You're unhappy, Li'l White." Irahi ambled up as she

reined her mount, his head coming up to her shoulder even on horseback. He set his hand on her arm, and she laid her free hand over his and traced the scar that ran from his thumb to wrist.

"You stopped a blade meant for me. That damned Aevar mercenary looked surprised when you punched him while his sword was still dangling from your hand." She wrapped her fingers around his thumb and index and squeezed gently.

She slid down, tethering the horse beside the other one at the wagon.

"I remember. And you're evading a real answer as well as you did that sword." She felt her cheeks heat. He chuckled, glancing over at the wagon paused five yards behind them. She followed his gaze. Janus wore several days of stubble, giving him a piratical look, and his hair didn't look as if he'd combed it in even longer. Like everyone, his attire was the worse for the wear, though even on the best of days, Janus tended to be rumpled.

He looks like death warmed over. I heard him pacing all night, but he wouldn't leave her side. It reminds me of us, so long ago... but it's different, too. I never saw him so at ease. There was something that made him dig in, even when Inspector Ritsuko was trying to shoo him away.

"Honestly," the other woman said, her voice carrying, "if you don't stop hovering, I won't do any paperwork for a month. *You* can explain all of this. In triplicate. In writing."

Saskia didn't know if all women were this way, but as she watched them, she wondered what was lacking in her—that she couldn't evoke the same response from him. At one point, she'd loved him desperately, and even now, the feeling lingered in a lonely echo. *There's no going back, but—*

"That's well past and done, Li'l White." Irahi squeezed her fingers gently, breaking her train of thought and drawing her attention. His thick brows were furrowed with concern. It was beyond her to think of a time when he *hadn't* been there.

"I know. I knew the first time I saw them together. But hope makes fools of us all."

The late-morning light made his hazel eyes blaze gold. She managed a smile, releasing his hand to run her fingers along his smooth-shaven jaw and up into his dark hair, newly and neatly retied into a thick topknot. The move surprised him, but that wasn't all. His eyelids flickered, and his broad chest swelled in a sudden breath. Her old friend was quiet as she struggled to make sense of his reaction: that flare of his nostrils and the pain in his furrowed brow when he registered her words.

When he answered, his voice was soft. "I know that all too well, Alexandra Braelan."

She bit her bottom lip at the wistful note in his words. She looked over at him—truly *looked at him*, for the first time in years. There were hints of gray in his long hair; when they had first met, his leonine mane had been dark as starless night. His broad shoulders strained the thin leather of his simple tunic; he'd become thicker with age but not soft. The doctor's bag he'd scavenged in Eldheim swung in counterpoint to the battered scabbard of his heavy cutlass—she was surprised that he'd managed to hang on to that in the chaos of the last few days, but on further reflection she remembered that he never let go of what was important to him.

Family, friends. Me. Bronze gods, we've quite literally been to hell and back now, Irahi Hu. In all their long years together, she'd never been quite so aware of his strength and quiet determination.

But then, we've spent far more time smuggling than fighting dragons. That sort of thing tends to change us, and how we view the world... and each other.

"You're staring, Li'l White."

"Just making sure you don't fall off the side of the mountain again." She pulled up her white scarf to try to hide the flush of her cheeks.

Why did you never tell me?

But deep down, she knew. First, it was her devotion to the company and later, her entanglement with Janus. *How difficult it must've been to hold your silence all of these years. To watch me stumble, oblivious.* Saskia didn't know exactly how she felt, but warmth swept over her. *Every woman should be loved like this, quietly and infinitely, a wheel without end.*

Suddenly, her eyes stung for all of the wasted years and the lost opportunities. Before she could think better of it, she rose up on her tiptoes and cupped his face in her hands. His eyes were dark, solemn, and slightly puzzled. She answered the silent question he was asking by kissing him. Irahi responded as if he needed her to live.

When she broke free, she was dizzy, elated, confused, stunned into silence.

"We'll be taking a break," the doctor called. "I've been waiting for this moment for almost twenty years. I'm not waiting a minute more."

Then he swept her up into his arms and strode toward a cluster of trees. Over his broad shoulder, Saskia glimpsed two startled faces and tipped her head back in silent laughter.

26

To say Ritsuko was surprised would be an understatement.

She watched the doctor stride over the rise and out of sight, but she was smiling as she did so. It was good to see him getting what he wanted, knowing how long he had been in love with Miss Braelan. Of course, that left Mikani and herself stalled beside the worn footpath that served as a road. The horses didn't seem to mind the break, grazing placidly beside the cart.

"Be honest," she said to Mikani. "Did you see that coming?"

He frowned, looking down the road where Irahi had carried Miss Braelan. "I never thought he'd get drunk enough to try. Let alone do it sober." He shook his head and turned back to her. "So, no."

Ritsuko hesitated. His expression seemed troubled, though her truth-sense indicated he'd answered honestly. "Are you all right?"

That was, possibly, a laughable question, given that she was wearing a robe borrowed from the landlord's wife. The burns didn't permit her to wear normal clothing yet, and the pain was a constant blaze on her skin. At first glance, anyone comparing the two of them would say that Mikani was in far better shape. He just had the normal scrapes and bruises.

Looks like business as usual for him.

He looked back toward the hill. "I'm happy for Hu, I think. Saskia's a handful, but she'll be good for him. And bronze gods know, he'll be good for her." Mikani patted the horse's flank, finally turning back to her. He smiled faintly. "To answer your question, yes. I believe I am."

The note was fainter this time, but not discordant; though she was still learning the nuances of her gift, she felt relatively certain that he was being mostly truthful. Ritsuko pondered the implications. *Does that mean part of him is sorry it didn't work out between them?* There seemed to be a thousand unspoken questions hanging in the air between them, but she lacked the courage to pluck one of them down and learn the answer.

So instead, she said, "Well, it seems we're having a rest. We should enjoy lunch as I'm sure we'll be traveling late tonight to make up for it."

"We could always spend some time admiring the view and taking the scenic route. But I'm bloody tired of this mountain." He tethered the horses to a low-hanging branch and rummaged in the saddlebags of Miss Braelan's horse for bread and cheese. "And the sooner we get to Northport and let them know what happened, the sooner that someone can start sorting out the mess. Hopefully, without us." He ambled toward her, juggling three bundles and a bottle of white wine.

"*Everything* may be without us. I suspect we could end up on the penal farms for this." She didn't like to consider the consequences, but it was hard not to imagine everything she'd worked toward burning to ash before her eyes.

Mikani unwrapped some rye bread and broke off a piece; he offered it with a hunk of cheese. She fiddled with the two, pressing the white into dark and spreading it with her fingers. That was a nervous habit, one she wasn't sure if he'd registered. At last, she took a bite, hearing all sorts of things in his silence.

Finally, he spoke as he uncorked the wine. "Well, the northern farms aren't horrible. It had to be done, partner. All of it. And I'm hoping *someone* on the Council has wit enough to see that." She didn't need the discordant chime to know he was lying. "And if they're not, we'll find a way. Hells and Winter, Ritsuko. We've survived meetings with ancient Ferishers, an army of raiders, and a dragon. What's a bunch of angry nobles after all that?"

"They're the ones with all the power. After this, I'm afraid we can't simply return to work. How can they allow it?"

He offered her the wine. Ritsuko pulled directly from the bottle, reckoning it was better to numb the dread. Never in her life had she known this exact combination of fear, exhaustion, and foreboding. There were so many potential snarls and complications, so few people she felt they could trust. *Will Gunwood have our backs after this?* The risks were especially great for her, as her promotion hadn't been a popular decision.

Mikani reached out and took her hand. His callused fingers squeezed hers. "I don't know what will happen, Ritsuko. Bronze gods, I barely know what I'll be doing when I wake up each morning. We saved a lot of lives. I have to believe that will count for something, with someone. Otherwise, what the hells have we been working for the last few years?" He took the bottle with his free hand, not breaking eye contact as he took a deep swallow. "Besides, if any of them tries to lay a hand on you, I'll shoot them."

Truth.

She was surprised into silence. He wasn't usually so... earnest. There was no levity in his expression, none of his customary insouciance. She didn't know how to handle this Mikani. Ritsuko studied the shape of his fingers wrapped around hers, listening to the increased thump of her own heart. His knuckles were scarred from countless fights; she'd watched him thump walls in frustration and anger, but years ago, she'd never imagined that he could make her feel this way with the touch of his hand.

It wasn't a decision she made as much as an irresistible impulse. She traced the ridges of his knuckles, valleys between his fingers, and back up to the tips. He was a topography of unspeakable beauty and mystery, and it was awful to feel such a wicked twist of longing when she'd watched his love affairs catch fire, time and again.

Not him. Why does it have to be him?

Her voice was husky when she replied. "I'm not sure shooting people would solve any of our problems."

Not what she wanted to say—it was what came out. But she didn't pull her hand back.

Mikani set the bottle carefully down next to her. He was close enough that she felt his warmth against her side; he frowned at her bandaged legs. She suspected he felt responsible for those injuries, though she'd suffered them of her own volition.

He spoke in a low voice, pauses making it seem as if he weighed every word. "I know. I could mow them all down, and it wouldn't matter. But I won't just stand by, Ritsuko... Celeste." He met her gaze once more with shadowed blue eyes that held more than a hint of the vicious streak she knew all too well. "I have no idea how, but we *will* be all right. We saved the bloody Architect's daughter. If we hadn't stopped that madman, every city and town in Hy Breasil would have fared worse than Eldheim by now. They *owe* us, and I'll be damned if we will let them forget it."

Ritsuko slipped her hand from his and laid it on his chest, feeling how his heart thundered. He tensed at her touch, though she wasn't sure why. She wished she could be as certain as he was; his fierce conviction was almost sufficient to quell her anxiety. *He needs me to believe that we'll be fine.*

Bronze gods, I want to. She was a realist, but she trusted him enough to permit the reassurance.

"Things will work out, one way or another."

Mikani let out a long breath as he relaxed under her palm. His face was tired and impossibly dear, new lines etched beside eyes and mouth. The quick washup at the inn hadn't altered his perpetually scruffy appearance, though she didn't look much better. Ritsuko couldn't remember the last time she'd had her hair cut. It must be a shaggy mop by now.

He set his hand over hers, trapping it against his chest. "I'm sorry. I get carried away. This *should* be the easy part, heading home to a hero's welcome after defeating the monsters."

"That part troubles me," she said softly. "Who are the monsters in this scenario? The elementals, for burning our homes, or us, for using them without their consent?"

"There are no innocents in this mess, partner. Our ignorance is no excuse for their enslavement; the massacre the elementals wanted is hardly any better, though."

She nodded, comforted by the steady thump of his heart. Probably she should move her hand away, but for once, she couldn't make herself do the smart, prudent thing. Ritsuko wished she could be as brave as Irahi; she'd lived her life defined by rules and boundaries, working as hard as she could. It was somewhat astonishing to realize that sometimes, making all the right choices might not matter.

Quietly aching, Ritsuko slipped her hand out from under Mikani's and pressed her palm to his cheek, reveling in the prickle of his whiskers. "If we're not fired, it's quite likely they'll separate us. I'll be demoted and reassigned. What will you do without me?"

* * *

What would I do without her? Hells and Winter… I have no idea.

He leaned into her touch instinctively. Her fingers were warm and soft against his jaw; he slowly rubbed against her hand, seeking the contact. Her thumb skimmed downward, over his cheek, toward his jaw, narrowly missing his mouth. *I'm having a hard time even drawing away; I can't begin to imagine life without her.*

Somehow, he managed to reply, "I don't think Gunwood'll be too keen to keep me on without you. Hells, he's been looking for an excuse to get rid of me for years. I may well give him an early holiday present and walk out."

The thought of leaving the CID had never seriously crossed his mind, despite Gunwood's constant threats and complaints. *Until now. With Ritsuko gone, I'm sure I'd end up back at the docks or worse, in no time.* Over the years, she'd become his trusted partner, able to shield him from the repercussions of using his gift. Now, though, he couldn't think of the right word for her. "Partner" no longer seemed deep or wide enough.

"Somehow, I doubt the choice will be left up to you. I'm debating just how severe our punishment will be." With a faint sigh, Ritsuko shook her head. "But there's no point in speculating. Let's talk about something else."

It was hard to step away from her touch, more difficult than it should've been.

Careful to not jostle her legs, he hopped onto the cart next to her, the bottle of wine between them. "Agreed. We'll have plenty of time to fret once we're back home. How's Higgins? I don't remember seeing him around headquarters recently." He was the man who worked in the morgue and paid altogether too much attention to Ritsuko.

Ritsuko raised a brow at him. "That's an extremely odd question, Mikani."

He met her gaze. "Is it? It was the first thing that came to mind."

Her expression seemed to be a mix of two emotions,

bewilderment and curiosity. "Then... he's well, so far as I know. I believe he requested some personal time to take care of his ailing mother. I pop around now and then to bring pastries. She's fond of apple tarts."

He was genuinely puzzled. The complexities of social interaction had never been of interest to him; the ability to sense the underlying emotions and little lies in everyday exchanges made it difficult to keep up the pretense properly. *It's part of why I became an inspector; I get paid to find out the truth, not to play nice.*

"You visit his mother? You're quite... surprising, sometimes, partner."

"In what way?"

"I just didn't think you knew them that well."

She aimed a sly little smile his way. "I see. I also read to orphaned children on Sundays. Did you know that?"

"No. Wait, really?"

"No. But you should see your expression. It's priceless."

"When I first met you, I didn't think you had any sense of humor at all."

"And I thought you were an obnoxious dullard."

"I hope I've improved upon acquaintance, to just obnoxious."

The amusement faded from her brown eyes, leaving a steady, if slightly unnerving regard. Mikani had the feeling she could see straight through him. *Actually she can, what with the truth-sense and all.* But she'd always been better at reading his moods than most.

"There's no one I care about more in the world," she said softly.

The weight of her sincerity caught him off guard; he took another drink of wine in a bid for time as words failed him. *The feeling's mutual, Celeste. What do I say? How do I say it?* Their relationship had grown complicated and fraught, no longer as simple as it once was but even more important for the knots and tangles.

If I thought there was a chance—

"You're quiet. Was that too much?"

"No. It's just... I'm not good. With the talking. At least, about this." That seemed to work, as she could decide what he meant by "this." And he was ever aware that if he spoken in evasions or half-truths, she'd know.

I don't want to hurt her.

"I didn't mean to make you uncomfortable." Her tone was apologetic. "But maybe that's part of why I'm always hearing stories about women who left, hm?"

He considered that for a moment. "They get tired of giving, yes. Sharing parts of themselves and their feelings." He waved a hand in front of his face. "When they're being honest, when they share the truth? The emotion seeps through the words. I have to shut them out, so I don't feel like I'm prying beyond what they want to share. And when they lie? That stays with me." He frowned. *Bloody hell; I've never tried to explain this. I'm not sure that I can.* "At the best of times, I'm keeping a tight rein on myself, Ritsuko. Not just my gift, everything. It's what kept me sane, yes? It's... difficult... to let that slip."

"Not quite what I expected. But... understandable. And it's a bit of a question, isn't it? How anyone could ever love someone who knows when you lie." She tipped her head forward so that her hair veiled the curve of her cheek; only the tip of her nose and chin were visible.

The realization was quick. *Hells.* He reached out, a fingertip to her chin, tilting her face up gently so he could seek her eyes.

"You need to really trust someone. Or it all goes to pieces with the first word."

"I've been listening to the same half-truths and social lies for a while now. No emotions, but the minute and infinite deceptions are enough. I know that Gunwood lies when he says he's pleased with his decision to promote me. I know that the man who sells me my tea wishes I hadn't left the Mountain District."

"Well. For what it may be worth, I'm glad you got promoted and stuck with me. And if you'd not left the Mountain District, I would never have had the chance to know you. Their lies don't make them right, and you know that."

"But each one is a little cut I didn't feel before. I understand why you've isolated yourself, at least to some degree. I'm tempted to find some remote location and become a scholar of obscure lore, so I don't have to talk to people."

"I'd tell you it gets easier, but it really doesn't." He offered her the bottle.

She took several pulls from it, head tilted back to examine the blue sky overhead. It was past noon, so the sun was high, playing peekaboo through some gauzy clouds. The altitude kept them cool even with the brightness. Part of that came from the Winter Isle as well. He watched her, trying to decide if he'd ever known a woman's face so well. He could probably draw her from memory, all the little dips and curves, the birthmark on her forearm. At the moment, she hardly resembled the precise perfectionist he'd been partnered with years before, but the changes were more than superficial. The past months had altered them both.

"I find something to believe in. If you're lucky, you meet a few people… and you'd rather have them be brutally honest than hear polite lies from anyone else." He paused. "Of course, it took me a while to realize that. And I took some rather uncomfortable turns along the way."

"I don't think I'd be very good at drinking and brooding. I suspect I could manage as a bitter recluse, however."

While he watched, she ate the rest of her tortured bread and cheese, more mechanically than with any real enjoyment. He could see that she was troubled, possibly still worried about the job or her future. Mikani was once more tempted to read her. He had been repressing that urge more often of late, but he didn't have the right to impose in that way—and with her least of all.

"I would much appreciate it if you held off on your impulse to become a hermit. We're quite the pair, Celeste Ritsuko. I'd be well and truly lost without you."

She smiled at him, then she did the most astonishing thing. Ritsuko leaned over and kissed his cheek. "Don't worry. I'll take you with me."

Mikani started, lifting a hand to where her lips had brushed his cheek. Before he could come up with a response, though, Hu's deep laughter rolled over them, followed by Saskia's voice, getting closer. *They sound... pleased with themselves.*

"Are you two ready to get moving?" Hu called.

Turning, he saw that they were walking hand in hand. Saskia was smiling, a sweet but wistful light in her eyes. Mikani sensed her reservations, strong enough to penetrate without him trying to pick them up. *She knows she'll always have that wanderlust. And someday, Hu will want to take her to the Seven Sisters to stay. But I hope they're happy until then.*

Nearby, Ritsuko wriggled toward the back of the cart. It was a reflex to help her, settling his partner for travel before responding to the others.

"More than," he answered, loud enough to carry. "I've had enough of Mount Surtir."

27

NORTHPORT WAS A welcome sight after five long days on the road. Ritsuko found it taxing to be so limited in what she was permitted to do, and she was tired of jolting in the cart. So when they approached from the low hills to the west, she was glad to recognize the buildings clustered on the coast. This trip had gone relatively smooth—no elemental attacks, no craggers—but the distance between inns seemed to increase by the day.

Mikani pointed at a train, motionless on the tracks a couple of miles from the city. The heavy engine, marked with the prominent crest of House Skarsgard in flaking paint, had split along the riveted seams. The flat cars lined up neatly behind it were piled up with the remains of steam cars and smaller engines; they were all ruptured and thrashed into heaps of barely recognizable iron and brass. Ritsuko could only hope that the conductor had been able to get away before the bound elemental had finally burst its bonds in a blast of superheated steam and flying metal debris.

"It looks like they've been busy. I can't hear any explosions, at least." He motioned farther along the track, where she saw at least three more debris-laden trains stretching back to the city proper.

"That's good. I'd rather not fight today," Ritsuko answered.

"Me either," Irahi added.

Miss Braelan looked tired as well, and the horses were in no better shape. If they'd had more mounts, they might have been able to speed their journey. As it was, slow and careful had ruled the day. So she was glad things seemed to have settled in Northport, though they couldn't be sure how bad it was until they actually entered the town proper.

The streets showed signs of fire and shattered windows. Some of the walls bore marks of gunfire; but on the whole, whatever chaos had been unleashed in Northport seemed to have been contained. People went about their business, sweeping and cleaning up. The faint aroma of fresh-baked bread wafted to Ritsuko, and she could not help a smile at the small sign of normalcy. A few of the townsfolk waved as they rode past. A woman came up to Mikani and pushed a small basket into his hands before heading back to her store. He gave Ritsuko a puzzled look when he peered inside the basket to find some sweet rolls and fruit.

They must think we are refugees. And to look at us, I cannot say I blame them.

"I was expecting worse. We must have stopped the worst of it before hell rained down on the city." Mikani took a bite from an apple and offered her the rest of the basket.

She chose a cake, as it had been days since they'd had anything besides dry meat or stale bread. Mikani drove the cart through the city to the docks. Evidence of the fighting was stronger here. A number of half-submerged steamers dotted the harbor; the water wasn't deep enough to swallow the vast frames, so the waves rose and fell against broken hulls as if the ships were part of some rusted reef. Surviving vessels had cannons out, even in dock. She saw holes in buildings that could only have come from a barrage. Some piers were damaged or charred in places.

Worried, she scanned for the *Gull* and found it relatively unscathed. The hull had been obviously repaired, and the sails were patched, but to her inexperienced eyes, the vessel seemed seaworthy. Ritsuko waved away assistance in hopping down from her perch on the cart; her skin felt dry and tight, but the pain wasn't as bad as it had been. Ritsuko felt self-conscious in her robe, which must smell dreadful by now.

Since the crew had no warning of their arrival, there was no welcoming party, and they made their way aboard without fanfare. Sailors were busy scrubbing at burn marks and sanding spots where new wood had been hammered over old. The *Gull* needed a proper refinishing to gleam like it did the first Ritsuko saw it. But she was relieved that it hadn't ended up at the bottom of the sea.

As soon as the boatswain spotted them, she hurried over, a wide smile softening her hard features. "I'm glad to see you made it back," Miss Oliver said.

"How did you fare?" Miss Braelan asked.

Mr. Ferro broke from supervising a group of crewmen reinforcing the mainmast. "Now that's a story. Why don't you freshen up, and I'll have cook put a meal together. Then we'll talk."

It was doubtless a testament to the ordeal, but even the first mate sounded less taciturn, warmer to Ritsuko's ears.

Miss Braelan nodded. "That sounds good. I was starting to feel as if I were growing into the back of that horse."

"Speaking of the animals," Mr. Loison said. "What would you like me to do with them?"

"Hire a local to return them to Eldheim. It was kind of Mr. Kurtz to let us borrow them, but I'm sure his brother can use them back." Miss Braelan smiled fleetingly, touched Irahi on the arm, then headed for her cabin.

"We need to see to those burns, Celeste. At least change

the bandages." The doctor took her arm gently, guiding her to the *Gull*'s infirmary.

Mikani stayed a couple of steps behind her. "I can help."

"Go wash up. The point of the infirmary's that it's clean." Irahi grinned at her partner; Mikani scowled. "I promise she'll be fine. You can see her at dinner."

Ritsuko held his gaze, aiming for a reassuring look. Eventually, he nodded and headed for his cabin with a mutter. "Bloody doctors."

Her legs looked simultaneously better and worse. The scars were tight and ugly, red, but the skin was starting to heal, which meant there was a light, thin layer growing over the burns. It gave her calves a peculiar, lizardly look. She winced as Irahi washed them, patted them dry, then applied some ointment from his store of medicines.

"Did I hurt you? I might have a topical analgesic—"

"No, it's fine. It looks worse than it is."

"That's not true." He commended her stoicism, but Ritsuko really wanted him to finish the treatment so she could have a bath, too. And Irahi must've sensed her impatience because he wrapped her legs efficiently. "There, that's done it."

"Thank you. I'll see you in the captain's quarters?"

"Indeed. As if you weren't tired of my company by now."

"Not that. I'm just rather grubby."

Before he carried Miss Braelan off, he would've said something charming about her appearance, but today, he only smiled as she excused herself from the infirmary. In her cabin, she found a ewer of water, a pot of soap, and a clean cloth. Ritsuko made good use of them, tidied her hair, then changed into clean trousers, cut wide enough not to bother her legs. Shoes were a problem, however, as her boots had been destroyed, and Mikani had been carrying her as if she had no feet at all. Sighing, she donned a pair of stockings, folding them down above her heels, so they didn't touch the bandages. Then she went to join the others.

Miss Braelan sat at the head of the table, sipping a glass of white wine. She had washed and changed so she seemed much as she had at the beginning of their journey. When she looked at the doctor, she looked better, if anything—but Ritsuko noticed a lingering shadow in her eyes. Irahi was smiling, chatting with Miss Oliver and the first mate. The cabin boy stood ready to serve, but Sam nodded at her when she stepped in and took her seat.

Ritsuko was about to ask after Mikani when he stepped in. He'd washed but not shaved. His hair was slicked back and sleeves rolled up to show some fresh scars she'd not noticed earlier. He sat next to her with a grin, exchanging perfunctory greetings with the others.

He was wearing his bowler hat.

Mr. Loison cleared his throat, and more than one of them started in surprise. He had been quietly standing in the corner behind Miss Braelan. "It is good to have you all back. During your absence, repairs to the ship were completed to satisfaction. We have replenished our store of supplies and are quite ready to head for home, Mistress."

"Thank you, Loison." Miss Braelan reached up to squeeze the clerk's arm; he seemed surprised. She turned back to her first mate. "Mr. Ferro?"

"The agreement with the Free Traders and House Magnus held. There was some trouble last week, but things settled the last few days. Lost three more men. It'll be a tight run, but we can make it." He handed the captain a couple of sheets of paper; Miss Braelan's lips had pressed to a thin line at the mention of more losses, but she offered Mr. Ferro a smile with her thanks.

"We'll see to their families. We've all lost far too much on this trip… but their sacrifice was not in vain."

Ritsuko settled in to listen to the rest of the news—and to eat a proper meal. *After all, I'll need my strength. We still have to report to the Major General.*

* * *

Once the shoes arrived from the cobbler, Ritsuko was ready to set out. Mikani waited for her to finish getting dressed, then they went on deck.

"You're sure we can't come with you?" Saskia asked. The doctor stood beside her, frowning. Saskia and Hu weren't pleased at being left behind.

"No, it's best this way."

Sorry, I know we've come a long way together.

In the end, they saw the wisdom in preparing the *Gull* for immediate departure. If Thorgrim reacted as he feared she would, he and Ritsuko might end up in irons or worse, and they'd need friends on the outside. *The Houses are too fond of making problems disappear. We've found more than our share of those "problems" floating in the river back home.*

Mikani checked his sidearm for the third time and nodded to Ritsuko. He led the way along the docks and warehouse district toward the Major General's palace, trusting Ritsuko to keep up. She was walking much better; he had full confidence that she'd make a full recovery between Hu's skills and her innate courage. He knew he could trust her at his back, so he scanned the side streets while they moved. He could see a checkpoint a half dozen blocks up a main avenue: soldiers flying Magnus colors, probably guarding a nobleman's warehouse or shipping concern. As they climbed up the hills toward the palace, he saw another Magnus and two Skarsgard checkpoints. Thorgrim squadrons patrolled the near side of the streets and down to the edge of the docks.

Like wolves. Watching their territory. The common citizens ignored the soldiers for the most part, talking and shouting. Going on with their lives, or doing their best to.

"You'd never guess that we were moments away from a fiery apocalypse." Mikani spoke at Ritsuko as she caught up with him.

"It's obvious in their faces. In their voices, too." She tilted her head at a group of women, chattering nearby. "They're a little too loud, lingering a little too long. Normally, they'd speak a few words and go about their business, you see? There's work to be done. But watch how they stand in clusters. They're afraid to go home, afraid it'll start all over again, and they'll be alone."

Mikani studied them for a few seconds, loosening his hold on his gift to taste the air properly. "I see what you mean."

He also saw the shadows she'd mentioned, both beneath the women's eyes, which spoke of sleepless nights, and the skittish dart of their eyes as they watched other people on the street. It would take time for the people of Northport to forget what almost happened here.

Thoughtful, he strode on toward the Major General's palace. As he came up to the main gates, the largest of three guards stepped forward and signaled for them to stop. "State your business, please."

"Inspectors Ritsuko and Mikani. On Council business with the Major General. I'll wager she's expecting us."

With a frown, the sergeant motioned for one of his men to run up to the main building, and he turned back to glare at Mikani. They waited five minutes or so before a runner dashed down to guide them to Lady Thorgrim.

"I'm nervous," Ritsuko whispered.

He knew that already, not from reading her but from the way she twisted her fingers as they walked. The Major General's complex had come through unscathed. There were more servants and guards moving through the corridors than last time; as the troubles outside had simmered down to a tense standoff between the three Houses, she must have pulled her men back home. No one challenged their passage, though a few gave them curious looks.

Lady Maire waited for them in her study. She sat behind an ancient desk, cluttered with piles of reports and maps.

She did not rise when they entered but offered a wan smile that seemed sincere. She had dark circles under her eyes, and a few strands of dark hair had escaped their bonds to frame her round face.

"Inspectors. Since my city's not burned to the ground and our steam engines have stopped trying to kill my citizens, I must assume that you were successful in closing that portal."

Mikani exchanged a look with Ritsuko. The Major General noticed the hesitation and rose, coming around her desk.

"We managed to put an end to the fire-elemental rampages, Lady Thorgrim."

"So I noticed. But the mirrors are still dead and there is not a wind crystal left unshattered in Northport, if not the whole Winter Isle. It may be best if you told me exactly what happened. Spare no detail, please; I'm *very* interested in hearing this story."

"Are the chalices still working?" Ritsuko asked. Water elementals bound to crystal cups, the ice chalices were the primary means of medical attention for serious injuries. Healers were reputed to treat their bound elementals with the same respect and care as weather witches did their familiars—once an eccentricity, now a godsend.

The Major General nodded. "If they weren't, there'd be a lot more families in mourning today. And several golems helped in putting out fires and stopping the rampaging fire elementals that broke free from their spheres during the worst of the troubles."

"That *is* good news," Ritsuko said.

"Make yourselves comfortable," Lady Thorgrim said. "Shall I ring for refreshments?"

Mikani took a seat in an ornate chair that looked better than it sat, with carved arms and thin brocade upholstery while Ritsuko sat nearby on a small settee. The Major General turned to the young man who had guided them into the room and spoke in a low tone. He guessed she was asking for a tray of tea and sandwiches, polite but unnecessary. Once the staff footman left, Lady Thorgrim folded her hands and regarded them expectantly.

"I perceive from your hesitation that you have bad news. I'd rather have it straight."

Ritsuko's silence told Mikani that she meant to let him do the talking. *Are you sure that's wise?* Nonetheless, he laid out what had happened, sparing no detail of what had gone on in Eldheim. By the time he finished, the older woman wore a look of comical shock. Before she could respond, however, a light tap on the door interrupted the proceedings.

At her quiet call of permission, the servant brought a silver salver laid with a variety of finger sandwiches and small cakes, along with a formal tea service. It seemed like excessive hospitality for the reception of two public servants, but Ritsuko took a cream cake, probably to show appreciation for the woman's generosity. She was prone to attending to the niceties.

Once the door closed behind him again, the Major General pushed to her feet, pacing to the window and back again. She wore a ferocious frown. "I can hardly credit it."

"I assure you," Ritsuko put in. "Everything Inspector Mikani has relayed is the truth."

"I'm sure it comes as no surprise, but... the two of you have grievously overstepped your authority. Some might even name what you've done treason, actively working to topple the great Houses, particularly Skarsgard. And my own, of course."

Mikani caught a glimpse of a frown from Ritsuko. He loosed his senses enough to take her measure. Under the circumstances, he didn't think she'd mind. She was deeply troubled. In doing so, he also read the Major General, and she was hiding her true emotional state beneath a calm facade; the older woman boiled with barely suppressed excitement. Abruptly, he had the sense of unseen currents hidden beneath a thin layer of ice.

"Do you feel we're guilty of treason?" Ritsuko asked. "Have we harmed your house?"

"No, my dear. You did what you thought best."

"So you're not arresting us?" Mikani was surprised, but it seemed as if the woman had already dismissed them from her mind, as if she had more pressing business.

Bronze gods if I know what. Something about this smells off.

"Definitely not. That would be exceedingly ungrateful. Unfortunately, I lack the political power to protect you from the storm that will surely sweep you up." She gestured at the town, and the sea beyond, tinged red by the approaching evening. "House Skarsgard will demand your blood for destroying the mines. House Magnus will recover... earth elementals are easier to find, and apparently more willing to work with humans." She turned toward them. "My House, Thorgrim... we'll be hit hard. But I am honor-bound to let you go. You saved Northport from the raging salamanders... and from a fleet of cragger savages, according to your story and Lord Magnus's scouts. You will need friends when everyone realizes that steam engines are gone for good, and you're to blame. Perhaps you have some allies elsewhere?"

"Yes," Ritsuko said.

She put down her untouched cream cake. "If that's all, my lady, we should return to Dorstaad to make our report there as well."

"I don't envy you that task. But thank you for everything you've done." The Major General moved to the door and opened it with an air of abstraction.

This isn't the reaction I expected at all.

Mikani didn't say a word until they left Lady Thorgrim's property, then he and Ritsuko both began speaking at once. "That was—"

"She was lying."

"About what?" Mikani asked, quickening his pace. He

had the feeling they needed to get away before the woman changed her mind.

"Everything. I don't know what to make of it, but she seemed *pleased* by the damage we've done to the Houses, albeit unintentionally."

"But she's Thorgrim," Mikani said, frowning. "Without the mines, they'll lose prestige and income, almost as much as Skarsgard."

Ritsuko glanced over her shoulder. "It doesn't ring true. She's letting us go for her own reasons. I just don't know what they are."

"Me either. But it makes me nervous."

His partner nodded, and Mikani hoped they'd be clear of Northport before Lady Thorgrim's scheming caught up with them.

28

THE *GULL* SHOWED signs of readiness when Ritsuko examined it down the length of the pocked pier. She picked a careful path around the holes in the wood. Close-up, she smelled the remnants of burned wood. *We're lucky the whole thing didn't collapse.* She hurried up the gangplank to find Irahi and Miss Braelan waiting on deck.

"How did it go?" the other woman asked.

"Eerily well."

Miss Braelan nodded. "I must admit, I was expecting to have to mount a rescue to pull you and Janus out of the Major General's dungeons."

"You were looking forward to it, you mean." Mikani smirked as he stepped off the gangplank and onto the *Gull*'s deck.

Miss Braelan lifted a shoulder, but she wore a smile that suggested Mikani might have a point. "Well, this is certainly easier. We'll set sail at dawn. I'm sure we're all eager to put Northport behind us."

"I don't like this," Ritsuko said.

"We were due a break." Mikani did not sound fully certain, though. "All the same, let's knock on wood and get back home before our luck turns."

She nodded. “If you don’t mind, I’ll retire for a rest.”

Though she didn’t let on, healing was exhausting work. The others murmured their assent, and she headed to her cabin. Ritsuko lay down on her bunk, but she took a notebook with her, where she documented everything that had happened since they left Dorstaad. *I’ve been slacking. How can I be expected to remember everything?* Once she had a record of recent events, she set aside the pen and paper and closed her eyes.

She didn’t mean to sleep so long, but when she opened them again, her head felt thick and achy, as if she’d been out for hours. *I’m surprised nobody came to check on me.* After sliding off her bunk, she put on her shoes, combed her hair, and stepped into the hall, where she followed the sound of voices, punctuated by the occasional burst of laughter, to Miss Braelan’s cabin. *It must be dinnertime.*

Her stomach gave a growl, reminding her that she hadn’t even eaten that cream cake at the Major General’s. She hesitated over the etiquette; technically, she hadn’t been invited. So her hand fell away from the door and she wheeled in the narrow corridor, instead making her way to the galley. The cook seemed surprised to see her.

“Can I help you, miss?”

“I was hoping you had something left?”

“Of course! You could’ve sent Sam for a bite.”

She suspected he was serving in Miss Braelan’s quarters, and she hadn’t spent enough time on the ship to be sure of proper decorum. “It was no bother to come myself.”

Smiling, the grizzled sailor fixed her a plate of poached fish and vegetables, simple fare, but impressive for being cooked on a ship. She took the tin dish up to the deck for some air, where she leaned on the railing and gazed across the water to the flickering lights of Northport. *In the morning, we put all of this behind us.*

A soft sound caught her attention. It sounded like low

voices, and she was about to dismiss them as dockworkers out late when she realized they were coming from the side of the ship away from the pier. She scanned the dark waters for a moment until she spotted a darker shadow bobbing up and down on the waves.

That's odd. I would think they'd light a lantern. They could smash on any of the wrecks, or even a ship.

The faint splash pulled her attention back to the *Gull*; a longboat pulled up to the clipper with the scrape of wood on wood. Ritsuko did not need to see the men clambering up along the side of the ship to know they were not meant to be there. Heart racing, she ran to the bell meant to alert the ship to the possibility of invaders and yanked on the rope with all her might. The resulting clamor echoed over the deck. Sailors came in response to the alarm, and the boarders scrambled up faster, vaulting on deck while unsheathing weapons. The *Gull*'s crew grabbed what weapons they could reach—poles, clubs, and hatchets meant to cut rigging in an emergency.

The raiders were dressed in dirty, ragged clothes. Their weapons looked new and well cared for, though; Ritsuko had a close look when one of them swung at her and she barely avoided the blow. She darted around the mainmast, but the brigand froze when he got a good look at her features.

Then he swore, his expression ripening to murderous intent. "Got one!"

He advanced on her as she scrambled back, seeking a weapon of her own.

They're looking for someone particular? For me*? Who are they? What do they want?*

She spun and ran aft through the chaotic melee as ill-prepared sailors tried to fend off the surprise attack. Despite their appearance, the raiders were too well organized for common thugs. They pressed their attacks with too much precision, and while Ritsuko did not recognize the barked orders, she could tell these men were highly trained.

She stopped short. A knot of six invaders blocked the way belowdecks. She recognized Mikani's voice swearing at them, then she glimpsed the flash of an axe and one of the attackers stumbled back. His sword landed at her feet.

Ritsuko had no experience whatsoever with a weapon of this type, but it seemed better than nothing. She snatched the blade up and tried to remember how to hold it. A skilled swordsman could probably wield this one-handed, but she needed two. Before she could wade in, Irahi smashed through the wooden wall next to the door in a burst of shattered planks and splinters that did nothing to disguise his rage. The three assailants who could still walk pulled back; Irahi grabbed one and bashed him into the deck, while Mikani pushed through the hole, swinging his axe wide.

The blade thunked into the cretin's neck and opened his throat in a gurgle of blood. His comrade tried to run, but Irahi took him down with a ferocious kick to the back of his knees, then his dagger flashed. Ritsuko remembered using that in battle herself—and with more skill than this sword. But the danger wasn't past.

All around, the ship swarmed with more and more invaders, all armed and calling out to each other when they spotted Ritsuko and Mikani. A torch flared nearby, and the moving light trailed over something on the fallen man's skin. Suddenly cold, she knelt to examine the tattoo on the man's forearm; the movement pulled her burned skin taut, but she ignored the pain.

"We have to fight," Mikani growled. "There's no time."

Knowing he was right, she pulled a knife from the dead man's thigh strap. *I can use this, at least.* She dropped the sword and followed Mikani. Irahi was already pushing to defend the boatswain, who had a pistol in one hand and a truncheon in the other. Her men were gathered around her, but most of the sailors weren't properly armed; a few were fighting with broom handles or buckets. She guessed they had been caught during late-night chores.

A shot rang out up high. One of the boarders fell, clutching at his chest. Taking advantage of the distraction, Miss Oliver and Mikani pressed forward with a half dozen men. Another shot, another man fell.

Mr. Ferro shouted from high on the mast, "Watch your flank!"

Ritsuko spun just in time to avoid a blade in the side. She blocked with a forearm and slashed low, nearly nicking the thug's femoral artery, but he danced back in time to soften the slice into a superficial wound. He bit out a curse and came at her again. She was distantly aware of the melee all around, but she was too focused on keeping this man from gutting her to be sure of what anyone else was doing. The soldier rushed again with his dagger, making her wonder why they weren't using sidearms.

They have orders to kill us quietly, perhaps. So much for that.

"Put us out to sea!" Miss Braelan shouted from somewhere to the left.

She couldn't tell if any of the sailors could fight free to get them away from the reinforcements swarming over the side of the ship. Ritsuko took a slice to her forearm in the next rush, but she timed her attack better, sinking her knife into the man's chest. It required more brute force than she'd realized; she felt the impact all the way up to her elbow, soft squelch of flesh and pop of bone as the blade popped through. Her stomach lurched.

No, that's the ship moving.

The sails swelled as someone hauled on the rope. She spun to see the attackers reacting; apparently, they weren't prepared for a long voyage. Some of them dove overboard rather than continue the fight on the open seas. Ritsuko stabbed another one as he tried to escape. Her hands were slick with blood, and she stood panting as Mikani and Miss

Oliver cleared the remaining attackers from the deck with brutal efficiency.

"What the hells just happened?" the boatswain demanded.

* * *

Mikani grabbed onto the rail, his hand slipping on warm blood. The *Gull* listed as they tore away from the docks and rushed into the darkness of the bay. A couple of men pushed past him, clambering over the railing and hanging precariously from the fore of the ship.

"Two points port! Obstruction ahead!"

Lookouts. We're running at full sail through a narrow space choked with debris. We'll be bloody lucky to get out of here in one piece.

He looked around, stumbling his way from the railing and back toward amidships. The boatswain was helping some sailors at the foremast, straining to get the rigging secured and running sails unfurled. Ferro called out instructions from his perch high on the mainmast; Mikani could not make out most of them, but he hoped that Saskia could. He could see a blotch of white at the wheel, Hu's big bulk next to her.

Ritsuko must be with them. A sailor nearly bumped into him as he ran past, vaulting over bodies and the debris of battle. *And bronze gods know, I'm little use down here.*

Mikani stumbled along the swaying deck and up the stairs toward the wheel. The ship lurched, and he fell, hard, against the railing. He hissed in pain and grabbed tight with both hands, while the roar of waves and pained creaking of the ship being pushed to her limits filled his ears. He dragged himself up the last four steps, more by sheer bloody mindedness than intent.

"Hells and Winter, Saskia—" He stopped when she turned the wheel hard, again, threatening to slide him off the side.

"We're being chased." Her hair was flying loose in the

wind. Hu was holding Ritsuko's arm to keep her steady; they were both looking back toward three ships that had broken their moorings and were quite definitely coming after them.

"Who did you piss off?" Mikani peered, trying to make out the ships' banners.

"Idiot. That's more your forte." Amusement laced her voice even as she pushed her ship to the limit.

"It's House Skarsgard," Ritsuko cut in soberly. "I recognized the insignia inked on the dead man's arm."

"Skarsgard. Because of the mines." Hu shifted his weight, his knuckles whitening where he grasped the railing.

"They cannot be pleased about that. But they found out much sooner than I'd hoped." Mikani grabbed a loose rope and lashed himself to the wheel post to keep from toppling every time Saskia turned the wheel. A muted boom rolled over them, followed by a splash a few dozen yards to their left.

"They're getting a range on us. We need to get out to open waters, where we can outrun them properly, and soon. Those frigates carry two dozen guns apiece. They'll shred us apart in minutes if they catch us." Saskia corrected her course, grinning like a wild woman.

She's enjoying this.

"I strongly recommend that they don't, then." Ritsuko sounded strained.

"Li'l White?" Hu pointed off to their left. "I do believe the Magnus's ship is moving up ahead of us."

Bronze gods. If they attack us on both fronts, we're done for.

Two smaller ships were moving alongside the *Pride of the North*. They easily outpaced the war cruiser, then turned toward the *Gull* with a thunderous flapping of sail that Mikani could hear even at that distance. "We need to open the gunports, get ready."

"We open up, we take in water. That slows us down and we're well and truly sunk... trust me, Janus. I know those ships." Saskia leaned hard on the wheel, aiming for the sloops cutting across their path.

Damned stubborn woman. But she usually knows what she's doing. I hope she's not wrong this time.

They were silent but for shouted orders and warnings for the next ten minutes. Mikani felt as if he held his breath that whole time; he held tight on to the railing until they were nearly abreast of the *Pride* and the sloops. Saskia held a steady course. The *Gull* raced past the smaller ships; they dropped their sails and turned toward the frigates as soon as the clipper had passed.

"Well, bloody hell..." Mikani looked back as they ran by; he could see a stout figure laughing and waving at them.

"That's Captain Lev." Saskia sounded relieved, though. "Met him while you were ashore that first day." She was keeping an eye on the big Magnus warship, now.

"Did you get a chance to make friends with Lord Magnus, too?" Ritsuko asked. They were all watching the massive ship looming closer by the moment.

"No." Saskia chewed her bottom lip and focused on steering the *Gull* in her mad dash for the bay's mouth. A series of sharp cracks made Mikani turn: one of the Skarsgard frigates had turned aside thanks to Saskia's friends; the quick shift in direction had tangled their sails and it was losing speed, fast. The other two Skarsgard ships had turned aside—their gun ports were open and he could see the smoke-dulled flash of Skarsgard guns as they opened fire on the fleeing *Gull* with their full broadsides.

A half dozen shots speared the water around them, shooting up thick spray that stung his cheeks. One landed a glancing strike against the *Gull*'s side, rocking the sleek ship with a loud sound of tearing wood. Before the Skarsgard ships could reload, though, the *Pride* opened fire.

Mikani lost his footing as the thunderous discharge of the cruiser's guns rolled over them like a physical blow; the *Gull* creaked and shuddered... but the shots sailed well above their heads, splashing wide of the House Skarsgard squadron. The smaller ships, friend and foe alike, scattered to gain some distance from the behemoth.

"Well." Saskia was wide-eyed, barely holding on to the wheel. "I guess Magnus hates House Skarsgard more than he hates us. But we're clear."

Mikani shook his head, barely able to hear her above the ringing in his ears. "The question is, how in the hells did Skarsgard know to come after us?"

The doctor wore a black scowl. "I have no idea. Did any couriers pass us on the road?"

As slow as they'd been moving, if a fast rider had blazed by, Mikani felt fairly sure he'd have remembered it. "Not that I saw."

Ritsuko asked, "Is there a better route than the one we took? Quicker?"

Mr. Loison joined the group. Mikani didn't know where the man had been during the fight, but he was disheveled, as if he'd done his part. "There is not. The train would be a more direct route, but the stations are closed. And the mountain trail you took on the way up is... unusable."

A sailor tapped Hu on the shoulder, murmuring about the injured on deck, so the doctor excused himself to tend the wounded. Mikani caught a movement from Ritsuko, and he turned instinctively. There was a question in her eyes. If she was thinking what he was... he nodded.

His partner cleared her throat. "I think I know how Skarsgard got word of what happened in Eldheim."

"Enlighten us," Saskia said.

Ritsuko explained, "We made a full report to the Major General, but... her reaction seemed wrong. She was too kind even though we cost her House a substantial amount of coin and hurt their business interests."

"It tracks," Mikani agreed. "She might have told Skarsgard, hoping they would eliminate us. That way, House Skarsgard deals with all inquires from the CID and the Council... and Thorgrim is free to claim we were working for Magnus, or whoever else best serves their interests."

Saskia seemed thoughtful, one hand resting on the wheel. "Some House scions tend to work that way. They prefer not to dirty their hands directly. And I can't think of how else Skarsgard would've found out, if not from the Major General."

Ritsuko wore an ominous look. Her clothing was stained in dark splatters, grisly remnants of the battle. "I wish she'd just clapped us in irons. There's no reason so many men should've been injured in trying to dispatch us."

Mikani knew her well enough to realize she was bothered by the violence on all sides, both the sailors Saskia had lost and the ones who had died because some Skarsgard lordling ordered them to. Without a thought, he wrapped an arm around her shoulder, and she leaned on him slightly. As comforting gestures went, it might not be enough, but he couldn't think what else to do. He remembered how she'd climbed into his lap after killing her first man, and a rush of warmth surprised him.

"We're away now," Mr. Ferro interrupted. "Pursuit well behind us, as we've caught the wind. There's no catching us unless they've a weather witch on board."

"Don't even joke," Saskia warned the first mate.

Agreed. That's a complication we don't need... the situation's bad enough already.

29

SASKIA LET OUT a breath she hadn't realized she was holding as soon as they cleared the headland for Northport bay. She looked over her shoulder; the *Pride* was following them at half sail, her gun ports still open. In the narrow passage of the harbor, the big warship effectively blocked the Skarsgard squadron's pursuit.

Smart. They'll probably claim they were firing on us as we made our escape, and Skarsgard will have little choice but to play along or start a war.

"He's as devious as any Magnus scion, that one," she said.

Ritsuko glanced back toward port. "What about the other Free Trader ships?"

Good of her to be concerned about them.

"They slipped out ahead of the cruiser, while Skarsgard was focused on us. I'm guessing they'll make for a sheltered cove up the coast to repair and refit before heading home." Saskia scanned the horizon for a moment, then pointed left. "There they go. I'm more worried about us. As soon as they clear the harbor, those frigates will chase us at full speed."

On the deck below her, Irahi and a couple of volunteers did what they could for the wounded. Saskia refused to look too closely, afraid to see how many more men she'd lost. The *Gull* had taken a blow near the rear mast; Nell was directing the repairs, her arm in a sling and a bloodied bandage around her right calf. She seemed to feel her captain's gaze, for she looked up and smiled through the grime shadowing her face.

"She'll hold, ma'am. Get us out of here!"

Saskia nodded at the other woman, her lips twitching. *She knows me too well. They all do. Bronze gods, this had all better be worth it.*

She closed her eyes and tilted her head up. One hand rested lightly on the wheel, keeping her wounded clipper steady. Saskia raised the other to the sky, splaying her fingers in an invocation. The rush of wind served to focus her, the cold salt spray a caress on her skin more familiar than any lover's touch. She called to her spirits with a whispered chant cast into the air.

Saskia felt the thrum of energy along her arms, surging from deep within.

Then she frowned. Though her senses stretched far and wide, she could barely feel a glimmer of her elementals—where they had always rushed forth at her summons, this time, they were reticent. Their cool presence tugged at the very edge of her awareness, circling and swirling but seeming afraid to come closer.

Oh, no... Not you, too. You're not slaves, you were never servants. She strained, reaching wider. Trying to reassure the spirits, murmuring entreaties. "You know me, you remember. I need your help. Don't run from me."

She was surprised when one rushed in, the arctic gust of its dash stealing her breath away. The sylph curled around her, wailing with a voice like icicles scraping the walls of a hidden cave. Saskia reeled, opening her eyes and blinking away tears. Janus and Ritsuko each grabbed an arm, and Mr. Ferro took the wheel; she saw them moving their mouths, but all she could hear was the keening of the wind spirits.

"Bronze gods. They're terrified." She shook her head and stumbled upright. "Something's wrong. They're scared, but not of me—" Her throat felt hoarse, and she realized that she was screaming when Janus held a finger to his lips. She let him help her against the railing, and waited for the cacophony in her head to recede.

"Who's scared?" Janus crouched before her, and Inspector Ritsuko offered a glass of water, which she downed gratefully.

"My air elementals. Only my family's ties to them are preventing them from making full speed for the open sea."

"Has anything like this ever happened before?" Ritsuko asked.

"Never."

Janus was frowning. "I take it they won't be granting us any speed for the escape?"

"Not under these conditions."

"What could scare them like that?" Mr. Ferro put in from his post at the wheel.

"That's an excellent question." Saskia's head felt too big, swollen with the echoes of the sylph's outburst.

Nell Oliver strode up, a knot of sailors at her back. "The lead Skarsgard vessel is gaining ground, ma'am."

She'd counted on her familiars to make a clean getaway, as she had done so many times before. But it didn't seem to be possible this time. "We need a new plan. Ideas?"

Janus exchanged a look with his partner, who lifted one shoulder. The first mate's silence didn't seem to spring from his taciturn nature this time. *It's possible the* Gull*'s made her last lucky escape.* But she wasn't ready to give up just yet. The *Pride* was still keeping pace, blocking the smaller Skarsgard warship, but she couldn't expect Viktor Magnus to risk his ship and command while covering their retreat.

"If we lighten the load, we might put on some speed," Ferro finally said.

The boatswain aimed a daggered stare at him. "Those

provisions have to last us past the Sisters. You want us to starve?"

"I'd rather come in thin than be bombarded with cannonballs, take on water, and drown."

Bickering wouldn't solve anything. The two inspectors didn't know that much about ships, so they couldn't be expected to solve this. She studied the ships behind them, a glimmer of an idea forming.

I hate this. If I am wrong, we're all dead.

"We may have a chance," she said finally. "Mr. Ferro, bring the ship about."

"Are you jesting?" Inspector Ritsuko wondered.

"No. Brace yourselves. This will get rough."

She took the wheel back from Ferro, who gave her a dubious look. The *Gull* turned hard, her timbers protesting the abuse, until they were facing the *Pride* and the first Skarsgard ship, both of which were nearly clear of the harbor mouth. Saskia's men scurried to the rigging and over the deck, securing lines and pulling at ropes to brace the sails as the new angle gave them a burst of fresh speed—in the wrong direction. They were rushing headlong toward the Skarsgard frigate. Janus regarded her as if he were trying to decide if she had lost her wits.

"Ramming them seems unlikely to yield a desirable outcome." Inspector Ritsuko gripped the railing with white-knuckled hands.

"I'm hoping her captain feels the same way, Inspector." She tightened her grip on the wheel; they were a couple of hundred yards from the Skarsgard warship and coming in at full speed. As the *Gull* passed the *Pride*, the Skarsgard ship turned hard, away from the *Gull*'s seemingly suicidal dash.

The wake of the gargantuan Magnus cruiser hit the Skarsgard frigate at the wrong angle as it turned; enhanced by the shallow and narrow channel at the port mouth, the waves hit the ship hard enough to topple it over.

Saskia pulled on the wheel and held firm. The *Gull* rocked and bounced on the same waves with a thunderous crash. She bit hard on her bottom lip as ropes snapped and one of the foremast's yards broke under the strain. The loose sail flapped with the crack of a giant's whip, but her clipper turned at last and raced off westward along the coast. Saskia finally looked back. The Skarsgard frigate was on her side; she could see two dozen men trying to get away from the sinking ship. The Magnus cruiser was swinging around to help, but the wreckage would block the second Skarsgard ship from pursuing them anytime soon.

The *Gull* limped away from the chaos and toward open water. Saskia's head pounded again. Her sylphs hadn't settled down. If anything, the conflict made it worse, so that they were the elemental version of hysterical. Their keening rose and fell like the waves beneath the ship, leaving her with a spinning, nauseated ache in her stomach, driven by the relentless sound.

"Take the wheel," she said to Mr. Ferro, hoping she wasn't shouting again.

With a narrow-eyed look, the first mate complied, and Saskia stumbled toward her quarters. It was a narrow thing, but she made it to the privacy of her cabin before vomiting in a basin. She shook all over as she rinsed her mouth. *This needs to stop. I have to get to the bottom of this, or I'll have no choice but to send the spirits away for good. My family might never forgive me… nor would I forgive myself.*

A tap on the door proved a slightly unwelcome interruption. She didn't feel up to dealing with another crisis, but it wasn't as if she could take the night off. With a smothered sigh, she answered, trying to look calm and capable. "Yes? Oh. Janus."

"You don't have to sound so dismayed."

"Idiot. It's not that. I'm not… at my best just now."

"So I noticed." He strode into her quarters as if he owned the place. "Obviously, something's gone haywire with your elemental bond. I think we need to sort you out."

"I could use some sorting," she admitted with a shaky laugh.

"Tell me what's happening?"

"As I mentioned, they're frightened, but that's not all. It's like... they're being tugged away from me when I try to call them. Whatever it is, they're terrified... and they cry out, and I hear it, all through my head, down into my bones. That probably sounds mad."

Janus raised a brow, as if to remind her who she was talking to, but all he said was, "That's not the oddest thing I've ever heard. Is there a way for you to... show me?"

"I'm not sure that's wise."

"Right, because I'm the epitome of wisdom. We'll be brief, I promise."

"Very well, then. Give me your hand."

Janus took her hand in his, and she was surprised to find it was only the comforting clasp of an old friend. *How things do change.* She sucked in a bracing breath and she whispered a call to the sylphs. The response was instantaneous—and agonizing. At the same time, she opened herself to Janus, so he could hear the endless keening, worse than the dying cries of a hundred men. Her skin crawled as their horror and pain razored down her nerves. The wind spirits were... caught, somehow, pulled taut through a force not of their own making. If there was a trap—

She cut the connection and dropped Janus's hand. He was pale, and he regarded her with shadowed blue eyes. For a few seconds, he didn't speak, and she mustered a semblance of aplomb, pretending she didn't want to sick up again.

"That... I've heard something like that before. I didn't feel it. But..." He trailed off, seeming unsure.

"Tell me. This is no time to be delicate."

His mouth twisted wryly. "Since I'm known so much for it. Ritsuko and I heard spirits wailing like that inside the mirrors at a station in Dorstaad."

"They were probably air spirits bound against their will," she said, quietly horrified.

All this time, I never knew. Those silver mirrors are a prison.

"Does that mean someone is trying to bind *yours*?" Janus asked. "Is that even possible?"

"I have no idea. It shouldn't be. But a practitioner of sufficient power and insufficient morals can find a way to do nearly anything."

"Then we need to figure out who it is and stop them." Janus curled a hand into a fist, looking as wary as she'd ever seen him.

"You have an idea, I take it?"

"Remember how I found Ritsuko?"

She nodded.

"Now that I know how your sylphs... feel, for lack of a better word, I can probably track them, as I did her. But it'll be... taxing."

"Maybe there's another way—"

"There isn't. Don't worry. I don't plan to die sober and at sea."

"What can I do to help you?"

"Nothing. Just... some peace and quiet. You can stand post outside my door if you like."

Saskia inclined her head. "I'll send your partner, actually. I should check in with Irahi, then find out how Nell's doing with the repairs. I'd hoped we could put into a cove for some patching, but it appears we don't have time. Good luck, Janus."

30

RITSUKO WAS HELPING Irahi tend the last of the wounded when Miss Braelan came looking for her. At first, she stepped aside, as the other woman seemed tired and more than a little ill. She imagined that Miss Braelan needed some medical attention.

Instead, she took Ritsuko's arm and drew her aside. "Janus needs you. Can you come?"

What's he done now? Below the aggravation, however, lay a thread of genuine worry. One of these days, he'd go too far, crawl out on a ledge from which she couldn't pull him back. Nodding, she hurried after Miss Braelan, but the woman stopped outside Mikani's cabin. Inside, it was all stillness and silence.

"Is he hurt?"

"No. Well. At least, not yet. But he needs you to stand guard."

Ritsuko stopped, a hand on the handle. "Pardon me?"

Then Miss Braelan explained that the complication with her familiars had reminded Mikani of the screaming mirror spirits. She finished with, "So he's trying to track down whoever's attempting to compel them."

"And I'm meant to keep everyone out while he does so." Her lips firmed.

He'll kill himself with nobody to stop him.

"If you don't mind."

Ritsuko did, but she merely nodded, scowling at the door so that it should've burst into flames from her ferocity as Miss Braelan strode away. For the first few moments, she was determined to do the job she had been assigned without interfering. But she couldn't get the potential for trouble off her mind, so with a muttered curse, she nudged the door open and slipped inside. Mikani stood with his back to her, hands flat against the wooden wall of his cabin. The small space was in disarray, his clothing and personal effects scattered throughout—unusual, even for his usual chaos.

"Close the door." He did not turn to her, but the strain in his voice was razor-sharp. She latched the door and stepped closer. The swaying ship nearly sent her tumbling into him. "I think I found them. Hell, I found *something*." He pointed back east, toward Northport.

"Where?" she asked, quietly taking stock of the damage.

Mikani turned to face her. He was pale and haggard; his eyes were clenched shut, a thin trickle of blood dripping from the corners of his eyes. After massaging his temples, he wiped at the red smears on his cheeks with clumsy hands. Ritsuko closed the door behind her. *It's never been this bad before.* She wondered if he had any pills handy that would dull the pain.

"Near as I can tell, her familiars are caught near the Major General's palace. Along with every air spirit, sylph, and wind elemental for miles around." His expression was stark. "I just felt a half dozen of them die. I'd rather not do that again."

When he stumbled, she reached him in seconds, putting her shoulder beneath his arm. His weight was almost enough to take her down, but she braced on the wall and helped him sit. Mikani looked shaky with exhaustion and horror. She perched beside him, despite the pull on still-healing skin on the backs of her calves.

"Whatever that damned Thorgrim woman's doing, we need to stop it. Let me catch my breath, and we can head out." He leaned back with a groan and went limp.

"The Major General's binding Miss Braelan's elementals?" Ritsuko repeated it just to make sure she understood.

"Saskia made that comparison. I only tracked them." He shook his head. "I don't know what she's doing to them... or with them. They feel somewhat like the tormented spirits in the mirrors, back in Dorstaad..." He opened bloodshot eyes, and looked up at her. "But there's something different, as well. Whatever she's doing tastes *rotten*. Like ashes and carrion... a lot like Lorne's ritual."

"Then this is too big for the *Gull*. We need reinforcements."

Damn shame we're essentially alone in this and already acting well outside our authority. Her time with Mikani had clearly corrupted her since that didn't bother her as much as it once would have. She'd once believed that all governmental rules existed for the protection of its citizens, but the longer she worked as an inspector, the more she saw regulations offering perks to people because they had wealth or power or both.

"You're right. Let's gather the others." He tried to rise and nearly collapsed again. "All right, new plan. Please call them in here, while I try to keep from passing out."

Ritsuko touched his hair lightly as she pushed to her feet. She rested her hand on his head for a few seconds, and he closed his eyes, leaning into her touch. If matters weren't so pressing, she would've stayed longer. Instead, she hurried off to summon the others.

Two hours later, she was in a skiff. Irahi trimmed the sails, carrying the small vessel away from the *Gull*. Mikani stood on deck, looking worried, and Ritsuko raised her hand partly in farewell, partly to reassure him that it would be fine.

"Thanks for coming with me," she said.

"Someone has to keep you out of trouble." Though his tone was light, his dark eyes were serious.

"That's usually my job, with Mikani."

"And you do it admirably. You're a good influence on him."

Ritsuko laughed as Irahi trimmed the sails, turning the skiff toward the harbor. Several hours later, the looming Magnus cruiser came into sight. It was a dark, overcast night with glimmers of the gibbous moon overhead trickling through the clouds in spatters of light that gave Irahi an odd aspect, reinforced by the lurch of the waves. The knots in her stomach tightened into tiny nooses when she contemplated all the ways this scheme could go wrong.

Magnus could clap me in irons. Chuck me overboard.

But there was no time for doubt. The Major General had to be stopped. There was no good reason for her to betray them to House Skarsgard or to be summoning elementals and slaughtering them. *And she has so many soldiers at her command.* Suppressing a shiver, Ritsuko accepted the doctor's hand as he helped her stand.

"State your business," the sentry shouted from the crow's nest. "Failure to do so will get you shot out of the water."

"I'm Inspector Ritsuko of the *Gull*. This is Dr. Irahi Hu. It's urgent that we speak with Commander Magnus at once."

"Hold your position. Comply, or we turn the cannon on you."

Since she had no idea how difficult it was to control a sailing ship of this size, Ritsuko turned worried eyes to Irahi. "Is that a problem?"

"I can manage."

A few minutes later, the man shouted, "I'm dropping a ladder. Board at once. The commander will see you."

She didn't feel much confidence as she took hold of the damp, slippery fibers and hauled herself up the side of the huge ship. Pings of pain accompanied the movements, but she couldn't falter. Irahi was climbing behind her, and she swung over the deck railing first, hauled up by hard hands. Sailors stared at them, many wearing Magnus ink on their skin. A man pushed through the crowd to beckon impatiently.

"You don't want to keep him waiting."

The mate escorted them to the captain's quarters and closed the door behind them. Viktor Magnus sat behind his desk, a pistol within easy reach. A man nearly Irahi's size stood behind him, holding a carbine trained on them.

"Inspector. You people seem to attract trouble like carrion does vultures." He regarded them with dark eyes, his mouth set in a grim line.

"We're here to deal with it, Commander. I'm afraid that means that we're only needed when there's a mess to be tidied up."

He laughed and held up a hand. His bodyguard put up his short rifle but did not take his eyes off them. "I'm sure that will make those Skarsgard bastards feel better about your shutting down their mines and sinking one of their frigates." He stood and poured some wine into a couple of goblets. "Maybe you should come work for House Magnus. We can always use people with a talent for chaos." He pushed one of the glasses toward her. "As long as we point you in the right direction, of course."

"Thank you, Commander Magnus. I'm afraid we already have a job." *Hopefully we do. For now, anyway.* "But we'll bear your offer in mind, as long as it still stands after what I have to tell you. You see, we need your help. Lady Thorgrim has captured a significant number of air elementals, and we believe she's planning to use them for something dire."

He regarded her in silence for a moment. Then he called out, "Hergrim! Bring the Windworkers in here! Now!" He motioned for them to sit as he took his own chair.

"Commander—"

He caught her gaze and raised a hand, signaling that she should wait. *We need his help. If he wants us to sit quietly, then we will.*

Five long minutes later, the door opened. Two men came into the cabin, weatherworn and with the air of those who hadn't slept in days. They could've been twins, lanky and with mousy, disheveled hair down to their shoulders that jingled lightly with the beads knotted into their braids.

"Tell them what you just told me." Commander Magnus motioned to the men. Ritsuko took a deep breath and relayed what they had gleaned, from the mirror incident back in Dorstaad to Mikani's findings.

"My lord," one of the mages murmured, when she was finished. "That would explain why we've been forsaken by the winds."

"If the bonds were broken, that's what killed Yngrid, my lord." The other weather worker mumbled a quiet prayer, then glanced at Ritsuko and Irahi. "Our eldest sister. We all felt a tearing pain deep within, when we were working our rituals last evening. She did not survive."

"We mourn your loss. But this is just the beginning," Ritsuko said somberly.

Viktor Magnus met her gaze. "What would you have me do?"

He knows, she thought. *That this is over his head, too. If he wades into this fight, there will be consequences.*

Taking a deep breath, she told him.

* * *

Mikani checked his sidearm and made sure the axe was strapped to his back. He gripped the railing when the *Gull* crested a wave. "Hells and Winter. This is a bloody stupid idea."

"It's *your* plan." Saskia corrected their course, putting a little more distance between the *Gull* and captain Lev's ship, the *Deva's Flight*.

"Yes, well. Even more reason to think it's bloody stupid, then, right?" He peered into the horizon. Dawn was fast approaching, the dark before the coming dawn staining the ocean jet and casting dark crimson shadows over the waters.

I hate ships. I hate the sea. I hate that Ritsuko's not here.

"Trust me, Janus. If we had a choice, none of us would be doing this."

She's right, of course. Bronze gods know it took all her skill and reputation to get Lev, Olson, and Beales to agree to help us.

He glanced over his shoulder. A few hundred feet behind the *Gull* and *Deva's Flight*, two other free merchantmen followed their lead.

"We're all fools, that's what we are."

"They're brave men." Saskia's voice was soft; he could barely make out her words over the rush of wind and waves. "And they know the stakes. Now get ready. I can see the lights of the headland."

He narrowed his eyes and leaned forward. Three darker shadows bobbed into view. He pointed toward them. "I'd wager those are the Skarsgard ships."

Saskia followed his indication, and frowned. "Then what are the others?"

"Complications."

Their small squadron exchanged signals and barked orders, sliding into a single line as they neared Northport. With the rising sun, they could make out the Skarsgard frigates as they spread out on a broad front. Three barques, flying Thorgrim colors, had taken up formation behind the larger warships, plugging the gaps between. Four or five smaller sloops sailed at the far end of the formation, undisciplined and almost erratic.

Mercenaries. Which means they're bristling with guns and probably boarding parties. Wonder where Thorgrim scrounged them up on short notice.

"All hands, ready for battle!" Saskia sounded scared, excited, and very much alive, just then. He unslung his rifle and watched as sailors slid down from the rigging and manned the *Gull*'s light cannons. "Here... we... go!" Saskia spun the wheel. The *Gull* bucked like a thing alive, heading for the smaller ships. The Skarsgard and Thorgrim ships turned more slowly, having to fight their own weight and the shifting morning winds.

For an endless time, all that he could hear was the sea and the creak of the ship. Then they broached the mercenary line, and the world exploded around him in concussive thunder and the sharp stink of gunpowder.

The Free Merchant ships weaved through the loose sloop formation, firing their guns in tandem as they slipped between the smaller ships. The nearest Skarsgard frigate opened fire with a rippling line of crackling cannons; two found their mark, tearing ragged holes in the side of the *Deva's Flight.* Most of them splashed harmlessly around the swiftly moving clippers, but one of the smaller mercenary ships exploded with a sudden and vicious flare. Debris rained all around them in a cloud of billowing smoke; when Mikani glanced back toward the burning wreckage, he saw that another of the sloops had caught fire from the explosion.

"That idiot must have been overflowing with powder. They're like floating magazines just waiting for a spark." Saskia turned away as the burning ship blew behind them. It was close enough to the Skarsgard frigate to cause some heavy damage, the flying fragments of burning wood and iron tearing a gash along the larger ship's flank and nearly to the waterline.

"There's your opening." Mikani pointed at the crippled Skarsgard ship.

"And there's your Inspector. And she's bringing friends." Saskia grinned and nodded toward the Magnus war cruiser, bearing down with full sails behind the Thorgrim and Skarsgard ships. The *Pride* opened fire with a full broadside that obliterated one of the smaller Thorgrim ships in a hail of hot iron and tore the mainmast off a second Skarsgard ship.

"That's going to cause an incident back home." Mikani grinned. *If they're here, Ritsuko's safe and well. And, she managed to convince a House Magnus scion to possibly start a war. I really must be a bad influence.*

"Idiot. Let's survive this, then worry about politics." Saskia laughed and turned her ship straight down the throat of their enemy. The nimble ship skipped over the waves, guns firing in staccato cracks of deafening sound. Mikani grabbed onto the railing and laughed with her, watching the other merchantmen converge on the wounded frigate like wolves. The lighter vessels danced closer, ripping the warship apart… a magazine exploded deep within the warship, rolling out a cloud of dark smoke over the debris-strewn waters.

The *Gull* slipped behind the remaining frigates as they turned to face the threat of the *Pride*. The Thorgrim barques were more stubborn, and two of them started chasing after them.

"You picked up a couple of suitors." Mikani looked back toward the harbor; on the deck below, Ferro was already preparing the remaining longship. A dozen armed men helped push the slender craft to the side, ready to release it as soon as they came close enough to shore.

"I'm used to it. I won't let them down easy, though. Now get to the skiff, find that Thorgrim wench, and give her hell."

"You do know just what to say to a man. Keep safe, Saskia; you're our only way home, after all."

"Idiot. Go." She laughed again, and he jogged for the skiff. He vaulted on board as Ferro gave the command to release the ropes; Mikani had to bite back a curse as his stomach lurched when the small skiff fell several feet into the churning waters around the speeding *Gull*.

He grabbed an oar as Ferro barked out their rhythm. For endless minutes, his world became the stinging sea spray and the strain of pulling against the waves. Ferro barked, they pulled. He started when they smashed with a grinding sound onto the rocky beach under a pier.

"Out, move, move, move!" Mikani rolled over the side and hefted his rifle. While Ferro's men disembarked, he spared a look back toward the harbor. The *Gull* still had two ships chasing her, but one of them had already lost a mast and seemed to be listing. One of the merchantmen was burning as it limped out to sea with a mercenary sloop chasing it. The *Pride of the North* looked torn up but still eager for a fight; it was exchanging broadsides with the two remaining frigates in a brutal match of sheer firepower.

"Look." Ferro slapped his shoulder, turning his attention down the beach with his characteristic lack of enthusiasm.

Two longboats slipped onto the beach a couple of dozen yards away. Thirty or forty heavily armed men in Magnus colors jumped ashore and scrambled to secure a line along the beach; three figures detached from the main body and headed toward them.

Ritsuko. Hu. And... hells. Viktor bloody Magnus.

His feet were moving before he made the decision to go to her. Mikani ran full out, splashing through the water. Somebody could shoot him in the back, and it wouldn't matter. When she spotted him, she put on speed, too, breaking away from whatever Magnus was saying to her. He caught her and whirled her around; she was laughing and batting at him, but he didn't put her down until he'd squeezed her tight.

"Worried about me, were you?" she whispered.

"It was a long time, at least eight hours."

Viktor Magnus stepped up beside them, arching an imperious brow. "Did you think I'd have her beheaded?"

"No, but I thought you might use her as a bargaining piece with Thorgrim."

"Some might make such a move. I prefer more straightforward engagements."

Studying Magnus, Mikani could well believe that. Despite his noble blood, he had the look of a soldier. "I'm glad you're on our side, then."

Mr. Ferro and his men caught up with them. The Magnus guards gave the Free Merchant sailors dubious looks, but there was no dissent in the ranks. *Just as well, we can't afford any.* The first mate skimmed Magnus up and down and seemed not to hate what he saw. *That's a first.*

"If you're through jawing, we need to get this force moving before they get bored and decide breaking windows and setting fires would be more entertaining."

Magnus aimed a dark look at him. "My men have more discipline."

"They're sailors at heart." Ferro spat as if to emphasize his point.

"I agree," Ritsuko said. "It's time to sack Northport."

31

RITSUKO SKIMMED OVER the collective forces assembled onshore, mentally tallying the number, and it was lower than she'd like.

Between Houses Skarsgard and Thorgrim, there would be at least a couple of hundred guards ordered to stop their progress by any means necessary. Irahi pressed his dagger into her hands, and she nodded a thank-you. Magnus had taken command of the ground forces, and he was going over last-minute stratagems—to the boredom and bemusement of most of the Free Merchant sailors. They had the sense not to interrupt, however, even if they weren't interested in a quick lesson on tactics.

"We don't have enough men to split our forces, or I'd send a diversionary force to throw them off. So we'll have to move fast and push through the alleys to the Major General's palace," Magnus concluded.

Nobody questioned how he had come to be in charge. House scions that ended in the military turned one of two ways—they were either nebbish dilettantes bursting with ennui or born commanders, sure of their right to rule from the cradle. It seemed Viktor Magnus was the latter. He was also arming the men with some makeshift siege equipment, hastily constructed from ship beams and coils of rope.

Mikani stood beside her, weapons in hand. He looked somewhat recovered from before, but she still worried about the lasting effects of pushing his gift. As if sensing her eyes on him, he touched her arm, and she smiled. *Not long now.*

Lady Thorgrim couldn't be permitted to bind all the elementals to her will. That kind of power was unthinkable in a single person's hands. There was no end to the damage the Major General could cause. Eventually, if they didn't stop her, the woman's strength would be sufficient to force all the isles to bow before her.

"Let's go," Magnus shouted.

His House Guards led the way, with the Free Merchant sailors close behind. The alleys of Northport were narrow and choked with refuse. In some of them, the stench was so bad Ritsuko had to put away Irahi's dagger and cover her nose and mouth with her forearm. It was impossible for fifty men, give or take, to move silently, but Magnus hadn't lied about his soldiers' discipline. None of them broke off, though some of the sailors in the back were doing so.

Citizens stepping out their back doors to see the small force sweeping through went immediately back inside. *Clever folk. It's not a day to be abroad. Best to stay indoors until the dust settles.* As they passed through town, she glimpsed the milkman on his delivery route and the baker heading into his shop. After the chaos of the past weeks, it was somewhat miraculous for Ritsuko to realize that the little civilities were still being tended—that somewhere, there was a pot of tea on the stove. That knowledge reinforced her resolve to see this through.

This is why we fight. For them. For those who can't.

By creeping through Northport via back lanes, they emerged at the base of the hill leading to the Major General's palace. There was no telling how many guards and mercenaries were waiting behind those solid stone walls. *If reinforcements come from the docks, we'll be caught betwixt anvil and hammer.* But Viktor Magnus didn't hesitate.

"To arms!" he called out.

And the motley squadron roared in response as they charged the gate. Irahi was on the wooden beam along with Magnus's second in command; together, they slammed it into the gate. Once, twice, and the door shuddered, then cracked and gave. Two more hard strikes, and it broke wide, so that their forces charged past.

Gunshots rang out immediately, and Ritsuko dove. She rolled behind a hedge and got out her gun, bracing to fire. A sailor dropped beside her, a bloody hole in his chest. The daylight helped with target differentiation, and she aimed at the Thorgrim guard who'd killed Miss Braelan's crewman. She shot him in the thigh, starting the count to keep track of her ammunition. Another rushed toward her; he had no pistol or he wouldn't be trying to force a hand-to-hand fight. She drew her dagger and sliced his Achilles tendon, then she shot him as his leg crumpled under him.

That's two.

In this scrum, it was impossible to find any of her friends, so she focused on staying alive. The defenders were frantic, and a couple tried to run, presumably to request reinforcements or maybe just to hide, but Magnus's soldiers had no compunction about shooting them in the back. Ritsuko told herself it was necessary… and did the same when one of the men taking aim at her broke and fled toward the manor. It sickened her when he stumbled and dropped, but everything about this situation did.

A Magnus guard nearby took a blade through the neck, spattering Ritsuko with blood. She stumbled back just in time to avoid the same. From the look of her opponent, this was one of Thorgrim's elite men. He was tall and well muscled, and his eyes were wild, not with fear, but exhilaration. *He enjoys killing.* The way he tossed his knife from hand to hand felt like a taunt and a promise.

"You're going to die," he said. "All of you."

She raised Irahi's dagger in her left hand without responding. *I'm not trained for this.* Which was why when he was watching her position the knife with apparent amusement, she whipped her revolver up in her right and shot him. *Hard to miss at this range.* He looked surprised when he fell, as if she'd done something she wasn't supposed to. *That's three.*

A large hand grabbed her arm and pulled her along; she tripped and nearly lost her balance. She raised her gun—and recognized Irahi.

"Sorry, Celeste, but we have to move." He glanced behind him briefly, then hurried to catch up with the men rushing up the path to the palace.

Ritsuko stumbled along, passing a knot of men tangled in close combat. The shifting mass of bodies made it impossible to tell who was winning, but Irahi did not pause to help either side. He paused, and she turned at the sound of gunfire behind them.

A large group of Skarsgard guards, thirty or forty of them, was rushing toward the broken gate at the bottom of the hill. A few Magnus marines were slowing them down with sporadic fire, but they'd be in the palace compound in a matter of minutes.

Mikani stepped up beside her. He had picked up a carbine somewhere but seemed to have lost his axe. "We need to get in the manor quickly. We can fend them off there and look for Lady Thorgrim."

"We won't be able to hold them off for long, even in there." Ritsuko could see a group of Thorgrim guards making its way toward the broken gate from the docks. *They were scattered through the city, hoping to spot a landing on time. Now they know where we are.*

"We only need long enough to stop her." Mikani turned and headed back up the hill; Irahi waited for her to start up the path before bringing up the rear.

Fresh gunfire plowed into the dirt around her and cracked slivers of stone from a fountain nearby; she ducked alongside Irahi, taking cover behind the marble stonework of a decorative column. Magnus's men and Free Merchant sailors crouched behind low walls and trees all around. She peered over the edge of the fountain.

The Major General's palace was a sprawling structure with graceful walkways and courtyards open to the fresh sea breeze. Now those arches and the broad second-story windows held snipers, the long barrels of their rifles shifting slowly in search of targets. The constant crackle of gunfire and cries of wounded men filled the air, while the bitter smell and growing pall of gunpowder made it hard to breathe. Ritsuko spotted a defender leaning out too far from one of the windows to aim, and she took her shot. The man fell back with a cry of pain; she wasn't sure where her bullet went, but she'd definitely hit him.

Four. Need to reload soon.

Ritsuko had twenty bullets in a pouch, so that would have to be enough to get this done. She surveyed the property for any sign of weakness, but the ground level seemed to be well fortified. *She'll crush us here if we don't move.* The defenders held the high ground, and there was no way to know how long the Magnus marines could corral the reinforcements down by the gate.

"The direct route is always best," Mikani said.

Irahi looked wary. "What'd you have in mind?"

"Follow me. I have an idea."

That never ended well. Nonetheless, she and Irahi crept after him as he inched around the side of the manor. It was unlikely that Lady Thorgrim had men sufficient to post guards in every window. Shots rang out as they moved, peppering the ground before them. Mikani kept to statuary and hedges when possible, but sometimes they had to run from point to point.

Eventually, he stopped at a small wooden door, half-hidden by overgrown grass and weeds, nestled at an odd angle against a solid wall. The wood looked old and weathered, the hinges rusted to a dark reddish brown.

She sniffed the air. "That smells like..."

"Coal delivery shaft," Mikani said. "Connects to the basement. Most old houses have them, especially when there's no gas used in cooking."

The doctor nodded. "Let's do this."

Ritsuko didn't know if it was a good idea to leave the others behind, but she didn't have a better one. "I'm in."

* * *

Mikani pried the doors open with his carbine; the hinges gave way with a dull snap, but the barrel of the short rifle was ruined. He tossed it aside and slid into the dark shaft, trusting Ritsuko and Hu to follow.

He landed with a clattering of coal and a cloud of black dust in the half-full bin, toppling it over. He rolled to his knees, coughing and trying to clear his eyes. The stone basement was dark, musty, and empty. *Good thing. We're not being quiet about this.*

Ritsuko landed into the pile of coal with a muffled grunt; he helped her to her feet and pulled her aside just as Hu rolled down with a loud clatter of the metal passage and a crash of the wooden bin collapsing with the big man's arrival. Hu stood, fragments of coal and dust sloughing off him like a dark waterfall. He gave Mikani a look that seemed distinctly unamused.

"Trust you to find the messiest way into anything."

Mikani grinned at him, and they all made their way up

the stairs to a wooden door. Mikani opened it carefully and peeked through. The kitchen was empty, the servants either fled or hiding in their quarters somewhere up above. He led them through and out to the main corridor. The sounds of fighting were muted by the thick doors of the atrium off to their left. The palace's private areas, including the Major General's suite, would be to their right, deeper in the complex.

"Let's find the Major General."

Hu shook his head. "You two go, and be careful. I need to open the front doors for our people outside before they're crushed."

Mikani frowned. "Hu, we need—"

His friend placed a hand on his shoulder and pushed him toward the stairs. "We each do what we must, old friend. Go stop the witch. I have lives to save." He grinned down at Ritsuko, then, his teeth the whiter against coal-stained features. "Keep him safe, Celeste."

Damn'd be, Hu. Mikani clapped the bigger man on the arm and headed toward the palace's private wing.

"This is how it should be," Ritsuko said quietly. "You and me, together at the end."

"Not the end of everything. Just Lady Thorgrim." Mikani flashed a determinedly cheerful look, hoping she wouldn't notice that he wasn't sure of that.

The way her lips compressed said she registered the half-truth. *Bloody hells. That'll cause me problems down the line.*

"We can do this." Her voice was firm, and he took comfort in it.

"Bronze gods know I'd rather not do this again, but we have to hunt her down. Watch my back, partner?"

"Always."

She took his arm as he closed his eyes. Mikani released his control slowly and felt his fists clench in anticipation—the wave of nausea was new, but the rush of pain was all too familiar from his earlier efforts. Even with his senses narrowed, the sensation was nearly unbearable from this close-up. He turned slowly, seeking the source of the flaring pain.

Like deciding where it hurts the most after being tossed into a bonfire. The skin peeling off my back, or the boiling— there it is.

He forced his gift down and opened his eyes. A red film obscured everything, but the throbbing memory of pain was clear. "This way," he mumbled.

His tongue felt thick, and his lips burned. Ritsuko slung his arm over her shoulder, and they scrambled along the corridor. His sight was clearing, and after a few steps he managed to walk on his own by bracing a hand on the wall. He stopped at the corner where another corridor crossed their path. Up ahead was a thick wooden door. Peering around the corner on his left revealed three men nervously guarding another set of double doors.

"She's behind those doors, somewhere close. Whatever she's doing, it's getting worse."

Beside him, Ritsuko took a knee, bracing her revolver. "We each take one. The last will get to cover if he can. Let's try not to let him."

"Agreed. On three?"

She whispered the count, then together, they popped out from around the corner and shot one guard each. Mikani nailed his target in the head, more by luck than design. Ritsuko went for the chest shot. The remaining guard returned fire as Mikani scrambled back around the corner. A bullet nicked the floor behind him, so he felt the shattering tile as he moved. Ritsuko was already there.

"He can't know when we'll come at him again."

Mikani heard the guard pounding on the door, but there seemed to be no response from those within. "Now."

They swung out together and shot the soldier as he wheeled to face them. As the guard dropped, Mikani raced toward the double doors. They were heavy and solid, unlikely to be shifted by two tired inspectors. Ritsuko knelt to examine the lock.

"Can you open it? Brute force isn't always the answer."

"I can try. Otherwise, we have to wait for Hu to bring the surviving marines and sailors."

An ominous sound from within—a sort of low, dull roar—likely made Ritsuko shake her head. "That'll be too late."

Mikani dropped to his knees beside her and got out his lockpicking kit. *Always be prepared for a little larceny.* He felt none too steady after the recent taxing use of his gift, but everything depended on stopping the Major General. So he applied rods to tumblers with dogged persistence.

After a couple minutes of work, the lock mechanism clicked. "We're in."

He pulled on the latch and pushed through, sidestepping behind a pile of chairs and a low banquet table that had been pushed nearly to the wall. Ritsuko slipped in to crouch beside him. They exchanged a look, then looked over the table.

Lady Thorgrim stood alone before a swirling vortex of silver and light. Mikani could make out vague shapes in the maelstrom; faces and impossibly elongated humanoid shapes. He shivered in the arctic cold of the ballroom, his breath steaming before him. When he saw the elaborate scrollwork at the edges, realization hit.

It's a mirror, like the ones we use to send messages, only I've never seen one this big. It's half a ton of pure silver.

"What the devil is she doing?" Ritsuko whispered.

"Don't care. It stops now." Mikani whipped out his sidearm and aimed, searching out a weakness in the mirror. *Hells and Winter. There's only one certain soft spot in this arcane mess.*

He shot the woman in the calf.

The spirits surrounding her shimmered and screamed, audible to Ritsuko as well, if her expression was anything to judge by. They swirled around Lady Thorgrim in a furious circle, then spiraled outward in a widening arc, then a pillar of light pierced the ceiling, funneling from the house in a deafening explosion, similar to what they'd set off in the mines.

Except without a grenade. That was his last coherent thought for a few seconds as the shock wave blew him back toward the wall. He slammed into it hard; as soon as he was able to move again, he started crawling toward Ritsuko, dimly aware of Lady Thorgrim shouting curses. *So she's still alive. Good. I want answers.* His partner found him with blind hands; she was bleeding from a cut on her forehead. When Mikani stood, his leg nearly buckled.

That'll leave a mark. His ears rang, and his entire body was a mess of aches and pains... but the keening wail of the suffering air spirits was fading, fast. *They're free.*

"You imbeciles! You could've killed us all," the Major General shouted from her position on the floor. Her once-matronly features were contorted with rage. From the look in her eyes, if she had a weapon, she'd cheerfully murder them both.

Mikani crouched, then sat near the Thorgrim woman when his knee gave out. Ritsuko stood beside him. She'd found her revolver and kept an unsteady bead on the woman.

"Sorry about that. We were improvising; you forgot to tell us your plan to steal away the air elementals when you were sending us off to fight salamanders. So, really." He leaned forward to tap Lady Thorgrim on the forehead with a finger, causing her to flail and snarl at him. "You're as much to blame as we are, for that, yes?"

"Get your hands off me, you bloody mongrel! I am Lady Maire of Kare, and I will not be manhandled by some animal."

Beside him, Ritsuko drew in a shocked breath. Mikani turned to her with a questioning glance, and his partner explained, "The Kares were a defunct bloodline from the old stories. Her line died out after the Ferisher princess slew her human husband rather than commingle—"

"We did not! The line of Kare lives on in the polluted halls of other so-called Houses." She shifted, wincing as she sat up straighter. "The Unbound Ferishers, founders and matriarchs of House Kare, still rule the deep places beyond Olrik's thrice-damned barrier. If they knew what's befallen their progeny, how you *beasts* have abused them..."

"You were trying to call them back." Ritsuko was looking up at the mirror, and Mikani finally understood.

A massive, heavily enchanted silver mirror. She was trying to call the ancient Ferisher Lords through the barriers between the worlds: the strain of reaching through the veil must have killed the spirits... she was using them as fuel for her summons.

Mikani ran a hand through his hair. "That's why you were binding the air elementals... but why the salamanders?"

Maire of Kare looked away and toward the window. "Those damned fire snakes... when the gate didn't open properly two months ago, thanks to that imbecile Nuall, there was enough of a rent in the veil to jolt the salamanders awake. Every time I tried to bind air spirits to the mirror and complete the summoning, a handful of fire elementals broke their fetters. They ran wild, disrupting the ritual... and as more elementals were freed, more and more started waking up throughout Hy Breasil."

"The salamanders... all those people dead, because of you." Ritsuko's voice shook slightly, with anger and grief.

"I was trying to finish what you spoiled in Dorstaad. This was my last chance!"

"You were Lorne Nuall's patron," Ritsuko said.

Mikani had already guessed as much from Lady Kare's furious rant.

"Of course I was. He was far too stupid and self-centered to manage on his own; he thought I meant to bring back the Shining Ones. He believed they would crown *him* king of a restored House Nuall, taking Saermine's place in a restored monarchy... as if I'd have any part in ruling you animals instead of exterminating you all. Now stop staring and get me some medical attention. I'm bleeding!"

Mikani said to Ritsuko, "I don't think Lady Thorgrim—that is, Lady Kare, understands how much her circumstances have changed."

"Not yet. But she will."

32

MIKANI TUGGED THE former Major General to her feet, ignoring the constant stream of insults as he slung her arm over his shoulder. "We need to get her away from the mirror and check on our people at the doors. It's been a few minutes since I last heard gunfire."

Ritsuko hadn't noticed the sudden silence until then. "You tracked the elementals… can you check to see if they're still bound?"

"Take her. Don't let her move."

She did, and her partner closed his eyes. His irises twitched beneath his lids as his face went beyond pale to green, and blood trickled from his nostrils. Mikani was gasping when he snapped back to the present. If she wasn't already supporting Lady Thorgrim, who was cursing in a low and virulent tone, Ritsuko would've offered him a shoulder.

"Anything?" she asked.

He nodded. "Best I can tell, they're all free. I suspect I disrupted her concentration when I shot her."

"The soldiers should've been enough to keep everyone out long enough for me to finish what I started," Lady Kare snarled.

Before the woman could say more, there were distant shouts; the palace echoed with faint footsteps along stone hallways and the occasional indistinct voice.

"Someone's coming," Ritsuko said.

Mikani took possession of the prisoner once more.

She pulled her revolver and stepped to the side of the door. *Just in case. Best not to presume they're friendly.* Her partner seemed to share the thought and clapped a hand over Lady Thorgrim's mouth to prevent her from calling for help. She waited in taut silence until the man stepped through the heavy doors. Ritsuko lowered her weapon when she recognized Viktor Magnus's first lieutenant.

"You have the traitor in custody?" he asked.

Casting a glance toward Mikani, who was holding the older woman, still struggling in his grasp, she nodded. "We stopped her in time. What's the situation?"

"The *Pride* sank the third Skarsgard frigate an hour ago. After that, they were eager to talk. That man of yours, Loison? He negotiated for a cease-fire. When Skarsgard stopped fighting, most of the Thorgrim forces laid down arms." He started walking down the main hall, so Ritsuko and Mikani followed. There was fresh debris and clouds of dust in the air; a sizable hole had been blown in the palace wall. "This was the last holdout," the lieutenant explained as he stepped over broken masonry. "The *Pride* persuaded them to surrender."

Mikani growled a curse. She turned to see his hand fall away from Lady Thorgrim's mouth. "She bit me," he said, looking incredulously at his fingers.

"This can't be happening," the old woman said numbly. "Not after all my plans and preparations."

The lieutenant regarded her curiously. "I assure you, ma'am, Northport is now under Magnus control and is likely to remain so, long after you're hung for treason."

Lady Thorgrim's face... collapsed. Her mouth tipped

down, and her head drooped as if she was about to faint. Ritsuko took a step closer, and as she did, the older woman struggled in earnest, lashing out with arms and legs. It took all Mikani's strength to hold her, but she broke free for a few seconds. Instead of running, however, she put her hand to her mouth. Ritsuko didn't have a good look at what happened, but her partner swore.

"Spit it out."

In seconds, pink froth bubbled from the woman's mouth and she went into convulsions, shaking so hard it appeared her bones might snap. As Mikani stretched Lady Thorgrim out on the floor, Ritsuko knelt and pulled her tongue away from her teeth. But she had insufficient medical knowledge to do more. The Magnus lieutenant ran in search of Irahi, but by the time they returned, it was too late.

Irahi knelt, checked her pulse, then raised his head with a sorrowful look. "I'm sorry. There's nothing I can do."

"Damn'd be!" Mikani stood. He was livid, and for a moment Ritsuko feared he might kick the corpse, but he turned to strike at a wall with an open hand. "Damn her bloody soul to—" He struck the wall again, and let out a hard, shuddering breath.

She put her hand on his back to console him. "It wasn't your fault."

He tensed for a moment, then relaxed as he turned back to her. "I know. Bloody coward, killing herself instead of facing justice... I'm fine. Let's go."

"My men will see to the body. This way." The lieutenant waited for Ritsuko, Mikani, and Irahi to join him, then resumed his trek.

They passed through the manor, and in the reception room, Ritsuko paused. With a gesture silently requesting patience from Mikani, she crossed to the antique coin collection that had drawn her eye during the first visit. With a rueful smile, she tapped the glass case. Though they weren't identical to the ones Nuall had used, they *were* old and stamped from the same era. *It might've been enough to make me suspect her if we had been investigating Lorne Nuall's patron instead of the elemental troubles.*

"Find something?" Mikani asked, behind her.

Ritsuko didn't need to say anything; she waited two beats, then he swore. "Like to like, it seems."

"Exactly what I was thinking," she said.

The soldier who had charge of them cleared his throat in apparent exasperation, and she let herself be herded out the front door. *Better than the coal chute.* Magnus soldiers patrolled the palace grounds in twos and threes. A group of Skarsgard guards were stationed near the gates, and Ritsuko felt the weight of their hostile stares as she passed by, but the soldiers didn't move from their assigned posts.

Good thing, too. We're in no shape to fight on.

The streets of Northport bristled with activity. People peered out through cracked windows as Magnus and Skarsgard patrols maintained order: word of the fall of the Major General must have spread like wildfire. Ritsuko saw a small group of teens fleeing from a Skarsgard patrol while holding on to armfuls of trinkets and food. *Looters. Not surprising. I hope it doesn't get worse.* The harbor was abuzz with sailors returning to their vessels. Some wore bloody bandages, and others were singing sea shanties in celebration of a battle well fought. They held on to each other's shoulders as they went up the gangplanks. Ritsuko smiled at the antics of the cabin boys, who swung from the riggings in visible glee.

It's not every day you bring down a House scion. And they were part of it.

Ritsuko knew there would be repercussions, but she wasn't eager to face them. Though she had a bit of coin put by, there wasn't much to spare on an honest inspector's salary, so if she lost her employment, it wouldn't be long before the wolf was at the door. Sighing, she put those thoughts aside and turned to the lieutenant, who wore an expectant look.

"Commander Magnus is waiting on the *Pride*."

"Lead on," Mikani said.

"I'm heading back to the *Gull*," Irahi cut in. "I should check on Saskia and see if we've any injured who need me."

Mikani nodded. "Tell her we'll be along as soon as we can manage. As long as we're not in chains."

Irahi grinned at them. "It wouldn't be the first time, mate. If you avoid the brig, we'll be leaving Northport before the week's end."

Ritsuko thought that sounded welcome. "I'm ready."

The lieutenant tapped an impatient foot, so she quickly said a temporary farewell to the doctor and followed the man to the Magnus war cruiser. The massive vessel was damaged, but as near as Ritsuko could tell, it had fared well enough. Men scurried along her sides and on deck, repairing and hauling off wreckage. They seemed in good spirits, though. Their guide knocked at the captain's door and ushered them in quickly.

Viktor Magnus dominated the room. Two men in Skarsgard uniforms flanked him, and a sullen-looking woman in Thorgrim colors sat facing him. They all looked up as they entered.

Ritsuko paused at the sheer hatred from the Skarsgard men, whereas the Thorgrim woman seemed resigned. Magnus waved them in. As she stepped forward, she sensed Mikani at her side; she almost reached for his hand. Then Mr. Loison cleared his throat and took position on her other side, offering a smile as he pushed his glasses up on his nose.

"You two have caused more trouble in the last couple of weeks than I can easily recount." Commander Magnus rose as he spoke. "Fortunately for you, it benefits me."

He sounds more amused than angry. What's going on?

Mr. Loison leaned in to stage-whisper in her ear. "The commander has been made to see the advantages of a House Magnus regent being appointed to Northport while this mess is being sorted out. It could take years."

The Magnus scion nodded. "House Thorgrim will need to explain their Major General's actions. Lady Teresa of Thorgrim denies all knowledge of her cousin's plans—"

The Thorgrim woman shook her head and spoke in a voice barely above a whisper. "She acted on her own. House Thorgrim will support any punitive action taken, of course, but the Council must understand that our House cannot be expected to stand idly by while Magnus usurps our authority here."

She's lying. Those are empty words. It felt odd to sense that, and by the gleam in Viktor Magnus's eyes, he knew it as well. *Now that he has hands on the wheel, he won't yield the driver's seat anytime soon.*

"House politics are not our concern," Mikani put in. "So why'd you bring us in, Commander?"

Ritsuko was wondering that, too.

* * *

Mikani narrowed his eyes, considering. *He needs to cement his claim with Skarsgard to retain control of Northport. And what Skarsgard wants most right now is us.* Mikani cast a quick look around the room. The door behind them was locked and probably guarded; they'd have to go through the room and over the commander to get to the large windows behind Viktor Magnus.

Not the best plan even if we weren't battered and bruised.

"Captains Boehr and Phylos of Skarsgard *requested* your presence."

The older Skarsgard captain started to rise. "We demand that you turn over—" Mikani tensed and started to crouch. *If I can take out the one on the right, we stand a chance.*

But Magnus slammed a fist on the table, cutting the man short and pulling Mikani's attention back to him. "You are here as my guests, Captain. And you will *not* forget that.

If it weren't for this lot, the Thorgrim witch would have ripped Northport apart, and gods only know what else. Right beneath your noses." The smaller man glared at the commander for a moment before sitting back down. Mikani relaxed slightly but didn't let down his guard.

So we're not the sacrificial goats?

Mikani started when Loison spoke. "Ladies. Gentlemen." The bookish clerk offered a smile and stepped up to the table, making Lady Teresa shift aside. "We're not here to assign blame, much as there is of *that* to go around." He held the gaze of each Skarsgard captain and Lady Teresa, and they all looked away after a moment.

Mikani frowned; he sensed faint but distinct sparks of fear when Loison made eye contact. *Who the hells are you, really, Loison?*

Commander Magnus addressed them all, but Mikani noticed he kept glancing back at the clerk. "Northport remains under joint Magnus and Skarsgard control until the Council decides otherwise. Thorgrim will cede all authority until that time; their men will be confined to barracks, under Lady Teresa's command. The Free Merchant ships will sail back to Dorstaad under escort, to be judged by the Council about their involvement in this affair."

Captains Boehr and Phylos rose together, and the former spoke for the two of them. "Skarsgard officially objects. This is on your head, Magnus."

Boehr strode out, snapping orders to his subordinates as he went. Phylos wore an identical look of outrage in stomping out of the cabin. *They took that well.*

Lady Teresa Thorgrim stood more sedately and curtsied to them all. "We'll welcome the Council's judgment on this matter." She turned without another word.

She probably has a half dozen plots ready to regain her position. I don't envy Viktor Magnus. But he looks like he can keep what he's won by conquest.

With a wary expression, the commander watched her leave, then took his seat. "I should have clapped you two in chains when you first came aboard this ship."

Ritsuko said, "I assure you, Commander, that what Lady Kare was plotting would have been far more trouble than anything we could have managed."

Viktor Magnus narrowed his eyes and leaned back in his chair. "The last of the Kare line were hunted down a thousand years ago."

Mikani shook his head and met the commander's gaze. "Seems they missed some. She was using the elementals to try to finish what her family started long ago... wiping mankind from Hy Breasil and bringing back the ancient Ferishers."

Magnus muttered an unintelligible oath. "Sit. Tell me everything."

Mikani sat across from Magnus while Ritsuko claimed the chair beside him. The telling didn't take long, and by the time Mikani completed his account, Magnus looked incredulous but alarmed. The commander shook his head, rubbing a hand over a jaw bristling with silver whiskers.

"Do you have any idea how far she got in her ritual? Was she close to finishing?"

"I'm not sure," Ritsuko said, "but from what Mikani sensed, it seems so."

Mikani sighed. "Things were bad enough after what happened in Dorstaad. I've no idea if this will make things worse, but if there was anyone out there who could've helped her or completed her work, I don't think Lady Kare would've killed herself."

"I agree." Ritsuko frowned, probably over the old woman's death.

"That's good news. We've had precious little of that of late." Magnus seemed weary, but it didn't seem to Mikani that the man would see peace anytime soon. The commander turned to Ritsuko. "You know, I was serious when I offered to hire you, Inspector."

Mikani glanced at his partner with a raised brow. "You had time to go looking for a new job?"

A blush rose to her cheeks as she explained, "He did suggest that House Magnus might benefit from our propensity for wreaking havoc, so long as he could direct our efforts."

Mikani turned back to Magnus. "I think we've had enough fun up in the north for a while, Commander. Afraid we'll have to decline."

"I thought you might. You don't look the type to follow orders. The harbormaster will see to it that your ship will be ready to sail in three days." He motioned toward the door.

Ritsuko rose. After a brief hesitation, Mikani followed suit.

It could have been worse. Neither Viktor Magnus nor the Council would let Skarsgard murder them in their sleep, at least.

"I was wondering, sir." Ritsuko paused. "Did they find any trace of the mine management? Have you heard?"

"They came into town earlier this morning, hungry and somewhat worse for wear. They're holed up in the Skarsgard compound."

She nodded. "You should know… they left a number of miners to die after the salamanders attacked.

"Cowards." Magnus wore a look of pure disgust.

"You can speak to Mr. Evans or Kurtz if you require confirmation or evidence." She seemed to assume there would be punishment, and Mikani hoped so, too.

"That's no longer your concern." Magnus's tone brooked no argument. They were at the door when he spoke again, in a milder tone. "Inspectors." Mikani looked over his shoulder. "Thank you. You did good work. I cannot offer you anything officially—"

"We couldn't accept anyway," Ritsuko interrupted.

"Then we're in accord. If I see you after your ship's ready to sail, you'll be clapped in chains and delivered to Skarsgard instead of the Council. As for your escort, I'm short on men *and* ships, so after the second day, you're on your own. I trust you know your way to Dorstaad."

Clever bastard. Always cover your arse. "We do," Mikani answered.

Magnus saw them off the *Pride*, and as Mikani stepped onto the dock, Ritsuko said, "We need to talk about our next step."

At her somber tone, he studied his partner. The skin beneath her eyes was bruised from lack of sleep, and worry lines formed a crease between her dark brows. Without even trying, he sensed the anxiety rolling off her in waves. It was enough to make him want to take her in arms and shelter her from the coming storm.

"If we head back home, Skarsgard and Thorgrim will do their damnedest to see us in prison or dead." He paused, considering the ramifications. "Gunwood might try to help, but they'll just roll over him, if not worse. Whatever favor we earned stopping Nuall *might* get us sent to the penal farms instead of the dungeon."

"I'm tired, Janus. And... I'm *really* scared." Her voice was very soft.

His heart clenched. Without thinking, he gave in to the impulse and slipped his arms around her, pulling her to his chest. "We'll be all right, love. I won't let anyone hurt you."

Her arms wrapped around his waist, and she put her cheek to his shirt. She let out a long breath. "Is that offer to meet your family still good?"

Though she sounded like she might be joking, he nodded. "Sod it, let's go. The CID can wait."

She lifted her head to stare up at him. "Are you serious?"

"Why not? It would at least buy us some time. We'll make them work to catch us."

"Bronze gods. I always wanted to be a fugitive from justice." But she was smiling at least, better than the fear from before. "You make my life inexpressibly exciting."

I can't bear it when she's sad.

"If I may be so bold." Loison had apparently followed them from the *Pride*, though Mikani hadn't been aware of him until that moment. "You two have earned your rest, and your family's address could easily be… *misplaced*, Inspector Mikani, making it rather difficult to track you down."

He frowned. He couldn't read the clerk clearly. Unlike Lorne Nuall, Loison was a constantly shifting pattern of emotions when Mikani gave in to temptation and reached out with his gift. *That's not something you see every day… hells, don't think I've ever seen anything like it before.* "If you can pull that off, Saskia's not paying you enough."

Loison smiled and bowed his head slightly. "Mistress Braelan is unaware of some of my talents. I may need to ask for a raise. But let's return to the *Gull*, shall we?"

Mikani waited for him to be out of earshot. "Do you trust him?"

"Not entirely. But that applies to the whole world, apart from you."

Mikani smiled down at her. "Good. I thought I was getting paranoid in my old age. Watch my back… and I'll always watch yours, Celeste."

She hurried along the quay, turning not toward the *Gull*, but for the nearest mirror station a couple of blocks away. But inside, the silver surfaces were dead and dull, just platters now, devoid of the spirits that had whispered from place to place. Ritsuko stood for a few moments, lost in thought, then she stepped out onto the street. Mikani followed.

"New plan. I'll write up a full report and dispatch it with a courier."

He nodded. "I wouldn't want to go renegade without filing the paperwork first."

33

SASKIA SAT ON her precarious perch at the prow of the *Gull*. The sea spray stung enough to keep her from drifting into sleep, and the rush of wind made her feel closer to her familiars. She could feel them again, just close enough to comfort her with their wordless whispers. She hadn't attempted to ask for their help since they'd left Northport a week ago.

I'm still afraid they might not come if I call. She'd have to try, sometime, just to know if she was still a weather witch… or if the Kare lunatic had stolen that from her. A creak of wood and a tug on the rigging bracing her jury-rigged nest made her look up. Janus made his way along the rail, gripping the ropes with white-knuckled hands.

She hesitated for a moment, then called out. "Watch your step. If you fall, it'll be an hour before we can get turned around to pick your soggy self back up."

He looked up at her, and if his gaze were daggers, she'd be pierced a dozen times. "You're not funny. Why in hells' name are you hidden all the way out here, anyway?"

Saskia laughed, casting an arm out as if to take in the sea all around. "I'm not hiding. I just needed the breeze to clear my head."

She shifted to give him some room as he reached her and sat, legs braced around the bowsprit. "I never did understand your love of the water. Salty, deep, full of things just waiting to feast on you if you slip."

"I love the sea's freedom, not the water." She studied him. He hadn't shaved in the last few weeks, his jaw covered in a dark scruff that would soon become a full beard. His shaggy mane had grown to near shoulder length, making his dark blue eyes shine bright from a face grown quite feral. "Bronze gods, Janus. I think we stripped the civilization out of you with this little jaunt."

He laughed and looked into the horizon. "Guess I'll have to trust Celeste to find it again."

Saskia waited for the pang that usually accompanied a mention of Ritsuko, but it didn't come. "She'd be the one to do it." She smiled and leaned in closer. He turned toward her, squinting against the sea spray. "I'm glad you found someone to give you some peace, Janus."

"I'm not sure that I'm quite there yet, Saskia." He reached over to wrap his fingers around her hand. "But I do think she's the one to show me the way."

She chewed her bottom lip and held his gaze. "I know. I suppose it's past time to admit that we are better as adventuring companions than lovers."

"Well, I can't promise you that we'll always have insane sorcerers and dragons to fight, but I'll always have your back, Saskia." He grinned and looked even more wolfish as he did.

"No? I'm disappointed." She smiled, glad to have found a new ease with him. "Now move, will you? I need to see my ship to port. We're nearing Summer's north shore." She pointed toward the east, where a verdant shore, wooded and undulating with gentle hills, had come into view. "We'll have you safe and sound on land in hours."

"Can't bloody wait. Love the company, hate the ship."

Janus made his way gingerly back to the deck, and she followed with a laugh. He waved without turning and headed for his quarters; she started aft to relieve Mr. Ferro at the wheel. When she reached the mainmast, she spotted Irahi lounging near the stairs up to the stern castle.

We haven't had much of a chance to talk since we left Northport.

When he spotted her, the doctor smiled. There was a warmth in his dark eyes of which she'd only recently become aware. So she measured her steps toward him with an answering smile. "All the men patched up?"

"They just need time now. I've done all I can."

"The same could be said for us all," she murmured.

"Isn't that the truth?" He leaned down to kiss her lightly, and she reached up to caress his jaw, lingering before easing back. "So Li'l White, does this mean you'll be at sea again? Or are you going back to your dusty ledgers?"

Saskia frowned. "I... I'm not sure, Irahi. The company needs to be run, but I missed this. I'd forgotten what it was like to feel the sea beneath me and the wind in my hair." She wrapped her arms around his and leaned back, grinning up at him. "Full sails, good wind, and a different port every week, like the old days."

"Not quite," he said softly.

Better now. But it wasn't the time to discuss serious matters, not during a quick chat on deck on her way to the stern. So she smiled up at him.

Saskia tugged, pulling him toward the stairs. "If we go back to Dorstaad, we'll be held in some dingy Council office while we answer endless questions. At best. At worst, well, we might end up locked up. I do *so* hate being locked up."

"I'm well aware of that, woman. Might as well try to cage the wind." Irahi followed her up and waited while she dismissed Ferro.

Breathing deep, she took control of the clipper, exulting in the way the ship leapt over the waves at her command. "Is this where we talk about our future?"

"I'd rather not. I'm afraid you'll tell me we don't have one." Though the doctor was smiling, she caught a serious undertone in his voice.

"Oh, Irahi. We have a future... just don't ask how long. Live for today, with me." She turned to him, her hand steady on the wheel. "Will that be enough?"

"Since it's more than I ever thought I'd get with you, it's perfect." He came up behind her and wrapped his arms around her.

She leaned back against him, ignoring curious looks from sailors nearby. They gossiped like old women, but Irahi was worth a little talk. *If he hears them, though, they might end up overboard.* At a glance from Saskia, they went about their work, and the vessel skimmed along the sea, ever closer to their destination.

* * *

A few hours later, just before sunset, Saskia turned the *Gull* back over to the first mate. The sky was alight with a brighter sunset than they'd seen since leaving the Summer Isle. Clouds hung low in the sky, pierced through with streaks of amber light, swirls of pink and dark umber. Lower still, there were violet lines that served as a reminder of those she'd lost.

It's good to leave the travails of Winter behind.

Rising on tiptoes to peer toward the rapidly approaching shore, she inspected Celbridge. She hadn't visited Janus's home before, and it was surprisingly picturesque. Weathered stone buildings lined the harbor, with small piers spaced evenly around the curved coastline. Most had brightly painted boats bobbing nearby, sleek enough to be sailed by one or two men, and others were so small that one man likely crewed them, equipped with oars and a net. In the twilight, the sea gleamed deep blue out past the jagged rocks, tinged green closer to the rocky beach where the algae grew in slick bursts. Tile roofs brightened the village, contrasting with the patchwork of green and brown farther inland, farms framing the cluster of homes in the town proper.

Bronze gods, they'll sink us.

The small harbor wasn't accustomed to ships the size of the *Gull*, and the local dockworkers almost managed to run her aground. Distracted from the view, she strode along the deck, inspecting their progress, then glaring at the dockhands. "Secure her properly, or I'll hang *you* from the gunwales to keep her from scraping the pier!"

She waited for them to tie the lines again before sounding the bell to signal their official arrival to port. "Mr. Ferro! Get the men sorted and a watch set up. We sail tomorrow, first thing; anyone not back on board can learn to herd sheep or whatever they do up here."

"They breed horses and grow wheat, actually." Janus walked toward her, Ritsuko at his side. "Sheep are more of an eastern thing."

"Looks like a fishing village to me," Saskia muttered.

"It's lovely," Ritsuko said. "Peaceful. Do you know, I've never been out of Dorstaad until recently? Now it appears as if I'm to see the world."

"I'm hoping for a brief respite before doing any more world-seeing. And I'd rather we do it by land for a while." Mikani smiled at Ritsuko. "But first things first; let's get a hot meal and some cold beer. Unless they finally managed to wreck it, the local inn's a quarter mile up the road."

In the morning—after a wild night of drinking and merriment—the officers stumbled out to meet Saskia in front of the Tankard and Tackle. Mr. Ferro was disheveled and red-eyed, and though the man could hold his drink, he'd put away a lot, even for him. Of them all, Irahi looked the best, with Nell Oliver coming in second. Saskia suspected her own hair seemed as if she'd combed it with an egg whisk.

Worth it.

For a few moments, she thought Janus might sleep through their leave-taking, but he burst out the front door seconds before she decided to set off for the harbor. Ritsuko joined him shortly thereafter, tidier and put together. The village was so small, there was no transport apart from her two feet, so she led the group back to the *Gull*.

Several sailors were still passed out on deck. *Hope they're not too hungover to set sail.* If they were, Nell Oliver would shout them deaf. Mr. Ferro called to the mate on deck, who lowered the gangplank with a wooden clatter. *This is it.*

Somber, she turned to Janus and his partner. "I haven't thanked you properly for everything you did. It was neither easy nor painless, but we did the right thing."

"There were no better choices," Ritsuko said. "But I'm glad we helped you if we did."

"You know I'll always do anything I can for you, Saskia." Janus was smiling despite a tired, worn expression and a hint of something darker.

"I should think so. You still owe me a favor, Janus, and I'll be along to collect."

He widened his eyes in mock dread. "I can only imagine what you'll ask for next."

Mr. Ferro paused beside the group, brows lifted in what looked almost like a friendly expression. "You weren't entirely useless. Fair winds, safe travels, and suchlike." With that, the mate went past and boarded the *Gull*, where he immediately set to work.

And that's why I keep him on.

"He's a charmer," Janus observed.

Saskia grinned. "He does remind me of you."

Nell Oliver offered Janus and his partner a hearty handshake. "You were both handy in a crisis, and you didn't make my job harder. Can't ask for more."

Ritsuko smiled at the boatswain. "I was truly impressed with how you keep the men in line. Perhaps I need lessons."

"Gods spare me," Janus murmured.

That left Saskia standing beside a silent Irahi on the pebbled shore, waves lapping toward her toes. They needed to get under way before high tide ended, so she had to make this quick. Throat thick, she reached for Janus first, squeezing tight around his neck. Then she turned to the other woman, hesitated, and Ritsuko bobbed a little nod, which she took for permission. It was a quick hug but sincere for all that. When she stepped back, Irahi took her place, drawing both of them into a clumsy embrace. He thumped Janus on the back and kissed Ritsuko's forehead.

"Be safe, both of you. I'd tell you to behave, but I know that one too well." He tilted his head at Janus.

"I won't say good-bye. Come, Irahi."

Saskia turned and boarded the *Gull*. The sails swelled with a fair and friendly wind; the ship turned with Mr. Ferro's expert handling. Each whispering swell of the waves seemed to sing of bittersweet partings. She moved along the rail to keep her friends in sight until they were only small specks on the beach, and the sea carried her away.

34

It didn't take long for Ritsuko to gather her few possessions; the journey through the Winter Isle had left her with precious little. Once she had everything, she met Mikani in the inn's common room. He'd washed but not shaved, and his shirt had several permanent stains. Since she didn't look any better, she didn't mention it.

She felt unaccountably nervous about meeting his family, so she fiddled with her bag. "How far is it?"

"Two miles, give or take. Let's go."

As they walked through Celbridge, people took a second glance at Mikani, then called out a greeting or lifted a hand to say hello. Some, she noticed, didn't look entirely pleased to see him, while others seemed delighted the prodigal son had returned home. A woman who was stacking apples for display tossed one to her partner.

"Does your mother know you're back?"

Mikani caught it, shaking his head with a conspiratorial expression. "It's a surprise." With a wink, he touched his index finger to his lips and walked on as the fruit merchant laughed.

"This is a pretty place," Ritsuko said, admiring the scenery.

"It is." Though she didn't ask why he'd left, he sensed the

question. "But it wasn't quite big enough after my father disappeared. I saw his shadow everywhere. I found that I couldn't just step into his shoes and take on everything."

"So you moved to Dorstaad and went to work for the CID."

He flashed a wry smile. "Eventually. I explored other options first."

"I feel odd about descending on your family uninvited. And I'm concerned about the consequences for sheltering us."

"I'll warn them. Whatever you may think of me, I don't lie to my mother." He wore an oddly sheepish expression.

Ritsuko found it disconcertingly adorable. Mikani was known for being a quick-tempered rogue, fast with his fists, and she added this small tidbit to the storehouse of information she'd been collecting on him for the past several years. She thought about the way he always scanned a crowd until he found her in it and how he only relaxed when he knew she was safe. That subtle slip of his shoulders had come to mean a great deal to her.

And now I'm meeting his family.

But it wasn't for personal reasons. They just needed a place to hide while waiting for the furor to die down in Dorstaad. She hoped Mr. Loison could keep his promise about expunging information from Mikani's file. Otherwise, the authorities would be here in a matter of days.

"No, I didn't think you did. I was just worried."

"You worry too much. Haven't I said we'll be fine?"

Her lips twitched as she gave his words back to him. "You say many things."

"And I mean them all where you're concerned." Mikani quickened his step, heading for the narrow wagon path leading out of town. "I've cousins farther up along the coast. If need be, we can introduce you to the whole clan while we stay ahead of trouble."

The two-mile walk over level ground was easy compared to recent travel. In less than an hour, Ritsuko was standing on the path before Mikani's family farm, sprawling with a couple of additions tacked on here and there; she could tell which was the oldest by the different levels of weathering on the stone. Roughly shaped like an E, the house had been recently whitewashed, a contrast with the outbuildings that lay farther from the main dwelling.

A cluster of fruit trees grew on the far corner of the property, perfuming the air with the sweetness of ripening apples. There was also a verdant smell, probably from the crops nearly ready to come to harvest in distant fields, underscored by the tang of freshly turned earth. Ritsuko pulled in a deep breath, and Mikani regarded her with curiosity.

"What?"

"Incredible. There's no soot in the air. No smoke. I've never known anything like it."

He grew up here... and he chose to go away. I don't think I ever could. But then, she'd never left Dorstaad until recently.

"It is... clean," he admitted.

She glimpsed conflict in his face, likely driven by memories of his father. He strode toward the front door, painted a glistening red. Ritsuko wondered if he would knock, but no, he pushed it open and strode through into a warm and welcoming room, decorated in the same haphazard style she'd first seen in his own cottage. There were knickknacks and wall hangings, bits of sewing and embroidery scattered about. Deeper in the house, she heard children calling to each other and a woman's lower tone admonishing them.

"Is that any way to greet a hungry wanderer?" Mikani called out.

The sound of pottery shattering followed, then the quick patter of footsteps. For a moment, Ritsuko was overwhelmed by the number of people, mostly women, who ran into the front room. She identified his mother straightaway, both from the graying brown curls and the incredibly bright blue eyes. The woman was tall and solidly built, with a stained white apron wrapped around her middle. She pressed a hand to her mouth as she skimmed Mikani from head to toe, then she grabbed him in a tight hug. Women she took to be his sisters closed in either side, all talking at once. He hugged them all, kissing heads in turn.

A dash of color in short pants squealed and ran in full tilt, clambering over a chair to leap in the air and toward them. Mikani barely had time to step back and catch the boy in his arms, stumbling back against the wall and knocking a vase to shatter on the floor.

“Bloody hell, young Janus, you’ll prove your mum right in saying I’m a bad influence.”

“*Janus*, both of you! Language! Bronze gods, what are you doing here?” The taller of his sisters seemed torn between crying and laughing. *That must be Helena.* Her hair was longer and features softer, but she was definitely the twin. Mikani merely shook his head, and they exchanged a look as he handed her gleefully squealing son back to her.

Ritsuko had no experience with children and less with families. Life with her grandfather had certainly never been this noisy or… warm. *That’s the word.* She saw their gladness in every word, every gesture. The little ones were fairly bouncing for his attention, stretching up on tiptoes to rummage through his pockets. *He usually brings sweets, I suppose.*

Someone tugged at Ritsuko’s split skirt. She found a girl, no more than six, studying her intently. “Are you my auntie? Mum said Uncle Jay wouldn’t be back until he got married.”

Much as she would’ve liked to tease Mikani, Ritsuko shook her head. “I’m his partner, Celeste Ritsuko. It’s a pleasure to meet you.” She extended her hand, wondering if manners applied to people under a certain age.

The girl tilted her head before taking her hand in small fingers. “How do you do. I’m Lena, and I’m almost seven.” Her smile revealed two missing front teeth.

“A very respectable age,” Ritsuko said.

She faintly hoped someone would save her from this conversation, and her wish was granted when the smaller of Mikani's sisters set a hand on Lena's head, frowning at her brother. "Is there some reason you haven't performed the introductions?"

Too many curious eyes focused on her. Ritsuko worked not to fidget. *I wish I was making a better impression. I look like I've fallen off mountains and nearly drowned and been terrified by a dragon and then faced a would-be Ferisher queen.* She would give a lot for an immaculate suit, a tidy haircut, and perhaps a spritz of her favorite perfume. Ritsuko couldn't even remember the last time she'd worn any.

"I was being assaulted by a wild Janus." He gave his nephew a look, and Ritsuko could see the love for the little boy in his eyes. "Celeste Ritsuko, this is Agatha Mikani, my mother. Helena Brunn and Daphne Signael, my sisters."

The three women pressed closer, and Agatha ignored the offered hand to pull Ritsuko into a close embrace. She'd never been hugged by a stranger before, but she did her best not to seem awkward or unfriendly. Then she shook hands with his sisters and offered polite greetings to the children milling about her legs.

"She's his partner," Lena piped up.

Mikani added, "You've met Lena. Irena's the shy blonde in the corner, and Cassia's the eldest. The little flying goblin's Janus; though I still think the Ferishers switched my sweet nephew for an imp when he was born."

Helena smiled at her brother, then slapped the back of his head. "He's your spitting image in *everything*, gods keep us."

Ritsuko felt the weight of scrutiny from Mikani's mother. "Look at the both of you. Did you bring her to see us on the back of a potato cart?"

"The potato cart was busy, we had to walk." He grinned briefly, looking around. "Where are Karl and Mac?"

Daphne answered. She was shorter than Ritsuko and

blond where her family was dark. "Karl's out fishing. My Mac's at the forge."

Mikani nodded. "I'll say hello to them later."

"If you'll pardon my saying so, my dear, you need a proper bath and some clean clothes." Agatha Mikani frowned at her son, which made Ritsuko fight a smile. "You still have some things in your room. As for you, Celeste? I think you can wear one of Daphne's old dresses. They don't fit her anymore anyway."

"Are you saying I'm fat, Mum?" But there was none of the offense she'd expect in Daphne's tone, only genuine affection.

"Of course not. But you've had children. Come along, Celeste."

Before she could offer more than an alarmed glance, Mikani's relatives swept her away. She wasn't used to the chatter, but it was all good-natured, and soon Agatha had her in a bath and was trimming up her messy hair, just as if this was normal. Ritsuko couldn't remember ever being naked in a room with strange women before, but they acted like this was customary.

As if I'm family.

For obvious reasons, she didn't protest.

* * *

Four hours later, they gathered around the table in the spacious dining room. The children had eaten earlier in the kitchen and gone to bed despite vigorous protests. Mikani offered to help, but his mother shooed him out of the kitchen. With Daphne and Helena's help, she carried out platters of food for them to eat family style: lamb stew, roasted chicken and potatoes, green peas and onions, along with fresh bread. It smelled delicious and reminded him of so many meals eaten at this table over the years. For once, his father's shadow didn't fall across everything as he studied the smiling faces in the firelight.

Helena's husband, Karl, a tall lean fellow a little younger than Mikani, was tidied up with his hair slicked back. Mac, Daphne's man, was a burly, dark-haired blacksmith who crafted all the tools for the farm. The work had left his hands scarred and callused, his shoulders thick as a well-made door. Ritsuko had her hands folded in her lap, and she wore a gray dress. He couldn't recall ever seeing it on Daphne, but it suited his partner. She was the picture of refinement amid his boisterous family, and he was surprised at how much it meant to see her here, as if his world was whole at last.

"That's done it," his mother said, blowing a wisp of hair out of her face.

Along with Karl and Mac, he stood until the women took their seats at the table. *Seven of us. That's supposed to be a lucky number, right?*

The meal passed with friendly teasing and chatter. Ritsuko was quiet, taking it all in. He wondered if she found his relatives overwhelming. *She's not used to this.* Things got embarrassing when his mother commenced telling stories from his childhood.

She concluded, ". . . and then, I came out of the bakery, and what did I see? Janus Mikani, racing down the street naked as the day he was born."

"I only did that because Helena dared me. She promised me her share of pudding for a month." Though he pretended chagrin, it was worth it to see Ritsuko smiling.

"Did you get it?" his partner asked.

"He got his hide tanned," his mother said with a twinkle in her eyes.

"How old was he?" Ritsuko wanted to know, probably to picture the scene.

"Nine or ten," Daphne replied.

Ritsuko's smile widened into a grin. "I never did anything like that. My grandfather would've disowned me."

"We never will," said Mrs. Mikani.

Once everyone finished the butter cake, Mikani set down his coffee cup. It was time for explanations. He'd seen the questions in his mother's eyes, but this was harder than he'd expected—to admit how dire the situation and how much he needed their help. When he'd left home, he had been running from his father's ghost.

With a deep breath, he recounted their travels and troubles. Shocked exclamations rang out at every other sentence, including, "You did *what*?" from Helena.

Finally, he came to the end of the tale. He glanced over and met his mother's gaze. "We decided to let things settle down in Dorstaad. Loison said he'd see to it that the Council couldn't track us here… and I'm inclined to believe him. That said, we can be gone in a day or two—"

"Don't be daft, Janus. This is your home. Of course you're welcome, for as long as you need." His mother looked at each of them in turn, making sure Ritsuko knew she was included in that statement.

His partner pressed her palm to her sternum, as if it hurt, and he thought he knew why. Since her grandfather's death, she had been alone. No family. And to hear suddenly, *This is your home*, must feel startling. Painful even. Mikani wanted to reiterate the words. He didn't, mostly because it had been a long time since he felt like he belonged anywhere. Even here.

But I belong with her, wherever that may be.

"Thank you," Ritsuko said huskily. "But everyone must agree. I won't endanger the children without parental consent."

Mac nodded right away, the stout blacksmith tapping a thick finger on the table as he spoke. "We'll keep you safe. Let those southern city fools come looking, and we'll show them a proper Expanse welcome, we will."

Karl seemed more reticent. "The men who will come hunting you, what kind are they?"

"I don't know," Janus said honestly.

He'd never heard of a crime like the one he and Ritsuko had pulled off. It was bigger than the penal system typically encountered. Men were shipped off to the farms for lesser offenses, and though executions were rare, they did happen.

And this is bigger still.

Helena thumped her husband on the arm, addressing her words to Mikani. "Don't worry, little brother. We'll keep the big bad men from finding you."

She's enjoying this far too much. I'll never hear the end of it.

"You're plotting to hide me in the compost heap, aren't you?"

His sister smiled. "Of course not. I'd never do that... to Celeste."

"I'll help hide you," Karl finally said. "And I'll get you away if possible. But I won't do anything to risk my little ones."

Mikani nodded. "I'd expect nothing less."

Afterward, everyone pitched in to tidy up the table and clean the kitchen. It wasn't so in all households, but Mikani had grown up helping with what some men would call women's work. *A good thing, too, or I'd have starved.* His father had always pitched in, too, when he was home. He remembered his saying, *There's plenty of work on a farm. No need to be particular about it.*

The last dish was dried and put away when his mother kissed him on the cheek. "I'll see you in the morning."

His sisters added their good-nights, and his brothers-in-law clapped him on the shoulder as they passed. In the fluttering lamplight, Ritsuko looked shocked. Her face was pale, and she didn't seem to know what to do with her hands, now that the work was done.

She took a deep breath, then said, "I need some air."

Mikani waited a few seconds before following her. Outside, it was chilly and clear, the stars visible as they rarely were in Dorstaad. Ritsuko stood with her hands wrapped around her arms as it to stave off the frost in the air. Without thinking much about the impulse, he put his arm around her shoulder. *Because it's cold.* It occurred to him to take it one step further, and he shrugged out of his jacket to drape it around her.

"Better?"

"Yes, thanks."

"So you survived meeting my family. There's still time to go turn ourselves in rather than face another day with them, if you'd like."

She cut him a reproachful look. "They're lovely, and they clearly adore you."

"Madness runs in the line. Come, or we'll wake the little ones. Then *Helena* will have our hides. She's worse than the Council, trust me." He started across the field, toward the copse of trees bordering a small stream.

"Did you carve your initials into any of these trees?" Ritsuko's tone was wistful, as if she'd only read stories about such things.

He smiled but didn't answer until they reached the stream. "Once. It was a long time ago. There." He pointed at a small carving high on the trunk of an old elm, almost faded away entirely with age.

To his surprise, she dug her fingers into the bark and scrambled up, using the lowest limb to pull herself into the tree, where she kept climbing until she was close enough to trace the weathered initials. "It must be nice to have roots sunk in so deep that you can leave for years and return to find your mark still upon a place."

He looked back at the farm and over the fields all around them. There was enough moonlight to make out the far edge of the property, where the patch of woods he'd played in as a boy marked the start of their neighbor's lands.

Before the old man left, I never even considered spending my life anywhere else.

"Honestly, I haven't thought much about it. But I guess

we all take the most precious things for granted sometimes."

Acting on impulse, he scaled the tree he'd climbed so often as a boy and came to stand beside her. The view had changed a little, and he was taller, of course. Without telling her what he meant to do, he got out his pocketknife and dug into the tree, carving her initials next to his. He ached to do something else, something more, but this was what he felt would serve. Here. Now. But he hid a quiet ache, fired by seeing her surrounded by his family.

"There. Now you have roots, too."

Her smile was worth everything. "Thank you."

"I never thought I'd see you up a tree." His heart squeezed in his chest, protesting the space between them.

"There have been lots of those moments between us over the years. Surprising, *I can't believe this* sort of things."

There have, indeed, Celeste.

She touched the "C" first, then the "R," her face uptilted to the moon, and its light rained down silver, gilding the lines of her face. He could've drawn them with his eyes closed.

I want to kiss her.

The impulse passed. This wasn't the time to complicate things, not when they had so many other problems barreling toward them like a wailing train.

If this is meant to be, our moment will come. I'll get it right with her. I have to.

"What do you suppose will become of us? How bad will it be?" she asked.

He could've said so many things—that if he knew anything about the Houses, they loved coin and power. Their actions had cost Thorgrim and Skarsgard the most, but the ripples and consequences would take weeks and months to be fully felt as the elemental trade died down. While it was impossible to predict how Magnus would react, given their gains in Northport, the former two Houses would prove implacable enemies.

But maybe Olrik still feels grateful enough to help us... He wouldn't count on it.

Aloud, he only said, "Whatever happens, at least we're together."

ABOUT THE AUTHORS

A. A. AGUIRRE is the pseudonym for Ann and Andres Aguirre, a husband-wife writing team. She specializes in compelling characters; he excels at meticulous world-building. By day, she's a *New York Times* and *USA Today* bestselling novelist, and he is a pharmaceuticals tycoon.

Born in Mexico, Andres spent his early years traveling and getting in trouble everywhere else. Along the way, he got a degree from Pepperdine in economics and international business. Ann was born in the Midwest and has a degree in English literature from Ball State. She's traveled less than Andres and gotten into less trouble, but scaling Machu Picchu should count for something, right? Now settled, if not fully domesticated, Andres lives with his love, Ann, their fantastic kids, three adorable cats, and two delightful dogs.

Together, they form Megatron. Or not. Actually, they write books. Visit them online at aaaguirre.com.